THE APEX BOOK OF
WORLD SF

"This ongoing anthology series allows English-language readers the opportunity to explore speculative visions of the future, past and present from writers around the world—including those who don't publish in English."

An NPR notable book of 2014
The Apex Book of World SF: Volume 3

Also from Apex Publications

The Apex Book of World SF 1

"These stories deserve to be heard!"
—Frederik Pohl

The Apex Book of World SF 2

"**The Apex Book of SF** series has proven to be an excellent way to sample the diversity of world SFF and to broaden our understanding of the genre's potentials."
—Ken Liu, winner of the Hugo Award
and author of *The Grace of Kings*

The Apex Book of World SF 4

"Important to the future of not only international authors, but the entire SF community."
—*Strange Horizons*

www.apexbookcompany.com

THE APEX BOOK OF
WORLD SF

EDITED BY
Lavie Tidhar

An Apex Publications Book
Lexington, Kentucky

Apex Book of World SF: Volume 3
Edited by Lavie Tidhar
ISBN: 978-1-937009-34-2
Cover Art © 2015 by Sarah Anne Langton
First Edition, April 2013
Second Edition, August 2015

Published by Apex Publications, LLC
PO Box 24323
Lexington, K.Y. 40524
www.apexbookcompany.com

TABLE OF CONTENTS

Introduction

I t seems, to use the old cliché, only yesterday—and yet so long ago!—that the first *Apex Book of World SF* anthology came out and, alongside it, the first post on the accompanying World SF Blog appeared.

I am writing this introduction some time before the actual book comes out, as is always the case. The World SF Blog, started in February 2009, has recently celebrated four years online, and has just, as I write this, won the BSFA Award for Best Non-Fiction. Only some weeks back, it was given a special Kitschies (the "Black Tentacle") Award, for "an outstanding contribution to the conversation surrounding genre literature". This seems as unlikely as doing an anthology of international SF/F short stories had seemed to us back in 2008 or so, when Jason Sizemore of Apex and I first began to kick the idea around. Neither of us, I think, imagined those awards, nor the changes in the landscape and discourse around speculative fiction that has emerged, nor that we would be publishing a third volume—the one which you are now holding.

I am, naturally, excited about this anthology. I got to include more longer stories this time, and it is a thicker volume than its predecessors. Women dominate—twelve to five (one story is a collaboration). I was able to draw on a wide range of sources, many more than I had access to in 2009, amongst them the excellent *Afro SF* anthology (edited by *Apex Book of World SF 2* contributor Ivor Hartmann), anthology *Breaking the Bow*, edited by Vandana Singh, and *The Apex Book of World SF* contributor Anil Menon, and even the World SF Blog itself! In that I am indebted to my two excellent fiction editors for the site, first Debbie Moorhouse and later Sarah Newton.

As before, these stories run the gamut from science fiction, to fantasy, to horror. Some are translations (from German, Chinese, French, Spanish, and Swedish), and some were written in English. My thanks in particular go to the indefatigable Ken Liu, who continues to translate Chinese SF stories into English, two of which are reprinted here. The authors herein come from Asia and Europe, Africa and Latin America. To me, their stories are all wondrous and wonderful, and showcase the vitality and diversity that can be found in the field. They are a conversation, by voices that should be heard, and I am, once again, tremendously grateful for the opportunity to publish them.

Lavie Tidhar

London
April 2013

Courtship in the Country of Machine-Gods

Benjanun Sriduangkaew

One of the most exciting young writers of speculative fiction working today, Thai author Benjanun Sriduangkaew exploded onto the scene in 2012 with a string of high-profile novelettes, of which this lyrical tale is one.

In the shadow of machine-gods I tell wayfarers of a time when my people were a nightmare the color of hemorrhage and glinting teeth.

There are other narratives, but this is the one they want to hear most, the one they pay with their adoration and bright-eyed want, for they've never known us for anything but peace. Conflict juts out from the skein of Pojama's history, broken glass-shard, rupturing and ruptured.

I smile; I oblige. Though the story is for me, there are parts that I share simply for the reality of speaking it out loud, for the virtue of being heard.

My mouth moves, output for one of my cranial chips. My fingers sketch, autopilot, the forms of our heroes and enemies from a continent whose name and life has now been lost. My voice murmurs the tragedies and sings the heroics of Kanrisa and Surada, rising for climax, falling soft for denouement. The visitors' district is machine-dead. What a thrill it must be to hear the thunderclap notes of my gloves, behold the psychedelic fires that pour from my nails.

Once, they interrupt. The figures of our enemies do not seem real. They are right: with sagging eyes the hues of cheap jades and faces like skulls, even for villains they are too fantastical, too unhuman.

"My great-grandmother told of them so," I say and shrug. "Perhaps she was senile." With a motion, I turn the figures into shapes more familiar, shapes more like ours.

Inside the vessel of my thought—a garden of sliding intelligences who whisper to me, childhood mates grown to adults next to my ventricles and lungs—a different story unfolds.

I met my betrothed Kanrisa in our second cycle.

A garden festooned with lights, on a day of the scythe. I was in academy uniform, narrow skirt and sigil-carved sleeves, surrounded by girl age-mates. I tried to look severe, and mature, and to be taken seriously. I can no longer remember what the gathering was about, albeit I recall that someone was terra-sculpting on the fly. The earth twitched and jolted, forcing us to hover. For an hour or so, I tolerated this, making stiff comments to my age-mates. The ground eventually stilled—I thought the mischief-maker had simply had enough; the hush that fell on everyone told me otherwise.

A garden patch smoothed into an impromptu landing pad. The craft touched the grass quietly, which was not extraordinary until I realized that the engine had been off long before it touched the ground. It had shed altitude with nothing save clever maneuvering and air resistance. Brave. Reckless.

Its hatch lifted, and out came echoes in training, each fitted in muted flexskin, their throats metallic with Bodhva implants that'd let them synchronize with machine-gods. The last of them, the pilot, stepped out. She stood taller than most.

My age-mates rippled, whispering. "Oh her—" "The prodigy, my sister said." Breathlessly. "Graduating soon, at our age." "No, she's a little more senior...look how she moves."

I looked, compulsively. Kanrisa was dressed no differently from the rest, but she set herself apart in the sinuous fluidity of her steps. Where other echoes were soft and pared, she was hard and full-figured.

Now I remember why I was there, that day.

I moved through the wave of giddy students on tiptoes at the sight of rarely-seen echoes, basking in reflected prestige and exotique. Most of us had been taught the theories of Bodhva training; few saw it in person, and even close observation told little. How did one stretch a mind to accommodate the multi-threading of machines?

"She's lovely, birthed to an echo, I think." "Oh no you don't, that's not legal anymore—the molding matrices, surely not!" Someone sighed. "It was legal when she was made. Is she even entered into the Abacus? I'd guess not, a shame..."

One last line of young ambigendered and I was through. From her angle I must have looked as though I'd materialized out of nowhere, scandalized susurrus given flesh. Kanrisa glanced at me, over her shoulder, over a tight little smile: she wasn't pleased to be here, preferred to be back in meditative spheres or else out flying. For that was the privilege of Bodhva.

We surprised each other. I didn't expect to catch her; she didn't anticipate anyone to touch her at all, let alone to clasp her hand and say, "I'm Jidri. You are to be my wife."

A few heard, her fellow echoes mostly. One or two behind me, part of the academy crowd.

Kanrisa's smile didn't change, though she didn't dislodge me or pull away. "You must be mistaken, student. The Abacus doesn't rattle my name."

"It will." Courage or unreason moved me to draw closer. "Put your name in. It'll match us."

Until that day, I had never met her: had no personal knowledge of her, let alone desired her. All she'd been to me was a name, output to me by a modified copy of the predictive algorithm that gave the Abacus its sapience.

Kanrisa submitted her name, out of either curiosity or an angry impulse to be proven right that the exercise was pointless, and within the week we were declared matrimonial potentiates. We would make a union of two, against the average match of four point five.

The land of our enemies had a name. But we called it Intharachit.

For centrids untold, it was an enigma, first the preoccupation of dreamers then that of physicists: a spatial distortion cordoned Intharachit, locking it from sight and opening it to imagination. And then the Intharachit turned up, leaving us speechless, which said much—as a tribe we were tremendously difficult to shock.

It was a vast continent with a long history. Not a gentle one, for in their memory-paper I read the eradication of another indigenous group followed by a theological scourge—born of some snake-woman-fruit myth—that swept through their states, incinerating reason as it went. Eventually, recovery happened, but they'd spent so long in that quagmire it was a wonder to me, to us, that they overcame the barrier that kept them from the rest of the world.

I imagined myself in that first voyage with its crackling heat, the air just breathable, oxygen supply kept low against spontaneous combustions. And then, emergence into the unknown. A horizon stretching without end.

To this day, historians debate the why. Why it is that they were drawn to our shore; why they made first contact with us, and not with any of the other city-states or sovereignties...there are entire disciplines dedicated to this question. Some are determined in their belief that, had they met Tisapk first, or Mahuya perhaps, conflict could have been elided. (Elision, not avoidance, a distinction of some importance.)

All moot. The foreign ship landed on our shore, and there we were under the shadow of our machine-gods. We offered them hospitality, seeing no threat in them beyond their extreme alienness, and my elders took a portion of them into our home. We were curious.

One day I came home—back from a week in Umadu where I learned matrix-splicing—and found two Intharachit navigators housed with us. Like empty canvases their skin stretched, open to sun-stains that reddened their cadaverous cheeks and pointed snouts. Hair in thin yellow and dried-offal red clung lank to their skin, which poured salt and sick-smells. They did not look human.

Among the children of the house, I reacted least badly to them: our elders, then, tasked me with the aliens' care. "Aren't they grown?" I asked sharply. "They aren't children. I am."

"The female has seen less than a cycle, and the male under half that. With great care do treat them," one of my ungendered parents told me. "For they are infants who think themselves complete."

I didn't hide my aversion, but the aliens didn't remark on it, having opted to take our hospitality at surface. They were eager to believe us welcoming, eager to explore any corner large enough to admit their ungainliness. We didn't consider it necessary to inform them that we restricted them to the visitors' quarter.

"I've never seen anything like your city," the female said as we went through the artisans' street. She spoke her own tongue, which our software had been compiling into a lexicon through analysis of physiological cues. "Most—unique."

Her fellow navigator said something in another language, one dialectically related to hers. My chip picked that up. *Most primitive, more like,* he corrected her.

"Speak your home to me." I enunciated the syllables carefully: it wasn't pleasant, this barbaric syntax. They mistook my formulation of it, in as near a form as I could draw to Pojami, for inarticulate stupidity.

Regardless this request launched them into a double-voiced monologue. "We have such machines—" "To warm us in winter, and cool us in summer." "Our records are carried in contraptions the size of your finger." "And in one of them alone, we can store an entire library ten times the size of your home."

By their gesticulations, I understood that I was to be impressed. I didn't oblige, but I did have the courtesy not to inform them that what they had listed was nothing to be proud of. It didn't do to tell a toddler that perambulating on two legs was no accomplishment to adults.

The Bodhva compound was visible in the distance; having decided I wasn't fit for language, the aliens flapped their hands to indicate interest. I consulted my linguistics. Nothing in their languages answered the connotations of *Bodhva, machine-gods,* or *echo.* "A temple to mathematical faith, where acolytes train to be god-speakers mediating between us and our deities."

They looked at each other. "This institution is important to you?"

"The very most. For the gods make our skies what they are."

It was not my intent to deceive; again the matter was one of linguistic disparities. In retrospect perhaps I should have communicated in kennings.

"May we see this temple?"

"No," I said. "I haven't the authority with which to permit you. Even if I had, I would not. You are not to go there. This is definite."

Again they shared that glance, but did not press the issue.

That night they tried to breach the Bodhva compound; summarily drones executed them. I'd warned them—the entire expedition was cautioned against certain entries, certain acts. Still it could have been written off, if we cared to, the deaths smoothed over in the diplomats' laps. We did not try: we reported the pair's demise to them, stating that they'd violated one of our few rules. The expedition anticipated apologies, some efforts to compensate and reconcile.

By this point it was evident we would gain nothing from them, and our engineers had collected what they needed from the Intharachit ship, to replicate and refine the spatial compensation.

Other indiscretions happened. We hadn't yet perfected hematocyte synthesis, and a number of outsiders had come to Pojama for education, paying for tuition with their blood. One such student—to whom I'd taught a class in haptics—told the expedition what she did, as amicably as she discussed her studies.

But more than that discovery, it was the hairline crack in their story that they couldn't bear. Their records were littered with moments of first contact that'd proceeded predictably: trade, abjection, conquest. We did not desire the first, had no interest in pretending the second, so what was there for the aliens to do but seek the third? They had to refit us into a narrative they could understand; we must be made to exist in relation to them, ciphered in their language.

The expedition went home carrying what they believed were our secrets, and what they thought was a schema of our architecture and small limited sciences.

War, then, two segments in the making.

To their credit, the Intharachit deliberated, presenting arguments and counter-arguments among themselves. Nuptials dictated by lottery-engine, lives shaped by primitive worship, and sustenance from the arteries of thralls. What came to be known as the League of Intharachit determined it their duty to erase Pojama, liberating the peoples of our continent to freedom under Incharachit rule. They would be benevolent and generous. Tisapk and Umadu and Mahuya would bow to them in gratitude.

Intharachit first struck Sitembru, one of our few offshoot cities. Damage was little, their force eliminated, but we'd suffered civilian casualties. Even so, we tried to moderate our response; we ran analyses and plotted out the trajectories of their actions. We eavesdropped on exchanges not only between their military and rulers but also between family, friends, lovers united against a city they had never seen or breathed.

More than that, they needed land. It was this that drove them, when all pretensions were cast aside. It was this that would make them try, and try again, until they had removed us and claimed this continent for their own.

Their biotech was little. They never detected the monitoring symbiotes that we had put in each member of that first expedition. It must be said: they weren't entirely backward. In their fact-finding mission, they detected an absence of a certain element in our city and, noting that there was no photosynthetic life within our walls, arrived at the conclusion that this could not be without reason. They set to manufacturing reactors and explosives that would bathe us in artificial sunlight.

But for this, even in spite of their flailing assaults, we might have let them alone.

During that time, I graduated, making frequent contact with Kanrisa, who remained careful around me: negotiating a space, circumscribing terms she could work with. "Do you find me intolerable?" I asked one day in the sanitarium as, lying side by side, we each received our portion of hematocyte.

"I find you intriguing. It's only—I've never been courted before, not properly." Kanrisa frowned. "How can you be so blunt? You don't look it. You're just *academy*. I'm the one who's supposed to be forward."

I smiled up at the ceiling which, itself a mirror, let me smile at her too. We shared a bed large enough that we didn't have to keep close. Nevertheless, we did, our outlines overlapping. "Academy girls are more than we look."

"How did you predict the Abacus?"

It was the sanitarium, and we were taking sustenance. Privacy was ours by right. "I didn't."

"Are you telling me it was a lucky *guess*?"

At this I turned to her, lips to ear. "I recreated the Abacus in miniature; I just needed the matchmaking protocols. I input names. Mine, that of my age-mates and a few within the range, including the ones whose names weren't in the system yet."

"Copying the Abacus—"

"I said recreate, not copy. Copying is easy. Recreating...I approached it from a different angle, really. Accelerated the evolution process. Admittedly, it's easier when you know what the end result should look like."

Kanrisa's lips tightened. "That's dangerous. You insane girl."

"My name was floating in the system for a while. Nothing. Then I tried that, to see if I could, and it gave me just the one match."

"Me."

"You." Our fingers curled, twining thumb to thumb, as of two hands belonging to one body.

Raising Kanrisa nobody ever thought to ask: What is she? Much of the information behind her conception was first classified, then diluted into gibbercrypt, then buried so far under it might as well have been scourged clean. It did not cross the mind that she mightn't have been made to flex; that she could function only as part of a unit, a piece of a whole, in the teams that formed through Bodhva regimens. They didn't know what to do with Kanrisa, so why not put her to a purpose for which she was made? It was a kindness and, at the same time, useful. She exceeded expectations when integrating with her machine-god; no questions were put forward. Her compatibility indices were subzero in the Abacus, but what did that matter? Her happiness was beside the point.

I miss her. I miss our shared time, which lives in my breast flickering like the last pulses of dying cortices.

"Are you coming to Viraya's wedding?"

I sit down at the edge of a fountain. Ice crystals tinkle and shatter in my lap, unmelting. Half the city is in the throes of winter, the other enjoying a rainy spring. Meteorologic manipulation has become the rage this last segment. It won't last. We all know it's unhealthy and pointlessly ostentatious, but our current council is led by a whimsical woman rarely content with any one temperature. "I'm very bitter about weddings, Manop. Padon."

"You can tell which one I am," he chides. "I learned to like you that way, you know, even if it took some doing."

"Would it have helped if I'd hit you? Physical contact is the syntax of romance." I sweep aside flecks of ice. More fall to replace them, grazing my cheeks with knife facets. "Why did you go along with your brother?"

"That's not—"

"My business, not that either of you ever respected it when I said that."

He rocks back into the fountain, turning his face up to the harshsoft fall of frozen drops. His tongue darts out, catching the cold. "My brother was convinced you'd keep us together."

"Ah."

"He also liked you as a person; still does. You aren't doing *that* for a living, are you?"

I draw off my gloves, the little performance paraphernalia, and tuck them away. "No." My work as a data savant pays more than enough, even if a quarter goes toward Kanrisa's care. The light-marionette show merely helps me relive the story, externalize it beyond the confines of my dataspshere. "You've just come back from Umadu. Did you see…her?"

"I visited. She's up and walking so there's something in that. They are making progress, but—haven't they been sending you reports?"

"My chip goes through them for me. Notifies me if there's anything of note." I can't make myself read them, not anymore. The same repetitious nothing, over and over.

"They are trying. Last month this one splicer made a breakthrough."

"Until they can do something for Kanrisa, I don't want to hear about it." I stand. Icicles fall from my clothes and my skin. "How did it go so wrong? I should have noticed, shouldn't I? I was there; I was with her."

"You aren't an echo. What would you have known?" He puts a hand over mine, briefly. "Have you had any luck with authorization?"

"I'm a nobody. Her engineering was illegal to start with and who likes to admit a mistake?"

"If you ever need funds—"

"Thank you." I wipe away the rime that's formed over his brow, the way you would a child. "You're a good friend."

A number of solutions were put in metaphor-bowls, and sampled across diverse palates. Many tongues flicked, and their opinions were recorded.

We would send out echoes, and the machine-gods would go to war for the first time in centrids. Incharachit infrastructure would be destroyed, along with their armaments. Once they were set back to a pre-industrial stage, we'd have time to decide what to do further, if anything.

On the day this was announced, Kanrisa came to my home. Our households are hardly alike—hers a suite in one of the Bodhva towers, mine a sprawling ancient beast in a compound shared between our extended family. It tilts at an angle, finial-tipped, built like a heart where each ventricle is divided between siblings. "I can see myself living here," Kanrisa said as she entered what I used as my study.

"Maybe."

"Well, I certainly can, no maybes about it." I held her hand, just as I'd done that first day we had met.

Her fingers gripped mine. For a moment I wondered if she might bring them to her mouth. I thought of that often, her mouth. "Is this where you grew your version of the Abacus?"

"Maybe," I said, mimicking her timbre. Around us screens and cortices hummed in standby, processing, calculating, dreaming the curious dreams of pure mathematics. They made the room cramped; made us sit knees to knees, so close we breathed upon one another. I thought, *This is where we will kiss for the first time, and learn the secrets of each other's skin.*

"You heard about—it."

"Yes." Murmuring, not declaring, war. I watched the pulse jump in her throat where the implants hadn't yet covered flesh.

"Because this hasn't happened since...since anyone can remember, they'll be collecting data in real time. Each cadre is taking specialists with them to monitor the voices." That's what echoes call the machine-gods: voices. "To keep up diagnostics on the fly. Our voices won't have any processing power to spare in combat."

"You can choose just anyone?"

"If they're qualified." Kanrisa was very close, now. "Would you like to? I'd understand if you don't. It could be dangerous. You've never been near the voices before."

Laughing I threw my arms around her. "What do you think? Of course I am. I'm coming with you."

That was the first time that I saw them. Not the titans which stand guard over Pojama, but smaller, sleeker machine-gods crafted to synchronize with echoes.

The sight of them filled an absence in me I hadn't known existed.

Five shared space with Kanrisa's voice (her terminology already transmuting mine), each a chassis of gleaming ceramic alloy with six gaunt limbs clad in rippling permutative metal. At each machine's center sits its armored face, where the Bodhva would sit enclosed, folded into its system like a fetus in the womb.

I stood close to her as she introduced me to other echoes, and shivered. Excitement and something else that set my veins to a slow scalding heat. Coiled tight around this, I replied in monosyllables, remained quiet throughout the back-and-forth between Kanrisa and her fellows. They hadn't picked other field analysts yet it seemed, so among them I was the sole unbelonging presence.

"They are so..."

"There's no need to whisper, Jidri. And yes, I know what you mean. Overwhelming. You'll be spending most of the time in the carrier, though, which we will take turns piloting."

A young man named Tephem jabbed an elbow at her. "But we all know Kanrisa's the best at it."

"Only because she cheats." Viraya, this. Half-joke, half-honest. I glanced to see whether Kanrisa had taken it badly—whether it was meant as derision, or just something between friends. A little of both. Rivalry underneath thin surface tension.

The preparations were brief. Within days, I was abroad the carrier ship *Khrut*. "Carrier" makes it sound smaller than it is: the *Khrut* harbors a river cortex, sustaining an ecosystem of three hundred interdependent intelligences. Excluding analysts and echoes, the crew numbered eighty-nine. It was made expressly for war—as a people we didn't believe in everlasting peace. Species-wide cynicism perhaps, but we keep our battle engines refined and updated. Echoes grow up running battle simulations. The only addition the *Khrut* required was spatial compensation and thicker armor.

It was the first time that I socialized with data savants outside the academy. There were Manop and Padon, twin brothers from the same house as Viraya. Tephem's aunt Pattama was in her fourth cycle and the oldest of us. A few others. Not a large group. In a crowd I could have faded, but in a setting this small I had few excuses to keep to myself. I retained my distance, but the brothers were undeterred.

One of them approached as I sat down to lunch. "Is it true," either Manop or Padon said, "that you're engaged to...that girl?"

I looked up from my rice. "Which girl would that be, Manop? Or Padon. Whichever of you it is."

The boy cackled. I had intended to pique him but, as I later found, the twins loved nothing more than to be mistaken for each other. By birth their genes were identical; by efforts their predilections, mannerisms, and diction were as near alike as any two individuals could be without abusing virtualization. To them this similarity was a performance and, like bad actors convinced of their own greatness, they played it loud and blunt. "The girl! The prodigy. Kanrisa of course, did you know we might have become colleagues? My brother and I were echo material early on. When we were toddlers. Only by then they were up to their teeth in potentiates. What a generation that was—what a generation *we* are."

"Are you a geneticist?"

"Just a data-glutton, like you. Though Kanrisa's case is pretty fascinating, isn't it? Tailored just so. Ancestors bless, but what intricate work. Made to echo; born for a voice. Engineering made poetry."

To this day, I don't know what impelled me. An act like that wasn't in my nature.

Barely knowing how to do it, I punched Manop/Padon in the face. Knuckles to nose, my fist tightly shut.

He pitched over, the back of his skull thudding against bulkhead. Others abandoned their food; his twin came running and Viraya shouted above the din. Somewhere in all this, Kanrisa stood staring, wild-eyed, lips fluttering like gills.

"No, no!" The brother I'd hit was flinging up his hands, pushing away his twin and older sister. "I'm fine! I'm fine. It's all right, everybody please disperse, no Viraya be quiet, I'm not pressing charges. Also—" He paused, raised his head and stretched wide his arms to make the moment what it was: theatrics. Despite the blood streaming from his nose. "Also, I'm in love. Brother, we're in love and this is the woman we are going to court. The Abacus can go hang."

My knuckles bloomed bruises afterward.

Kanrisa came to see me in my cabin which, contrariwise to my preference, I didn't share with her. "Why did you do that?" was the first thing out of her mouth.

"I'm sick of hearing you referred to as some mad geneticist's pet project. Aren't you?"

"I am. I'm the one who's had to live with it, so what do you think? But I *am* a mad geneticist's pet project. The perfect match for my voice." She laughed, brittle. "I got over it, as you do, growing up. So why did you think it was a fine idea to do what you did? Did you suppose you were defending my honor?"

Behind my back I folded my hand, which had acquired shades new and strange. Blue-black and purple soon to make acquaintance with green. "That's what suitors do. Are you embarrassed?"

"Viraya is enraged. She is my closest friend—not DNA-knitted but at least a…an institution kid. We grew up together, as much as that means anything."

"Oh," I said, reading her half by instinct, half by familiarity grown from absorbing data detritus. My chest ground, like old reactors, like archaic hardware unable to breathe past debris and overheating components. "You have an interest in her."

"Long past. The Abacus has decided."

"It only suggests." I scuttled on my bed, making myself small, and rested my head against the viewport. Outside the sky raced by. "I didn't think."

"Not just the Abacus. I like you. It's just…with Viraya it was simple. But we were never going to wed or even have anything like a sustained relationship; two Bodhva are like two mirrors set opposite— endlessly reflecting. I'm not going to hide the thing with Viraya from you, Jidri. Please let me see your hand."

"I'll use a patch. It'll heal before the day's out."

"Even then."

I let her have it, the bruised hand. She cupped it and I contemplated the differences between us. Her fingers were blunt-rough, some of them tipped with implants that let her handle her voice; mine were long and thin, empty unmarked skin. Kanrisa pursed her lips, very lightly, on each darkened knuckle.

"Do I get a kiss?" I said, pushing. "A real one."

Her nod was almost shy; her mouth tasted of coconut, plum sugar, and implants. When I breathed her, my head turned bright with information overlays.

Alarms thrummed through our arteries. We were almost there, on the edge of Intharachit's field.

Before she was gone, Kanrisa would tell me about her training.

Bodhva immersive simulation sharpens the mind and opens it to thinking in, perceiving, six dimensions on its own. With augmens that enlarges to eight. The perception of an echo, and the potential that arises from it, cannot be matched. Being firmly outside both process and subculture, I couldn't comprehend it.

But there are other courses, where a Bodhva in training would be given the task of spinning permutations of herself. Living different lives, not echoes at all but ordinary Pojami—sometimes not even that. Kanrisa reimagined herself a weaver in Mahuya, a queen from the chronicles of Dakkhu, a general of Immarad, a hundred thousand variations of herself placed in a hundred thousand contexts. When she found one she thought useful, she would absorb pertinent information from it.

Any simulation is permitted, but some are less permissible than others. Kanrisa ran a version of herself as an Intharachit resident to gain a better understanding of them. She said she came away feeling soiled and ugly: theirs was a short life, choked by *do not*.

In the safety of my processing ecosystem, I'm doing as she did, my bare skin open to cold metal and optics. Without the necessary software assisting me, I've had to put on more links to facilitate the procedure. They bud in a line between my breasts, flourishing on body nutrients. I've been eating more lately, and increased my sanitarium visits. No one asks, much.

I gave in to the temptation, once, of creating a model of Kanrisa and putting her inside the same reality as one of my simulacra. Not long after—days in real time, segments in virtual—I killed the entire instance and banished it from memory.

Yet somewhere in this is a path to her, a way to reverse-engineer her genesis. The original plans may be gone, but within me, there are imprints of her, facets of her. Sufficient for associative algorithms.

All is numbers; all is data. From me the cortices keep no secrets.

The periphery of Intharachit was a ruin where nothing would grow. Passing through the field my teeth rattled. Colors tinkled against my gums.

Drones flitted out of the *Khrut*, hissing into chameleon state. We waited and watched. Other carriers were in range; each ship pulsed communications to the next on organic frequencies that, shifting in constant flux, matched no League signal.

The League had built machine-gods of their own, in the forms of long-legged, earthbound automata with graceless armed heads and hammerhead sharks that flew on rotating blades. No echoes. Our drones found one of the factories where the bombs and reactor cores were assembled, and Kanrisa's cadre followed.

Starbursts shredded the night, laying it bare: in the wake of this I breathed shallowly, so thinly my lungs trembled with need. I had seen the voices in still life—in motion they were something else.

League constructs were ugly. The voices were beautiful, and sang. *Engineering made poetry,* I thought, sounding out the brothers' phrase in spite of myself.

Kanrisa's voice spread its limbs, anti-grav wingblades fanning wide to let her hover as she coordinated other echoes. Mindless airborne drones rushed at her, and were swept away under disruption signals from the voice's vast mouth. They fell in a hail of dead metal and whirring mandibles.

Some semblance of order, now, in the factory. The larger machines lumbering into combat, sighting down ours. They were cumbersome, their targeting sluggish. Viraya swooped down, her voice's arms a blur of brilliant edges, and tore them apart.

Between all this I was tuned into Kanrisa's channel. My heart beat to her rhythm—I felt invincible and could have forgotten what I was meant to do had the instruments not reminded me. I mightn't have made friends among the crew, but I had made plenty among the cortices. Panels thrilled to my touches, loops of machine-ghosts whispering within me as I hoped Kanrisa one day would. In my hands the data streams knitted, flowed into a sea that washed over me in blue-white waves.

I was with her.

And so, well before anyone cupped in cradles that let us swim in the river cortex, I felt the anomaly. It made me shout with my physical mouth—and therefore useless—a warning that nobody ever heard.

It surged from beneath the mass of fabricators and generators, a matte-grey blur. None of our symbiotes had seen it, and later I would learn that the expedition had never known of it. Some of their engineers had been paranoid enough, vigilant enough, to keep secrets from the first contact party.

This construct was humanoid, four limbs, a head, and nearly as large as the machine-gods that stood guard over our home. A scan told me it carried life signs. Its arms wound tight around its torso as it rose;

its face was an oval of gold.

Hardly any reason to panic. On the *Khrut* we were shielded, well away from the battle. In the voices, each echo was secure. If the League thought merely the sight of an artificial sun would drive us insensate, they would be disappointed.

Then the construct reached out and caught Tephem's voice in three long, prehensile fingers.

He fought back with cold contempt; in one swipe he severed crude wrist-cords, but it held on. With its free hand, it tore off one wingblade. Permutative metal shifted rapidly, cycling through probability alloys, each invulnerable. But Tephem's voice was not entirely armored in that. All this creature needed was a puncture wound.

The League machine's face blazed. A soft, wet noise somewhere in my head and Tephem's data-stream went black, unraveling from the sea. My horror left my lips in a thin scream.

But he had been overconfident. Others darted out of reach and chipped away at the monstrosity's grey shell. It was welded in the same material that let League ships withstand spatial distortion; in the face of sonic-flux bursts, it was useless.

As it died in cascades of sloughing shrapnel, I heard the wails, subliminal, of the League men and women that piloted it.

It wasn't the only such machine—three had been successfully made, three unleashed against us. During that first foray, we lost four voices, four echoes.

In those days, Kanrisa spoke to no one, carrying out each attack as the orchestrating focus with precision matched by few other cadre leaders. Under her guidance, generators were torn into shockwaves that destroyed Intharachit cities. One factory after another unseamed into pulped flesh and melted slag. The League had tried for cycles to bring their growth under control, crowding more and more thickly into slivers of land, building upward and downward: ugly spires thrusting into the sky and stabbing roots deep into the earth. In five turns of night we quartered, then halved, their residential density.

Still I did not know peace.

Tephem had been a stranger. I don't believe we ever had a complete conversation together. To me he existed in sideway correlations— Pattama's nephew, Kanrisa's colleague, a lover, on and off, of Viraya's.

Even so, his death gripped me and would not let go. Perhaps entrenched in Kanrisa's channel at the time, I assimilated her grief for my own. Even apart from that, I couldn't comprehend that an echo was gone, so quickly and simply. Whatever else Manop/Padon had said, Bodhva who successfully integrated into a machine-god were rare. It was such a precious, intricate process. And now four had died, together with their voices. Irrevocably they had died. I relived, each time I slept, that one moment and imagined that I could reach across the ships and touch the other echoes, too, as they fell.

A communiqué was broadcast on League bands in stammering, erratic stabs. It found us, as it was meant to, and in their staccato language told us this: *We will not surrender. We will break your god-speakers. We hide, we rebuild, and while we live, we will not share this earth with you. You are few; we are many.*

The twin brothers sneered, jointly. "Like ants are many, and us crushing them underfoot by the colony. Don't they realize they're outgunned, outmatched, that they're barely more than shit-slinging apes? All that bluster."

No one laughed with them.

"Can they do that?" I had never seen Viraya show fear. A flicker of it crept down the roots of her hair, to limn the corners of her eyes. "Where did they get our forensic samples?"

Pattama shook her head. "They didn't. An idle threat, a bluff. There wasn't enough left of my younger sisters' son. Even if there were, I doubt they can manage the most elementary manipulation — let alone bioweapons. There's been no evidence they are capable."

How desperate I was to believe that she was untouched, impervious to loss. We all needed that.

Kanrisa stared at the screen where the words shimmered and said nothing. I was behind her, centimeters away. In a gesture as personal as I could ever make myself perform in public, I wound my arms around her waist. "They aren't all wrong, Pattama-elder. Number to number there are thousands of them to each of us. In time, they will rebuild and try to make good their promise. One way or another."

"What would you do then?" Pattama looked at me.

"Kanrisa," I whispered. "What do you want?"

She turned to me, my intended, and the honed point of her gaze made me ache. "I want them gone."

It contradicted our original objective, but none protested. In that we were aligned, as voice to echo.

The cortices wanted to soothe me out of mourning and my chip purred equilibrium protocols, webbing me in childhood fractals and haptics. I ignored them—the only time I ever did—and pored over League censuses: physiology metrics, mortality rates, and life expectancy. In the last I found sharp drops. Their population was still growing faster than could be sustained, but for some age brackets there were psychological fractures that culminated in random violence and suicide. In one of their administrative divisions, nine out of ten adolescent males had died of marrow poisoning. Within a capital city, there had been a period just before their exploratory mission where all infants born had emerged with tumors lodged deep within their cerebra.

I investigated further. There were genome models and a veritable library of DNA samples we had downloaded from their quaintly obsolete servhosts.

Their phenotype spectrum was vanishingly thin and their gene pool had diminished to a puddle. Each generation carried diseases and gave them to the next, conditions more and more hardcoded. The League was dying a protracted, incestuous death. They were inbreeding into extinction because they'd extinguished any genetic material not precisely like their own.

Knowing this made it simple. The analyses I ran after that were some of the most uncomplex I had ever done: cross-referencing the indices, diagnosing the common links and afflictions. I sent them to Pattama, who pinged back almost immediately requesting an optimal target.

"The northern city," one of the twin brothers said from a cradle adjacent to mine. This was the one who'd made acquaintance with my fist. "They are the healthiest. It'll demoralize them best."

"Yes." I sent that back to Tephem's aunt, remembering the female I had guided through Pojama. She had died painlessly.

"Where's Kanrisa? This is her idea. I thought she'd be looking over your shoulder."

"She is resting." Kanrisa hadn't slept much. When I could, I would go into her room, climb into her bed, and she would cup my body with hers, one hand closed over my stomach. Only then did she fall into dreams.

"Hey. I've always wanted to know, why Kanrisa? I know, the Abacus, but you don't seem like the type who'd just walk up to her and make such a scene—all those people, that day—just because the Abacus gave you a name."

"You were there?"

"I was landscaping."

I frowned. "You are such a child. And I didn't take her hand simply because of the algorithms. I saw her and chose." *I couldn't not have,* I did not tell him. Her pull had been gravitational, sun to my star.

"What about me then? I'm not that incompatible."

"I have Kanrisa. What do I want with you?"

He blinked, then widened his eyes. "You're a monogamist?"

My face must have colored. "None of—"

"My business, yes, but it's just I've never actually met... I swear, I've found more spontaneous cohesion in gibbercrypt than monogamists. So you'll live in your own household?"

"Sharing with my siblings. Why am I even telling you this?"

"Because you want to tell it to somebody. Honestly, though. Monogamy." He unlinked and threw up his hands. "Unbelievable. Are you sure?"

"Kanrisa and I are content with just one at a time. Now shut up before I punch you again."

A long sigh of bliss. "See? You can tell me apart from my brother after all. That's why I wish you would consider us. Maybe in half a cycle? People do change, you know."

I have decided to attend Viraya's wedding, after all. That is what friendships are like: a net of obligations and social niceties.

The old faces are all there, the familiar names. Both twin brothers, Pattama, Surada, the crews of the *Khrut* and the *Samutthevi*. I have even brought some of the *Khrut's* cortices, which I'd adopted as part of my compensation, and they chatter away in my wrists, at the back of my neck: recognizing and regaling each other with tales of this or that ship hand. It keeps me calm and reassured, to be surrounded by their dialogue.

It's a modest wedding. Viraya is marrying a man, an ambigendered, and two women. As matrimony goes, it isn't a large union (my parents began with six, and over time the conjugation grew to nine) and out of the would-be partners I know only Viraya and another, a quantum navigator recently instrumental to solar-systems crossing. These new ways of traveling, in leaps and bounds through space-time, make me feel old. I could be up there; affinity-class data savants are always in demand. But much keeps me earthbound. Out there in the beyond, communication can get tattered, too slow to catch up with vessel speed. Too many uncertainties, and these days I want the solidity of sureness. Of knowing where I am, what I do.

Most would be hard-pressed to believe I was part of the force that destroyed Intharachit. I'm so much less. Just another administrative worker with a monthly salary.

I don't dream of past glories. I don't dream of exhilarating voyages through doors spun out of herded probabilities. In my bed surrounded by the susurrus of cortices, I dream merely of her.

"Life is more than that," one of my sisters would say. "Find another, younger sister, and laugh again."

"This is the life I've chosen. I won't laugh until she is well."

The earth shudders; would-be spouses giggle, arms linked, as grass and soil swell.

"Life is more than that," one of my mothers would say. "Seek the stars, petulant daughter, and smile again."

"This is the life I've chosen. I won't smile until she is well."

I watch the brother who didn't visit Umadu as he brings his arms down and the ground cracks open, thrusting up a bounty of persimmons and chrysanthemums. I watch him as he accepts congratulations for a job well done and, disentangling, strides toward me on feet that don't quite touch the grass. "Jidri. I didn't think you would come. What a sight you are! So long unseen."

"Our careers branched apart."

"That they did. You don't belong there, webbed in those antique cortices, rerouting old tech. Up there is where you should be. Finding out just how many dimensions comprise our universe. Be part of the cutting-edge."

Life is more than that. "I like doing what I do."

He shakes his head. "You have changed, but then who hasn't.

Have you reconsidered?"

"I've been told you only wanted me to keep your twin from individualizing himself."

A disbelieving chortle. "My brother and his dog's mouth."

"For the record, I'd sooner marry him, if he didn't already belong to four spouses."

"Not sharing well even now?"

"I never will. A monomaniac, remember? That's what you called me after you were done with 'monogamist.' "

"You are, though I'm sorry for the tone I used then." He sighs and newly blossomed flowers rustle with him. "Please, Jidri. Life is more than Kanrisa."

"Kanrisa is the life I've chosen for myself."

From the strands of my indices and extrapolated models Pattama teased out an answer to Kanrisa's question.

The northern city was the wealthiest on the continent. I expected more from them than the swarming anthills of other Intharachit states. But what I saw was scarcely better, a riot of squalor and starvation. The air churned with disease, dust, despair. Pattama's cultivar wasn't going to be a retaliatory strike after all, but a mercy. A way out.

We introduced the strain into their rebreathers, which vainly tried to purify the filth it inhaled from the city's throats. We put it into the tanks that processed fluid waste and recycled it into a semblance of water.

During the first week little happened, and in this lull I spent my time with Kanrisa. We were past the negotiation stage and, ignoring nominal protests about chain of command (which barely existed and hardly mattered), she migrated to my cabin. We kept a touch of resistance so infinitesimal it couldn't be expressed numerically even as we stretched it out: testing its tensile strength, its elasticity. Anticipation of what we'd set in motion made it hard to think of anything else, even while we slept skin to skin. It was good to do so, all the same, each shared touch piquant. Tense.

(There were warning signs. A look in the distance. Fleeting instants when Kanrisa was not with me but went somewhere else, chasing Tephem's ghost. Back then I hadn't realized the extent of her unique nature. Why the way she functioned as an echo was unlike anyone else's.)

"I can't stop thinking how it might have been different."

"If you keep doing that you will end up like Zhuyi," I told her as I undressed and climbed into bed. She was warm from a fresh hematocyte intake and smelled of psychometric links. Intoxicating. With her I never needed simul-input bombardment, my addictive of choice, to fall delirious and trembling. "All his time spent in simulations, running that one moment through fifty, a hundred, a thousand scenarios."

"Who's that?"

Sliding my hand under the gap between her spine and the bed, I frowned. "One of my brothers? I must have told you about him—the one whose marriage fell to pieces, so he keeps replaying a sim to find out what he did wrong. It's all very sad and he refuses to put his name back into the Abacus."

Kanrisa tickled my collarbone with her tongue. "You might have mentioned him in passing. I forgot. Do you think I will regret this? Calling for what I did."

I wrapped myself tight around her. "Never. And if there's ever regret it will be mine, too. I won't let you carry it alone."

Our monitoring cortices went into a frenzy when the infected city came apart. I listened to some of the chatter. Cries for help. Emergency dispatches. Pattama's virus had targeted their arteries; out of everything, it was what we knew best. It thinned their plasma, and thinned it again, until what went through their veins was like water. From their pale, diluted mouths, they retched pale, diluted hemorrhage as they clawed themselves open. This fluid, not blood anymore, puddled in their streets and soaked the tiny rooms in their beehive houses. It lapped at their windows and gave life to frail weeds in the interstices of their walls. They wept it in deep, wracking shudders, and died in throes of asphyxiation as their lungs drowned.

In the midst of this, one of the other ships—the *Samutthevi*—pinged us with a set of coordinates and a message: *We have found them.*

What remained of League military command had submerged themselves in radio silence after broadcasting that one challenge. No communication of any kind, minimal power usage: they'd retreated, as deep as they could, into a pre-tech state. Only through chance did one of the *Samutthevi's* drones catch a glimpse of an engineer out to obtain food supplies. From there it divided itself, splitting into transmitter and receiver. The first latched onto him, integrating into his nervous system; the other returned to the *Samutthevi*. In discreet pulses it sent back schematics, an inventory of equipment and personnel.

"There's not much to them," said Surada, their cadre's commander. "Some two hundred holed up in a cave network underground. You will coordinate with us?"

"What do they have? Apart from—" Kanrisa motioned at the imaging of their tools, furniture, miscellanies. "These. They can't possibly hope to fight with that."

"I have good reasons to think they're culturing a strain that'd work against us. Of course, they haven't any sample—unless somehow they do. Our casualty..." Surada's expression flickered. "We collected her. There's no chance. It's best to proceed with caution regardless. We could bombard the whole area, which would be my preference, except the tunnels go deep."

"How about gas? Their ventilation can't be much good. Two of my people developed an agent that bonds to their circulation. It's been effective."

Surada gave a curt nod. "I've seen the footage. *Brutally* effective. Take a look at this, though." A shape sharpened into focus on the viewport. "Thermal take from the symbiote. That's a biomass right there."

"That," I said, measuring it against a scale in my head, "is very huge."

"And very dense. Estimates say a hundred fifty tall, eighty wide, and five to eight hundred heavy. What do you say to that, savant?"

"Her name is Jidri, Surada."

"They're cloning muscle tissue—too dense to be anything else. There's no organ, no anything except for a skeleton, also extremely dense and likely metal. They want to make..." I paused, remembering the makeup of the creature that had killed Tephem. "No radio, no anything. So it's all grown in a vat, organically, without machinery or circuits or electricity. And maybe...here, where it thins. A cavity, I think. Waiting to be filled."

Surada nodded. "With what, Jidri?"

"This is a pure educated guess. This construct isn't running on conventional energy—it's going to be powered by one of their own. A crude transplant." My rambling flung up a spume of disparate suppositions in my private sphere. I filtered them through my chip. "They are making another killing machine out of their own materials, controlled by a brain or a collective of brains. It will carry not a miniature sun but an anti-Bodhva weapon: physical, toxin, something. If we are to believe their threat."

"In line with my savants' conclusions. Yes. What are the chances of your viral agent working on this biomass? So far as my probe's been able to determine, what runs through its veins is crude fuel or possibly liquid alloy."

"Another approach then." Kanrisa ran her fingers over the displays. They rippled, briefly projecting imprints of her hands that chased the real ones. "I have an idea. It's not something I ever wanted to do. Circumstances have changed. Just to be sure we'll flush them out first."

We flooded the tunnels. Redirecting the nearest reservoir proved more trouble than anticipated—so few natural bodies of water existed in Intharachit—but there was enough. Their shelter was old and, though chambers were armored and sealed, structural integrity had been eroded by time and neglect. That first rush killed fifty who hadn't fled behind blast doors in time. Circuited synapses fired, machines coming awake under emergency routines.

A sudden spike in neural electricity. Their callsign; our warning.

Pulsating flesh so hot it flashed white on thermal take, stitched together by artificial sinews. Each ungainly piece must have been grown individually. Its head was distended, its torso a gaping red wound. From each pore, it oozed oil, pus, blood. Veins throbbed beneath its shell.

"Ancestors," one of the twins said. "What did they put into that thing?"

"Brains locked in sync." I ran a scan: whatever made up the skeleton blocked several of our sensors, but I could still measure neural voltage. "Twenty, no, sixty. Sixty brains transplanted, feeling in conjunction."

The other brother reared up from his cradle. "In a month they perfected that?"

"No," I said, "they perfected nothing." We brute-forced our way into what passed for its mainframe. A composite hastily thrown together without regard for compatibility or efficiency, orienting as fast as it could to new senses, new realities expressed in synesthesia. And what it felt, through ink-stain drops infiltrating its liquid consciousness, was pain. Each sensory input overloaded it, converting to agony until it knew nothing else. It found its level in the biomass, erasing intellect and sanity, channeling it into one single pinpoint purpose: to lash out. At us.

Kanrisa did not allow this. Once the biomass emerged she began.

She was—is—a centrifuge; her age-mate echoes belonged to her, operating as her adjuncts. Over their voices' output she wielded a fine control, able to reach in and weave, plait, and transfigure. That is the purpose of a Bodhva focus.

What she did that day hadn't been seen before and seldom since. Today we continue trying to replicate it, gnawing at the process with augmens, a cortex biosphere greater than the Abacus, and the best minds of our age. Progress is slow, with rare successes so miniscule they hardly count.

Kanrisa seized the voices' chorus and shattered it into sixty-five permutations of itself. It punctured situational probabilities where the laws of physics were rewritten for an instant.

When it ended, the biomass was gone, each particle threshed into nonexistence. The tunnels became a crater. So did twenty nearest cities within range of the blast. Half the spatial storm that enclosed Intharachit coiled and released under Kanrisa's guidance. Most coastal regions were drowned under tidal waves.

We still had to spread Pattama's virus to the surviving population, but it was a nominal gesture. Kanrisa had ended the war.

We came home with more diagnostics than anyone knew what to do with.

The aftermath was incandescent: as one we breathed, drinking in one another, as the city celebrated us not as heroes but as living stories. What we had done—decided by Kanrisa, mediated by me, brought into being by Pattama—was like nothing in living memory, and our living memory is immense in breadth and length. Pojama wanted for nothing but novelty, and we were that magnified many times over. Nothing seemed impossible. Kanrisa's stigma vanished overnight. Through centrids we had grown in peace, and that was stagnancy. This was the first occasion after so long that conflict would jolt us forward.

We were so much wanted back then, pulled this way and that, sometimes parted. Great bursts of advances were made. Optimizing the voices, evolving deep logics of our cortices at exponential rates, leapfrogs in cybernetics. Though Intharachit lay in ruins each savant had brought back libraries of DNA samples we would append to our biodiversity projects and assimilate into our virtualization programs.

Kanrisa and I didn't find time to marry properly, but we did put aside nights. Just as I had thought—had wanted—we secreted ourselves away in my cortex nest. I discovered the stretch marks on her breasts and thighs; I counted her epidermal implants, where they ridged her flesh, where they hardened the texture of her stomach. Her fingers digging into my hips, my nerves alight with her augmens output: a hundred compressed Bodhva songs.

I...

I can't recount this, even to myself. Even to my cortices, who already know, who understand and record and dream with me. It is difficult. It is impossible.

But when all else is gone there is the wreckage of our story, and within that, there is us. When I am done playing a small piece out for an audience and whispering it to myself, I will be able to begin again. I will go back to when we were young, and whole, and perpetual: a day of the scythe, in a garden festooned with lights.

It is hard to pinpoint where the disintegration began.

Minor lapses. She met my mothers, my siblings, and then she misplaced their names and their order: who was elder, who was younger. I told myself she had not been reared in a family but in an institution where no one claimed kinship to her. Why should I expect her to adjust overnight?

One morning she woke up not quite sure where she was.

The next she woke up unable to remember Viraya, Tephem, any of her unit.

After that, she could not remember me, and finally her implants went dormant: she could no longer echo.

(I can't speak this aloud. I can't include it for my audiences. I do not discuss it with my friends, my family. It is taboo to speak Kanrisa's name in my earshot.)

Perhaps she was built to function only once. Perhaps she was so centrifugal that without the orbit of other echoes she could not exist, and losing Tephem mid-chorus damaged her. Or perhaps what she did to shatter her age-mates' song, to manipulate Intharachit's spatial storm, broke something within her that made her Kanrisa.

Perhaps.

Today I think of my brother Zhuyi. The lost one, the tragic one.

I lie in my cradle, in an obscure division of the complex that cares for the city's network. It's dim and quiet, so as to least disturb previous -gen cortices that haven't yet made the leap and joined the great ocean of the Abacus. Most of my days are spent here, persuading them to become part of it, to join it in the tasks of monitoring the shields, maximizing compatibility, the processes that complete Pojama and keep it in constant growth.

Some are reluctant, others afraid. A few refuse and those I shepherd into lesser systems, where they can serve and know simpler joys. Regardless of their destination, it's necessary that their owners' signature is erased first: their original information will only weigh them down unnecessarily.

Nearly a cycle and a half have passed since I came to this division. My wait has been so long and precisely planned that when *it* finally shuffles into one of my arrays, there's no surprise. Existence is a series of coincidences. One may stand still until chances collide and result. I choose otherwise. I calculate, predict, and attain. Opportunity must be plucked out of, and strained from, churning randomness.

Tephem's personal cortex drifts into my lap. It's been in a protracted hibernation and will probably acquiesce to whatever I suggest. In spite of that, my breathing lurches and my heart palpitates unevenly, now sharp and exquisite, then dull and empty.

This will work.

It has to.

With delicacy—my physical fingers shake, even as the ones I've made in the administrative subreality move with surgical accuracy—I extract fragments of Tephem's memorabilia, consumption habits, training permutation back-ups, all the things that can be found embedded in any private chip. It's unambiguously, incredibly illegal. If found out I will be punished, my chips and cortices purged, some of my links disabled. It'll blind me, shackle me, halve my self. There are data savants who, so deprived, can't maintain sanity.

I don't care.

Once my shift is finally ended I leave, bloated with thieved data. Through the scanners I step, nearly on tiptoes, as they skim over my heart-rate, neural activity, blood pressure. None of which is in its regular state and I get past only by fooling the sensors with prefabricated readings I installed a week ago in anticipation of today.

For this my brain would be emptied, my genes scrambled until I'm no longer me; until the being known as Jidri is reduced to if-else strings.

I am not afraid. The tightening of my larynx, the hammering of my heart: they are biological reflexes.

Out in the streets, crowds buffet me, vendors trying to draw me in with flashes of sculpted light and funneled sound. A woman more cybernetics than flesh, her skin all facets, touches me with a jolt of seduction memes: inviting me to make love with her, glass to glass. I shrug her off and very briefly wonder if she's an overseer agent. They can be anywhere and my crime—

Kanrisa would have spat out her fear, as one would a morsel of spoiled food.

On the edge of the visitors' area is a small octagonal storeroom in a small octagonal building.

I pass into that room, where a cortex sleeps. It's had no contact with any other for two full segments. Gently I bring it awake but not online, wiring myself into it without tapping into a network. It comes out of standby with reluctance, only faintly recalling who I am.

To reconstruct a person is hard, to reconstruct a stranger long dead almost impossible. Even with a fully-powered, cognizant cortex with the latest ware. But I can't take the risk of using my own—I need to be anonymous, as far offline as I can go.

Over these last two cycles, I collected snippets of surveillance, records from sanitariums and trails left across the net, piecing together a picture of Tephem. With the personal data I've downloaded, the result is, theoretically, at least half-complete. Nevertheless, a whole life is not easy to transliterate into code. There's much to reconcile, a host of contradictions and phases I can't easily put in order.

The reconstruction is agonizing. I install updates to the cortex a little at a time, but it remains sluggish and unwilling. I persevere and coax. I can't return too often; sometimes I would manage three visits in as many days, sometimes almost none, and each can be measured in minutes. My nerves fray and I would keep away for fifteen, twenty days. I don't know if my theory is anywhere near correct or functional. This is all I have left, to reconstruct Tephem and that moment in Intharachit. To recomplete her inner system and make her the center of that unit again.

Unnatural winter persists over Pojama. I've been told they have found a way to localize the weather patterns. How quickly the world hurtles by.

When it is done, finally, I purge all remnant information. There would be no trace. A copy of the reconstruction lives in a partition of my chip, but that is the only one. I send it off, behind multidimensional proxies and the best encryption I can do.

"What is in it?" the splicer asks, when the packets have passed through dead drops in pieces and reassembled on his end.

"You don't need to know." I hold many secrets of his, and now have another: he would be my accomplice. "Put it in her treatment programs."

"But—"

"Please do it."

I cut contact and wait for word from Umadu.

It is the first day of summer and the city is festooned with lights.

I wander my family's home, where the trees are fruiting heavy and red, where the roofs are gestating blue pearls in each tile. It feels strange to be leaving; I've been in one place for so long. My work at the op-net is done with, and I am at last entering newer, stranger fields. Umadu continues to send reports, each emptier than the last.

Two cycles. It's time to be elsewhere, be someone else.

"It is good," one of my sisters said as I miniaturized my cortices to fit a single chip, drinking down protocols and matrices that would hibernate in my implants. "You will be holding stars in your hands, and how many dream of that?"

"Sister, I don't dream of stars."

She wound a mercury chain around my wrist. "Second best is not so bad. It is a life. I will think of you and hope you find peace."

There are gold-and-black fish in our pond, a hybrid Zhuyi has cultivated in his spare time. It has eyes like one of his former wives', he said, and in its swimming patterns he claims to see the imprint of her body. Above me, something sings with a human mouth, the favorite song of one of Zhuyi's once-husbands. He's turned our home into a memorial. We all indulge him, glad that he no longer spends all his time running those simulations. I'm on speaking terms with Varee, one of his erstwhile wives, and when Zhuyi isn't home she sometimes pays us a visit.

"It is good," one of my mothers said as I folded sheets of shiftcloth to fit into a single case, smoothing the permutative fabrics that would regulate my temperature up in the cold of satellite stations. "You will be conquering dimensions, and how many dream of that?"

"Mother, I don't dream of conquest."

She clinched an electro-carbon cube around my throat. "Second best is not unacceptable. It is a life. I will think of you and hope you find joy."

My contract is valid for half a segment; beyond that I will be free to renew it, or enlist as part of the force. It will be some time before I'm physically here again. I've already begun arrangements to transfer guardianship of Kanrisa to me officially—she has no one who can claim genetic relation to her—and cryogenics will be needed to slow down her aging. Where I'm going, time will move at sporadic paces.

My transport is here, a spindly thing running on sub-routines so unintelligent they spare me no acknowledgment. The research ventures I'll be a part of are secretive and I'll have scant opportunities to speak to my family, most of them monitored. But if there's a way for her, a way to her, it is in the probability crossroads—the noiseless impact between invisible dimensions—that I will find it.

Someone's trying to open a comm channel. I mute it. The vehicle irises open and I think of the worlds beyond, of what our world looks like from far above. Of being unfettered by the sun.

Footsteps behind me, bare feet pattering on pavement. A shadow falls, overlapping mine.

It is the first day of summer and the city is festooned with lights.

I turn.

"Your name is Jidri," she says, bringing my hand to her lips. "And you are to be my wife."

A Hundred Ghosts Parade Tonight

Xia Jia

(Translated from Chinese by Ken Liu.)

Chinese author Xia Jia began publishing in 2004 in a variety of Chinese SF magazines. She is a several-times winner of China's prestigious Galaxy Award for her short fiction, including one for the following story.

Awakening of Insects, the Third Solar Term:

Ghost Street is long but narrow, like an indigo ribbon. You can cross it in eleven steps, but to walk it from end to end takes a full hour.

At the western end is Lanruo Temple, now fallen into ruin. Inside the temple is a large garden full of fruit trees and vegetable patches, as well as a bamboo grove and a lotus pond. The pond has fish, shrimp, dojo loaches, and yellow snails. So supplied, I have food to eat all year.

It's evening, and I'm sitting at the door to the main hall, reading a copy of *Huainanzi*, the Han Dynasty essay collection, when along comes Yan Chixia, the great hero, vanquisher of demons and destroyer of evil spirits. He's carrying a basket on the crook of his elbow, the legs of his pants rolled all the way up, revealing calves caked with black mud. I can't help but laugh at the sight.

My teacher, the Monk, hears me and walks out of the dark corner of the main hall, gears grinding, and hits me on the head with his ferule.

I hold my head in pain, staring at the Monk in anger. But his iron face is expressionless, just like the statues of Buddhas in the main hall. I throw down the book and run outside, while the Monk pursues me, his joints clanging and creaking the whole time. They are so rusted that he moves as slowly as a snail.

I stop in front of Yan, and I see his basket contains several new bamboo shoots, freshly dug from the ground.

"I want to eat meat," I say, tilting my face up to look at him. "Can you shoot some buntings with your slingshot for me?"

"Buntings are best eaten in the fall, when they're fat," says Yan. "Now is the time for them to breed chicks. If you shoot them, there won't be buntings to eat next year."

"Just one, pleaaaaase?" I grab onto his sleeve and act cute. But he shakes his head resolutely, handing me the basket. He takes off his conical sedge hat and wipes the sweat off his face.

I laugh again as I look at him. His face is as smooth as an egg, with just a few wisps of curled black hair, like weeds that have been missed by the gardener. Legend has it that his hair and beard used to be very thick, but I'm always pulling a few strands out now and then as a game. After so many years, these are all the hairs he has left.

"You must have died of hunger in a previous life," Yan says, cradling the back of my head in his large palm. "The whole garden is full of food for you. No one is here to fight you for it."

I make a face at him and take the basket of food.

The rain has barely stopped; insects cry out from the wet earth. A few months from now, green grasshoppers will be jumping everywhere. You can catch them, string them along a stick, and roast them over the fire, dripping sweet-smelling fat into the flames.

As I picture this, my empty stomach growls as though already filled with chittering insects. I begin to run.

The golden light of the evening sun splatters over the slate slabs of the empty street, stretching my shadow into a long, long band.

I run back home, where Xiao Qian is combing her hair in the darkness. There are no mirrors in the house, so she always takes off her head and puts it on her knees to comb. Her hair looks like an ink-colored scroll, so long that the strands spread out to cover the whole room.

I sit quietly to the side until she's done combing her hair, puts it up in a moon-shaped bun, and secures it with a pin made of dark wood inlaid with red coral beads. Then she lifts her head and re-attaches it to her neck, and asks me if it's sitting straight. I don't understand why Xiao Qian cares so much. Even if she just tied her head to her waist with a sash, everyone would still think she's beautiful.

But I look, seriously, and nod. "Beautiful," I say.

Actually, I can't really see very well. Unlike the ghosts, I cannot see in the dark.

Xiao Qian is happy with my affirmation. She takes my basket and goes into the kitchen to cook. As I sit and work the bellows next to her, I tell her about my day. Just as I get to the part where the Monk hit me on the head with the ferule, Xiao Qian reaches out and lightly caresses my head where I was hit. Her hand is cold and pale, like a piece of jade.

"You need to study hard and respect your teacher," Xiao Qian says. "Eventually you'll leave here and make your way in the real world. You have to have some knowledge and real skills."

Her voice is very soft, like cotton candy, and so the swelling on my head stops hurting.

Xiao Qian tells me that Yan Chixia found me on the steps of the temple when I was a baby. I cried and cried because I was so hungry. Yan Chixia was at his wit's end when he finally stuffed a handful of creeping rockfoil into my mouth. I sucked on the juice from the grass and stopped crying.

No one knows who my real parents are.

Even back then, Ghost Street had been doing poorly. No tourists had been coming by for a while. That hasn't changed. Xiao Qian tells me that it's probably because people invented some other attraction, newer, fresher, and so they forgot about the old attractions. She's seen similar things happen many times.

Before she became a ghost, Xiao Qian tells me, she had lived a very full life. She had been married twice, gave birth to seven children, and raised them all.

And then her children got sick, one after another. In order to raise the money to pay the doctors, Xiao Qian sold herself off in pieces: teeth, eyes, breasts, heart, liver, lungs, bone marrow, and finally, her soul. Her soul was sold to Ghost Street, where it was sealed inside a female ghost's body. Her children died anyway.

Now she has white skin and dark hair. The skin is light sensitive. If she's in direct sunlight, she'll burn.

After he found me, Yan Chixia had walked up and down all of Ghost Street before he decided to give me to Xiao Qian to raise.

I've seen a picture of Xiao Qian back when she was alive. It was hidden in a corner of a drawer in her dresser. The woman in the picture had thick eyebrows, huge eyes, a wrinkled face—far uglier than the way Xiao Qian looks now. Still, I often see her cry as she looks at that picture. Her tears are a pale pink. When they fall against her white dress they soak into the fabric and spread, like blooming peach flowers.

Every ghost is full of stories from when they were alive. Their bodies have been cremated and the ashes mixed into the earth, but their stories still live on. During the day, when all of Ghost Street is asleep, the stories become dreams and circle under the shadows of the eaves, like swallows without nests. During those hours, only I'm around, walking in the street, and only I can see them and hear their buzzing song.

I'm the only living person on Ghost Street.

Xiao Qian says that I don't belong here. When I grow up, I'll leave.

The smell of good food fills the room. The insects in my stomach chitter even louder.

I eat dinner by myself: preserved pork with stir-fried bamboo shoots, shrimp-paste-flavored egg soup, and rice balls with chives, still hot in my hands. Xiao Qian sits and watches me. Ghosts don't eat. None of the inhabitants of Ghost Street, not even Yan Chixia or the Monk, ever eat.

I bury my face in the bowl, eating as fast as I can. I wonder, after I leave, will I ever eat such delicious food again?

Major Heat, the Twelfth Solar Term:

After night falls, the world comes alive.

I go alone to the well in the back to get water. I turn the wheel and it squeaks, but the sound is different from usual. I look down into the well and see a long-haired ghost in a white dress sitting in the bucket.

I pull her up and out. Her wet hair covers her face, leaving only one eye to stare at me out of a gap.

"Ning, tonight is the Carnival. Aren't you going?"

"I need to get water for Xiao Qian's bath," I answer. "After the bath we'll go."

She strokes my face lightly. "You are a foolish child."

She has no legs, so she has to leave by crawling on her hands. I hear the sound of crawling, creeping all around me. Green will-o'-the-wisps flit around, like anxious fireflies. The air is filled with the fragrance of rotting flowers.

I go back to the dark bedroom and pour the water into the wooden bathtub. Xiao Qian undresses. I see a crimson bar code along her naked back, like a tiny snake. Bright, white lights pulse under her skin.

"Why don't you take a bath with me?" she asks.

I shake my head, but I'm not sure why. Xiao Qian sighs. "Come." So I don't refuse again.

We sit in the bathtub together. The cedar smells nice. Xiao Qian rubs my back with her cold, cold hands, humming lightly. Her voice is very beautiful. Legend has it that any man who heard her sing fell in love with her.

When I grow up, will I fall in love with Xiao Qian? I think and look at my small hands, the skin now wrinkled from the bath like wet wrapping paper.

After the bath, Xiao Qian combs my hair, and dresses me in a new shirt that she made for me. Then she sticks a bunch of copper coins, green and dull, into my pocket.

"Go have fun," she says. "Remember not to eat too much!"

Outside, the street is lit with countless lanterns, so bright that I can no longer see the stars that fill the summer sky.

Demons, ghosts, all kinds of spirits come out of their ruined houses, out of cracks in walls, rotting closets, dry wells. Hand-in-hand, shoulder-to-shoulder, they parade up and down Ghost Street until the narrow street is filled.

I squeeze myself into the middle of the crowd, looking all around. The stores and kiosks along both sides of the street send forth all kinds of delicious smells, tickling my nose like butterflies. The vending ghosts see me and call for me, the only living person, to try their wares.

"Ning! Come here! Fresh sweet osmanthus cakes, still hot!"

"Sugar roasted chestnuts! Sweet smelling and sweeter tasting!"

"Fried dough, the best fried dough!"

"Long pig dumplings! Two long pig dumplings for one coin!"

"Ning, come eat a candy man. Fun to play and fun to eat!"

Of course the "long pig dumplings" are really just pork dumplings. The vendor says that just to attract the tourists and give them a thrill.

But I look around, and there are no tourists.

I eat everything I can get my hands on. Finally, I'm so full that I have to sit down by the side of the road to rest a bit. On the opposite side of the street is a temporary stage lit by a huge bright white paper lantern. Onstage, ghosts are performing: sword-swallowing, fire-breathing, turning a beautiful girl into a skeleton. I'm bored by these tricks. The really good show is still to come.

A yellow-skinned old ghost pushes a cart of masks in front of me.

"Ning, why don't you pick a mask? I have everything: Ox-Head, Horse-Face, Black-Faced and White-Faced Wuchang, Asura, Yaksha, Rakshasa, Pixiu, and even Lei Gong, the Duke of Thunder."

I spend a long time browsing, and finally settle on a Rakshasa mask with red hair and green eyes. The yellow-skinned old ghost thanks me as he takes my coin, dipping his head down until his back is bent like a bow.

I put the mask on and continue strutting down the street. Suddenly, loud Carnival music fills the air, and all the ghosts stop and then shuffle to the sides of the street.

I turn around and see the parade coming down the middle of the street. In front are twenty one-foot-tall, green toads in two columns, striking gongs, thumping drums, strumming *huqin*, and blowing bamboo *sheng*. After them come twenty centipede spirits in black clothes, each holding varicolored lanterns and dancing complicated steps. Behind them are twenty snake spirits in yellow dresses, throwing confetti into the air. And there are more behind them but I can't see that far.

Between the marching columns are two Cyclopes in white robes, each as tall as a three-story house. They carry a palanquin on their shoulders, and from within, Xiao Qian's song rolls out, each note as bright as a star in the sky, falling one by one onto my head.

Fireworks of all colors rise up: bright crimson, pale green, smoky purple, shimmering gold. I look up and feel as though I'm becoming lighter myself, floating into the sky.

As the parade passes from west to east, all the ghosts along the sides of the street join, singing and dancing. They're heading for the old osmanthus tree at the eastern end of Ghost Street, whose trunk is so broad that three men stretching their arms out can barely surround it. A murder of crows lives there, each one capable of human speech. We call the tree Old Ghost Tree, and it is said to be in charge of all of Ghost Street. Whoever pleases it prospers; whoever goes against its wishes fails.

But I know that the parade will never get to the Old Ghost Tree.

When the parade is about half way down the street, the earth begins to shake and the slate slabs crack open. From the yawning gaps, huge white bones crawl out, each as thick as the columns holding up Lanruo Temple. The bones slowly gather together and assemble into a giant skeleton, glinting like white porcelain in the moonlight. Now black mud springs forth from its feet and crawls up the skeleton, turning into flesh. Finally, a colossal Dark Yaksha stands before us, its single horn so large that it seems to pierce the night sky.

The two Cyclopes don't even reach its calves.

The Dark Yaksha turns its huge head from side to side. This is a standard part of every Carnival. It is supposed to abduct a tourist. On nights when there are no tourists, it must go back under the earth, disappointed, to wait for the next opportunity.

Slowly, it turns its gaze on me, focusing on my presence. I pull off my mask and stare back. Its gaze feels hot, the eyes as red as burning coal.

Xiao Qian leans out from the palanquin, and her cry pierces the suddenly quiet night air: "Ning, run! Run!"

The wind lifts the corner of her dress, like a dark purple petal unfolding. Her face is like jade, with orange lights flowing underneath.

I turn and run as fast as I can. Behind me, I hear the heavy footsteps of the Dark Yaksha. With every quaking, pounding step, shingles fall from houses on both sides like overripe fruits. I am now running like the wind, my bare feet striking the slate slabs lightly: *pat, pat, pat.* My heart pounds against my chest: *thump, thump, thump.* Along the entire frenzied Ghost Street, mine is the only living heart.

But both the ghosts and I know that I'm not in any real danger. A ghost can never hurt a real person. That's one of the rules of the game.

I run toward the west, toward Lanruo Temple. If I can get to Yan Chixia before the Yaksha catches me, I'll be safe. This is also part of the performance. Every Carnival, Yan puts on his battle gear and waits on the steps of the main hall.

As I approach, I cry out: "Help! Save me! Oh Hero Yan, save me!"

In the distance I hear his long ululating cry and see his figure leaping over the wall of the temple to land in the middle of the street. He holds in his left hand a Daoist charm: red character written against a yellow background. He reaches behind his back with his right hand and pulls out his sword, the Demon Slayer.

He stands tall and shouts into the night sky, "Brazen Demon! How dare you harm innocent people? I, Yan Chixia, will carry out justice today!"

But tonight, he forgot to wear his sedge hat. His egg-shaped face is exposed to the thousands of lanterns along Ghost Street, with just a few wisps of hair curled like question marks on a blank page. The silly sight is such a contrast against his serious mien that I start to laugh even as I'm running. And that makes me choke and I can't catch my breath so I fall against the cold slate surface of the street.

This moment is my best memory of the summer.

Cold Dew, the Seventeenth Solar Term:

A thin layer of clouds hides the moon. I'm crouching by the side of the lotus pond in Lanruo Temple. All I can see are the shadows cast by the lotus leaves, rising and falling slowly with the wind.

The night is as cold as the water. Insects hidden in the grass won't stop singing.

The eggplants and string beans in the garden are ripe. They smell so good that I have a hard time resisting the temptation. All I can think about is to steal some under the cover of night. Maybe Yan Chixia was right: in a previous life I must have died of hunger.

So I wait, and wait. But I don't hear Yan Chixia's snores. Instead, I hear light footsteps cross the grassy path to stop in front of Yan Chixia's cabin. The door opens, the steps go in. A moment later, the voices of a man and a woman drift out of the dark room: Yan Chixia and Xiao Qian.

Qian: "Why did you ask me to come?"

Yan: "You know what it's about."

Qian: "I can't leave with you."

Yan: "Why not?"

Qian: "A few more years. Ning is still so young."

"Ning, Ning!" Yan's voice grows louder. "I think you've been a ghost for too long."

Qian sounds pitiful. "I raised Ning for so many years. How can I just get up and leave him?"

"You're always telling me that Ning is still too young, always telling me to wait. Do you remember how many years it has been?"

"I can't."

"You sew a new set of clothes for him every year. How can you forget?" Yan chuckles, a cold sound. "I remember very clearly. The fruits and vegetables in this garden ripen like clockwork, once a year. I've seen them do it fifteen times. Fifteen! But has Ning's appearance changed any since the year he turned seven? You still think he's alive, he's real?"

Xiao Qian remains silent for a moment. Then I hear her crying.

Yan sighs. "Don't lie to yourself any more. He's just like us, nothing more than a toy. Why are you so sad? He's not worth it."

Xiao Qian just keeps on crying.

Yan sighs again. "I should never have picked him up and brought him back."

Xiao Qian whispers through the tears, "Where can we go if we leave Ghost Street?"

Yan has no answer.

The sound of Xiao Qian's crying makes my heart feel constricted. Silently, I sneak away and leave the old temple through a hole in the wall.

The thin layer of clouds chooses this moment to part. The cold moonlight scatters itself against the slate slabs of the street, congealing into drops of glittering dew. My bare feet against the ground feel so cold that my whole body shivers.

A few stores are still open along Ghost Street. The vendors greet me enthusiastically, asking me to sample their green bean biscuits and sweet osmanthus cake. But I don't want to. What's the point? I'm just like them, maybe even less than them.

Every ghost used to be alive. Their fake, mechanical bodies host real souls. But I'm fake throughout, inside and outside. From the day I was born, made, I was fake. Every ghost has stories of when they were alive, but I don't. Every ghost had a father, a mother, a family, memories of their love, but I don't have any of that.

Xiao Qian once told me that Ghost Street's decline came about because people, real people, found more exciting, newer toys. Maybe I am one of those toys: made with newer, better technology, until I could pass for the real thing. I can cry, laugh, eat, piss and shit, fall, feel pain, ooze blood, hear my own heartbeat, grow up from a simulacrum of a baby—except that my growth stops when I'm seven. I'll never be a grown up.

Ghost Street was built to entertain the tourists, and all the ghosts were their toys. But I'm just a toy for Xiao Qian.

Pretending that the fake is real only makes the real seem fake.

I walk slowly toward the eastern end of the street, until I stop under the Old Ghost Tree. The sweet fragrance of osmanthus fills the foggy night air, cool and calming. Suddenly I want to climb into the tree. That way, no one will find me.

The Old Ghost Tree leans down with its branches to help me.

I sit, hidden among the dense branches, and feel calmer. The crows perch around me, their glass eyes showing hints of a dark red glow. One of them speaks: "Ning, this is a beautiful night. Why aren't you at Lanruo Temple, stealing vegetables?"

The crow is asking a question to which it already knows the answer. The Old Ghost Tree knows everything that happens on Ghost Street. The crows are its eyes and ears.

"How can I know for sure," I ask, "that I'm a real person?"

"You can chop off your head," the crow answers. "A real person will die with his head cut off, but a ghost will not."

"But what if I cut off my head and die? I'll be no more."

The crow laughs, the sound grating and unpleasant to listen to. Two more crows fly down, holding in their beaks antique bronze mirrors. Using the little moonlight that leaks through the leaves, I finally see myself in the mirrors: small face, dark hair, thin neck. I lift the hair off the back of my neck, and in the double reflections of the mirrors, I see a crimson bar code against the skin, like a tiny snake.

I remember Xiao Qian's cool hands against my spine on that hot summer night. I think and think, until tears fall from my eyes.

A Hundred Ghosts Parade Tonight

Winter Solstice, the Twenty-Second Solar Term:

This winter has been both dry and cold, but I often hear the sound of thunder in the distance. Xiao Qian says that it's the Thunder Calamity, which happens only once every thousand years.

The Thunder Calamity punishes demons and ghosts and lost spirits. Those who can escape it can live for another thousand years. Those who can't will be burnt away until no trace is left of them.

I know perfectly well that there's no such thing as a "Thunder Calamity" in this world. Xiao Qian has been a ghost for so long that she's now gone a little crazy. She holds onto me with her cold hands, her face as pale as a sheet of paper. She says that to hide from the Calamity, a ghost must find a real person with a good heart to stay beside her. That way, just as one wouldn't throw a shoe at a mouse sitting beside an expensive vase, the Duke of Thunder will not strike the ghost.

Because of her fear, my plan to leave has been put on hold. In secret I've already prepared my luggage: a few stolen potatoes, a few old shirts. My body isn't growing any more anyway, so these clothes will last me a long time. I didn't take any of the old copper coins from Xiao Qian though. Perhaps the outside world does not use them.

I really want to leave Ghost Street. I don't care where I go; I just want to see the world. Anywhere but here.

I want to know how real people live.

But still, I linger.

On Winter Solstice it snows. The snowflakes are tiny, like white sawdust. They melt as soon as they hit the ground. Only a very thin layer has accumulated by noon.

I walk alone along the street, bored. In past years I would go to Lanruo Temple to find Yan Chixia. We would knock an opening in the ice covering the lotus pond, and lower our jury-rigged fishing pole beneath the ice. Winter catfish are very fat and taste fantastic when roasted with garlic.

But I haven't seen Yan Chixia in a long time. I wonder if his beard and hair have grown out a bit.

Thunder rumbles in the sky, closer, then farther away, leaving only a buzzing sensation in my ears. I walk all the way to the Old

41

Ghost Tree, climb up into its branches, and sit still. Snowflakes fall all around me but not on me. I feel calm and warm. I curl up and tuck my head under my arms, falling asleep like a bird.

In my dream, I see Ghost Street turning into a long, thin snake. The Old Ghost Tree is the head, Lanruo Temple the tail, the slate slabs the scales. On each scale is drawn the face of a little ghost, very delicate and beautiful.

But the snake continues to writhe as though in great pain. I watch carefully and see that a mass of termites and spiders is biting its tail, making a sound like silkworms feeding on mulberry leaves. With sharp mandibles and claws, they tear off the scales on the snake one by one, revealing the flesh underneath. The snake struggles silently, but disappears inch by inch into the maws of the insects. When its body is almost completely eaten, it finally makes a sharp cry, and turns its lonesome head toward me.

I see that its face is Xiao Qian's.

I wake up. The cold wind rustles the leaves of the Old Ghost Tree. It's too quiet around me. All the crows have disappeared to who-knows-where except one that is very old and ugly. It's crouching in front of me, its beak dangling like the tip of a long mustache.

I shake it awake, anxious. It stares at me with two broken-glass eyes, croaking to me in its mechanical, flat voice, "Ning, why are you still here?"

"Where should I be?"

"Anywhere is good," it says. "Ghost Street is finished. We're all finished."

I stick my head out of the leaves of the Old Ghost Tree. Under the slate-grey sky, I see the murder of crows circling over Lanruo Temple in the distance, cawing incessantly. I've never seen anything like this.

I jump down from the tree and run. As I run along the narrow street, I pass dark doors and windows. The cawing of the crows has awakened many of the ghosts, but they don't dare to go outside, where there's light. All they can do is to peek out from cracks in doors, like a bunch of crickets hiding under houses in winter.

The old walls of Lanruo Temple, long in need of repair, have been pushed down. Many giant mechanical spiders made of steel are crawling all over the main hall, breaking off the dark red glass shingles and sculpted wooden molding, piece by piece, and throwing the pieces into the snow on the ground. They have flat bodies, blue-glowing eyes, and sharp mandibles, as ugly as you can imagine. From deep within their bodies comes a rumbling noise like thunder.

The crows swoop around them, picking up bits of broken shingles and bricks on the ground and dropping them on the spiders. But they are too weak and the spiders ignore them. The broken shingle pieces strike against the steel shells, making faint, hollow echoes.

The vegetable garden has been destroyed. All that remains are some mud and pale white roots. I see one of the Monk's rusted arms sticking out of a pile of broken bricks.

I run through the garden, calling for Yan Chixia. He hears me and slowly walks out of his cabin. He's still wearing his battle gear: sedge hat over his head, the sword Demon Slayer in his hand. I want to shout for him to fight the spiders, but somehow I can't spit the words out. The words taste like bitter, astringent paste stuck in my throat.

Yan Chixia stares at me with his sad eyes. He comes over to hold my hands. His hands are as cold as Xiao Qian's.

We stand together and watch as the great and beautiful main hall is torn apart bit by bit, collapses, turns into a pile of rubble: shingles, bricks, wood, mud. Nothing is whole.

They've destroyed all of Lanruo Temple: the walls, the main hall, the garden, the lotus pond, the bamboo grove, and Yan Chixia's cabin. The only thing left is a muddy ruin.

Now they're moving onto the rest of Ghost Street. They pry up the slate slabs, flatten the broken houses along the sides of the street. The ghosts hiding in the houses are chased into the middle of the street. As they run, they scream and scream, while their skin slowly burns in the faint sunlight. There are no visible flames. But you can see the skin turning black in patches, and the smell of burning plastic is everywhere.

I fall into the snow. The smell of burning ghost skin makes me vomit. But there's nothing in my stomach to throw up. So I cry during the breaks in the dry heaves.

So this is what the Thunder Calamity looks like.

The ghosts, their faces burned away, continue to cry and run and struggle in the snow. Their footprints criss-cross in the snow, like a child's handwriting. I suddenly think of Xiao Qian, and so I start to run again.

Xian Qian is still sitting in the dark bedroom. She combs her hair as she sings. Her melody floats in the gaps between the roaring, rumbling thunder of the spiders, so quiet, so transparent, like a dreamscape under the moon.

From her body come the fragrances of a myriad of flowers and herbs, layer after layer, like gossamer. Her hair floats up into the air like a flame, fluttering without cease. I stand and listen to her sing, my face full of tears, until the whole house begins to shake.

From on top of the roof, I hear the sound of steel clanging, blunt objects striking against each other, heavy footsteps, and then Yan Chixia's shouting.

Suddenly, the roof caves in, bringing with it a rain of shingles and letting in a bright patch of grey sky full of fluttering snowflakes. I push Xiao Qian into a dark corner, out of the way of the light.

I run outside the house. Yan Chixia is standing on the roof, holding his sword in front of him. The cold wind stretches his robe taut like a grey flag.

He jumps onto the back of a spider, and stabs at its eyes with his sword. The spider struggles hard and throws Yan off its back. Then the spider grabs Yan with two sharp claws and pulls him into its sharp, metallic, grinding mandibles. It chews and chews, like a man chewing kimchee, until pieces of Yan Chixia's body are falling out of its mandibles onto the shingles of the roof. Finally, Yan's head falls off the roof and rolls to a stop next to my feet, like a hard-boiled egg.

I pick up his head. He stares at me with his dead eyes. There are no tears in them, only anger and regret. Then with the last of his strength, Yan closes his eyes, as though he cannot bear to watch any more.

The spider continues to chew and grind up the rest of Yan Chixia's body. Then it leaps down from the roof, and, rumbling, crawls toward me. Its eyes glow with a deep blue light.

Xiao Qian jumps from behind me and grabs me by the waist, pulling me back. I pry her hands off of me and push her back into the dark room. Then I pick up Yan Chixia's sword and rush toward the spider.

The cold blue light of a steel claw flashes before my eyes. Then my head strikes the ground with a muffled *thump*. Blood spills everywhere.

A Hundred Ghosts Parade Tonight

The world is now tilted: tilted sky, tilted street, tilted snow falling diagonally. With every bit of my strength, I turn my eyes to follow the spider. I see that it's chewing on my body. A stream of dark red fluid drips out of its beak, bubbling, warm, the droplets slowly spreading in the snow.

As the spider chews, it slows down gradually. Then it stops moving, the blue light in its eyes dims and then goes out.

As though they have received some signal, all the other spiders also stop one by one. The rumbling thunder stops, plunging the world into silence.

The wind stops, too. Snow begins to stick to the spiders' steel bodies.

I want to laugh, but I can't. My head is now separated from my body, so there's no way to get air into the lungs and then out to my vocal cords. So I crack my lips open until the smile is frozen on my face.

The spiders believed that I was alive, a real person. They chewed my body and tasted flesh and saw blood. But they aren't allowed to harm real people. If they do, they must destroy themselves. That's also part of the rules. Ghosts, spiders, it doesn't matter. Everyone has to follow the rules.

I never imagined that the spiders would be so stupid. They're even easier to fool than ghosts.

The scene in my eyes grows indistinct, fades, as though a veil is falling from the sky, covering my head. I remember the words of the crows. So it's true. When your head is cut off, you really die.

I grew up on this street; I ran along this street. Now I'm finally going to die on this street, just like a real person.

A pair of pale, cold hands reaches over, stroking my face.

The wind blows and covers my face with a few pale pink peach petals. But I know they're not peach petals. They're Xiao Qian's tears, mixed with snow.

Act of Faith

Fadzlishah Johanabas

Malaysian author Fadzlishah Johanabas has published short fiction both in Malaysia and abroad. When not writing, he works as a doctor in Kuala Lumpur. He maintains a blog at http://www.fadzjohanabas.com.

I.

Ahmad Daud bin Kasim lived alone. His wife had passed away almost ten years ago, and his only son spent more time mining Helium-3 on the moon than at home. And because Daud insisted on living alone, Jamil bought him an advanced household android when the model came out. RX-718 had cost him three years' income, paid in monthly installments. The old man, a relic from the early twenty-first century, at first thought the robot was a nuisance. When he woke for his predawn prayer—*Subuh*—to find a full breakfast plate (with reduced salt and carbohydrates to control his hypertension and diabetes) on the kitchen counter, he sat down, scratched his leathery chin, and stared hard at the tall, androgynous, and motionless robot.

"If I have to live with you, I cannot call you 'Eh.' "

The android remained standing at the corner of the kitchen, unflinching. Its outer shell of white aluminum and grey carbon-reinforced polymer gleamed in the automated built-in ceiling lights.

"What about Sallehuddin? I always liked that name. Even though you're a robot, I can't give you a woman's name. It's just wrong, you hear?" He wagged his finger at RX-718. "Do you like that name?"

"Voice-command recognition, Ahmad Daud bin Kasim, acknowledged." His voice was clear, with a slight metallic edge, just as in the advertisements.

"Call me Abah."

Sallehuddin cocked his head a fraction. "Abah is a common term for 'Father.' That is what Jamil bin Ahmad Daud calls you. Are you certain you want me to call you Abah?"

Daud flapped his olive-hued hands in dismissal. "Yes, yes. Less confusing for me. And call my son Jamil. Can you talk like a normal person?"

"I am unable to comprehend the question."

"That. Less of that, and more of talking like a real person."

Sallehuddin remained silent for almost a minute. "I have the ca-
pacity to adapt and learn, and I have wireless connection to the worldnet. In time, I will learn to talk like a human being would."

"Hmm. You do that." Daud poked the genetically-engineered chicken
breast with his fork, and took a tentative bite. "Hey, this is good!"

II.

Jamil leaned back against the aluminum bench at the edge of his father's aeroponic garden and smoked his cigarette—good, old fashioned
tobacco, none of that subcutaneous nicotine-releasing implant. For a
long while he sat in silence, with the rustle of the flowering plants and
the crackle of his cigarette. Sallehuddin stood beside him in the
moonlit garden, just as silently.

"That's where my outpost is, near the south pole." Jamil pointed in
the general direction of the full moon. "Peary Crater, where it's daytime all year 'round. Sometimes I miss the quiet, the darkness of night-
time. The Earth is beautiful from the moon, all blue and white and
brown. People say there used to be lots of green, but I see only brown.
It's still beautiful, though."

"You sound like you love it there."

"I do, actually. But I worry about my father. I can't believe he
made you call him 'Abah.' "

"Does it displease you?"

Jamil scrunched his face and rubbed three days' growth of stubble.
"Not that. It's just weird, I guess. But I've never seen Abah this content
since Mak passed away. Look after him while I'm not here. I'm counting on you."

"Affirma—I will."

"Maybe when I come back, I'll get you that human skin upgrade
with my bonus. You can wear my clothes. We're about the same size,
minus my waistline."

"It will not be the same."

Jamil raised both eyebrows. "What won't?"

"He talks about you all the time. He misses you and wishes you
would come home more often. I am not your substitute, and making
me look human will only make things harder for him."

"Can you actually refuse an upgrade?" His tone carried only curiosity.

"My processor is capable of evolution and judgment. I can advise you what I think is the proper course, but ultimately, I cannot disobey my owners if the command doesn't endanger their lives."

"Even if it's to save your own life?"

Sallehuddin cocked his head slightly to the right. "You mistake me for a human being, Jamil. As long as my processor remains intact, I can be transferred to another vessel. If not, so be it. But you expire easily, and my owners' safety is my first priority."

"Hmm." Even his facial expression was similar to his father's. "I have no choice but to work on the moon, I guess. A resource engineer like me has no work left on Earth; there's no energy source left to mine. But hearing you say what you said, I'm glad I invested in you." Jamil let out a chuckle. "I can't believe I was jealous of you."

"You are his only son. That will never change."

Jamil embraced Sallehuddin and rubbed the back of his smooth head. "Thank you. You take good care of Abah, okay?"

"May I suggest something? If you want to upgrade me, purchase an application to enable you to see through my eyes, and talk through my mouth, even from the moon. It is more expensive than the skin, but I believe it will benefit you."

"I'll think about it. Thanks, Sallehuddin."

III.

"The two of you had a long conversation last night," Daud said when he and Sallehuddin were tending his garden. "What did you talk about?"

"Jamil asked me to take good care of you."

Daud sniffed. "He's a good kid."

"He loves you."

"Yes he does, but how can you tell? I may be outdated, but last I checked, robots can only simulate human emotions when given the command. You cannot feel true emotions, can you?"

Sallehuddin cocked his head. "From the information I gathered on the worldnet, Dr. Rosalind Picard first postulated affective computing in 1995. It has been eighty-four years since then, and affective computing is a science on its own."

Daud raised both hands and smiled. "I'm just a retired *ustaz*. I taught Islamic lessons to schoolchildren—those whose parents still preferred physical, face-to-face teachers. What you're talking about is beyond my understanding."

"I can interpret emotions in your speech, movements, pupil size, and breathing and heart rates. I am also equipped with emotional reaction software. So yes, I *can* feel."

"Hmm. Do you know what separates humans from robots, apart from our manner of creation? Emotion. Free will is nothing; AI has been given free will since before I was born. But for a robot to actually understand and feel human emotions, I don't know if I should be happy or afraid."

Both of them continued gardening in silence for another hour, before Daud had to go to the mosque for the late afternoon prayer, or *Asar*. When he came back, he headed straight for the small library beside his room and Jamil's, and took out a thick, aged tome, its hardcover blue with Arabic cursive words.

"I thought about what you said, and what I said. If you can feel emotions, then maybe you're a child of God as well." Daud stroked the surface with reverence. "This is a Quran. It belonged to my father. They don't make them like this anymore; everything's digital. This is real paper, from wood and all, so be careful with it. Can you read Arabic?"

"I can download the language into my databank."

"Don't. I want to teach you to read the Quran the way I learned it, the way I taught Jamil and my schoolchildren. I'm sure you'll learn much faster than they did."

"It is a holy tome. Is it wise?"

"I don't know. The first word the Prophet heard from God's messenger was 'Read.' The Quran will enrich you, give you knowledge. You can never have too much of that, you hear?"

IV.

First Daud taught Sallehuddin Arabic letters and numbers. Then he taught Sallehuddin how to read the words based on the guide markers: the short pauses, the long pauses, the hard stop, the repeated sounds,

49

the inflections, the sighs, all the correct *tajwid* when reading the Quran. He taught Sallehuddin the meaning of the words, and before long his vocabulary grew.

During Ramadhan, the Islamic fasting month, Sallehuddin accompanied Daud in reading the Quran, a chapter a day. Daud seldom had to correct him, but after completing the twelfth chapter, Daud stayed seated opposite the android.

"When will you start reading with your own voice?"

"I do not understand. My voice is factory-standard, but if you want to, the pitch is adjustable."

"Not that. Your voice. Sallehuddin's voice. Not like how I read, not like the recordings of the imams you listen to at night. Each person has his own inflections, flaws, and strengths. You sound like a machine, too perfect, emotionless."

"Does my reading not please you?"

"Not that. I want you to put your personality in it. I want your reading to be individual."

Sallehuddin cocked his head slightly to the right. "I will need time to process this. I fear I may not be equipped to comply."

Daud gave him a look that he could only interpret as *faith*.

That night, while he sat plugged to the living-room socket, Sallehuddin reviewed his conversation with Daud. He played recordings of Quran recitals from all over the world, and studied the individual voices, comparing the differences, both subtle and obvious. He was astounded about how reading the same thing could sound so different from person to person. He then reviewed his entire existence, how his experience after coming out of his packaging was different from other RX-718s even though there were five units active in the same neighborhood.

When he read the Quran the next day, his recital was just as smooth and clear as before, but he sounded different, even though the change was subtle.

Daud stopped reading and gave a smile that creased his entire face with deep lines. "Now you sound like Sallehuddin." With that, and a nod, he resumed reading.

From then on, Daud taught Sallehuddin the Faith. When he was not learning from Daud, the android scoured the worldnet for more information. When Jamil came back toward the end of Ramadhan, Sallehuddin had learned more about Islam than Jamil had in his entire life.

"Has Abah been hard on you? He used to flick my knuckles when I read the Quran wrongly." Jamil sat beside Sallehuddin with a steaming mug of synthetic coffee in his hands. Daud was asleep upstairs, and Sallehuddin had updated Jamil on what he and Daud had been doing since the last time Jamil had come back.

"He is a good teacher, and I am thankful for it. I feel I have grown exponentially in his care."

"I thought you're the one who's taking care of him?"

"I feel that he takes care of me, spiritually."

"Hmm."

"He does that, too, all the time."

"What?"

Sallehuddin adjusted his pitch to mimic Daud's voice. "Hmm."

Jamil burst out laughing, filling the stillness of the night with his deep voice. "You sound just like him! I picked up his habit when I was a boy, I guess."

"Is that how it is, to have parents?"

Jamil rolled the mug with his hands. "I guess. Hey, if it makes any difference, I think Abah thinks of you as his son, too."

Sallehuddin cocked his head but remained silent.

In the predawn darkness, with Jamil asleep in his room, Daud walked down and gestured for Sallehuddin to follow him. "Come, let's do the Subuh prayer at the mosque."

The android followed without hesitation.

The mosque was still empty. The main chamber was spacious, with a high, domed ceiling, and slender support pillars arranged at regular intervals. The thick, carpeted floor was free from dust and dirt. But the emptiness was profound. Sallehuddin felt it even though it was his first time in the mosque.

"It's almost time. Connect yourself to the speakers and *Azan*. If anyone can call people to pray here again, it's you." Again, the old man's eyes conveyed unquestioning faith.

Sallehuddin complied, and recited the call for prayer, in his own voice. *"Allah hu-akhbar, Allah hu-akhbar…"*

When he'd completed the call and turned to face Daud, he saw tears streaming from the old man's eyes.

"Have I done it wrong, Abah?"

"No," Daud whispered, and wiped his face with the base of his wrists. "I forget how beautiful it sounds."

Within a few minutes, one person after another entered the main doors of the mosque, Jamil included. Most of them were elderly or middle-aged, but all came with curious looks on their faces. The Imam, who had been standing silently at the back of the main chamber, clasped Daud's hands. His eyes were equally red from tears.

"I have not seen this many people here in years. What software did you use for your robot? The recordings I play can never get the congregation to pray here."

"I didn't install any software. I taught Sallehuddin what I can, and he learned the rest on his own."

"*He*? It's a machine, Daud."

"That may be so. But Sallehuddin is a Muslim, Imam."

The Imam inhaled sharply. "That's blasphemy, Daud!"

"Is it? I have taught him the *syahadah*, and he follows the Islamic ways."

"Even praying? How is it possible, when it can't even take ablution?"

"He is waterproof, Imam. Even if he cannot risk getting water in his joints, Sallehuddin has learned to take ablution using fine-grained sand. Isn't that acceptable when you have no access to water?"

"Yes, but—"

Jamil knelt down beside his father and lowered his head to look at the two older men. "What's going on?"

"Talk your father out of this insanity, Jamil. He thinks the robot is a Muslim!" The Imam shook his head, his jaw set.

"Abah—"

Daud kept his gaze forward. "Everyone's waiting, Imam. Lead the prayer, already."

If the Imam was indignant at being reminded of his job, he did not show it. He stood up, walked to the front of the chamber, and gave Sallehuddin a cursory glance. *"Qamat."*

Sallehuddin nodded and recited a similar call as the Azan, only shorter. The Qamat was to inform the congregation to stand in rows behind the Imam, shoulder to shoulder. When he finished, Sallehuddin padded to the back, behind the last row. Then he saw Daud making his way to the back row, and signaled for Sallehuddin to join him by his side. The men around them muttered among themselves but did not stop Sallehuddin from joining the prayer.

It was then that Sallehuddin began to comprehend that he may be different from the rest of RX-718 models after all.

V.

"Abah, I know Sallehuddin means a lot to you. But to call him a Muslim?"

Daud plucked resilient weeds choking his orchids. "What's wrong with that?"

"He's an android, Abah."

"Who made the rule that only humans can be Muslims? There was even a time when people believed there were Muslim djinns and spirits. What's wrong with a Muslim android?"

"It's just—" Jamil sighed and slumped against the wall. "I'm worried about you, Abah. Maybe I should just stay home and take care of you."

"And have us live off my pension? We won't even afford Sallehuddin's monthly installments. I'm not going crazy, if that's what you mean."

"I don't want to have to worry about you when I'm not around."

"Then don't. I'm fine. I know what I'm doing."

Sallehuddin watched the argument between father and son in silence. They were angry with each other. He had done something to endanger their relationship. He felt the conflict in his system. When Jamil stormed into the house, Sallehuddin followed him to his room. "Forgive me, Jamil. I did not mean for you to argue with Abah."

Jamil shook his head. "You've done nothing wrong. It's Abah that I'm worried about. Has his behavior been erratic in any way?"

"From my observation, no. He is an exemplary model of human behavior."

"You know what, the Imam asked me to return you to the manufacturer, to reboot your system at the very least."

Outwardly, Sallehuddin did not even twitch. But his system jumped to overdrive, and his awareness worked furiously to interpret the strange, oppressive feeling that had suddenly invaded him. For the first time in his existence, Sallehuddin felt fear.

"But I'm not going to do that."

He actually let out a small sigh.

"I am going to take your advice, though. I'm buying the application so that I can observe Abah through you."

Sallehuddin nodded.

"But I don't want you to tell Abah about this. He won't like it, I guess."

The android nodded again in assent.

VI.

Sallehuddin continued to accompany Daud to the mosque for all five daily prayers even after Jamil left for another assignment. The Imam allowed him to recite the Azan, but only grudgingly; he had tried to play a recording one time, but the turnout was poor. Sallehuddin's recital differed subtly each time, much to everyone's surprise. Other Muslim owners of RX-718 and later models tried to duplicate Sallehuddin's feat, but none of them succeeded. The androids all sounded the same, every time.

Even though everyone loved Sallehuddin's Azan, they still had difficulty accepting him praying with them. Daud stood right at the back, always beside Sallehuddin. There was no smugness in him, nor disdain. He was the same as he ever was.

"You're right," Jamil said to Sallehuddin via their worldnet link. "I was wrong to worry about Abah."

"The Imam has kept his peace. He may not accept me, but I do not think he's rejecting me either. I'm glad Abah isn't having such a bad time with the rest of the congregation."

Jamil's chuckle reverberated through his consciousness. "It's still weird, hearing you call him Abah. But I don't mind having you as a brother, I guess."

"That is—" Sallehuddin cocked his head. "Unexpected. Thank you, Jamil."

"Maybe one day I can talk you into accepting humanoid skin."

"My opinion remains unchanged. I do not plan to be your substitute. You are his son."

"Well, two more months here and I'll be back for half a year. They're shutting this mining plant down, and I'll be doing paperwork for a while."

"That is good. Abah will be happy to hear this."

"No! You can't tell him you have this application, remember?"

"I assumed you were going to make a conventional phone call."

"Later, I guess. What are you doing with Abah today?"

"There is a storm outside, but he insists on going to the mosque to pray."

"Can't you talk him out of it?"

"Without success."

"Well, be careful then. Call me if you need anything."

Sallehuddin ended the connection well before Daud came down with an umbrella in his hand. The old man thumped the left side of his chest with his balled fist, and flexed his arms repeatedly.

"Is there anything wrong, Abah?"

"It's the storm and the cold. I feel it in my bones. That's what happens when you get old." His gentle smile lit his face and made him look more like his son.

"Maybe we should just pray at home."

Daud waved his hand. "Nonsense. Come, we don't want to be late."

Sallehuddin held the umbrella in one hand and wrapped his free arm around Daud's shoulder to steady him in the howling tempest. Tall trees swayed and bent around them, humbled by the force of nature, and both of them were soaking when they entered the mosque. The Imam was already there, less wet as his house was just beside the mosque. Sallehuddin ran a quick diagnostic sweep on himself, and did not find any aberrations in his system. Daud, on the other hand, was shivering, and his pulse had quickened. Sallehuddin held him close and gave off comfortable warmth.

When his teeth stopped chattering, Daud pointed to the front of the main chamber. "Go, it's already time to Azan."

Sallehuddin hesitated, but eventually nodded and complied. His amplified voice competed with the roar of the storm outside. The Imam waited for a good fifteen minutes after the Azan, but only three others turned up. He looked at everyone except for Sallehuddin, and they in turn nodded at him to go ahead with the prayer. Sallehuddin stood directly behind him, and even though the Imam looked uneasy, he did not say anything.

In the middle of their prayer, the doors by the side of the main hall banged open from the force of the tempest. The Imam stumbled in his recital at the distraction, but Sallehuddin guided him back, just audibly. It was the responsibility of the man standing behind an Imam to correct him when he stumbled, and Sallehuddin did this without hesitation.

A loud thump overhead, followed by an almost imperceptible crack, alerted Sallehuddin of another danger. In a split-second decision, he overrode his first commandment. He had to harm the humans in order to save them. Just as the glass dome overhead shattered, with an uprooted tree jutting into the gap, Sallehuddin pushed the Imam forward, toward a small alcove, and pushed the rest of the startled men away. He grabbed hold of Daud and lay atop him.

Glass shards bounded off his carbon-enforced polymer body and scraped the aluminum parts. He knew he had saved the men from harm, but jumped off Daud when the old man started to gasp for air. Daud clutched at his chest; beads of sweat rolled off his forehead. Broken glass lay around them, and the men could not come close.

Sallehuddin placed three fingertips over Abah's chest, where the vital points of his heart should be. Full diagnostic ECG was almost impossible with the old man thrashing about, but Sallehuddin managed to get enough readings to compare with worldnet database. "Ventricular fibrillation."

The Imam padded as close as he could. "Can't you do something?"

"I'm not equipped with medical capabilities. I cannot depolarize his heart safely. Please, Abah. Please hold on." Sallehuddin did the only thing he could do. He called Jamil.

"What's wrong, Sallehuddin? I'm in the middle of—" A short pause, and a sharp intake of breath. "Abah! What's happening to him?"

"He's having a heart attack, Jamil. I've called for help, but I cannot do anything to help him. He needs you now. Talk to him, through me."

"Abah." Sallehuddin's lips moved, but the voice was Jamil's.

Daud's eyes flared opened with feverish clarity. "Jamil?"

"It's me, Abah. Hold on. Help is coming."

For the briefest moment, Daud's grimace turned into a smile. Then his head lolled to the right, limp and lifeless.

Sallehuddin grabbed him and held him close to his chest. "Abah!" both of them wailed simultaneously. There was no telling which voice was human and which was android.

VII.

In the predawn darkness the day after Daud's funeral, Sallehuddin and Jamil walked side by side to the mosque. A temporary polyfiber sheet had been draped over the gap in the dome to keep the elements away. The Imam was already there, ready to play a recording of the Azan.

"Jamil. I thought, after your father passed away—"

"I would no longer pray?" Sallehuddin interjected. "I am a Muslim, Imam. For me to meet Abah again in Heaven when I expire, I have to be a good Muslim."

"You can't be serious."

Jamil rested his hand on Sallehuddin's shoulder. "Do you know how I pray up there on the moon? With the Earth rotating, the Kaaba is never at the same place to be my *kiblat*. And it's always daytime, so I don't have a guide for my prayer time. I place my mat facing my bunker door, and I set my alarm in time with our prayer times here. I just do it because I have faith that Allah will accept my effort all the same." He looked at Sallehuddin, then back at the Imam. "Sallehuddin believes that his prayers will be accepted, too. Maybe you should have the same faith in him as Abah had."

For a while, the Imam stared at them, stroking his white beard. Finally, he took a deep breath and sighed. "Do you truly believe you have a soul, Sallehuddin?"

The android cocked his head slightly to the right. "I do, Imam."

"Then go ahead and Azan. Call the congregation to pray with us."

Sallehuddin nodded and took his place.

The Foreigner

Uko Bendi Udo

Originally from Nigeria, Uko Bendi Udo currently lives in the United States. He is the author of several short stories and one radio play.

Edikan threw a stick a few yards in front of him. "Go get!" he said to Mboro, who froze in place and then turned his head sideways to show puzzlement. "*Ke bin!*" Edikan repeated in Milinan. Mboro hopped happily after the stick, fetched it, and returned it to Edikan, his yellow eyes flashing brighter with pride.

Edikan's gaze strayed and he noticed that the security guard in front of the Lagos Ministry for Intergalactic Services building had moved from his spot. Edikan acted quickly. He accepted the stick from Mboro, touched a model car icon display on his gloved left palm, and then waved his right palm over Mboro, changing him into a pocket-sized model car. Edikan pocketed the car, and ran across the street.

"*Yeye* boy!" a motorist cursed as his vehicle missed Edikan by a hair. The motorist's outburst drew attention to him, so he squeezed behind the glass wall of the Ministry building that faced Omotayo Street. Briefly distracted, he studied his image in the glass wall, and was reminded, sadly, of a few things about him that contributed to his "foreignness." His hair was a forest of dark black, spiky locks, and his boyish, doll-like face bore eyes that were at once familiar but unearthly.

A worker in a suit and tie walked up to the building's entrance, and pressed a thumb on a console. Edikan ran up and slipped into the building behind him. He walked briskly towards the glass door that led into a cavernous room with space travel and life form monitoring equipment.

A few workers in lab coats operated the equipment. A scanner checked an astronaut and his suit for alien particles. Seated three desks away from the scanner was Tolu Makinde, dressed in a suit and tie. Edikan ran up to his desk and sat in front of him, making Tolu jerk back in surprise.

"How did you get in here?" Tolu said, looking round. "Where is the security guard?"

"*Ayak no dok,*" Edikan said.

"Speak in English!"

"He let me come."

"You're lying."

"Go ask."

Tolu stood up and pointed at the door. "Get out!"

"*Yem eti fok*!" Edikan stood up. "My father Nigerian. You have proof!"

"I told you the last time you asked. We have no records to show that."

"Lie! Where paper from Milina?"

Tolu's brow squeezed tighter with more surprise. "What paper? What are you talking about?"

"NiMLAF say," Edikan said, and shoved a piece of paper at Tolu.

"The Nigerian-Milinan Legal Aid Foundation?" Tolu sat down as he read the paper.

"They help me. They say you have proof."

Tolu slowly ripped the paper into bits, fed them to the shredder, and leant closer to Edikan. "Since you have friends like this on your side, why don't you tell them to buy you a one-way ticket back to Milina where you belong? This case is closed, as far as the government is concerned. You're an illegal alien."

"I am Nigerian-Milinan. I belong here!"

"There's nothing here for you, Edikan. You have no proper papers, and no family."

"Nothing for me in Milina."

"But that's your home."

Edikan stood up. "Nigeria is home! My father born here!"

"Where's the security guard?" Tolu pressed a button on his desk, and then rose to his feet.

"Give me paper!"

Tolu reached across the desk and shoved Edikan, who staggered backwards, spilling to the floor. "Get out of here!"

Mboro rolled out of Edikan's pocket and transformed into a great big bear with yellowish eyes. It growled loudly, prompting the other workers in the office to let out ear-splitting screams, and a mad dash for the exit ensued. Mboro charged after Tolu.

"*Yak*!" Edikan said.

Mboro froze, its sharp, big claws only inches away from Tolu's face. Edikan walked up to Mboro, and waved his right palm, reversing him back into a model car, which he picked up and pocketed. Tolu remained frozen against the wall, his eyes bulging with fright.

A security guard burst through the door, gun drawn. Guided by Tolu's hysterical pointing, the guard turned to look. Edikan, however, was nowhere in sight. The guard ran around the office looking under desks and equipment.

Tolu pulled out a file from his desk labelled Edikan Usoro, and rifled nervously through it. He found a document, folded and pocketed it. He replaced the file and then searched for his Galaxy phone.

"Freeze!" the guard barked as he spotted and then chased after Edikan, who had emerged from hiding and now headed for the back exit. Behind them, police officers with sophisticated weapons drawn entered the office.

"What took you people so long, eh?" Tolu said, and pointed in the direction Edikan and the security guard had gone, adding, "this is 2080, for God's sake. Not 1999!" Tolu found his phone and quickly exited the office.

"Open driver's door," Tolu Makinde commanded as he nervously approached his 2077 Moonray sports sedan. The car, recognising his voice, lifted up the driver's door like a butterfly's wing, exposing an interior dominated by a curvy touchscreen console that spewed relevant info graphics.

He looked around him and jumped when he heard another car door open behind him. *I should've requested a police escort*, Tolu thought, *that Edikan boy is dangerous. Where did he get that...thing?* He'd heard of NiMi kids bringing strange toys back to Earth, but this one took the cake.

He entered the car, started it with another voice command, and drove out of the underground garage. When he emerged onto the surface streets, he saw that the security guard and the police officers had followed their quarry outside but were now looking around as if they'd lost Edikan.

Edikan must go, Tolu thought, as he gunned the car past his office building and onto Monsood Idowu Highway. He should've pressed on with the hire to eliminate the boy a month ago. He could've put this issue far behind him by now.

How did Edikan find out about the Milina Report? That lawyer group must have a snitch inside the government, or perhaps right inside Tolu's office. *Kai!*

Tolu swerved sharply to avoid hitting the traffic pole signalling flashed cars onto the highway entrance. He gunned the engine, but had to step on the brakes to avoid hitting another car in front of him, and he became mired in a traffic jam.

His thoughts went to Edikan Usoro Senior, Edikan's father and Tolu's cousin. *That old fool should've kept his zipper closed whilst up there on Milina.* Though it did not surprise Tolu that the man had fathered a child up there with an alien, because he was already a dedicated womaniser down here on Earth.

He must find a way to make Edikan go away. He would put in a forced deportation order on that boy. He must return to Milina, or die here on Earth. Either that or Tolu might as well kiss his plans and dreams goodbye.

Tolu frowned as he gazed ahead and realised that the traffic was still tight. A 2080 Lunar Amphibian sedan lifted off the highway in front of him and slowly flew away, leaving the traffic jam behind. Tolu wished that he could afford that car. Maybe with Edikan gone, everything—the house and the bank accounts left behind by his cousin—would be his. Then not only would he be able to afford the 2080 Amphibian, but also he could actually buy one of the just-listed houses on Callaway Moon, the new galactic moon approved for settlement by the Ministry for Intergalactic Services.

"Music," Tolu said, triggering a blast of atmospheric music in the car. He leant back on his seat and sighed deeply, but the car's phone rang, the music faded away, and Chinyere Oduma's face appeared on the console screen.

"Mr Makinde, where are you?" she asked.

Tolu sat up straight on his seat. "Boss. On break, madam."

"What happened here, Tolu? The police are looking for you?"

"Don't mind them, *jare*. They are too slow! This NiMi boy eluded security and came into my office. Can you believe that?"

"*Enh*, but you needed to stay and help the police with their report.

Come back to the office. This is a serious breach."

"Okay. I'm coming."

Tolu touched an icon on the screen, cutting off the call, and the music rose again. He frowned as he looked ahead for the next exit. Now he couldn't even quench the incessant hunger that was making his stomach growl.

A fly, with buggy yellowish eyes, landed outside on the car's windshield. Tolu leant forward to study it, and then jerked back when he noticed the coloration of the fly's eyes. The windshield's eyelid of a wiper automatically nudged the fly off.

Just as he was about to lean back in his seat, the fly appeared inside the car and settled on the windshield, directly in front of him.

He took wild swipes, but the fly zoomed directly at him, dodged his swipes, and settled on the exposed part of his neck. He felt a sharp sting just before he slammed his palm against his neck.

The car swerved sharply to the left and then quickly corrected itself by taking control. Tolu flailed, and then slumped forward in his seat, unconscious, as the car drove off the highway and onto surface streets, and then rolled to a gentle stop on a deserted one.

"Mr Makinde, are you there?"

Tolu sat up in his seat and strained to see clearly. A pedestrian glanced curiously at Tolu as she strolled past the car.

Chinyere appeared on the car's console and said again, "Mr Makinde, are you there?"

"Yes," Tolu replied. He frantically searched his pockets for the document he'd pulled out of Edikan's file in the office, found it, and sighed with relief.

"Where are you?"

"I don't know."

"You don't know?"

"I'm on Martins Street. Yes, I can see the sign now."

"Are you all right?"

"Yes. I'm fine."

"I spoke to you thirty minutes ago, asking you to return to the office. What happened?"

"I don't know."

"I'm sending the police."

"I'm fine! Ah, ah. I'm not a baby."

"We need you here immediately."

Tolu cut off the call, studied his reddened eyes in the visor mirror, and then said, "Start the engine." The engine did not start, he repeated the command, but again it failed to start. He took out the car keys from his pocket, manually started the car, and then drove off.

Edikan ran into the Nigerian-Milinan Legal Aid Foundation office and looked around, searching for John Obinna, a fellow NiMi and Edikan's legal counsellor. Spotting Edikan first, John got up from his chair and ran up to him.

"*Aki bam o*, where have you been?" John asked in Milinan as he embraced him.

"*Mme niye*, I have it!" Edikan exclaimed, jumping up and down with excitement.

"You have what?"

"The paper."

"What paper?"

"Come," Edikan said in English, and grabbed John by the hand and turned round in a bid to lead him out of the office. John grabbed him instead and pulled him into an empty conference room.

"Where have you been?" John asked in Milinan, fright in his eyes. "The police are looking for you."

"Why?"

"Why? Where were you this afternoon?"

"I went to see Mr Makinde."

"I told you not to go there. You don't listen!" John stood up and paced the room. "Now the police are looking for you."

"I didn't do anything wrong."

"How did you get into Mr Makinde's building?"

"I just did!" Edikan stood up and kicked at the chair. "Nobody wants to help me. Not you, not anybody!"

John grabbed Edikan by the hand and yanked him around. "Listen. I've stuck my neck out for you because I care about you and your case. The deal was that you were not going to do anything we didn't tell you to do. This is not Milina."

"I see that. Maybe I should just go back as Mr Makinde suggested and take my chances."

"That is not a good idea either. They will surely kill you for joining the insurrection movement. And what were you doing joining that group?"

"They're killing NiMis like me on Milina, Mr Obinna. Just because of our Earthling blood! Milina doesn't want us, and when we come here, Nigeria does not want us!"

"That is not so. Look at me."

"There are more of me than of you, Mr Obinna."

"That's not true. The problem is that you came in without papers."

"And I'm trying to tell you that I have the papers."

John moved closer to him. "What papers?"

"The paper the government will not release. The paper you have been asking Mr Makinde to show us that proves my father is Nigerian."

"Where is it?"

Edikan brought out Mboro, set him down, jabbed at an icon on his left palm, and waved his right hand over him, turning him into a computer tablet.

John jumped back. "Mboro is an Akan!"

Edikan beamed with pride. "Yes."

"How did you get one? I've asked people to bring one back for me, but they say the Milinan government banned their sale. I see why."

"You don't need it. You're not a kid."

"You're fifteen. That's three years removed from being an adult. Now what about this paper?"

Mboro beamed a video transmission from a pair of human eyes, whilst Edikan scrolled through video images on the tablet. "We need to find it. I saw it earlier. Then we need to print it."

John moved closer to the tablet as if approaching a spectacular phenomenon. "What is this?"

"Video from Mr Makinde's eyes."

An urgent knock on the conference room door prompted John to guide Edikan and Mboro behind a cubicle partition. John tip-toed to the door and cracked it open.

"The police are here," said a co-worker.

John grabbed Edikan and they escaped through the back of the office.

Tolu studied Edikan Usoro Senior's framed photo closely, and sighed. Yes, he had to agree, Edikan bore some resemblance to Edikan Senior. He remembered exactly the day of the photo. Edikan Senior's first trip into space, the family had been so happy. It silenced, at least for that day, the talk that Edikan Senior was a misguided Nigerian astronaut who was more interested in chasing skirts than chasing his dreams.

Tolu had been happy that day for a different reason. His cousin, who had always overshadowed Tolu's accomplishments and made him seem inconsequential in the eyes of everybody—especially Tolu's father—was blasting away to a different world, and would be gone for a few years.

It gave Tolu the space to breathe, and the chance for his family to notice him, especially his father. It gave him the opportunity to suppress the suffocating inferiority complex he felt around his cousin. Tolu had hoped—although it made him uncomfortable—that Edikan Senior would never return.

For if he never did, according to Nigerian law, and Tolu being the closest kin alive, Tolu would inherit everything Edikan Senior owned, both here on Earth, and everywhere else in the galaxy. This house, the ones in the village, and all the others on Milina, and all the other worlds his cousin had roamed in search of adventure. When his body returned back to Nigeria several years later, Tolu thought that his prayers had been answered.

Then, the NiMi boy showed up.

However, the little runt had made a big mistake, and was now going to be forcibly removed from the country, and good riddance. Tolu rubbed his eyes, and then ran up to the bathroom to see what was causing his eyes to itch a lot lately.

In the bathroom, Tolu leant closer to the mirror and noticed that his pupils reflected strange red dots that seemed to appear and disappear depending on how he tilted his head. He'd never seen such a thing before. He'd have to make an appointment with the eye doctor.

The doorbell chimed. Tolu touched the mirror and a projection of a video feed from the entrance showed Edikan standing at the front entrance with John.

"What do you want?" Tolu asked, irritation colouring his voice.

"Open the door, Tolu. We have something to show you," John said.

"Show it to the police."

"We have the document."

Tolu frowned. "What document?"

"Edikan is a citizen of Nigeria," John said, and held up the printed paper to the camera.

Tolu's legs almost gave way under him as he leant in to study the image projected on the mirror.

"You're lying! It's fake!"

"Your office has confirmed the existence of the original, Tolu. We need to talk."

Tolu swiped at the mirror, cutting off the image. He staggered out of the bathroom and flopped onto the couch in the living room. *How had they gotten the document?* He had the original. He stood up and stutter-stepped towards the door.

Tolu opened the door and yanked a document out of John's outstretched hand. Tolu studied the paper briefly, and then slowly sat down on the steps of the staircase.

"As of now, Mr Tolu Makinde, this house belongs to Edikan, by virtue of him being the verified son of astronaut Edikan Usoro Senior, who died on Milina in the year 2069. If you wish to contest this fact, I suggest that you file an appeal in court within the next thirty days."

Tolu sighed, stood up, and said, "Please come into the house."

The City of Silence

Ma Boyong

(Translated from Chinese by Ken Liu.)

Ma Boyong is a popular blogger, speaker, and one of China's foremost authors of speculative fiction. His novels include the Western-setting wuxia novel The Chronicles of European Heroes, *and the alternate history* A History of the Conquest of the Maya by the Shang Fleet. *He is also the author of many short stories.*

The year was 2046, the place, the Capital of the State. The State needed no name because, other than it, there were no states. It was just as the Department of Propaganda kept emphasizing: there are no other states besides the State, and It is who It is, It has always been and always will be.

When the phone rang, Arvardan was sleeping with his face on the desk in front of the computer. The ringing was insistent, sharp. He rubbed his dry eyes and got up unwillingly. His brain felt heavy and slow.

The room was cramped, the air stagnant. The only window was shut tight. Even if the window were open, it would not have helped — the air outside was even murkier. The room was only about thirty square meters. An old army-green cot stood in the corner, the serial number painted in white on one leg. Right next to the cot was a computer desk made from thin wooden boards, on top of which sat a pale white computer.

The phone continued, now on its seventh ring. Arvardan realized that he had no choice but to take the call.

"Your Web Access Serial, please." The voice on the other end was not in any hurry. Indeed, it contained no emotional content whatsoever because it was generated by a computer.

"ARVARDAN19842015BNKF."

Arvardan automatically recited the string of numerals and letters. At the same time, he felt his chest grow even more congested. He did not like these empty electronic voices. Sometimes he thought, *wouldn't it be nice if the voice on the phone belonged to a real woman, smooth and mel-*

low? Arvardan knew this was an unrealistic fantasy. But a fantasy like that still relaxed his body for a few seconds.

"Your application dated October 4th for an account to participate in the BBS discussion forums has been processed. The appropriate authorities have verified that the information you provided was in order. Please come to the processing center within three days with your Personal Identification Card, your Web Access Permit, your Web Access Serial Card, and other relevant documentation. You will receive your account user name and password then."

"Understood. Thank, you." Arvardan carefully chose his words, pausing between each.

It was time to get some work done. Arvardan sat down in front of the computer and moved the mouse. With a faint electronic pop, the screen came alive: "Please enter your Web Access Serial and name." Arvardan entered the requested information. Immediately the indicator LEDs on the front of the computer case began to blink rapidly, accompanied by the low hum of spinning fans.

Every Web user had a Web Access Serial, without which it was impossible to access the Web. This was the only representation of a user on the Web: it could not be changed or deleted. There was a homomorphism between the Web Access Serials and the names on the Personal Identification Cards that everyone carried. Thus, ARVARDAN19842015BNKF *was* Arvardan and Arvardan *was* ARVARDAN19842015BNKF. Arvardan knew that some people with poor memories would print their Web Access Serials on the backs of their shirts.

The appropriate authorities explained that the Real ID Web Access System was designed to make administration of the Web more convenient and rational, and eliminate the serious problems caused by anonymity on the Web. Arvardan was unsure what these "serious problems" were. He had never personally used the Web anonymously, and he knew no one who had—indeed, from a technical perspective, it was impossible for anyone to disguise himself on the Web. The appropriate authorities had given this careful thought.

"The appropriate authorities" was a semantically vague phrase that nonetheless was full of authority and the power to intimidate. It was simultaneously general and specific, and included within its meaning a broad range of references. Sometimes, it referred to the State Web

Administration Committee, which had issued the Web Access Serial to Arvardan. Other times, it referred to the server that e-mailed Arvardan the latest Web access announcements and regulations. Yet other times, it referred to the Web Investigation Section of the Department of Public Security. Still other times, it referred to the State News Agency. The "appropriate authorities" were everywhere and responsible for everything. They would always appear at the appropriate time to guide, supervise, or warn.

Now that the Web was almost equivalent to daily life, it was necessary to be ever vigilant and not allow the Web to become a tool for conspirators seeking to destabilize the State—so said the appropriate authorities.

The computer continued to hum. Arvardan knew this was going to take some time. The computer had been issued to him by the appropriate authorities, and he was uncertain about its technical specs and hardware configuration. The case was welded shut and could not be opened.

While waiting, Arvardan ferreted out a plastic cup from the mountain of trash at his feet and filled it with distilled water from the drinking spigot at his side. He swallowed a painkiller with the water. The distilled water went down his throat and settled into his stomach. The empty taste nauseated him.

The speakers on the computer suddenly began to play the national anthem. Arvardan put down the cup and refocused his eyes on the computer screen. This meant that he had signed on to the Web. The screen first displayed a notice from the appropriate authorities: plain white background, black text, 14-point font. The notice described the meaning of using the Web and the latest regulations concerning such use.

The notice quickly disappeared. What followed was a desktop background emblazoned with the slogan: "Let us build a healthy and stable Web!" Another window slowly floated up, containing several links: work, entertainment, e-mail, and BBS discussion forums. The BBS link was greyed out, indicating that choice was not yet available to him.

The operating system was simple and clear. The browser had no place to enter a URL. Only the bookmarks menu, which was uneditable, contained the addresses for a few Web sites. The reason for this was simple: all of these Web sites were healthy and positive. If other Web sites had the same content as these, then, logically, having access to these Web sites alone was sufficient. On the other hand, if other sites had different content, then, logically, those other sites must be unhealthy and vulgar and should not be accessed.

Some said that outside the borders of the State there were other Web sites, but those were only urban legends.

Arvardan first clicked "work." The screen displayed a menu of Web sites and software related to his work.

As a programmer, Arvardan's daily duty consisted of writing programs in accordance with instructions from his superiors. The work was boring, but it guaranteed a steady income. He did not know what the source code he wrote would be used for. His superiors never gave him such information.

He tried to continue the work left over from yesterday, but he soon felt he couldn't concentrate. He tried to entertain himself, but the "entertainment" link only contained Solitaire and Minesweeper. According to the appropriate authorities, these two games were healthy: there was no violence and no sex, and they would not give players criminal desires.

A system alert popped up: "You have new mail." Arvardan had finally found a reason to pause in his work. He quickly moved the cursor onto the "e-mail" link, clicked, and soon a new window appeared on the screen.

To:ARVARDAN19842015BNKF
From:WANGHENG10045687XHDI
Subject:Module/Already/Complete, Start/Current/Project?

WANGHENG10045687XHDI was the Serial of a colleague. The body of the e-mail was written with a series of individual words and certain fixed expressions separated by slashes. This was a format suggested by the appropriate authorities. Although modern mainframe computers could now process natural-language digital texts easily, this style of writing was a gesture on the part of the citizen to indicate that he possessed the proper attitude.

Arvardan sighed. Every time he received a new e-mail, he hoped there would be some fresh stimulus to jolt his nervous system, which was growing duller by the day. On some level, he knew that he would be disappointed each time, but he felt that keeping hope alive at least yielded a few seconds of excitement. It was like his wishing that the voice on the phone would be the smooth and mellow voice of a real woman. If he didn't keep for himself bits of remote, hopeless hope, Arvardan thought he would go mad sooner or later.

Arvardan clicked "reply," and then opened a text file with the name "List of Healthy Words" in another window. This file contained the words and fixed expressions that the appropriate authorities required every Web user to use. When they wanted to compose e-mails or use the discussion forums, they must find the appropriate words from this list with which to express themselves. If the filtering software found any Web user using a word not on this list, then the word would be automatically shielded and replaced with the phrase "Please use healthy language."

"Shielded" was a technical term. A shielded word was forbidden in writing or in speech. Ironically, "shielded" itself was a shielded word.

The list was updated constantly. Every revision meant that a few more words disappeared from the list. This forced Arvardan to exercise his brain to come up with other words to substitute for the words that were shielded. For example, "movement" used to be allowed, but then the appropriate authorities decided that this was a sensitive word, so Arvardan had to use "change of position" to express the same idea.

He referred to the list and quickly composed a response similar in style to the e-mail he had received. The List of Healthy Words forced people to compress as much information as possible into the fewest words, and to eliminate all unnecessary flourishes and figures of speech. The resulting compositions were like that cup of distilled water: flavorless. Arvardan sometimes thought that one day he would become as bleached out as the e-mails and distilled water because he wrote such e-mails and drank such water.

Arvardan sent the e-mail but could not save a copy for himself. His computer had no hard drive, and no slots for floppy disks or CDs or even a USB port. Broadband technology had advanced to the point where software applications could be hosted on remote servers, and individual users would not suffer any speed issues related to remote access. Thus, there was no need for end users to have hard drives or local storage. Every document or program a user wrote, even every movement of the mouse or keystroke, would be automatically transmitted to the public server of the appropriate authorities. This made administration easier.

After completing the e-mail, Arvardan once again fell back into his anxious, listless mood, which he could not express because "tired," "annoyed," and other negative words were all dangerous words. If someone wrote an e-mail to others to complain about such feelings, the recipients would only get an e-mail full of "please use healthy language."

This was Arvardan's life. Today was a little worse than yesterday, but should be a little better than tomorrow. But even this description was imprecise, because Arvardan himself was unclear what constituted "a little better" and what constituted "a little worse." "Better" and "worse" were variables, but his life was a constant, the value of which was "repression."

Arvardan set aside the mouse, tilted his head back, and gave a long sigh. (At least "sigh" had not yet been shielded.) He wanted to hum a song, but he couldn't remember any songs. Instead, he whistled a few times, but it sounded like a dog with tuberculosis barking, and he had to stop. The appropriate authorities were like specters that filled the whole room, giving him no space. He was like a man stuck in a quagmire: as soon as he opened his mouth, mud flowed in, so that he could not even scream for help.

He shook his head restlessly a few times, and his eyes happened to fall on the phone. Suddenly, he remembered that he still had to go to the appropriate authorities to finish the application for the BBS permit. He was glad of an opportunity to be temporarily free of the Web. On the Web he was nothing more than the sum of a series of dry numbers and "healthy words."

Arvardan put on his coat and covered his mouth with a filtering mask. He hesitated for a moment, and then picked up the Listener and put it over his ears. Then he left his room.

The Capital's streets had few pedestrians. Now that the Web was everywhere, most chores could be done there. Unlike in the primitive past, people no longer needed to go outside the home for the necessities of daily life. The appropriate authorities did not recommend too many outdoor activities, as they caused people to make physical contact with each other, and what happened after that was difficult to control.

The Listener, a portable language-filtering machine, was designed specifically to prevent that sort of thing. When the wearer said or heard some sensitive word, the Listener automatically gave a warning. Every citizen, before leaving home, must put on this device so that they could review and critique their own speech and conversation. When people realized that the Listener was present, they often chose silence. The appropriate authorities were attempting to gradually unify life on the Web and life in the physical world, so that they would be equally healthy.

It was November, and the icy wind drove clouds across a leaden, oppressive sky. Along both sides of the street, utility poles stretched out in two rows like dead trees. Pedestrians wrapped themselves tightly in black or grey coats, shrinking into themselves so that they appeared as quick-moving black dots. A thin miasma covered the whole Capital. Breathing this air without a filtering mask would be a challenge.

Has it really been two months since I last left my room? Arvardan thought, as he stood next to the sign for the bus stop.

A tall man in a blue uniform stood next to Arvardan. He looked suspiciously at Arvardan, wrapped in his black coat. Gradually, he shuffled closer, and, with pretended casualness, said to Arvardan:

"You, have, a, cigarette?"

The man enunciated each word, and paused half a second between them. The Listener was not yet sufficiently advanced to adjust to the unique rhythm and intonation of each person. In response, the appropriate authorities required that all citizens speak in this manner, so that it would be more convenient to check if anyone used words outside the regulations.

Arvardan gave him a quick glance, licked his own dry lips, and replied:

"No."

The man was disappointed. Unwilling to give up, he opened his mouth again:

"You, have, a, drink?"

"No."

It had been a long time since Arvardan had had any cigarettes or liquor. Perhaps it was due to the shortages, a common problem. But something was amiss: Arvardan's Listener had not issued a warning. In Arvardan's experience, whenever supplies of cigarettes, liquor, or other necessities suffered shortages, these words would temporarily become sensitive words that had to be shielded until the supply could be restored.

The man seemed exhausted. His puffy red eyes were a common sight these days, a result of long hours spent on the Web. His hair was a mess, and a few days' growth of stubble surrounded his mouth. A strong moldy smell dissipated from the collar of the shirt under his uniform. It was obvious that he had not been outside for days.

It was only now that Arvardan realized that the man's ears were unadorned. The space where the silver-grey Listener should have been was empty. Arvardan was stunned, and for a moment, he did not know whether to remind the man or to pretend that he hadn't noticed. He thought, *perhaps it would be better to report this to the appropriate authorities.*

Now the man inched even closer, and desire and yearning radiated from his eyes. Arvardan's heart squeezed tight, and unconsciously he took a step back. Was he going to be mugged? Or maybe this man was a sex maniac who had repressed his desires for too long? The man suddenly grabbed his sleeve. Arvardan struggled awkwardly but could not pull himself free. The man did not make another move, but gave a loud yelp, and began to speak to Arvardan in a rapid manner that Arvardan was no longer accustomed to.

"I just want to talk to you, just a few sentences. I haven't spoken in so long. My name is Hiroshi Watanabe. I'm thirty-two years old. Remember, thirty-two. I've always dreamed of having a house by a lake, with a small boat and a fishing pole. I hate the Web. Down with the Web Regulators! My wife has been poisoned by the Web. She only calls me by my Web Access Serial. This whole city is an asylum, and in it, the stronger inmates govern the weaker inmates and turn all the sane people into madmen like themselves. Fuck 'sensitive words.' I've fucking had it…"

The man's words poured out of him like soda from a bottle that had been shaken and the cap then popped. Arvardan's Listener beeped continuously. He stared in amazement but had no idea how to respond. Even more worrisome, he discovered in himself a sense of sympathy for the man, the sort of sympathy people who suffered from the same disease had for each other. The man had now gone from complaining to simply cursing, the most raw, direct kind of curses that had long been shielded. It had been five or six years since Arvardan himself had last cursed, and even the last time he had heard such language was four years ago.

But now this man was swearing at him in public, as though he wanted to say every single shielded sensitive word in a single breath. Arvardan's eardrums began to throb with pain from the decibel level and the constant beeping from the Listener.

Just then, two police vehicles appeared at the end of the street, and, lights flashing all the way, rushed toward the bus stop.

The man was still swearing when five or six officers in full riot gear rushed over and pushed him to the ground, beating him with their batons. The man kicked with his legs, and words poured out of his mouth even faster, and the curses grew even coarser. One of the officers pulled out a roll of tape, and with a sharp "pa" tore off a piece, which he stuck over the man's mouth. Immediately before his mouth was taped, the man raised his voice, and heartily yelled at the police-man, "Fuck you, you sonovabitch!" Arvardan watched as his expres-sion turned from madness to a contented smile, as though he were in-toxicated with the pleasure and release brought about by the swearing.

The police scrambled to push the man into one of the cars. One of the officers came to Arvardan. "Is, he, your, friend?"

"I, do, not, know, him." Arvardan responded in the same way.

The policeman stared at him. He took down Arvardan's Listener and checked its records. There was no record of Arvardan using any sensitive words. He put the Listener back on Arvardan's ear and warned Arvardan that everything the man had said was extremely reactionary, and he must immediately forget it. Then the officer turned around, and the police left with the arrested man.

Arvardan sighed with relief. Just now he had, for a second, an im-pulse to scream at the top of his lungs on this empty street, "Fuck you, you sonovabitch!"

The street quickly returned to its customary quiescence. Ten min-utes later, a bus slowly arrived at the station. The rusty doors opened with a clang, and an electronic female voice filled the empty space in-side the bus: "Passengers, please pay attention and use civilized language. Adhere strictly to the List of Healthy Words as you speak."

Arvardan wrapped his coat even tighter around himself.

About an hour later, the bus arrived at his destination. The cold wind blew in through the broken windows of the bus, frosting Arvardan's breath. The coal dust and sand in the wind stabbed at his face. He got up, shook the dust off himself like a wet dog shaking off water, and left the bus.

Arvardan needed to go to the appropriate authorities, the Department of Web Security in this case, responsible for processing BBS permit applications. Located across the street from the bus stop, this was a five-story building, cube-shaped, completely covered in grey concrete. If it weren't for the few windows, the building would be indistinguishable from a solid block of concrete: hard and dead. Even mosquitoes and bats stayed away.

It was also very difficult to obtain a permit to use the BBS forums. An applicant must go through close to twenty procedures and endure a long investigation process before being granted permission to browse the forums. Only after having had permission to browse the forums for three months could one be granted permission to post in designated forums. As for starting your own BBS, that was impossible.

Despite these obstacles, many used the BBS forums because this was the only place on the Web where one could have some limited conversation. Arvardan had decided to apply for a BBS permit simply out of a vague yet stubborn sense of nostalgia. He didn't know why he wanted to cause so much trouble for himself. Maybe it was just to bring a sense of excitement to his life. Maybe it was to emphasize the bits of connection between himself and the old times. Maybe it was both.

Arvardan vaguely remembered that when he was a kid, the Web was very different. Not that the technology was different, just the culture. He hoped to remember some of the things from that era through the BBS forums.

Arvardan walked into the building. Inside it was just as cold as outside, and even darker. There were no lights in the hallways. The walls, painted in a bluish white, were pasted over with Web-related regulations, policies, and slogans. Sucking the cold air into his lungs, Arvardan shuddered. Only the crack around the door at the end of the hall let in a sliver of light. On the door was a sign: "Department of Web Security, BBS Section."

Arvardan did not dwell on the irony that in order to use some virtual functionality of the Web, one had to physically come here to apply.

Once he was behind the door, Arvardan immediately felt a blast of hot air. The heat in this room was turned way up, and Arvardan's hands, feet, and face, all frozen numb, now tingled and began to itch. He wanted to reach out and scratch himself.

An electronic female voice suddenly burst out of the speakers in the ceiling: "Citizen, please remain still as you wait in line."

Arvardan put down his hand as though he had been given an electric shock, and respectfully waited where he was. He observed the room he was in: a long and narrow lobby, divided in half by a marble counter that rose in the middle like the Great Wall. A fence made of silver-white poles connected the top of the counter to the ceiling.

"Please proceed to window number eight."

The counter was so tall that Arvardan could not even look over it to see what was on the other side. But he could hear the sound of someone approaching on the other side, then sitting down.

"Please place your application documents in the tray."

The speaker on top of the counter issued the order. Unexpectedly, the voice this time was different. Even though it was still dry and cold, Arvardan could tell that the voice did not belong to a computer—this was the voice of a real woman. He tried to lift his head even higher, but he could see nothing. The counter was just too tall.

"Please put the documents in the tray."

The voice repeated the order. There was some impatience in the tone.

Yes, this is the voice of a real woman... Arvardan thought. The electronic female voice was always polite and never had any emotion in it. He put his Personal Identification Card, Web Access Permit, Web Access Serial Card, the record of sensitive word violations, and other similar documentation into a small metallic tray, slid the tray into a slot in the side of the counter, and closed the flap over the slot. Immediately he heard a faint *whoosh*. He guessed that the person on the other side of the counter—perhaps a woman—had pulled the tray out on her side.

"What is the purpose for your application for BBS service?"

The woman's voice from the speaker was business-like and professional.

"To, increase, Web, related, work, efficiency; to, create, a, healthy, and, stable, Web, environment; to, better, contribute, to, the, motherland."

Arvardan paused between each word, knowing that this was only a formality. All he had to do was give the standard answer.

The other side sank into silence. After about two minutes, the speaker came on again.

"The final procedure has been completed. You now have permission to use the BBS forums."

"Thank, you."

With a bang, the metallic tray bounced back out of the slot. In it, a few more pieces of paper had been added to the documents that Arvardan had provided.

"The appropriate authorities have issued you a user name and password for the BBS service, an index of available forums, a user guide, a copy of the applicable regulations, and the latest List of Healthy Words. Please also check your e-mail inbox."

Arvardan stepped forward, took out everything in the tray, and examined them. He was disappointed to see that his BBS user name was identical to his Web Access Serial. He remembered that when he was little, it was possible to pick your own BBS forum user name.

Memories of childhood were often mingled with fairy tales and fantasies, however, and might not match reality. The reality now was that you could only use the user name and password issued by the appropriate authorities. The reason was simple: user names and passwords also could contain sensitive words.

He shoved the papers into his coat pocket. The pieces of paper were actually meaningless, as the electronic copies had been sent to his e-mail already. But the appropriate authorities felt that formal documents on paper were helpful in inducing in users the proper feelings of fear and respect.

He hoped the speaker in the counter would speak a bit more. But he was disappointed by the sound of someone getting up and leaving. Based on the rhythm of the steps, Arvardan was even more certain that the person on the other side was a woman.

The empty electronic female voice again came from the ceiling: "You have completed the necessary procedures. Please leave the Department of Web Security and return to your work."

Arvardan wrinkled his nose in disgust, and turned to leave the warm lobby and return to the freezing cold hallway.

On the way home, Arvardan curled up in his seat on the bus without moving. The success of obtaining permission to use the BBS service gave him an illusory sense of excitement. His right hand fingered the documents in his pocket as he tried to remember the sound of that mysterious woman's voice.

It would be so nice to hear that voice again. At the same time, he rubbed his thumb lightly over the piece of paper on top of the stack in his pocket, imagining that this document had been touched also by *her* slender, graceful, ivory-like fingers. He was so excited that he wanted to yell, "Fuck you, you sonovabitch!" The sound of that man cursing was stuck in his mind, and again and again the curse rose to the tip of his tongue.

Suddenly, his finger felt something out of place on the back of the document. Arvardan looked around him, ascertained that there were no other passengers, and carefully took the document out and flipped it over. He examined it carefully in the light from the bus window.

Arvardan realized that the top right corner of the document had been lightly creased by a fingernail. The crease was so light that if Arvardan hadn't been fingering it so closely he would never have noticed it. The crease was unusual: it was a straight line, but at the end of the line, not far from it, was another very short crease, as though the person had meant to make a dot. The whole thing looked like an exclamation point, or, if you looked at it from the opposite direction, the letter "i."

He looked through the other papers, and soon discovered that the other four documents also had similar creases. They were shaped differently, but all seemed to be symbols of some sort. Arvardan recalled the order in which the woman from the speaker had mentioned the documents, and began to write the symbols found on each document in order on the steamed-up bus window:

t-i-t-l-e

Title?

The bus stopped, and a few passengers got on. Arvardan moved his body to cover the writing on the window. Then, pretending to yawn, he lifted his sleeve and erased the letters.

Arriving home, Arvardan took off his coat and filtering mask, and threw the Listener on the cot. Then he fell onto the cot and buried his head in the pillows. Every time he left home to go outside, he felt exhausted afterward, in part because his weakened physique was no longer used to being outside and in part due to the stress of being with the Listener.

When he woke up, he checked his e-mail. His inbox contained two work-related e-mails from colleagues and five e-mails containing the electronic copies of the BBS documents from the Department of Web Security.

Arvardan opened the index of BBS forums. All the forums were officially sanctioned. The forums had different subjects, but all basically revolved around how to better cooperate and respond to State directives and how to build a healthy Web. For example, on one of the computer technology forums, the main topic was how to improve the technology for shielding sensitive words.

Amazingly, one of the forums was about games. In it, the main topic of discussion was an online game about how to help others use healthy words. The player could control a little boy to patrol the streets and see if anyone was using sensitive words. If so, the little boy could choose to go up and criticize the offender or report the offender to the police. The more offenders the little boy caught, the higher the score and the better the rewards.

Arvardan opened a few other random forums. Everyone in them was polite, and spoke very healthy language, just like people outside on the streets. No, it was even worse than on the streets. People on the streets at least had opportunities to perform a few private gestures, like the way Arvardan had written "title" on the bus window in secret. But on the BBS forums, even the last bits of privacy of the individual were stripped away. The appropriate authorities could examine every mouse movement, every keystroke, every bit that passed through your computer, and there was nowhere to hide.

Disappointment and a sense of loss overwhelmed Arvardan. He closed his eyes and lay back. He had been so naive to think that the BBS forums might be a little more open, but now it was clear that it was even more suffocating than real life. He was stuck in an electronic quagmire, and he couldn't breathe. "Fuck you, you sonovabitch" once again rose to the tip of his tongue. The urge to shout was so strong that he struggled to contain himself.

Suddenly, he thought of the mysterious "title." What did that really mean? Five documents, five e-mails. Maybe the e-mails had something hidden in them? Perhaps they had something to do with "title?"

Arvardan turned back to the screen and carefully examined the five e-mails from the Department of Web Security. He opened the e-mails and saw that each one had a title in larger font at the top. He arranged the titles in the order indicated by the letters in the word "title," taking each creased letter as indicating the position its corresponding e-mail's title should be in.

"Navigate/With/Care:/Your/User/Name/And/Password"

"To/Our/Users:/Newest/Index/Of/Available/Forums"

"User/Basics:/Guide/For/New/BBS/Users"

"Education/In/Health/And/Responsibility:/Applicable/BBS/Regulations"

"Forum/Etiquette:/List/Of/Healthy/Words/For/The/Web"

The first word from each title, when put together, formed a sentence: "Navigate To User Education Forum."

Arvardan remembered that just now he had indeed seen a forum with the name "User Education Forum." He clicked the link for that forum, hoping that this was not just some coincidence.

The User Education Forum was an administrative forum. All the posts in it were suggestions or complaints about BBS management. The forum moderator was someone named MICHEAL19387465LLKQ. There were few posts and responses, and the forum had little traffic. Arvardan opened the index of all posts in the forum and clicked open each one. The posts seemed completely random, and he could see no pattern.

Arvardan was disappointed. He seemed to have hit another dead end. But he had not been this excited for so long. He stubbornly kept on staring at the screen, trying to hold onto the sense of discovery and excitement, even if illusory, for just a little while longer.

Suddenly, his eyes focused on the user name of the forum administrator. MICHEAL was not the usual spelling for MICHAEL.

He clicked through the posts in the forum again, and noticed that some of the posts were also posted by user names containing unusual spellings for common names.

Following the pattern from before, he took the initial words from the titles of posts by users with unusually spelled names and arranged them in the order of the number portion of the authors' user names to form a new sentence:

"Every Sunday at the Simpson Tower, fifth floor, suite B."

There must be some meaning in this. The documents, the e-mails, and now the forum posts: three times in a row he had put clues together that led to more clues. This was no mere coincidence. Who had hidden these messages in the official documents from the appropriate authorities? What happened every Sunday at the Simpson Tower, fifth floor, suite B?

Arvardan had finally found the excitement long absent from his life. The novelty of the unknown stimulated his long-numbed nerves. More important, these word games, planted in the middle of official documents from the appropriate authorities, gave him the satisfaction of breathing freely, as though a solid iron mask had been punched through with a few air holes.

Let us build a healthy and stable Web!

Fuck you, you sonovabitch!

Arvardan stared at the desktop background on the computer screen, mouthed the curse silently, and lifted his middle finger to the screen.

For the next few days, Arvardan lived in a state of constant, barely subdued excitement. He was like a kid who was trying to hide a mouthful of candy with an innocent smile, and who, after the adults had turned away, broke into a sly grin, enjoying the feeling of having a secret.

Day after day passed; the List of Healthy Words continued to shrink; the air outside the window grew even murkier. This was the way life was. Arvardan had begun to use the List of Healthy Words as a calendar. If three words had been deleted, that meant three days had passed. When seven words had been deleted, Arvardan knew it was Sunday.

Arvardan arrived at the Simpson Tower at noon. The clue that had brought him there did not mention a specific time. Arvardan thought it probably made sense to show up around noon. As he arrived wearing his dark green army coat, the filtering mask, and the Listener, his heart began to beat irregularly. He had imagined all kinds of possibilities for this moment, and now that the secret to the mystery was about to be revealed, he was nervous. *No matter what happens here, it can't be worse than my life now*, Arvardan thought.

He walked into the building, and noticed that there were very few people here as well. The empty halls were filled only with his steps and their echo. An old elevator car had advertisements for "Let's build a beautiful home on the Web," and a poster with a man whose face was imbued with truth and justice. The background of the poster was the Flag, and the man pointed at the viewer with his right index finger. Above him was the slogan: "Citizen, I need you to use healthy language." Arvardan turned away, and saw that the other wall of the elevator car had the exact same poster. There was nowhere to hide.

Luckily, by then he had arrived at the fifth floor. The elevator doors opened, and opposite was the door to suite B. The door was green, the paint chipped, and splats of ink covered the door frame.

Arvardan took a deep breath, and pressed the doorbell.

Arvardan thought the rhythm of the steps within the door sounded familiar, as though he had heard it somewhere. The door cracked open halfway, and a young woman held onto the doorknob as she filled the doorway, leaning forward to stare at Arvardan. She said, suspiciously:

"Who, are, you, looking, for?"

It was the voice behind the counter at the Department of Web Security, BBS Section. She looked beautiful: hunter green wool sweater, hair worn short in a tight bun in the typical style, skin so fair it was pale, and lips glowing with the flush of health.

Looking into the woman's eyes, Arvardan hesitated, and then raised his right hand: "Title."

Arvardan stared at the woman tensely. If the woman reported his strange behavior to the police, then he would be arrested and interrogated as to why he had gone to a stranger's home. The crime of "willfully lolling about" was only slightly less serious than the crime of "using sensitive words."

The woman nodded, barely perceptibly, and carefully gestured with her right hand for him to come in. Arvardan was about to speak, but the woman glared at him, and he swallowed and obediently followed her into the apartment.

Once they were in, the woman shut the door immediately, and then pulled a lead-grey curtain over the doorway. Arvardan blinked anxiously, and looked about him. The apartment had two bedrooms and a living room. The living room had a couch and a coffee table, on top of which there were a few bunches of red and purple plastic flowers. Next to one of the walls was a desk with a computer. A common white wall calendar hung on the wall, but the owner had taken care to decorate its edges with pink paper, giving it a homier feel. Arvardan noticed that the shoe rack next to the door held four pairs of shoes, all different sizes. This meant that he wasn't the only guest here today.

Arvardan was still uneasy. Suddenly the woman clapped him lightly on the back, indicating that he should continue inside. The two of them went across the living room, through a short hallway, and arrived at a bedroom. The bedroom door was curtained by the same kind of lead-grey curtain. The woman lifted the curtain and pushed open the bedroom door.

Arvardan saw three smiling individuals in a room decorated with real, fresh flowers. The room was also full of antiques that existed only in Arvardan's memory: an Impressionist painting, a wooden sculpture from Uganda, and a silver candelabra. But there was no computer.

As he hesitated, the woman entered the room. She carefully pulled the curtain closed and shut the door. She turned around:

"Welcome to the Talking Club!"

The Talking Club?

Out of habit, Arvardan did not say the words aloud. He wasn't certain if the words were healthy, and so asked his question only with his eyes.

"You can speak as freely as you like in here. This damned device won't work here." The woman pointed to his Listener. There was no warning beep. It didn't seem to hear the two sensitive words in her speech: "freely" and "damned."

Arvardan remembered the man he had seen a week ago at the bus stop. If he took off his Listener, would what happened to that man also happen to him? The woman saw that he was hesitant. She pointed to the lead-grey curtain at the door: "Don't worry. This can shield off the signal for the Listener. No one will know."

"Who, are, you? What, is, this, place?"

Arvardan took off the Listener. He spoke in a low voice. It was still too difficult for him to shift out of the manner of speech demanded by the appropriate authorities.

"This is the Talking Club. Here, you may speak as you like," said another man as he got up. He was tall and thin, the glasses over his nose particularly thick.

Arvardan mumbled, but could not speak out loud. He was embarrassed by the stares of the four others, and his face flushed bright red.

The woman who had opened the door for him gave him a sympathetic look: "You poor thing. Don't be so tense. Everyone is like this when they first arrive. Over time you'll get used to it."

She put a hand on Arvardan's shoulder: "Actually, we've met. At least I've seen you, but you haven't seen me." As she spoke, she reached up and let down her hair. The black tresses fell to her shoulders, and in that moment Arvardan thought she was the most beautiful woman he had ever seen.

Arvardan finally spoke a whole sentence, though the words still did not flow smoothly. "I... remember you, remember your voice."

"Really?" The woman laughed. She sat him on a couch, and handed him a glass of water. Arvardan noticed that this was an old-fashioned glass, etched with a flowery pattern. The water inside the glass gave off a faint fragrance. Arvardan tried a sip. The sweet taste was particularly stimulating for a tongue that had grown used to distilled water.

"This wasn't easy to obtain. Even we can't get it every week." The woman sat next to him, looking intently at him with her dark eyes. "How did you find out about us?"

Arvardan explained the process by which he had discovered the sequence of clues. The other four nodded in approval. "Smart man. Your brain hasn't become mush," said a thirty-something man with a few extra pounds. His voice was very loud.

The middle-aged man with glasses put his hands together in a gesture of agreement. "You are a natural for membership in the Talking Club."

"All right," the fat man said, "let's give a round of applause to formally welcome the new member."

The other four applauded, and the sound of their clapping filled the small bedroom. Arvardan lifted the glass to them, embarrassed. When the applause died down, he timidly lifted his head, and asked, "Can I ask a question? What exactly is the Talking Club?"

The woman who had brought him in responded:

"The Talking Club is a gathering where we can say anything we want. There are no sensitive words here, and no healthy Web. This is a space to release your soul and stretch out your body."

"Our principle is just this: talk," added the middle-aged man, and he adjusted his glasses.

"But, what can I talk about?"

"Anything. You can talk about anything in your heart." The middle-aged man smiled.

This is an audacious gathering. It's clearly criminal, Arvardan thought. But he found himself attracted to the idea of being a criminal in this way.

"Of course, we need to make certain things clear," the woman said. "Talking is dangerous. Every member faces the danger of arrest by the appropriate authorities. State agents may break through the door at any moment, and capture us under the charges of illegal assembly and using illegal language. You have the right to refuse to join us, and leave immediately."

Arvardan listened to the woman's warning. He hesitated. But he thought that if he left now, then he would go back to his life, suffocating in a quagmire. Arvardan had not known that he had such a strong yearning to talk.

"I will not leave. I will join you, talking."

"Perfect! Oh, why don't we start with self-introductions?" The woman was delighted. She stood up. "Let's start with me. My name is Artemis. As for my Web Access Serial? To hell with it. Who cares? I have my own name."

Her words made everyone, including Arvardan, laugh. Then she continued. "Still, Artemis is just a pseudonym. She's a goddess from Greek mythology."

"Pseudonym?"

"Right. It's not the same as the name on my Personal Identification Card."

"But, why?"

"Aren't you sick of the name they have for you in their files? I want to give myself a name that I like, even if there's just one place to use it. In the Talking Club we each have picked a name for ourselves. That's how we address one another."

Arvardan nodded thoughtfully. He understood Artemis's feeling. When using the BBS forums, he had hoped to pick a name that he liked, and not be assigned a user name.

Through Artemis's self-introduction, Arvardan learned that she was a staffer at the Department of Web Security, BBS Section. She was twenty-three, single, and hated cockroaches and spiders. Her hobbies included sewing and gardening, and the flowers in the bedroom were secretly cut and brought back by her from outside the Capital.

Next was the middle-aged man. His name was Lancelot. He was forty-one, an engineer at the Capital Electric Plant. The name "Lancelot" came from the Arthurian legends, and belonged to a faithful knight. Lancelot was married and had two children: a boy (aged three) and a girl (aged four). They liked lemon-flavored candy the most. Lancelot hoped that he would be able to bring the kids to the next gathering of the Club. The children were still learning to talk, and he wanted them to learn real speech.

The thirty-something overweight man was a Web Regulator for the Department of Web Security named Wagner. This surprised Arvardan. He had had the impression that Web Regulators were all cold, expressionless men, but the man before Arvardan was corpuscular, oily, and his mustache curled up spiritedly at the ends. He loved cigars and the opera, and took advantage of the special privileges available to Web Regulators to obtain them.

"Wagner got us the curtains that can shield the signals from the Listener," Artemis added. Wagner tipped an imaginary hat and bowed to her.

The fourth member of the Talking Club was a woman in a black uniform. She had just turned thirty. Her name was Duras, and she worked as an editor at the *Capital Daily Times*. She was even thinner than Artemis, and her high cheeks contrasted with her sunken eyes. Her thin lips didn't part much from each other even when she spoke, and never revealed her teeth. She liked cats and dogs, even though she had no pets now.

"It's you next," Artemis said to Arvardan. Arvardan took a minute to think, and then introduced himself to the group, stammering many times. When he tried to describe his hobbies, for a moment he couldn't think of any. He had never had to think about hobbies before.

Artemis put her hand on his shoulder again, and tried to help him. "Well, what's the one thing you really want to do?"

"I can really say anything?"

"Anything. There are no restrictions here."

Arvardan thought that he had finally found an opportunity. He cleared his throat, scratched his head, and broke into a loud, crisp shout: "Fuck you, you sonovabitch!"

All the others were stunned. Wagner was the first to recover. He held onto his cigar with his teeth and applauded vigorously. Then he took the cigar in his hand, and loudly exclaimed: "Fantastic! This should be our formal membership oath."

Artemis and Duras both giggled. Arvardan thought that beyond the novelty of speaking with the Club, he really enjoyed the sense of contempt for the appropriate authorities in voicing the string of swearwords.

Artemis tilted her head and asked him. "What do you wish to name yourself?"

"Ummm...Wang Er," Arvardan said. This was a Chinese name. He had once had a Chinese friend who loved to tell stories. In all his stories, the main character was named Wang Er.

The mood in the bedroom was now friendly and easy, and conversation became more natural. Everyone got into a comfortable position, and Artemis refilled everyone's cup from a kettle from time to time. Arvardan gradually let go of his tension, and felt that his brain had never been so relaxed.

Artemis filled his cup with sweet water again, "It's impossible to speak freely in our daily lives. We need this space. But we can't openly advertise for membership, and it's far too risky to try to find new members through physical contact. So Lancelot designed a system of clues and hints, and Wagner and I used our system access privileges to leave the clues in places. Only those who discovered and solved the clues would find the Club."

"My system wasn't designed just for safety," Lancelot said. He took off his glasses and carefully polished them. "It's also a qualifying exam for potential new members. Members of the Talking Club must be in possession of intelligence and wisdom, passionate, and full of yearning for freedom."

Wagner held his cigar between two fingers, flicked the ash into an ashtray, then said loudly, "In my experience, most applicants for permission to use the BBS service are nostalgic for the past or desire something new and fresh in their lives. They think that the BBS forums will show them something different from daily life—of course, reality is far otherwise, since the State's control over the BBS forums is even stricter than the regulation of e-mail—but their desire indicates that they want to be free. Thus, we hide our clues in the BBS documents so that only applicants for BBS service can find them. And only those who are smart and observant can find all the hints and follow their trail to find this place."

"You are the second person to find the Talking Club. The first was Miss Duras," Artemis said to Arvardan. Arvardan gazed at Duras in admiration. Duras lightly said, "It's no big deal. My job is all about playing with words."

Arvardan remembered the crazy man he had met at the bus stop a week ago. He told the others his story. When he was finished, Lancelot shook his head, and sighed.

"I've seen this sort of thing, too. It happened to a colleague of mine. This shows the necessity for something like the Talking Club as a pressure-release valve. Living constantly under the restrictions imposed by sensitive words will drive people crazy because they can neither think nor express themselves."

Wagner moved his heavy body to the side. "This is exactly what the appropriate authorities want to see. Then only the stupid will survive. A society full of stupid men is a stable one."

"You are also a member of the appropriate authorities, Mr. Wagner," Artemis said lightly as she refilled Wagner's cup.

"Miss Artemis, I'm an ordinary man just like any other, with the sole distinction that I'm allowed to use a few more sensitive words."

Everyone laughed. Arvardan had never seen so many people speak so much. He found, to his own surprise, that he quickly felt at home among these people. The distance and sense of unfamiliarity between them melted away quickly. Also, his dizziness and congested chest, problems that had become habits, disappeared.

Quickly the topic of conversation turned from the Talking Club itself to broader interests. Artemis sang a song; Lancelot told a few jokes; Duras told everyone about the customs of the southern provinces of the State; Wagner even sang an aria from an opera. Even though Arvardan couldn't understand a word of this last contribution, he did not hold back his applause. In a shielded corner of the Capital, five individuals unwilling to sink into silence were enjoying a most precious luxury—talking.

"Wang Er, do you know *1984*?" Artemis asked. She sat down next to Arvardan. Arvardan shook his head. "I only know that *1984* is part of my Web Access Serial."

"It's a book."

"Book?" This was an old word. Now that computer technology had advanced to the point that all information was contained by the Web, anyone could go to the online library to get the digital editions of published material. The appropriate authorities considered physical books to be an unnecessary waste, and they had gradually disappeared.

Wagner said, "It is understandable that the appropriate authorities prefer electronic books. With electronic books, all you need is FIND and REPLACE to eliminate all unhealthy words in a book and decontaminate it. But to correct and edit physical books would take forever."

"*1984* is a great book. It's what an old philosopher predicted about our modern world," Artemis said earnestly. "Long ago, the book perceived the struggle between restraint and freedom over the flesh and over the soul. It's the foundation of the Talking Club."

"How can one read this book?" Arvardan asked, staring into Artemis's dark eyes.

"We can't find a paper copy, and of course the online library won't have it." Lancelot shook his head, and then broke into another smile. He gestured with his left hand at Duras. "Our Miss Duras should be proud of her memory. When she was young, she was fortunate enough to have read this book, and could recall most of it."

"Wonderful! Then she wrote it out, right?"

"That would be far too dangerous. Right now, owning physical books is a great crime, and would risk exposing the Talking Club. Instead, every time the Talking Club meets, we ask Miss Duras to recite some of it."

Everyone quieted. Duras stood up and walked to the middle of the room. Arvardan casually put his arm around Artemis's shoulders, and she leaned toward him, her hair drifting between them. A faint feminine fragrance found its way to his nose and caused his heart to skip a few beats.

Duras's voice was not loud, but clear and forceful. Her memory was indeed amazing: not only did she remember the plot, but also she could recount many of the details and recite entire passages verbatim. Duras got to the part where Julia pretended to fall and secretly handed a note with the words "I love you" to Winston. Duras's retelling was so lively that she captivated everyone. Artemis was especially absorbed in the story and didn't notice Arvardan's eyes, which never left her.

"The author of 1984 predicted the progress of totalitarianism, but could not predict the progress of technology." Wagner gave his opinion as Duras paused for a drink. Arvardan thought that Wagner's appearance belied his quickness: he was a very perceptive technocrat.

"In Oceania, it was still possible to pass secret notes to each other and express one's hidden thoughts. But now things are different. The appropriate authorities have forced all of us to live on the Web, where even if we wanted to pass secret notes to each other the Web Regulators would see everything. There is no place to hide. And in real life? We still have to contend with the Listener." Wagner knocked his cigar against his thighs. "To put it simply: technology is neutral. But the progress of technology will cause a free world to become ever freer, and a totalitarian world to become ever more repressive."

"This seems like the pronouncement of some philosopher," Artemis said, winking at Arvardan. She retrieved some cookies from a drawer and handed them to everyone.

"Isn't this just like how the bits are just 1's and 0's, but some will make them into useful tools, while others will make them into malicious viruses?" Arvardan said. Wagner snapped his fingers happily. "Very good, Wang Er. That's exactly it. You are a credit to programmers."

Duras looked at the clock hanging on the wall, and reminded the other four that time was up. The Talking Club could not meet for too long each time. The longer their Listeners remained shielded and off the grid, the greater the risk of exposure.

"All right. Let's take the final half-hour to complete today's activities."

Artemis cleaned away the empty cups on the table, and Lancelot and Wagner both got up to stretch out their shoulders and backs, a bit sore from sitting for so long. Only Duras remained seated without moving.

"Activities? What activities?" Arvardan asked. *What would the Talking Club do other than talk?*

"Oh, right. We do have other activities." Artemis moved her bangs out of the way, and gave him a seductive smile. "We still have to have frank exchanges with each other."

"Frank exchanges?"

"Yes, fucking, to speak plainly."

Arvardan's face turned white, and his breathing quickened. His stomach felt as if it had just been injected with air chilled to thirty degrees below zero. He couldn't believe his ears.

Of course, the appropriate authorities *did* permit sexual activities, but only between married couples. And there was a complex set of algorithms that computed the legally permitted frequency and lengths of their couplings based on the couple's age, physical health, income level, professions, environment, climate, and record of rule-violations. As for unmarried individuals such as Arvardan, it was completely illegal to engage in any sexual activity whatsoever (including masturbation) or to read or view any material related to sex — all immoral words having been eliminated from the List of Healthy Words in any case.

"The Talking Club has freedom of speech, as well as the freedom to go to bed with anyone," Artemis said without any embarrassment. "We talk to each other, and then choose whoever we like to make love with, just as we choose to speak the words that we like."

Lancelot saw the awkward expression on Arvardan's face. He walked over and lightly clapped Arvardan's shoulders. He said, gently, "Of course, we won't force anyone. This is all built on the foundation of consenting adults. I still have to leave early to pick up my kids. You have just the right number without me."

Arvardan's face flushed bright red. He felt hot, like the CPU in his computer during the summer. He couldn't even lift his eyes to look at Artemis. He had desired female company for so long, but this was the first time he had been so close to that goal.

Lancelot said his goodbyes to everyone. Artemis left the bedroom to Wagner and Duras, and took the hand of Arvardan, who was close to panicking, and led him to another bedroom. This one clearly belonged to Artemis herself. The room was appointed simply, very neat and clean.

Artemis took the initiative. Under her seductive ministrations, Arvardan gradually let himself go, and allowed the primitive desires hidden deep within his heart to come out. He had yearned for any kind of release from his dry, boxed-in life by imagining the smooth, mellow voice of a real woman, and now his dreams were finally coming true. Arvardan did not know if there was a distinction between his desire for her and his desire to say "Fuck you, you sonovabitch," but now was not the time for analysis.

When he woke up, he saw that Artemis was lying beside him, her naked body like a white jade statue. Even in sleep, her pose was beautiful. He lifted himself, yawned, and then Artemis opened her eyes.

"Feels good, doesn't it?" she asked.

"Yes…" Arvardan didn't know what else to say. He paused, then said hesitantly, "Before, with Lancelot and Wagner, did you also… ummm, what I mean is, like we did just now?"

"Yes," Artemis said, gently. She sat up, her hair hanging over her shoulder to cover her chest. Her forthrightness confused Arvardan. There was an uncomfortable hush in the room, and then Artemis broke the silence: "You remember the story today? The woman in the story handed the man a note that said, 'I love you.'"

"Yes," Arvardan said.

"The word 'love' does not exist in the List of Healthy Words promulgated by the appropriate authorities." Artemis's eyes were filled with regret and loss.

"I love you," Arvardan said, without thinking. He knew that it was possible to say anything he wanted in this room.

"Thank you." Artemis gave him a perfunctory smile. She put on her clothes and hurried Arvardan to do the same. Arvardan was a bit disappointed. She had not responded as enthusiastically as he had wished, but as though what he had just said was not all that important.

By now Duras and Wagner had already left. Artemis walked him to the door, handed him his Listener, and then reminded him, "Once outside, remember not to mention anything about the Talking Club or anyone here. Outside of the Talking Club, we are strangers."

"I understand," Arvardan said. He turned to leave.

"Wang Er."

Arvardan turned at her words. Before he knew what was happening, two soft lips covered his lips, then a low voice sounded by his ear. "Thank you. I love you, too."

Arvardan felt his eyes grow wet. He put on the Listener, opened the door, and walked back into the suffocating world. But now, he was in a very different mood from when he had first showed up.

After this, Arvardan's mental condition clearly improved. He carefully treasured the joy of having a secret club. Every week or two weeks, the five members met. They talked, sang, or listened to Duras tell the story of *1984*. Arvardan enjoyed frank exchanges with Artemis a few more times, and occasionally did the same with Duras. Now he had two personas: one was Arvardan, who existed in real life and on the Web, and the other was Wang Er, member of the Talking Club.

At one meeting, Arvardan asked, "Are we the only ones who gather to talk in private in the whole State?"

"It is said that there are some places in the State, far from the Capital and deeply hidden in the mountains, where the truly radical not only gather to talk, but also organize for violence. They shout as they rush at the State's agents, and even curse at the firing squads as they are executed," Wagner said.

"Can we join them?" Arvardan asked.

"Only if you are willing to give up your safe and still-comfortable life. The radicals live in places so desolate that except for free speech there is nothing else, not even enough clean water," Wagner said, a little coldly.

Arvardan flinched and did not pursue the topic further. He certainly desired talk, but not to the point where he was willing to give up all that he had, little though it was. Distilled water was still better than no water. The Talking Club provided sufficient nourishment to sustain the dried husk of his spirit. Bottom line: he was easily satisfied.

At another meeting, the topic of conversation turned to sensitive words. Arvardan remembered that long ago—his memory was growing hazy—the appropriate authorities had actually issued a List of *Sensitive* Words. People who ran the various Web sites were told to refer to it secretly in administering the sites. He was not sure how that system had evolved into the present one. That day, Wagner brought a bottle of wine for the occasion and was in good spirits. He explained to them the history of the "shielding" system. As a Web Regulator, he had access to the historical records for this process.

Initially, the State only shielded certain sensitive words, but the State quickly discovered that this was essentially useless. Many simply mixed in special characters or numbers or misspelled words to get around the inspection system. The appropriate authorities had to respond by trying to shield these variant spellings. But, as everyone knew, the combinations of different characters to approximate the appearance of different words were virtually limitless. Provided you had some imagination, it was always possible to come up with a novel combination and get your meaning across. For example, the word "politics" could be written as "polit/cs," "政itics," "pol/itic$," and so on.

After the appropriate authorities finally caught on to the problem, they took a new tack. Since it was not possible to filter out all possible combinations of characters that might spell out a word, the solution was to forbid the use of anything except real dictionary words. This procedure was initially very successful. The number of rule-violators went down significantly. But, very soon, people discovered it was possible to use puns, homonyms, or rhyming slang to continue to express the same dangerous ideas. Even if the appropriate authorities filtered out all sensitive words and all possible puns and homonyms with those words, it was useless. Imaginative citizens gave their creativity free rein, and used metaphor, metonymy, analogy, etymology, rhyming slang, and other rhetorical tricks to substitute non-sensitive words for sensitive ones. The human mind was far more creative than the computer. The computer might shield off one path, but the people had many more paths to choose from.

This contest, under the surface, seemed to go the way of the people. But then, a man who could think outside the box appeared. It was unclear who he really was: some said that he was the chief administrator at the appropriate authorities; others said that he was a dangerous man who had been arrested for using too many sensitive words. He was the cause of the turn in the tide of the battle between the State and the people.

He suggested to the appropriate authorities that the regulations should no longer explain what was forbidden. Instead, the regulations should set forth what *could* be said, and *how* to say it. The appropriate authorities immediately took this advice, and issued new regulations. The List of Sensitive Words was eliminated, and in its place was the List of Healthy Words.

This time, the people were on the losing side. In the past, they had delighted in playing cat-and-mouse games with the appropriate authorities on the Web and in daily life. But now the appropriate authorities had them by the throat, since the entire framework and building blocks of language were now under their control.

Nonetheless, the people refused to give up. They began to select words from the List of Healthy Words and use them in novel combinations to express illegal meanings. For example, writing "stabilize" twice in a row meant "topple," "stabilize" plus "prosperity" meant "shield." The appropriate authorities had to keep an eye on this sort of trend, and day after day, eliminate more and more words from the List of Healthy Words to prevent their use in these new roles.

"So long as the world even contained two words or even two letters, then it would be possible to continue the free exchange of ideas—you know Morse code?"

Wagner paused, drained his cup, and gave a satisfied burp.

"But, the price for this war is the loss of language. Our ability to express ourselves continues to get poorer, and more dry and banal. More and more, people will choose silence. But this is a good thing as far as the appropriate authorities are concerned." Lancelot had a worried expression on his face, and rhythmically knocked against the desk. "If you think about it, isn't it the people's desire for freedom the very thing that's pushing language to the edge of death? Ironic, isn't it? The appropriate authorities will have the last laugh."

"No, no. They will not understand the emotion behind laughter," Wagner said.

"Actually, I think the appropriate authorities have always operated in a state of fear. They are terrified that people will have the use of too many words, and express too many thoughts, making their control difficult," Artemis put on the stiff, cold expression she wore for work, and imitated the common speech pattern: "Let us build a healthy and stable Web!"

Duras, Lancelot, and Wagner all burst into laughter. The only one who didn't laugh was Arvardan. He was stuck on the last thing that Lancelot had said: in the war between the people and the appropriate authorities, the final conclusion was the death of language. Then the Talking Club was nothing more than a chance to enjoy the brief, final quiet moment that came from pulling shut the curtains on the windows of a train speeding toward the edge of a cliff.

Duras could not attend the frank exchange phase of the Talking Club that time because it was her time of the month, and she left early.

Artemis washed the cups and smiled at the three men: "Should we try a three-on-one?"

Lancelot patted Arvardan on the shoulder. "I have some things I want to discuss with Wang Er. We'll stay here a bit." Artemis took Wagner to the other bedroom. Arvardan was confused, unsure of what Lancelot wanted.

Lancelot sat back on the couch. The engineer's expression became serious. "Wagner has told you about the radical organizations?" Arvardan nodded.

"What do you think of them?"

"I admire them. But I'm not sure if it's necessary to go that far. Men cannot live on words alone." Although Arvardan had never been to the mountains, he had heard plenty about their desolation.

Lancelot laughed bitterly and drained the coffee cup in front of him. "I was once a member of the radicals. But now I'm a deserter."

Arvardan stared at him.

"In the beginning, I had lots of ideals. I went to the mountains and joined them. But when the rush of freedom had passed, what followed was only constant deprivation and suffering. I wavered and finally abandoned my friends, snuck back to the Capital, and now I hide in a girl's bedroom, chat, fuck, and drink coffee, and say I'm satisfied with my life."

"You regret leaving?"

"My regret is not what's important." Lancelot handed a piece of paper to him. The paper was thin, light, and had a single address written on it.

"Memorize it and swallow the paper," Lancelot said. "This is how you get to the mountains and get in touch with them. If you change your mind about your life, you can go any time."

"Have you given this to the others, too?"

"No. The Talking Club is enough for the rest of us. But something is different about you. You remind me a lot of the younger me. Though you look quiet, inside you there is a dangerous spark. I have lost the ambition and the will to change the world, but I do not want to see everyone become like me."

"But I—"

"You don't need to promise me anything. This is only an option, that's all."

After returning home from the Talking Club, Arvardan lay on his cot with his hands under his head, and sank into thought. He was infatuated with Artemis and could not help himself. Arvardan envied Winston from Duras's telling of *1984*. He and Julia had their own room, a world that belonged only to the two of them.

(He also thought about what Lancelot had said to him about the radicals, but soon he put it out of his mind—the image of radicals hiding in the mountains was simply not as alluring as the body of Artemis.)

Once, when he was engaging in a "frank exchange" with Artemis, he had revealed his thoughts to her. She didn't answer him directly but only said that the relationship between them could not go beyond what they had—the limit of what was possible. The appropriate authorities would not be napping forever. "We can only compress our emotional lives into the weekly meetings of the Talking Club. It's already a great luxury," she said, as she gently stroked his chest. "In the Talking Club, we are Artemis and Wang Er. But any other time, you are ARVARDAN19842015BNKF, and I am ALICE19387465BJHD."

Arvardan could only sigh in response. He really shouldn't have asked for more.

Along with his emotions, the Web also changed. Ever since he had joined the Talking Club, Arvardan had gradually begun noticing some of the hidden aspects of the Web. Just as Wagner had said, the war between the people and the appropriate authorities never ended. Always, thought and speech leaked from the cracks.

Arvardan noticed that within the formulaic e-mails and BBS forum posts were hidden many details that were worth paying attention to, just like his "title." There were all kinds of codes and hidden meanings. These puzzles came from different individuals, and the format and decoding technique differed for each. Arvardan didn't know what was hidden behind some of the codes, but one thing was certain: the Talking Club was not the only underground gathering. Wagner was right: always, individuals were attempting to use "healthy" words to express "unhealthy" thoughts.

In the past, Arvardan had only vaguely felt that he was being constrained, but now he could see clearly the pulsing arteries and veins of this system, and the various tricks played on him by the appropriate authorities. The freedom that he enjoyed at the Talking Club only made him even more aware of the lack of freedom in his life.

"Fuck you, you sonovabitch!"

At every meeting, the three male members would shout this curse out loud. They understood very well that this had no effect on the appropriate authorities, but they loved the feeling the curse brought them.

One week, Arvardan was particularly busy. His colleague, for unknown reasons, had been shielded. This meant that the whole project fell on his shoulders. The project involved designing a piece of software for the appropriate authorities, which would be used to control the energy distribution for a new, high-powered, active Listener. (It was unusual for Arvardan to be told this much, but since his colleague was gone, his superiors had to give him the bigger picture.) The software was complex, and he had to spend more than twelve hours a day working in front of the computer, only pausing to eat, take a drink of distilled water, or nap briefly on his cot when his body could no longer take the abuse. His room was filled with the stench of sweaty socks and shirts.

Coincidentally, the heating system in his room failed. The grey radiators became ice cold and no longer circulated hot water. Arvardan checked them and realized the problem wasn't with the pipes. Since his neighbors were suffering the same fate, it meant that the heating system was failing as a whole. The one positive effect of this failure was that it reduced the stench in his room. The negative effect, however, was that his room turned into an ice cellar. The low temperature covered everything in the already-uncomfortable room with an additional layer of frost. The only source of warmth in the room was the computer. Arvardan put on all his winter clothes, crawled into bed, and pointed the exhaust fans of the computer toward him.

The appropriate authorities decided that "heat" and "furnace" and other similar words were also temporarily sensitive words, so Arvardan had no way of drafting a complaint to the heating supply agencies. All he could do was to wait quietly. Other than his fingers moving over the keyboard, he tried to remain very still, so as to conserve body heat. On the fourth day after the heating system had failed, the radiators finally began to clatter and rattle with the sound of hot water flowing through them. The room warmed up again, and "heat" and "furnace" and similar words returned to the List of Healthy Words. So e-mails and BBS forum posts were filled with sentiments like "We congratulate the appropriate authorities for restoring heat so quickly to bring warmth to the people in need!" and "The people's government loves the people!" et cetera.

But this was too late for Arvardan. He fell sick with a cold, a terrible cold. His head hurt as though someone had shot a dumdum bullet into his skull. All he could do was lie on his bed and wait for the doctor. The doctor arrived at his home, put him on an IV, gave him some nameless pills, and told him to rest. This sickness lasted several days, and he had to give up that week's Talking Club meeting. His body just wasn't up for it, and Arvardan thought he was going to die.

Arvardan lay on his bed, filled with regret. The Talking Club was his only joy in life, and now he couldn't even go. He covered his head with his blanket and thought, *Would Wagner bring something special to the meeting this time? Would Lancelot bring his two children? And Artemis... If Arvardan weren't there, who would she have a "frank exchange" with? Wagner or Lancelot?* He also thought about Duras. At the last meeting, Duras had reached the point in the story where Winston told Julia, in their secret meeting room, "We are the dead." Julia also said, "We are the dead." And a third voice then said, "You are the dead."

Duras had stopped when she got to this point. Arvardan had desperately wanted to know what happened next. Who was the third voice? Was it the Party? Would Winston and Julia be arrested? What was going to happen to them?

"Let it be a cliffhanger," Artemis said to him. "Then the whole next week our lives will be spent in the joy of anticipation." And then the two went back to the joy of frankly exchanging.

Arvardan's sickness lasted ten days. The first thing he did after he felt well enough was to get up and look at the calendar on the wall. Today was Sunday, a Talking Club meeting day. Arvardan had missed one meeting, and he felt like a man dying of starvation. Even in his sleep, he dreamed of talking at the Talking Club.

Arvardan washed his face and carefully shaved off his thick stubble with a rusty razor. He brushed his teeth and smoothed down his bed hair with a towel and some warm water. Due to his sickness, the appropriate authorities had issued him some extra supplies, including two croissants, two ginger beers, and a packet of fine sugar. He wrapped these carefully in a plastic bag, and put the package inside his coat pocket to bring to the Talking Club to share with everyone.

Arvardan got off the bus, felt for the package hidden inside his coat, and walked toward the Simpson Tower. Halfway there, he lifted his head, and an icy chill seized his heart, forcing him to stop in his tracks.

Something was very wrong.

He looked up to the fifth floor. Before, the window from Artemis's apartment that faced the street had been covered by pink curtains, but now the curtains were pulled to the sides, and the window was wide open. If there was a meeting of the Talking Club today, Artemis would never have left the shielding curtains open. And keeping the windows open was odd, period. In the Capital, the air outside was terribly murky. No one would have opened the windows to let in "fresh air."

There was no Talking Club today. Something else was going on. Arvardan stared at the window, and his heart began to beat furiously. He took his hand out of his pocket, put a cigarette in his mouth, then leaned against a utility pole, and forced himself to be calm so as not to raise the suspicion of passing pedestrians. Suddenly he saw something that made him almost faint. A single idea filled his mind.

"There would be no meeting of the Talking Club this week. There will never be a meeting again," he mumbled to himself, his face the color of ashes.

He saw a contraption that looked like a radar dish, hidden in a corner on this side of the street. Arvardan knew exactly what this was. It was what he had been designing the software for: the new, high-powered, active Listener. The device was capable of sending out active electromagnetic waves to capture vibrations made by voices against walls and windows from a distance, and examine such speech for sensitive words.

If such a device had been installed right near Artemis's home, then that meant the Talking Club was completely exposed to the view of the appropriate authorities. The active Listener's penetrating waves would easily pierce through the lead curtains, and transmit the Club members' words verbatim to the ears of the appropriate authorities.

This invention defined a new era. The appropriate authorities no longer had to wait passively for warnings. Instead, they could at any time actively inspect any speech made by anyone. Arvardan could easily imagine what had happened next. Everything that Artemis and the others said was recorded by the appropriate authorities. Then the police broke into her apartment and arrested all the members of the Talking Club who were present. After they conducted a search, all that was left was the empty room and the empty windows.

Arvardan felt a knife was being twisted inside his heart. He did not think that he was fortunate to have escaped capture. His stomach churned, and nausea rose from his stomach to his mouth. He wanted to vomit, but he couldn't—"vomit" was itself a sensitive word. His body, only just recovered, could not take the hit. He began to shake as though he was suffering chills.

He dared not continue forward. He turned around, boarded another bus, and shut his mouth even tighter. When Arvardan returned to his own building, he saw that another active Listener was being installed nearby. The dark antenna extended into the sky, and along with the other antennas around the Capital, it wove an invisible, giant Web in the sky that covered everything.

He dared not stop to look. Keeping his head low, he walked past the active Listener, and returned home without stopping. Then he hid his face in the pillow, but dared not cry out loud. He couldn't even say, "Fuck you, you sonovabitch."

After that, Arvardan's life returned to normal—just as before, it was stagnant, restrained, passionless, healthy, and without any vulgar joys. Lancelot had said that the result of the war was that the people's desire for freedom would push language to the edge of death. The death of the Talking Club led to the deletion of "talking," "opera," "frank," and "exchange" from the List of Healthy Words.

Although it was still possible to use numbers, the number "1984" was shielded. One morning, without any warning, Arvardan was simply assigned a new Web Access Serial that no longer contained that string of numerals. This also meant that programmers like Arvardan had to constantly ensure that their programs did not compute illegal numbers. This added greatly to the workload, and Arvardan was even more exhausted.

What happened later in *1984* Arvardan would never know. Duras, the only one who did know, had disappeared completely. So what happened to Winston and Julia would forever be a mystery: like the fate of Lancelot, Wagner, Duras, and Artemis.

He worried the most about Artemis. Every time he thought of that name, Arvardan could not control how depressed he became. What happened to her? Was she completely shielded? If that was the case, then the only trace she left in this world would be a pseudonym in the memory of a programmer.

Three weeks after the disappearance of the Talking Club, everything remained calm. No one came after Arvardan. He thought maybe it was because the others had refused to give up any information about him. Or maybe it was because they didn't really know who he was — the person they knew was a programmer named Wang Er. In the Capital there were thousands of programmers, and Wang Er was just a pseudonym.

Life went on peacefully. No, to be precise, there was one bit of difference. That would be the List of Healthy Words: words disappeared from it at a faster and faster pace. Every hour, every minute, words vanished from it. As the pace of revision for the List quickened, e-mails and BBS forum posts became more and more vapid and banal. Since people had to use an extremely limited set of words to express an inexpressibly wide range of thoughts, everyone more and more preferred silence. Even the secret codes and hidden clues became fewer.

One day, Arvardan lifted his head from the computer. He stared at the grey, hazy sky outside the window, and his chest spasmed. He coughed in pain, and drained the distilled water from his cup. He threw the disposable plastic cup into the trashcan, also made of plastic. Listening to the dull sound of plastic hitting plastic, he thought his own brain was also filled with a pile of trash. He rapped his knuckles against his skull. Indeed, the same empty dull sound came out.

He put on his coat and filtering mask and walked out the door. He did not wear a portable Listener because it was no longer necessary. The Capital was filled with active Listeners, ever vigilant for the presence of sensitive words. The entire Capital was now just like the Web, healthy and stable.

Arvardan had a legitimate excuse for going outside. He had decided to turn in his permit for BBS service. It was no longer necessary to use this service. E-mail, BBS forums, Web sites—everything was now the same.

The calendar said it was spring, but outside it was still very cold. Tall, grey buildings stood like a forest of stone in absolute zero. Gusts of wind carrying yellow sand and polluting exhaust gas rushed between them and filled every available space, making it impossible for anyone to escape their suffocating presence. Arvardan put his hands in his pockets, shrank into his coat, and continued to the building for the Department of Web Security.

Suddenly, he stopped, his feet frozen in place, incapable of movement. He saw Artemis, standing under the streetlight before him and wearing a black uniform. But what a change had come over her! She seemed at least ten years older, her face full of wrinkles. There was none of the vitality of youth left in her. She heard his steps, turned around, and her dark eyes seemed especially empty. She stared past Arvardan into the distance, without focus.

Arvardan had never expected to meet her at this time in this place. His heart, long dormant, now was lit by a few sparks. But his dull and exhausted nerves were incapable of feeling the simple emotion of "excitement." The two stared at each other for a while. He finally walked next to her, and tentatively moved his lips, as though he wanted to say something to her. But when he took out the latest edition of the List of Healthy Words distributed earlier that day, he found it was empty—even the last word had been shielded by the appropriate authorities.

An address flashed in his mind—luckily, it was not yet possible to shield the mind with technology. Perhaps it was now time to take a trip to the mountains. He had nothing more to lose.

Someone has to do this.

And so, Arvardan maintained his silence. He passed by the expressionless Artemis, and continued his forward progress. His silhouette eventually melted into the equally quiet, grey crowd.

The whole city seemed especially silent.

Planetfall

Athena Andreadis

Athena Andreadis is a Greek author resident in the US, where she is a researcher in molecular neurobiology. She is the author of To Seek Out New Life: The Biology of Star Trek, *and edited the feminist SF anthology* The Other Half of the Sky.

I. In the Depths of the Sea

Nine generations past planetfall

Through the haze of her dark blue mane, the mershadow gazed sternly at her youngest. She had often warned her not to go near the shore. Afterward, forever would she long for the hostile land, where her skin would crack and she would wither.

The youngster, eyes as smoky as her mother's, felt unrepentant. She already knew starfire—they spent many nights on the foam. She knew of the landers, too. They had not been here long, said the Elders. They could not understand the People's singing—yet they trod as lightly as the whisper of a calm sea. Many came to rest in her people's domain, bearing the gifts of their kin. She longed to catch more glimpses of them. She wanted to encompass the whole world, sea and land, for her lays.

It eased the elder's mind that, for a while, her child would have to stay near. Her turn had come to watch the Sea Rose.

The Sea Rose...the great burden and joy of the mershadows. It bloomed unpredictably once every thirteen cycles of the wanderer that cast light on the night. Between dusk and dawn, a single blossom came alive. It granted to its watcher one wish, so the Elders sang. In exchange, for each cycle of the Wanderer, a vigilant mershadow guarded it and nourished it with her salty, greenish blood.

And so, as soon as the Wanderer started waxing, the youngster dutifully nested near the mound where the Sea Rose slumbered. It stood on a leafless stem, bluish-black like its guardian's hair, at the bottom of a deep crevasse filled with slate-green pebbles.

As the last night of her watch started to lighten into dawn, she sighed with regret and relief. The Sea Rose would not bloom in her turn. She was looking forward to recovering her strength and seeing the dry gardens once again, filled with all those blossoms that had no names in her tongue.

And just then, the water turned transparent, so transparent that she could see the pale sliver of the wanderer. She could distinctly hear the dream birds' trills, the mist cats' hunting calls, all the way from the distant hills of the dry lands. On the barren seafloor, the Sea Rose slowly unfurled. Its angular petals glimmered blue-green, like the precious nodules that her people occasionally found on the ocean floor. The water around it broke into jeweled prisms.

The youngster knew what she wanted to ask of the Sea Rose—she would ask for songs that might help the landers understand her people. But just as she prepared to sing her plea, an intricate object slowly twirled from the waters above and came to rest gently upon the blossom.

Hesitantly, she touched it—and a storm of yearning broke in her mind. Endless striving, anxious love, fear, longing... Meanwhile, alerted to the unfolding of the Rose, the mershadows began to congregate around the mound and its guardian.

"My child, what did you ask?" said her mother.

"I did not think to wish," whispered the youngster. "The landers' amulet—it spoke to me..."

And at that moment, they realized that the Sea Rose had not folded. For the first time, the only time, the sunrays touched it. It burned in colors of the fires that fueled the star cores. Then it closed.

She became her people's greatest bard. And her lineage kept the amulet until they returned it to the landers, on the night that the two Peoples sang together—and understood each other's words.

II. The Sea of Stars
Four generations past planetfall

Four generations after planetfall, strife arose on Glorious Maiden. The planet, beautiful but stark, almost entirely ocean, sorely tested mettle and resources. Some hearths wanted to start ocean farming, despite the decision made even before planetfall to leave no footprint on the planet. The argument got bitter enough that several tanegíri withdrew from the council and armed their hearths.

So Sefanír, tanegír of the Sóran-Kerís hearth, first among equals, fitted herself into her kite, snapped the struts taut, and flew to the storm-guarded southern archipelago, seeking to end the conflict.

"Why should we trust people who would separate us into powerful and powerless? Who no longer enter the Dreaming?" asked dark-voiced Sháita, tanegír Dhaíri. The Dreaming…as dangerous as following the songs of the dwellers of the deep. People were known to never emerge from it. They wandered inside it, eyes half-open, till they died.

"I will Dream," replied Sefanír, drawing herself up to her considerable height. "But if I emerge from it," she added, her blue eyes flashing, "will you agree to a truce and return to the council?"

Sháita chuckled, her long silver braids floating like cirrus clouds on her black tunic. "If you emerge," she said, "you won't need my agreement. The southern hearths will follow you without question or demur."

Next dawn, Sháita led her to a tiny room facing the small inner courtyard. It was bare and windowless but for an opening high up that showed a patch of sky. She lowered the marís bowl on the stone floor, then put her hand on Sefanír's shoulder.

"I would rather that our people were not divided and that we stayed true to our original resolution. But if we're to unite them, I cannot be seen to let you bypass this test," she said quietly. "Remember this if you have forgotten it. If a man enters your vision whose hair is as pale as winter seagrass, come out of the vision in any way you can. Or you won't come out at all."

She waited until Sefanír had emptied the bowl, then left. Sefanír hummed a song to keep herself calm. *Show no fear, no hesitation…the people's future depends on it…on me.* She felt little effect from the marís beyond its smoky aftertaste. Time went by. Consort in unclouded glory briefly appeared in her skylight, then passed. A bright dot of shimmering light hurried past—the *Reckless*, still in orbit, though now lost to her people. Finally, when the color leached from the patch of sky, she rose from the floor, determined to ask for another try on the morrow. She had given her word to her hearth that she would not return till she succeeded in healing the rift—or died in the attempt.

As she emerged into the larger outer courtyard, she saw a man seated by the murmuring fountain. He was muffled at dusk against the evening chill in garments the color of the evening sky.

"I am looking for Tanegír Sháita," she said.

"I will take you to her," he replied in a voice as soft as a mist cat's pad. *They make beautiful men, the Dhaíri, and they are said to bless their consorts with daughters, as well,* thought Sefanír, her gaze sliding over his fluid body lines. *If only we could get more living girl children... Madness to split into factions, when our need to keep all the lines is dire.*

Through narrow corridors they wended. *Strange,* mused Sefanír, *the dwelling seemed smaller from the outside.* He led her to a room lit by a small torch.

"We'll await my kinswoman here," he said and gracefully lowered himself onto the thick carpet. Sefanír imitated him. After a brief interval, he reached over and idly trailed a fingertip along her collarbone. A feather would have been heavier than his touch. Waves of heat, then cold coursed through Sefanír.

"It may take her a long time to come," he whispered. "I have pleased many. I could please you, too."

If he is offering, he is not handfasted, thought Sefanír. *And it may help the truce take hold.*

As she leaned toward his scented warmth, he pressed her against him. She caught the spicy whiff of newly budded leaves. Sefanír's hands slid over the wild silk of his clothes. Then, under the thin fabric she felt scars embroidering his back. Disconcerted, she gripped his shoulder; and there she felt the raised edges of a handfasting brand.

Instantly sobered, she pulled at his sleeve and the fabric ripped with a long-drawn sigh. On his shoulder glared the divided circle of the Night. He laughed, and the room filled with the wingbeat of wheeling dream birds. Sefanír's abrupt movement had dislodged his headscarf. Now he discarded it, revealing hair as pale as the midwinter sun. His eyes became star-filled pools.

"You are strong-willed," he murmured. "Even my Tanegír gives in when I caress her. Why do you insult me? Shall I tell her you think her judgment in consorts is wanting? She is the only one allowed to criticize me."

"You tried to trick me," retorted Sefanír. "If I had given in, it would be an even worse trespass on her prerogatives. And all tales of the Night tell how easily she is aroused to anger."

"In that they are right," he conceded. "Those scars you felt are signs of her temper. But I suffer the fire gladly in exchange for the sweet moments. Besides, I lost fairly. Had I prevailed..." and he laughed again, the Morning Star, the First Consort of the Night. "We hunted the Two Sisters, I and all my brothers. The Elder sister had borne a child that one of us had fathered. We wanted it. Long they evaded us, but at last we overtook them, burdened as they were with the child.

"Yet the Younger would not surrender, nor leave her sister. When I saw her falter with fatigue, I grew careless and ventured close. She was prepared: her firewhip wrapped around my throat. So I bargained—in exchange for my life, I and all my brothers became her consorts. To prevent us from taking her sister's child, she sequestered herself and us in the darkside. Now the Two only touch palms at dusk and dawn. Let me please you, Tanegir. Then I can let you go without losing honor."

Sháita's warning rang in Sefanír's mind. Now she knew why so few survived the Dreaming. He, of course, guessed her thoughts.

"Perhaps my Tanegír will not notice. Perhaps I will not tell her. Who knows?"

"If each choice brings death," decided Sefanír, "I can at least take bliss as my last memory." She laughed and opened her arms. "Please me, then, First Consort. Should you not, I myself will complain to your Tanegír when she weaves me as another fireflitter in her dark braids."

"Bravery like yours deserves a gift," he said. "You will see something few have seen and none has lived to tell." Very gently, he eased Sefanír back into the pillows. And when he embraced her, his long hair gleaming in the torchlight, he unfurled over both of them a multihued pair of wings. Joined, they soared, their outlines bathed in his brothers' dim radiance.

Sefanír returned north with the catamarans of the Southerners behind her like a flock of seabirds. But all across her body she also bore tracks of lightning, and for a long time her dreams were consumed by fire. For the Night valued courage but she was also exacting about her Consorts' fidelity.

III. The Dagger Sheath
Nine generations past planetfall

My evening star, my sweetest spring,
How has your beauty set!
From the lay of Rodhánis the Storm

"Impaired, I say!" teased Kíghan. "Admit it, sister, your thinking grows less sharp if he's involved."

Rodhánis shook her head, exasperated. "I stand by my decision. He is the best navigator on this planet! Is it his fault that he is also beautiful?"

"Those golden eyes of his, who would not want a mist cat padding in their wake!" replied her brother, chuckling. "And you're right, he seems to be as good among the stars as he is on the seas. But you cannot give him your brand and name him consort. You are tanegír Yehán—a son from every hearth is vying for…"

"Are you that eager to be pushed out of the hearth?" she interrupted him.

"I will remain as long as you need me but the Yeháni must have an heir, Storm, and I'm only a man." He took her in his arms. "I know about the two miscarriages you tried to hide from the hearth members, my heart. The desolation on his face was clue enough; he is not schooled in deception. But at least it means you can conceive. They are circling you, if you don't choose soon there will be slaughter. Seeing a wanderer in your bed is not improving their mood. And no matter how carefully you choose, they will still kill each other below your windows."

"All these men, left to roam…" mused Rodhánis. "How did it come to this? It was not so when Captain Semira Soranakis and her Keegan arrived on the *Reckless*."

"It has been so ever since planetfall," he said quietly, "ever since Glorious Maiden chose to selectively harvest our women. We can barely keep our numbers steady, and neither the miscarriages nor the duels are helping. Perhaps you will know soon how family matters ran on the *Reckless*. Are you sure about the risks of this expedition? I should never have agreed…"

"And let Eridhén Kálan or one of his allies be the first to board the arcship?" burst out Rodhánis. "Not while I stand upright."

"I cannot believe I'm recommending this, but take his eldest as your consort," he said reluctantly. "Anáris is handsome, more even-tempered than his father—and he wants you. It may stop Eridhén from constantly raising the winds of discord."

"Eridhén wants power too much to be deflected by kinship, and Anáris will heed him even as Yehán," answered Rodhánis. "And with his tanegír ailing and no daughters yet, Eridhén will do anything short of declaring himself tanegír Kálan."

"We would kill him if he did," growled Kíghan. "At planetfall, the crew of the *Reckless* agreed that the hearths on Glorious Maiden would be headed by women. Their reasons were sound then, and even more so now. But Eridhén is too canny to make a mistake. He always hugs the shore, never ventures into blue water."

The derelict arcship shone with reflected sunlight like Wanderer at his fullest. Images flashed across the console of the *Seastorm*. Rodhánis stopped the engines and went into freefall, using the thrusters to match the larger ship's motion.

"The bubble must be the command center…that has to be the engine compartment, there on the tether…" She turned to her companion. "All frequencies open?"

He nodded, his golden eyes reflecting the vessel in the viewport. "Only background hiss. Amazing that the orbit-boosting mechanism still works. After all this time planetbound, to lift free of the atmosphere once again and board the ship that brought us here! Perhaps reclaim it…"

"Yes," she said yearningly, putting her hand on his shoulder, "finally take to the stars, even find the first home in time…"

He turned, kissed her fingers. "Will I be your astrogator, my soul?"

She let her palm linger on his face. "When I bid for your contract, little did I know what seas we would cross, you and I. But I must choose a consort when we return, I promised my hearth."

He half-smiled. "You promised Kíghan, who counts more than everyone else combined. Yet it seems to me that if you choose none of the mighty, it will be less likely to cause strife."

"If I had a sister, I would let her have both the power and the burden. I would go back to exploring the wilds with you." She exhaled as he left the seat and wrapped around her like a twining vine. "Or we could stay here, bring the *Reckless* back to life… Keep your mind on your task, cub!" she scolded him fondly, as he began to plant kisses under her jawline.

"Just awaiting my tanegír's orders…" he defended himself, hiding a smile against her neck. He glided back into the navigator's seat, keeping a hand on her thigh. Deftly, he maneuvered the *Seastorm* next to the larger ship. Its hull was pitted and blistered, the plates unevenly hued, reflecting several rounds of replacements. "The blaze…" he pointed.

"The Sóran-Kerís starburst," she marveled.

"Yes," he whispered, averting his eyes. And suddenly in her mind's eye she saw a spare woman with hazel eyes holding a boy with tousled auburn hair. *A wanderer's child and a son at that… How can I acknowledge you as Captain Semira's descendant, call you Sóran-Kerís? It might start another round of vendettas, the men have become so jealous of the lineages…*

"There's a hatch," he observed, his voice even once again, "let's try to dock." As gently as floating a toy catamaran on a glass-calm pond, he turned the *Seastorm*. He tucked it against the arcship's hatch, forming a soft seal.

"Negligible radiation, no leakage from the engine," she noted, looking at the gauges.

"Keep the comm open," he said, attaching magnets to his boots. She began to object, but he silenced her with a gesture. "You are the foremost explorer of Glorious Maiden, but you are also tanegír Yehán. On this I agree with your brother, you put too much at risk." He grinned. "If it hurts the vanity of the hearths, the records can show that you were the first to board."

He pressed her hands against his lips, lingered a moment. Then he turned on the deep-sea breather they had hurriedly adapted. He went through the hatch and Rodhánis sealed it behind him. She leaned against the hull, the cold seeping into her. *We're re-opening the gate to the stars after the long wait…and all I can think of is the danger of losing him.* She waited forever, or so it seemed, fingering the corroded pendant of Keegan Jehan, first science officer of the *Reckless* at planetfall, passed down the line to each tanegír Yehán.

"Can you hear me?" finally came his soft rasp through the comm.

"Yes!" she replied, letting out the breath she wasn't aware she'd been was holding. She felt the arcship starting to rotate, taking the *Seas-*

torm with it.

"The air is breathable, though there is an ozone smell... I managed to activate the gravity generators. I found the heat coils, too, but it will take a while for the temperature to rise."

Dank, chilly darkness awaited her on the other side of the hatch, but at least the gravity was nominal. She made her way carefully to where he was outlined against the blue runner lights that barely lit the corridors. He enfolded her hand in his own warm one, the one solid object in this domain of ghosts.

"Shall I light one of the flares?" he suggested.

"Keep them in reserve," she decided, "let's use them only if we must."

After a few wrong turns they reached the bridge, a cavernous vault with a wraparound viewport, filled with navigation, engineering, and communication banks. By trial and error, they found the controls for the starcharts and comms. They agreed not to disturb the other consoles. "This," he said, touching a seat decorated with the starburst motif, "must be where Captain Semira Soranakis sat..."

"Want to try sending a signal?" she asked.

"We should be in range," he replied, adjusting dials. She was surprised to find herself shivering, and not just from the chill. Only now did the enormity of it all fully register. Sensing her trembling, he embraced her. She tried to pull away, but he tightened his hold and she relaxed in his arms. "Nothing to be ashamed of, my light," he murmured into her hair. "Not every day do we enter the starship that brought us here." Still nestled within his arms, she turned toward the comm bank.

"Oránis, do you read?" she said into the primitive contraption. There was a burst of static, then a young man's voice sprang from the receiver.

"Oránis port."

"This is Rodhánis Yehán from..." and she took a deep breath, met his eyes. He gave his lopsided grin and nodded. "...from the *Reckless*... we boarded it successfully, I am calling from the bridge...Captain Semira's bridge."

A long silence followed her words. Then the receiver crackled again. "I will transmit your message to the entire network. This is a moment to remember, Tanegír!"

Then Kíghan's voice emerged from the comm. "How long is it safe to stay there? Don't get carried away, Storm!"

"We will be quick," she replied. She heard him inhale anxiously. "We will return within the safety window!" she reassured him.

Her companion's long-lashed eyes glinted with amusement. He laughed, filling the age-chilled bridge with the sound of swirling leaves. "I would give much to see the faces of your rivals... Shall we explore a bit? We can start here," he said at her eager nod, steering them to a door on the side of the bridge.

They pressed a few buttons but the door remained stubbornly shut. Finally, he attached his magnets to it and winched it open. They gained entry into a narrow room containing a cot with a console next to it. The rest of the room was taken up by a large table buried under datapads. The viewport occupied an entire wall, now filled with blue Glorious Maiden and ivory Wanderer in jewel-like splendor, bathed in Consort's golden-reddish light.

"The Captains' ready-room," said Rodhánis. "They dreamed the path from here..." He pressed a button on the console. A set of blue lights came on along the floorboards and next to the ceiling, turning the room into an underwater cavern. He pressed another button—and a husky, clipped voice rose amid crackles and hisses.

"Is étos ek fyghís pentekatón eksínta tríton, eghó, Semíra Ouranákis, kyvernís astéron plíou..."

"Captain Semira," whispered Rodhánis. "This must be the last log before the planetfall."

"She sounds young," he murmured. "I wonder what the words mean. Was she happy? Eager? Frightened?" Suddenly his eyes emptied out. She grasped his shoulder.

"What do you see?"

"I see... I see fire consuming this room..." He stopped, trembling. "What future did we bring with us through that hatch?"

"Surely you are not afraid, beautiful man?" she asked him softly, cradling him in her turn. "We faced near death in the Southern seas, our catamaran got smashed on the Fangs, we almost suffocated when we first launched the *Seastorm*..."

"That was different," he said, sheltering against her. "That was just us. This, this may affect all the people..."

She started kissing him, counting on the distraction to calm him. *Rock-steady in danger, but often undone by his visions, my evening star!* And then, as he filled her senses, her caresses went from consoling to ravenous.

"Here?" he asked hesitantly, his hands embarking on their own exploration.

"Yes, here!" she replied, parting his clothes. "Where better than the Captain's eyrie to dispel the ghosts, reclaim the *Reckless* for the living?"

"When you bestow your brand..." he said, his eyes darkening.

"I bestow to whom I choose!" she declared defiantly.

"Yes, as long as he is not a wanderer," he corrected her gently. "Or a man who is unable to give you..." and he looked away, biting his lip.

"Look at me!" she said softly. "Here, now, no one can reach us, nothing can touch us."

He subsided onto the cot, taking her with him. Growing rough with the need, he clamped his mouth on her breast, his teeth grazing her nipple.

"Drift, wanderer!" she commanded. "Wander over me..."

"My sandy cove!" he sighed. And as he arched into her, a wisp of flame licked her mind. *Give the brand to whom you will — I am yours, yours as long as I draw breath...*

"This is the man who risked his life to board the *Reckless!*" said Rodhánis, her voice rising.

"I understand that you were the first to board the arcship, Yehán," replied Eridhén Kálan, smiling lazily. "Even if what you say is true, it matters naught. I am within my rights to issue challenge on behalf of my hearth, my son is among those asking for the privilege of your brand."

A low murmur of agreement accompanied his words. Rodhánis looked around. His allies were there in force, he knew when to strike. Teráni Sóran-Kerís was absent, the rest were neutral at best. And she was aware that her reluctance to choose a consort had rankled as much as her making history on the *Reckless*.

"Need we hew so closely to the customs?" she began again in a conciliatory tone. "I promised to decide upon my return. Does the opening of the star gates mean nothing, hearths?"

"Precisely because we can now take to the stars, we must not forget who we are," said Eridhén.

"I will choose a consort now, if you leave him alone," she countered.

"No," answered Eridhén, his teeth glinting. "He has been clouding your mind, impeding your decisions. I stand by my challenge; he is a danger even if you refuse to see it. I am doing you a favor, Tanegír. Continue on your present destructive course, and I will call your brother and all the Yehán men to account."

"No need to go that far, Kálan," interposed Fáhri Haissé. She turned to Rodhánis. "Because of your gifts and your contributions, we gave you extraordinary leeway, Yehán, while the rest of us abided by the customs. Withdraw your protection from the wanderer and there will be no vendetta against your hearth. Shield him and we cannot prevent the issuing of challenges. Is one man, and a wanderer at that, worth so much?"

Rodhánis went through the permutations. If she complied, they would all duel him in turn, and her hearth would owe the winner a debt. If she refused their terms, the men of her hearth, Kíghan…no, not Kíghan. She was tanegír Yehán. She stood up.

"I will duel the wanderer, tanegíri."

"No!" sprang from both Kíghan and Eridhén, but she cut them off with a glance.

"This takes precedence over all other challenges. He was contracted to my hearth."

"What have you done?" asked Kíghan after the gathering. She rounded on him.

"The only thing I could do to protect the Yeháni."

"At such reckless risk to yourself? Without you—ashes in the wind, the Yeháni!"

"After all that he did," she whispered. "The best navigator in…"

"You don't understand," interrupted her brother heavily. "The more he accomplishes, the worse for him. The same goes for you, but the hearth name and being a woman stands between you and any harm. He, on the other hand…"

"He can go away until the storm subsides," she said. "In time, they will forget." She grasped her brother's shoulder. "Send him a message. If anyone knows where to hide on this world, it's him."

That night, that short night, she paced the courtyard looking up at

Wanderer's pale disk, at the bright fast-moving star that was the *Reckless*. That they should be reduced to blood pride, when the stars were beckoning!

"My heart," came a whisper from under the arch.

"Didn't you get Kíghan's message?" she hissed.

"Yes, Tanegír," he replied and she could hear the smile in his voice. "But not to hold you in my arms? No navigator leaves his captain in such straits!" And he pressed her against him.

"Take the *Seastorm* and go!" she urged him, shaking with anxiety and need.

He did not reply, busy undoing the fastenings on her clothes. She sank into him, nails and teeth, not caring if she drew blood. When the first light pierced the darkness, she saw her marks on him. As she started touching them, aghast, he imprisoned her hand and kissed the knuckles.

"Calmer now, Storm?" he asked. "Ready to face the hearths?"

"Promise me you will be far away when I do!" she implored.

Before he could answer, Kíghan entered the courtyard carrying her weapons. "It's time," he said. His eyes burned on the other man. Then he lowered his eyes and bowed.

All the tanegíri of Oránis and their consorts stood watchfully silent around the stone beach by the shore. All but Teráni Sóran-Kerís. And then, Rodhánis' heart became a stone in her breast. Appearing over the rise, he approached the throng in the meager finery that she had torn in her frenzy, defiantly flashing his lopsided grin. Her face draining of color, she went up to him.

"I told you to go!" she groaned in anguish under her breath.

"You will have multiple vendettas against your hearth," he replied in a low voice. "They won't let it rest, now that they have taken notice. And if I go into the wilds, they'll hunt me down. Better like this." Strands of his hair floated in front of his face. Reaching over, she tucked them behind his ear.

"You didn't braid it," she said. He smiled.

"Only you can do that properly, my life…"

Neither bothered with the preliminary feints. They had practiced together so often in the past that it had become a dance. He knew she was over-quick with the dagger, just as she knew that he relied too much on his reflexes. They circled closer and closer. The pounding of her heart was deafening. Because of the wind, the firewhips would occasionally go astray, but rarely missed. Soon the ground was decorated with an intricate design of blood drops that marked their weaving.

The cold and wind started taking their toll. He slowed down; her wrists started aching. Her anger and self-disgust vanished—now she was filled only with the desire to be done, to sit down out of the bite of the wind. On one of the seemingly endless rounds, he passed very close. She stabbed at him, expecting his guard to come up, when she realized that he was no longer holding his dagger. Hers went into his side up to the hilt. He stumbled, then in slow motion went to his knees.

All the observers rushed toward them, but she slashed a circle around the two of them with her whip. "Away!" she snarled. They stopped in their tracks. She cradled him against her but before she could stop him, he extracted the dagger. His eyelids flickered as he tried to focus on her.

"You are so bright, my sun," he whispered. Blood trickled out of the corner of his mouth. She held him tightly.

"Let a healer see to it," she pleaded, "it does not look mortal!"

"You must end it," he murmured. "They will never cease tormenting you otherwise."

"No!" she uttered through gritted teeth, her fingers clenching around the dagger. He buried his face against her breast, gave a small sigh, as he always did before sailing into sleep. Then he wrapped his hand around her wrist and moved her hand, pressing the edge of the dagger against his throat.

"I'll scout the twilight for you." He opened his eyes, fastened them on hers. "Look at me…" Without warning, his fingers suddenly tightened on her wrist, making her hand jerk. His grip slackened. A gush of blood poured over her hand and he grew inert in her embrace.

Wordlessly, everyone slowly left. For the entire length of the Consort's crossing, Rodhánis huddled, rocking her burden. At dusk, she began to scream. She wailed through the night, the seawaves her echo. Fine cracks started to vein windows in Oránis. The wind took her voice into the Yehán hearth where Kíghan wept, drawing fine lines across his arm with his own dagger. Into the Kálan hearth where Eridhén sat still, his nails digging into his palms. Into the other hearths of Oránis where everyone kept vigil, wondering what price the Storm would exact for her loss.

Wanderer had set and the sky was getting light when Rodhánis finally lost her voice. Kíghan went to the cove sheltering the Yehán fleet and chose a small, finely wrought catamaran, the vessel that the hearth children used to learn their deep-sea skills. He sailed it to where Rodhánis crouched, and beached it soundlessly. He approached her, gingerly enfolded her.

"Let us give him to the sea, sister..." She nodded numbly, her face raw from the rivers of salt water that had scraped and scored it.

It took a while to line the catamaran, there was not much drift-wood on the shore. They placed him on top of the dry wood, laid his dagger next to him. Then Rodhánis removed Keegan Jehan's pendant from her neck and lowered it across the red line on his throat. She pressed her cheek against his, now ice cold.

"From one star traveler to another," she murmured hoarsely. "You wanderer, you drifted away from me, despite all your avowals. Who will be my astrogator now?"

As the tide turned, the undertow strengthened. The catamaran swayed, slowly started moving away from the shore. Kíghan lit a torch and flung it into the vessel. Eager flames sprang up in the freshening dawn breeze.

"Go," cried Rodhánis, her voice cracking, "kiss the two tiny shades for me!"

When the vessel had become a dwindling star in the distance, Kíghan lifted her in his arms and started homeward. Three turns later, the Yeháni asked for a gathering. When Rodhánis entered the council room, silence spread like an early snowfall. The men of her hearth followed, armed and braided for battle.

"There is no need for more fighting, Yehán," said Vónis Táren. "Everyone is satisfied."

"Everyone?" asked Rodhánis, her voice a hoarse whisper. "I am not satisfied."

"Even had he borne your brand," countered Eridhén Kálan, sounding much less assured than his wont, "he would not be recognized by the hearths as your consort. He was a wanderer, he had no standing." A small sound escaped Teráni Sóran-Kerís, but she said nothing.

"That may be," replied Rodhánis evenly, "but since I killed him at your behest, I can now make a claim on you, hearth Kálan. A favor as large as the one you received from me." Eridhén went white.

"You wouldn't..." he started.

"Am I within my rights?" asked Rodhánis quietly and winds swept the room. Teráni Sóran-Kerís raised her head.

"Yes," she said clearly and steadily, her hazel eyes boring into Eridhén.

"You were eager to give me one of your sons, Eridhén," said Rodhánis. "Which one will you give me now?" He started trembling. "You will not choose? Then I will take them both."

He fell to his knees before her. "Have mercy, Storm!"

"Mercy?" she repeated, smiling bleakly. "Did you have mercy when you issued the challenge? He was worth more than both your sons."

"Take me," he pleaded abjectly, "take me, spare them! I beg you, spare my younger at least, this will kill their mother...!"

"I will take them both," resumed Rodhánis, "into my hearth, into my bed, teach them not to thirst for power. And perhaps one night I will stop calling them by the name of the one whose face constantly rises before me." Her voice filled the room. "We want to regain the sky, tanegíri. Will we take this senseless killing with us to the stars? These customs that condemn our men to loneliness, because there are not enough women? We cannot leave so many of them without caresses, angry and bereft. Don't you wish to stop fearing for your brothers? For your sons? Use your power, unite behind me!" She paused, then resumed, her voice wavering. "If our men ask for the brand, let it be only for love."

She sat still for a very long time. Then she raised her eyes. "The Night took all the Stars as her consorts, so the lays tell. Nothing in the customs forbids it. Aye or nay, hearths?"

Vónis Táren hung her head. "I offer you my Edánir, if you will have him," she said.

"And I, my Keméni," added Fáhri Haissé.

Teráni Sóran-Kerís remained silent. But as people were leaving, she came up to Rodhánis.

"I was a coward and a fool," she said in a low, ragged voice. Her fingers dug into the younger woman's arm. "I should have acknowledged that brightness. Captain Semira would deem me unworthy, and rightly so. I won't ask you to forgive me, I only entreat you not to let this sunder our hearths." She took her hand abruptly away. "I will make no claims. I forfeited that right."

Within three generations, duels and vendettas ceased and wanderers became rare jewels, to be prized and cosseted. Eridhén's tanegír died in her next childbirth, taking the child and the Kálan hearth with her. They found his cold body next to hers, his hair spread across her chest.

Kíghan never left the Yehán hearth, remaining at his sister's side. Soon after Rodhánis handfasted her four husbands, she had a golden-eyed daughter, Semíra. After taking her daughter to the sea for her naming ceremony, Rodhánis went to the Sóran-Kerís dwelling and put her in Teráni's arms. They say that Teráni wept when she held the child. Rodhánis did not quicken again, though her husbands did their utmost to make her smile. She organized all subsequent expeditions to the *Reckless*, but never returned there herself.

Rodhánis sang the story to her daughter even when the child was too young to understand the words. Nor have the people forgotten. They still sing it under Wanderer's light, on the ships crossing the starry lanes. And the lay names him Consort of Rodhánis, the lost astrogator, her beautiful man.

IV. Falling Star
Planetfall

Traveler from afar who sailed to our shores — ask the Sea Rose for a gift...

In the year five hundred and sixty-three after the Launch, I, Semíra Ouranákis, captain of the starship *Reckless*, hereby enter the last log before planetfall.

It now fills our viewports, the world that pulled us by a thin thread of dreaming. When the *Reckless* lifted, all they knew was that the planet was earth-like, had oxygen in its atmosphere and orbited a G-type primary. The world they left had been beautiful once, but was at the brink of destruction — drained resources, genocides driven by hot hatred or cold greed. Had they waited, the window would have closed forever. Flames fanned by ignorance and fear were already consuming starship launch pads and the people who built them. Still, they took a terrible chance, leapt into the dark trusting that a place waited to welcome them at the other end. They loved and raised children in this ship, lived and died without ever sleeping under open skies...though their views of the stars were glorious.

The planet's system is embedded in a nebula studded with young blue giants that swept away much of the gas and dust when they ignited, but its own yellow sun is stable. In the last four generations, as the *Reckless* got closer, they launched automated probes, then scoutships with exploration teams. Amazingly, the planet resembles the home we left, which I know only from wavering images: a world of seas and island chains, with a large moon, breathable air, and a biochemistry compatible with ours.

The planet is bursting with life. In particular, there is an aquatic species that shows every sign of sentience, including communication through sound tones as well as rudimentary technology. I remember the long, heated discussions they held when I was a child, about what we should do upon arrival. In the end, they decided not to use the frozen stocks of plant and animal embryos in our cryoholds. Some were initially dubious about the wisdom of this, but eventually all agreed that we should not repay the bounty of a new home by destroying it, as we did to our birth planet.

Despite the planet's beauty, survival on it will be difficult, even with our technology. Its weather is violent and its oxygen content is at the low range for our lung function. But living in enclosed domes would make us prisoners, not explorers. So my parents' generation made an irreversible commitment. They studied the genetic material of the planet's sea dwellers, determined what sequences facilitated the processes unique to the planet. Then they spliced these into the chromosomes of children at the beginning of gestation, after testing them first on cells, then on smaller mammals in our laboratories.

As captain before me, my mother set the example. I was the first to receive tiny pieces of the new world. Her command crew followed suit with their children. And I, in my turn, had it done to the little sphere of cells that became my daughter Ethiran, even as my heart pounded fearfully in my chest.

Wonder of wonders, the material took hold, yet did not harm us.

On the contrary, it has given rise to abilities that were considered the stuff of fantasy in the world that we left—telepathy, precognition, even glimpses of clairvoyance and psychokinesis. Those who have been altered show increased mental and physical prowess, are unusually lovesome and uncannily beautiful. The next generation is all modified, the boy growing in me among them. I wonder if we will ever be able to thank the native inhabitants for the gift they gave us, that has bound us to them as blood relatives.

I long to see the new home with my own eyes, but the captain should never leave her ship until it reaches harbor. I have steeled myself to wait until we settle the *Reckless* into circumpolar orbit. I will take the voice-activated command crystal with me when we go downplanet. It is gene-keyed to me and Keegan Jehan, to make sure the starship is never inadvertently activated.

There are moments when I think of all the danger and labor ahead...and my head swims. Then only Keegan's arms feel safe— Keegan, who laughs at obstacles and burns my fears away with his kisses, Keegan who perfected the chimeric chromosomes and the augmented mitochondria that will allow us to breathe unaided on the planet's surface.

I did not name the new world, though it was my prerogative as commander of this mission. Because of the breathtaking nebula around the system, my girl began calling it Kore Dhoksas—Glorious Maiden— and the moniker stuck. She also named its sun and moon, Maiden's Consort and Wanderer. A crack linguist already, she speaks all the mother languages of our crew.

And what of her brother? Will he come intact through the pregnancy? Will he survive on this new world with all its unknowns? Ariven I will name him, from the old scroll. Perhaps he will sing lays as haunting as those of the long-lost sweet-blooded young Celt, who gave his life for a single night with one of my ancestors.

Ethiran and others in her generation have persistent visions, and I cannot tell if they are dreams or premonitions. They hear songs in a language that whispers and caresses, they see women as radiant and merciless as the dawn, and bewitching men with shimmering lights in their streaming hair...

Will they bless or curse us? Will they even remember us, who came as reckless and as jaunty as the hope that launched us? And what will they become, now that we started them on this path? All I can do is take Ethiran and Keegan's hands, step outside, and make a wish—that this place becomes a haven and a starship for our children...that they root and blossom here.

We will stride in the sky, or die trying. We have no need of small lives.

V. Nightsongs

Nineteen generations past planetfall

The darklit voice of my wanderer falls silent when he finishes translating Captain Semíra's words, and I lie back into the bower of my consort's arms. As Adhísa puts down the crystal that holds our past and our future, the scent of juniper from his braids fills the night air. A mershadow's long moan wafts in, like mist from the bay, letting us know they're starting their migration south on the morrow. "They wished well, they who sailed on the *Reckless* across the ocean of stars," he murmurs.

"They did more than wish. They wrought tirelessly to make it come true," whispers Arivén and his embrace tightens, "as you did, my soul..."

I pick up the command crystal, feeling the mild sting of its protective field. My two bright stars close their hands over mine, homage and blessing.

"The gift of Semíra, of Rodhánis, of the mershadows that gave us back the *Reckless* and all its glories," I say. "The records, the logs, the activation command sequences... Had I wished upon the Sea Rose, I could not have asked for more. "

And now...what is your wish now...heavenly fire...? My breath catches in my throat as they nestle closer, start to caress me like warm breezes with lips and fingertips.

Beloved...

They flow over me as gently and irresistibly as the rising tide. I float into their minds, into their hearts, the yearning, dazzling men of Captain Semíra's line with their scarred breasts, their roughened hands. Changelings, shapeshifters—falling stars, ships with fragments of sky as their sails, that have come home from long journeys to rest in me at last.

Jungle Fever

Ika Koeck

Ika Koeckis a young Malaysian writer, with stories published in the anthology Ages of Wonder *and elsewhere. She lives in Kuala Lumpur, where she is working on new fantasy novels.*

I can't remember *when* I came by the scratch on my left arm. But I remember *how* more than I remember anything in my short, young life. It was a prize given to me during one of my weekly trips to the jungle to collect herbs for my uncle's apothecary. In my eagerness to dance and twirl with an imaginary warrior of the Sultan's court, I had tripped on an upturned root and scraped my arm against the massive, red, rotting plant that had been lying in wait on the jungle floor. At least, I *think* it was a plant.

It had been a ghastly…thing, a large, flower-shaped mass of red and black pocked with thousands of ugly white warts. Its delicate, five round petals would have lent it a friendlier look, but the foul, horrid stench it released had driven me away before I could even think to investigate it.

Still, it is a tiny scratch, not worth worrying over. And while it hasn't bothered me much beyond sending a ripple of unbearable itching through my flesh every now and then, it *has* begun to release an unpleasant smell. One very much like the plant's. I stare at the scratch in growing exasperation whilst I wait for the next boat to arrive. The humidity at the pier tears at my patience, and I tap the wound as rapidly as I can with my fingers, resisting the urge to dig my fingernails into the purpled flesh and bulging veins surrounding it. Am I imagining things, or has the wound somehow grown larger since I last looked at it?

The man waiting next to me leans closer, to my discomfort. I recognise him as one of our neighbours from across the paddy fields that separate my uncle's house from the others, but I cannot remember his name. I don't intend to. Commingling with the neighbours will invite my uncle's displeasure, something all of his eleven children, five nieces and two nephews have quickly learnt to avoid. Besides, I have an errand to run, and reminding a poor family upriver that they haven't yet paid for taking one of my uncle's remedial unguents could take all day.

"Nasty scratch, that," my neighbour points out the obvious, oblivious of my discomfort. His breath stinks of coffee and pickled boar, but it is no match for what is now wafting out of my arm. "You should show it to your Uncle Suntong. He'll have a salve to fix it right up." His nose wrinkles in obvious disdain, but he tries to maintain a semblance of honest concern.

"I will," I lie with a sigh, dismayed by his pretence at ignorance. My uncle isn't exactly a paragon of compassion. He tolerates his four wives and the younger children as long as they stay out of his way, but the rest of us who are close to marrying age are subject to his tyrannical rule and foul temper. One would have to be the village idiot not to know that.

"You're the smart one aren't you? His dead brother's daughter?" My neighbour presses. Perhaps he *is* the village idiot after all. We do not speak of our dead. "I hear tell that your parents worked as translators and scribes for the desert tradesmen and the governor. That must've been some life, huh?"

A distant, different life—filled with the wonders of books, explorations, modernity, love, and laughter. The memory of my parents' fatal accident only a year ago is still raw. Images of a raging storm, an upturned boat, and my parents' hands flailing above the water makes my stomach lurch. Or perhaps it is the foul smell from the scratch again. I tuck my arm behind me and nod sullenly, hoping the gesture will relieve some of my discomfort. But the smell couldn't be masked. My neighbour steps back from the stench to offer a kindly, if patronising smile.

"You know, you could also try the physician upriver." He pinches his nose. "I hear he's got better medicine than your uncle does. Suntong *doesn't* know everything, after all."

I offer the man an equally unpleasant grin, the best I can muster despite my embarrassment, hoping the gesture will somehow soften the displeasure and send him away. Yet he pales, as though the gesture frightens him. His eyes widen into massive saucers, and he averts his gaze, stumbling away from the pier like a man who has just seen a ghost. It wasn't the reaction I'd expected.

It is only when I catch a reflection of myself in the crystal-clear water below that I realise my teeth are covered in blood. A loose tooth slips out of my gum and plunges into the water even as I yelp in surprise. I stare at a macabre version of myself in the water without comprehension, my eyes as wide as my neighbour's had been.

The terror that sweeps through me throws me back several steps. Horrified, I turn and run down the pier, run past the line of waiting villagers, ignoring their alarmed calls, forgetting my errand, and run even further until the black, wet earth of the riverside turns into the verdant green of the jungle floor.

And there I hide, sobbing, crying. Afraid for my life.

I am late.

The gravedigger birds have begun their loud, sinister thumping calls, marking the arrival of dusk. My uncle will not be pleased, but I didn't want to return to the longhouse until I had washed all the blood away. At least three more of my teeth have fallen out since the incident at the pier. I hide in the space between the ground and the house's raised floor, desperate not to make a sound. If he doesn't see me, he won't suspect that anything is wrong, but it is a foolish, childish thought. He *will* be looking for me.

For all the blood that had stained my teeth at the pier, it is strange that I can taste nothing. A feeling of numbness has begun to spread through my body, strongest where the scratch is. I am convinced now that whatever is wrong with me is associated with my encounter with the plant in the jungle. What else could have caused it?

A man's deep-throated bellow startles me. The sounds of flesh striking flesh, and the shrill cry of a young girl pierces through the quiet evening, silencing even the gravediggers.

I can see my cousin, Visak, from where I stand. My uncle has her by the arm, dwarfing her with his immensity. He is like a wild boar when he is infuriated, a cowardly one, for striking those who cannot fight back.

I can only imagine the pain my cousin feels, as she squirms underneath his vice-like grip. Her face is a contortion of agony, whilst his is a mask of pure hatred and fury.

"I told you not to speak with any of the village's young huntsmen!" My uncle yells at her. "You belong to *me*! You have no right to choose! I will choose a husband for you when I find a man who will offer me something lucrative in return, do you understand?"

My heart aches to hear her sob, but there is nothing I can do. She tries to beg for forgiveness but he strikes her again, and her head snaps back. When blood begins to drip down her mouth and her nose, something inside me stirs. My sense of taste, numbed for hours, returns with an intensity that startles me.

My body instantly stiffens. My mouth fills with saliva and an unexpected rumble passes through my stomach. I am shocked by the change, and even more troubled to realise that the notion of her blood is somewhat...appealing.

"Sailin!"

The man's shout rattles the floorboards above my head. A multitude of voices in the house whisper silence and obedience, mothers to their children, no doubt. I flinch, pressing my back against one of the many wooden stilts that hold the house up above the ground. Here it comes. *My* reckoning.

"I see you hiding under there. Come out here!" He snarls. I can see the ant-eater scales of his skull-cap flashing under the torch lights as he paces next to my cousin. All I can see of her is a glimpse of the patterns on her beautifully woven skirt, now torn and ragged.

"Sailin!" He screams again.

"Yes, uncle?" My fear is evident in my voice. I despise my terror of my uncle, almost as much as I despise the man himself.

"Where the hell were you?" He demands, advancing. His tattooed arm is already swinging when I emerge from under the house. I am on the ground before I realise he has struck me but it is strange. I...feel no pain this time.

"You're late. You're supposed to be back here hours ago!" he says, spittle flying through his beard. I roll to my knees and stand quickly, knowing that if I stay curled-up any longer he will not hesitate to kick me.

"Where were you? You look like shit!"

No thanks in part to his generosity, of course. I turn my head to spit more teeth to the ground, not certain whether they have fallen out because of his blow or because of my condition.

"I got lost," I mumble. I learnt when I was first brought here not to look him in the eye. I can feel his rancid, rice-wine scented breath on my forehead as he looks down on me, instantly reminded of the tale in the books my parents left behind. The one with the giant and the boy who defies it with a sling. Glad as I am to feel no pain, I wish I had the boy's courage to face my uncle.

"Lost? Again?" My uncle reaches for my arm and yanks me closer. I shut my eyes, not because I fear looking into his, but because I worry that if he sees my wound he will cast me out of the house. I am certain that none of the villagers will take me in with this malady, and to live off the jungle requires health and wisdom—neither of which, I have.

"Where's the money I told you to fetch?" He shakes me and strikes his hand across my face. "Did you ask them for my money?"

Again, I feel no pain, but it will do no good to show him that. I twist my expression into shock and despair and stutter, "N…no…I g… got lost! I couldn't find their house!"

"Devil's slut, you *smell* like shit, too." He shoves me away, repulsed. "I'll get the money myself. Make sure you get all your weaving done by noon tomorrow or I'll give you a reckoning that'll send you straight to hell!"

I can only nod. My uncle stalks back to the house, but not without a final glare of warning to my cousin, who lies curled on the ground, sobbing. I hesitate to approach her, for a part of me is still drawn to her blood.

The door slams shut—my uncle's way of telling us that we are to sleep outside tonight. The silence Suntong leaves in his wake is deafening, to say the very least. There is neither hair nor shadow of the other children or their mothers, but I do not blame their refusal to interfere. Suntong keeps only the most meek and obedient in his lot. The ones the coward finds difficult are quickly sent away, or have the defiance beaten out of them. In the end, I kneel next to my cousin.

My body twitches, eager as I reach forwards to pick her up.

"Sailin, you smell bad," my cousin says, her voice a mere whimper. It is good that she buries her bruised face in my shoulder when I lift her to her knees. Otherwise she would have seen the hunger in my eyes and resisted when I clutch her head with my hands and twist as hard as I can, until I hear her neck snap.

Her body is still twitching as I drag her behind the chicken coop. And there, under the watchful eyes of three dozen silent birds, I sink my teeth into her neck, savouring the taste of her flesh. My eyes roll back of their own accord as I am rewarded with the savoury feel of her meat sliding down my throat. In that haze of hunger and violence, I am absolutely horrified by my actions, absolutely terrified of the consequences. Yet above all else, I am absolutely satisfied.

My uncle and his entourage of wives and older children have gone for the day, searching for my cousin, but it will be a futile effort. They are convinced that she has run off with her secret lover, and it will take them half the day to make a trip downriver, to where the suspected young huntsman is staying. Another half a day to get back, which leaves me plenty of time to weave.

I have weighted Visak's remains down with a stone and rolled her into the river before washing myself clean of her blood. My soiled clothes I buried behind the chicken coop. It *should* trouble me as to how mechanical my actions have become, and how detached I have been about disposing her body. But it doesn't.

I moved on with today's chores without a second thought for the brutality of her murder, as though her life meant nothing to me.

As the hours pass, I watch in a mixture of horror and morbid fascination whilst the strange malady brings more changes to my body. The purple scratch, so minor just yesterday, has turned into a ghastly, oozing wound. Warmed by the afternoon sun, I shut my eyes against the throb within my skull and try to concentrate on weaving. My fingers are numb, where they should have been deft—my woven mats bulky, when they should have been a feat of artistry. Suntong will not be pleased, but that part of me that is so fearful of him is fast becoming distant.

"Sailin," a young voice calls.

I try to concentrate. My fingers make clumsy work of the strips of bark my young cousin, Kamit, cut for me earlier. He sits next to me now, the concern stamped on his face making me feel more agitated than loved.

"Sailin!"

"What?" I snap at him and pause to scratch for the hundredth time that hour. Kamit is merely concerned for me; I know that for a fact, but I cannot help myself.

"That looks bad," he points at the scratch, handing me the next strip with unmasked trepidation. "And you're looking awfully pale.

Are you sick?"

No, but I am hungry, my thoughts echo an answer. I can't help noticing how soft his young skin is. How succulent he looks. The smell of his body—a combination of sweat, smoke, and youthful innocence, wafts through my nostrils at the next passing breeze. I find myself wondering how *he* would taste and lick my lips at the notion of sinking my teeth into his flesh.

Then I catch myself. *No, not again!* I shake my head, trying desperately to banish the thoughts from my mind of his head on a platter. *No, no, one murder is enough! I have already sated my hunger on Visak. That should be enough!*

"Father won't fix you, but we can go see the shaman," my young cousin offers. "He'll know what's wrong. Fix you right up—-"

His mention of the shaman sparks a wave of contempt within me. The shamans here are no different from my uncle—superstitious old men who prey on the ignorance of a people who live by the primitive rules and laws of the jungle. "The Shaman can do nothing. I'm fine!" As I say these words, I lace my fingers through my hair and irritably brush the dark locks away from my eyes.

The sound of something tearing, and the look on my cousin's face stops me. It takes a second of contemplation before I muster enough courage to bring my hand forwards. Laced within my fingers are clumps of my hair, and worse…patches of skin. Rivulets of blood ooze down my head and my cousin's mouth drops open as he draws a breath to scream. He could barely manage a squeak before I reach forwards and clutch my fingers around his throat. I see a reflection of myself in his terrified pupils and hesitate, just for a moment.

Then, the desire to feed overwhelms me.

My head hurts.

It's hard to think. I see faces in my head, faces I should know but don't. A young woman's twitchy body; a young boy, small and soft. She sobbed, he screamed. They both tasted glorious and sweet in my mouth. I cannot remember why I am walking out here by the riverbank, but I keep hearing the words *physician* and *fix* in my head. It is very dark, but I can't go back to that house with the large, angry man, whoever he is. I've already come so far.

"Stop right where you are!"

The voice halts me. I look around; see nothing but the rushing river to my right, and the dense leaves of the jungle to my left. I am afraid, of *what*, I am not so sure.

"Who…you?" I've arranged so many other words in my mind, but my tongue feels thick. I shake my head to try and ease the confusion, but it does nothing. *Why am I here again?*

"I'm who you're looking for, I hope. No-one comes all the way up here to see the tigers. I am the physician," the voice answers. He speaks in the same tongue as I do, but it sounds strange coming from his lips. He is not from around here. But it doesn't matter. Physician means fix.

The leaves rustle. I turn round to see shadows and the darkness. Where is the man hiding?

"Physician!" I call out. "Fix me!"

"You've already fed yourself," the man speaks again. "I can see that from the roundness of your stomach. Which organs did you take? The heart? The lungs?"

His words trigger another wave of images. I see the boy within my head again. He is on the ground this time, and I see my hands, my fingers, tearing at his body. The satisfaction of burying my face into his open chest to feast on the organs inside makes me giddy with pleasure. I catch myself, knowing that I should feel guilty. I *should*. But I don't.

"I…not…no breathe…anymore…" I say, pounding my chest to try and control my emotions. "I thought…best…eat *his* lungs. To fix mine."

"Your brain is no longer functioning the way it is supposed to." The voice says. "And from what you're telling me, you've stopped breathing."

So many words. I furrow my brows and scratch the itch on my arm. "I no… I don't understand."

"You should have come to me sooner. This isn't a malady that is to be cured through the witchcraft and sorcery of your shamans!"

"You fix me now?"

"I can't," he sounds sad, which makes me nervous. He is supposed to *fix* me in some way. It is all my aching head is telling me. "You're already dead, and rotting," he rattles on. "You're not the first to be plagued by the corpse flower, and if this goes on, you won't be the last.

I have tried many weeks to find another infected victim, like you, but they either rot too quickly or wander off into the jungle before anyone can track them."

The leaves rustle again, and this time a tall, dark man appears on the path before me. He holds something long, curved, and sharp in his left arm. It is all I can see of him. Instinct warns me of danger, and an even stronger feeling urges me to take a step away from him.

"Wait, please. You're already dead. I can't fix you, but I can help you stop your actions. You want to stop eating your own people, don't you?"

Eat. Yes. I must eat soon. I will be hungry.

I am unsure of myself. My instincts tell me that if I stay, I will surely die.

"Come with me, please," the man says. The shiny thing in his hand flashes. It looks like it could hurt me, and I shake my head.

"No," my jaw hangs open. Spit and blood dribble down my chin. "Noooooo!"

"Please! Come back with me," the man reaches out a hand, and I turn to run. "No, girl, wait!"

I do not wait or look behind to see if he is pursuing me. The dense undergrowth of the jungle blurs out of focus as I blunder forwards, moving as fast as my legs can carry me. I need to get away. Away from the man who is supposed to fix me but can't...and back to where I know I can have a feast.

The girl re-emerges from the dense undergrowth of the jungle onto her uncle's lawn at the start of dawn. Her eyes are glazed over. Her skin, torn apart and bloody, is swarming with flies. Corpse-like, she ambles across the yard without a care for her appearance, dragging a stick behind her.

The owner of the house pauses at the bottom of the stairs that lead to his front door. The sight of the girl raises bile in his throat, and he snarls out of pure hatred and fury.

"Sailin? Where the hell were you?" The man bellows at the top of his lungs. "What happened to you?"

She ignores him and continues to close the gap between them. She is no longer breathing, but her pace quickens, and she tightens her rotting fingers over her stick.

"Kamit is gone, do you know that?" The man continues to shout. "First Visak, then Kamit, and then y—"

The stick slams into the side of his head with enough force to snap the weapon in two. The large man's head swings sideways, then back, following the momentum of his heavy body as he falls backwards to the ground. He can only gurgle when the girl lifts what is left of the stick and slams it into his skull. Again, and again, and again.

Some small part of her feels horrified at the viciousness of her actions, but the other part, the more dominant and primal one, continues to bash her uncle's head until his skull cracks open. The sight of clumps of meat and wetness oozing out of the open wound makes her smile. She scoops the organ up with her fingers and sucks on the juices, feeling more satisfied than she has ever been in her entire life. She is dead, but now, she has the energy she requires to survive in this form and to wait until others like her come out of the jungle. And from the sound of the terrified cries and panicked voices inside the longhouse, she knows she will have enough to eat for a little while.

To Follow the Waves

Amal El-Mohtar

A first generation Lebanese-Canadian, Amal has been nominated for a Nebula Award for her short fiction and published the prose and poetry collection The Honey Month. *She currently lives in Glasgow.*

Hessa's legs ached. She knew she ought to stand, stretch them, but only gritted her teeth and glared at the clear lump of quartz on the table before her. To rise now would be to concede defeat—but to lean back, lift her goggles, and rub her eyes was, she reasoned, an adequate compromise.

Her braids weighed on her, and she scratched the back of her head, where they pulled tightest above her nape. To receive a commission from Sitt Warda Al-Attrash was a great honour, one that would secure her reputation as a fixed star among Dimashq's dream-crafters. She could not afford to fail. Worse, the dream Sitt Warda desired was simple, as dreams went: to be a young woman again, bathing her limbs by moonlight in the Mediterranean with a young man who, judging by her half-spoken, half-murmured description, was not precisely her husband.

But Hessa had never been to the sea.

She had heard it spoken of, naturally, and read hundreds of lines of poetry extolling its many virtues. Yet it held little wonder for her; what pleasure could be found in stinging salt, scratching sand, burning sun reflected from the water's mirror-surface? Nor did swimming hold any appeal; she had heard pearl divers boast of their exploits, speak of how the blood beat between their eyes until they felt their heads might burst like overripe tomatoes, how their lungs ached with the effort for hours afterward, how sometimes they would feel as if thousands of ants were marching along their skin, and though they scratched until blood bloomed beneath their fingernails, could never reach them.

None of this did anything to endear the idea of the sea to her. And yet, to carve the dream out of the quartz, she had to find its beauty. Sighing, she picked up the dopstick again, tapped the quartz to make sure it was securely fastened, lowered her goggles, and tried again.

Hessa's mother was a mathematician, renowned well beyond the gates of Dimashq for her theorems. Her father was a poet, better known for his abilities as an artisanal cook than for his verse, though as the latter were full of the scents and flavours of the former, much appreciated all the same. Hessa's father taught her to contemplate what was pleasing to the senses, while her mother taught her geometry and algebra. She loved both as she loved them, with her whole heart.

Salma Najjar had knocked at the door of the Ghaflan family in the spring of Hessa's seventh year. She was a small woman, wrinkled as a wasp's nest, with eyes hard and bright as chips of tourmaline. Her greying hair was knotted and bound in the intricate patterns of a jeweller or gem-cutter—perhaps some combination of the two. Hessa's parents welcomed her into their home, led her to a divan, and offered her tea, but she refused to drink or eat until she had told them her errand.

"I need a child of numbers and letters to learn my trade," she had said, in the gruff, clipped accent of the Northern cities. "It is a good trade, one that will demand the use of all her abilities. I have heard that your daughter is such a child."

"And what is your trade?" Hessa's father asked, intrigued, but wary.

"To sculpt fantasies in the stone of the mind and the mind of the stone. To grant wishes."

"You propose to raise our daughter as *djinn?*" Hessa's mother raised an eyebrow.

Salma smiled, showing a row of perfect teeth. "Far better. *Djinn* do not get paid."

Building a dream was as complex as building a temple, and required knowledge of almost as many trades—a fact reflected in the complexity of the braid pattern in which Hessa wore her hair. Each pull and plait showed an intersection of gem-crafting, metal-working, architecture, and storytelling, to say nothing of the thousand twisting strands representing the many kinds of knowledge necessary to a story's success. As a child, Hessa had spent hours with the archivists in Al-Zahiriyya Library, learning from them the art of constructing memory palaces within her mind, layering the marble, glass, and mosaics of her imagination with reams of poetry, important historical dates, dozens of musical *maqaamat*, names of stars and ancestors. *Hessa bint Aliyah bint*

Qamar bint Widad...

She learned to carry each name, note, number like a jewel to tuck into a drawer here, hang above a mirror there, for ease of finding later on. She knew whole geographies, scriptures, story cycles, as intimately as she knew her mother's house, and drew on them whenever she received a commission. Though the only saleable part of her craft was the device she built with her hands, its true value lay in using the materials of her mind: She could not grind quartz to the shape and tune of her dream, could not set it into the copper coronet studded with amber, until she had fixed it into her thoughts as firmly as she fixed the stone to her amber dopstick.

"Every stone," Salma said, tossing her a piece of rough quartz, "knows how to sing. Can you hear it?"

Frowning, Hessa held it up to her ear, but Salma laughed. "No, no. It is not a shell from the sea, singing the absence of its creature. You cannot hear the stone's song with the ear alone. Look at it; feel it under your hand; you must learn its song, its language, before you can teach it your own. You must learn, too, to tell the stones apart; those that sing loudest do not always have the best memories, and it is memory that is most important. Easier to teach it to sing one song beautifully than to teach it to remember; some stones can sing nothing but their own tunes."

Dream-crafting was still a new art then; Salma was among its pioneers. But she knew that she did not have within herself what it would take to excel at it. Having discovered a new instrument, she found it unsuited to her fingers, awkward to rest against her heart; she could produce sound, but not music.

For that, she had to teach others to play.

First, she taught Hessa to cut gems. That had been Salma's own trade, and Hessa could see that it was still her chief love: the way she smiled as she turned a piece of rough crystal in her hands, learning its angles and texture, was very much the way Hessa's parents smiled at each other. She taught her how to pick the best stones, cleave away their grossest imperfections; she taught her to attach the gem to a dopstick with hot wax, at precise angles, taught her the delicate dance of holding it against a grinding lathe with even greater precision while operating the pedal. She taught her to calculate the axes that would unlock needles of light from the stone, kindle fire in its heart. Only once Hessa could grind a cabochon blindfolded, once she'd learned to see with the tips of her fingers, did Salma explain the rest.

"This is how you will teach songs to the stone." She held up a delicate amber wand, at the end of which was affixed a small copper vice. Hessa watched as Salma placed a cloudy piece of quartz inside and adjusted the vice around it before lowering her goggles over her eyes. "The amber catches your thoughts and speaks them to the copper; the copper translates them to the quartz. But just as you build your memory palace in your mind, so must you build the dream you want to teach it; first in your thoughts, then in the stone. You must cut the quartz while fixing the dream firmly in your mind, that you may cut the dream into the stone, cut it so that the dream blooms from it like light. Then, you must fix it into copper and amber again, that the dream may be translated into the mind of the dreamer.

"Tonight," she murmured quietly, grinding edges into the stone, "you will dream of horses. You will stand by a river and they will run past you, but one will slow to a stop. It will approach you and nuzzle your cheek."

"What colour will it be?"

Salma blinked behind her goggles, and the lathe slowed to a stop as she looked at her. "What colour would you like it to be?"

"Blue," said Hessa, firmly. It was her favourite colour.

Salma frowned. "There are no blue horses, child."

"But this is a dream! Couldn't I see one in a dream?"

Hessa wasn't sure why Salma was looking at her with quite such intensity, or why it took her so long a moment to answer. But finally, she smiled—in the gentle, quiet way she smiled at her gems—and said, "Yes, my heart. You could."

Once the quartz was cut, Salma fixed it into the centre of a copper circlet, its length prettily decorated with drops of amber, and fitted it around Hessa's head before giving her chamomile tea to drink and sending her to bed. Hessa dreamed just as Salma said she would: The horse that approached her was blue as the turquoise she had shaped for a potter's husband a few nights earlier. But when the horse touched her, its nose was dry and cold as quartz, its cheeks hard and smooth as cabochon.

Salma sighed when Hessa told her as much the next day. "You see, this is why I teach you, Hessa. I have been so long in the country of stones, speaking their language and learning their songs, I have little to teach them of our own; I speak everything to them in facets and brilliance, culets and crowns. But you, my dear, you are learning many languages all at once; you have your father's tasting tongue, your mother's speech of angles and air. I have been speaking nothing but adamant for most of my life, and grow more and more deaf to the desires of dreamers."

Try as she might, Hessa could not coordinate her knowledge of the sea with the love, the longing, the pleasure needed to build Sitt Warda's dream. She had mixed salt and water, touched it to her lips, and found it unpleasant; she had watched the moon tremble in the waters of her courtyard's fountain without being able to stitch its beauty to a horizon. She tried, now, to summon those poor attempts to mind, but was keenly aware that if she began grinding the quartz in her present state, Sitt Warda would wake from her dream as tired and frustrated as she herself presently felt.

Giving in, she put down the quartz, removed her goggles, rose from her seat, and turned her back on her workshop. There were some problems only coffee and ice cream could fix.

Qahwat al Adraj was one of her favourite places to sit and do the opposite of think. Outside the bustle of the Hamadiyyah market, too small and plain to be patronised by obnoxious tourists, it was a well-kept secret tucked beneath a dusty stone staircase: The servers were beautiful, the coffee exquisite, and the iced treats in summer particularly fine. As she closed the short distance between it and her workshop, she tried to force her gaze up from the dusty path her feet had long ago memorised, tried to empty herself of the day's frustrations to make room for her city's beauties.

There: a young man with dark skin and a dazzling smile, his tight-knotted braids declaring him a merchant-inventor, addressing a gathering crowd to display his newest brass automata. "Ladies and gentlemen," he called, "the British Chef!" and demonstrated how with a few cranks and a minimum of preparation, the long-faced machine could knife carrots into twisting orange garlands, slice cucumbers into lace. And not far from him, drawn to the promise of a building audience, a beautiful mechanical, her head sculpted to look like an amira's head-dress, serving coffee from the heated cone of it by tipping forward in an elegant bow before the cup, an act that could not help but make every customer feel as if they were sipping the gift of a cardamom-laced dance.

Hessa smiled to them, but frowned to herself. She had seen them all many times before. Today she was conscious, to her shame, of a bitterness toward them: What business had they being beautiful to her when they were not the sea?

Arriving, she took her usual seat by a window that looked out to Touma's Gate, sipped her own coffee, and tried not to brood.

She knew what Salma would have said. *Go to the sea, she would have urged, bathe in it! Or, if you cannot, read the thousands of poems written to it! Write a poem yourself! Or,* slyly, then, *only think of something you your-self find beautiful—horses, berries, books—and hide it beneath layers and lay-ers of desire until the thing you love is itself obscured. Every pearl has a grain of sand at its heart, no? Be cunning. You cannot know all the world, my dear, as intimately as you know your stones.*

But she couldn't. She had experimented with such dreams, crafted them for herself; they came out wrapped in cotton wool, provoking feeling without vision, touch, scent. Any would-be dream crafter could do as well. No, for Sitt Warda, who had already patronised four of the city's crafters before her, it would never do. She had to produce some-thing exquisite, unique. She had to know the sea as Sitt Warda knew it, as she wanted it.

She reached for a newspaper, seeking distraction. Lately it was all airships and trade agreements surrounding their construction and de-ployment, the merchant fleets' complaints and clamour for restrictions on allowable cargo to protect their own interests. Hessa had a moment of smirking at the sea-riding curmudgeons before realising that she had succumbed, again, to the trap of her knotting thoughts. Perhaps if the sea were seen from a great height? But that would provoke the sen-sation of falling, and Sitt Warda did not want a flying dream...

Gritting her teeth, she buried her face in her hands—until she heard someone step through the doorway, sounding the hollow glass chimes in so doing. Hessa looked up.

A woman stood there, looking around, the early afternoon light casting a faint nimbus around her, shadowing her face. She was tall, and wore a long, simple dark blue coat over a white dress, its embroidery too plain to declare a regional origin. Hessa could see she had beautiful hands, the gold in them drawn out by the midnight of the blue, but it was not these at which she found herself staring. It was the woman's hair.

Unbound, it rippled.

There was shame in that, Hessa had always felt, had always been taught. To wear one's hair so free in public was to proclaim oneself unbound to a trade, useless; even the travellers who passed through the city bound knots into their hair out of respect for custom, the five braids of travellers and visitors who wished themselves known as such above anything else, needing hospitality or good directions. The strangeness of it thrilled and stung her.

It would perhaps not have been so shocking were it one long unbroken sheet of silk, a sleek spill of ink with no light in it. But it rippled, as if just released from many braids, as if fingers had already tangled there, as if hot breath had moistened it to curling waves. *Brazen,* thought Hessa, the word snagging on half-remembered lines of English poetry, *brazen greaves, brazen hooves.* Unfamiliar words, strange, like a spell—and suddenly it was a torrent of images, of rivers and aching and spilling and immensity, because she wanted that hair in her own hand, wanted to see her skin vanish into its blackness, wanted it to swallow her while she swallowed it—

It took her a moment to notice the woman was looking at her. It took another for Hessa to flush with the understanding that she was staring rudely before dropping her gaze back to her coffee. She counted to seventy in her head before daring to look up again: By the time she did, the woman was seated, a server half-hiding her from Hessa's view. Hessa lay money on the table and rose to leave, taking slow, deliberate steps toward the door. As soon as she was outside the coffee house, she broke into a run.

Two nights later, with a piece of finely shaped quartz pulsing against her brow, Sitt Warda Al-Attrash dreamed of her former lover with honeysuckle sweetness, and if the waves that rose and fell around

141

them were black and soft as hair, she was too enraptured to notice.

Hessa could not stop thinking of the woman. She took to eating most of her meals at Qahwat al Adraj, hoping to see her again—to speak, apologise for what must have seemed appalling behaviour, buy her a drink—but the woman did not return. When she wasn't working, Hessa found her fingertips tracing delicate, undulating lines through the gem dust that coated her table, thighs tightly clenched, biting her lip with longing. Her work did not suffer for it—if anything, it improved tremendously. The need to craft flooded her, pushed her to pour the aching out into copper and crystal.

Meantime, Sitt Warda could not stop speaking of Hessa, glowing in her praise; she told all her wealthy friends of the gem among dream-crafters who dimmed all others to ash, insisting they sample her wares. Where before Hessa might have had one or two commissions a week, she began to receive a dozen a day, and found herself in a position to pick and choose among them. This she did—but it took several commissions before she saw what was guiding her choice.

"Craft me a dream of the ruins of Baalbek," said one kind-eyed gentleman with skin like star-struck sand, "those tall, staggering remnants, those sloping columns of sunset!" Hessa ground them just shy of twilight, that the dreamt columns might be dimmed to the colour of skin darkened by the light behind it, and if they looked like slender necks, the fallen ones angled slant as a clavicle, the kind-eyed gentleman did not complain.

"Craft me a dream of wings and flight," murmured a shy young woman with gold-studded ears, "that I might soar above the desert and kiss the moon." Hessa ground a cabochon with her right hand while her left slid between her legs, rocking her to the memory of long fingers she built into feathers, sprouted to wings just as she moaned a spill of warm honey and weightlessness.

Afterward, she felt ashamed. She thought, surely someone would notice—surely, some dreamer would part the veils of ecstasy in their sleep and find her burning behind them. It felt, awkwardly, like trespass, but not because of the dreamers; rather, it seemed wrong to sculpt her nameless, braidless woman into the circlets she sold for money. It felt like theft, absurd though it was, and in the aftermath of her release, she felt guilty, too.

But she could not find her; she hardly knew how to begin to look. Perhaps she had been a traveller, after all, merely releasing her hair from a five-braided itch in the late afternoon; perhaps she had left the city, wandered to wherever it was she came from, some strange land where women wore their hair long and wild and lived lives of savage indolence, stretching out beneath fruit trees, naked as the sky —

The flush in her cheeks decided for her. If she couldn't find her woman while waking, then what in the seven skies was her craft for, if not to find her in sleep?

Hessa had never crafted a dream for her own use. She tested her commissions, sometimes, to ensure their quality or correct an error, but she always recast the dream in fresh quartz and discarded the test stone immediately, throwing it into the bath of saltwater steam that would purify it for reworking into simple jewellery. It would not do, after all, for a silver necklace or brass ring to bear in it the echo of a stranger's lust. Working the hours she did, her sleep was most often profound and refreshing; if she dreamt naturally, she hardly ever remembered.

She did not expect to sleep well through the dream she purposed.

She closed shop for a week, took on no new commissions. She hesitated over the choice of stone; a dream crafted in white quartz could last for up to three uses, depending on the clarity of the crystal and the time she took in grinding it. But a dream crafted in amethyst could last indefinitely—could belong to her forever, as long as she wanted it, renewing itself to the rhythm of her thoughts, modulating its song to harmonise with her dream-desires. She had only ever crafted two dreams in amethyst, a matched set to be given as a wedding gift, and the sum she commanded for the task had financed a year's worth of materials and bought her a new lathe.

Reluctantly, she chose the white quartz. Three nights, that was all she would allow herself; three nights for a week's careful, loving labour, and perhaps then this obsession would burn itself out, would leave her sated. Three nights, and then no more.

She wondered if Salma had ever done anything of the sort.

For three days, she studied her only memory of the woman, of her standing framed in the doorway of Qahwat al Adraj, awash in dusty light; she remembered the cut of her coat, its colour, and the woman's eyes focusing on her, narrowing, quizzical. They were almost black, she thought, or so the light made them. And her hair, of course, her endless, splendid, dreadful hair, curling around her slim neck like a hand; she remembered the height of her, the narrowness that made her think of a sheathed sword, of a buried root, only her hair declaring her to be wild, impossible, strange.

Once the woman's image was perfectly fixed in her thoughts, Hessa began to change it.

Her stern mouth softened into hesitation, almost a smile; her lips parted as if to speak. Hessa wished she had heard her voice that day — she did not want to imagine a sound that was not truly hers, that was false. She wanted to shift, to shape, not to invent. Better to leave her silent.

Her mouth, then, and her height; she was probably taller than Hessa, but not in the dream, no. She had to be able to look into her eyes, to reach for her cheeks, to brush her thumb over the fullness of her lips before kissing them. Her mouth would be warm, she knew, and taste —

Here, again, she faltered. She would taste, Hessa decided, of ripe mulberries, and her mouth would be stained with the juice. She would have fed them to her, after laughing over a shared joke—no, she would have placed a mulberry in her own mouth and then kissed her, yes, lain it on her tongue as a gift from her own, and that is why she would taste of mulberries as Hessa pressed a hand to the small of her back and gathered her slenderness against herself, crushed their hips together...

It took her five days to build the dream in her thoughts, repeating the sequence of her imagined pleasures until they wore grooved agonies into her mind, until she could almost savour the dream through her sleep without the aid of stone or circlet. She took a full day to cast the latter, and a full day to grind the stone to the axes of her dream, careful not to miss a single desired sensation; she set it carefully into its copper circlet.

Her fingers only trembled when she lifted it onto her head.

The first night left her in tears. She had never been so thoroughly immersed in her art, and it had been long, so long since anyone had approached her with a desire she could answer in kisses rather than craft. She ached for it; the braidless woman's body was like warm water on her skin, surrounded her in the scent of jasmine. The tenderness between them was unbearable; for all that she thirsted for a voice, for small sighs and gasps to twine with her own. Her hair was down soft, and the pleasure she took in wrapping it around her fingers left her breathless. She woke tasting mulberries, removed the circlet, and promptly slept until the afternoon.

The second night, she nestled into her lover's body with the ease of old habit, and found herself murmuring poetry into her neck, old poems in antique meters, rhythms rising and falling like the galloping warhorses they described. "I wish," she whispered, pressed against her afterward, raising her hand to her lips, "I could take you riding—I used to, when I was little. I would go riding to Maaloula with my family, where almond trees grow from holy caves, and where the wine is so black and sweet it is rumoured that each grape must have been kissed before being plucked to make it. I wish," and she sighed, feeling the dream leaving her, feeling the stone-sung harmony of it fading, "I wish I knew your name."

Strangeness, then—a shifting in the dream, a jolt, as the walls of the bedroom she had imagined for them fell away, as she found she could look at nothing but her woman's eyes, seeing wine in them, suddenly, and something else, as she opened her mulberry mouth to speak.

"Nahla," she said, in a voice like a granite wall. "My name is—"

Hessa woke with the sensation of falling from a great height, too shocked to move. Finally, with great effort, she removed the circlet, and gripped it in her hands for a long time, staring at the quartz. She had not given her a name. Was her desire for one strong enough to change the dream from within? All her dream devices were interactive to a small degree, but she always planned them that way, allowing room, pauses in the stone's song that the dreamer's mind could fill— but she had not done so with her own, so certain of what she wanted, of her own needs. She had decided firmly against giving her a name, wanting so keenly to know the truth—and that voice, so harsh. That was not how she would have imagined her voice...

She put the circlet aside and rose to dress herself. She would try to understand it later that night. It would be her final one; she would ask another question, and see what tricks her mind played on her then.

But there would be no third night.

That afternoon, as Hessa opened her door to step out for an early dinner at Qahwat al Adraj, firm hands grasped her by the shoulders and shoved her back inside. Before she could protest or grasp what was happening, her braidless woman stood before her, so radiant with fury that Hessa could hardly speak for the pain it brought her.

"Nahla?" she managed.

"Hessa," she threw back in a snarl. "Hessa Ghaflan bint Aliyah bint Qamar bint Widad. Crafter of dreams. Ask me how I am here."

There were knives in Hessa's throat—she felt it would bleed if she swallowed, if she tried to speak. "...How?"

"Do you know," she was walking, now, walking a very slow circle around her, "what it is like—" no, not quite around, she was coming toward her but as wolves did, never in a straight line, before they attacked, always slant "—to find your dreams are no longer your own? Answer me."

Hessa could not. This, now, felt like a dream that was no longer her own. Nahla's voice left her nowhere to hide, allowed her no possibility of movement. Finally, she managed something that must have looked enough like a shake of her head for Nahla to continue.

"Of course you wouldn't. You are the mistress here, the maker of worlds. I shall tell you. It is fascinating, at first—like being in another country. You observe, for it is strange to not be at the centre of your own story, strange to see a landscape, a city, an ocean, bending its familiarity toward someone not yourself. But then—then, Hessa—"

Nahla's voice was an ocean, Hessa decided, dimly. It was worse than the sea—it was the vastness that drowned ships and hid monsters beneath its sparkling calm. She wished she could stop staring at her mouth.

"—Then, you understand that the landscapes, the cities, the oceans, these things are you. They are built out of you, and it is you who are bending, you who are changing for the eyes of these strangers. It is your hands in their wings, your neck in their ruins, your hair in which they laugh and make love—"

Her voice broke, there, and Hessa had a tiny instant's relief as Nahla turned away from her, eyes screwed shut. Only an instant, though, before Nahla laughed in a way that was sand in her own eyes, hot and stinging and sharp.

"And then you see them! You see them in waking, these people who bathed in you and climbed atop you, you recognise their faces and think you have gone mad, because those were only dreams, surely, and you are more than that! But you aren't, because the way they look at you, Hessa, their heads tilted in fond curiosity, as if they've found a pet they would like to keep—you are nothing but the grist for their fantasy mills, and even if they do not understand that, you do. And you wonder, why, why is this happening? Why now, what have I done—"

She gripped Hessa's chin and forced it upward, pushing her against one of her worktables, scattering a rainfall of rough-cut gems to the stone floor and slamming agony into her hip. Hessa did not resist anything but the urge to scream.

"And then," stroking her cheek in a mockery of tenderness, "you see a face in your dreams that you first knew outside them. A small, tired-looking thing you saw in a coffee house, who looked at you as if you were the only thing in the world worth looking at—but who now is taking off your clothes, is filling your mouth with berries and poems and won't let you speak, and Hessa, *it is so much worse.*"

"I didn't know!" It was a sob, finally, stabbing at her as she forced it out. "I'm sorry, I'm so sorry—I didn't know, Nahla, that isn't how it works—"

"You made me into your *doll.*" Another shove sent Hessa crumpling to the floor, pieces of quartz marking her skin with bruises and cuts. "Better I be an ancient city or the means to flight than your *toy,* Hessa! Do you know the worst of it?" Nahla knelt down next to her, and Hessa knew that it would not matter to her that she was crying, now, but she offered her tears up as penance all the same.

"The worst of it," she whispered, now, forefinger tracing one of Hessa's braids, "is that, in the dream, I wanted you. And I could not tell if it was because I found you beautiful, or because that is what you wanted me to do."

They stayed like that for some time, Hessa breathing through slow, ragged sobs while Nahla touched her head. She could not bring herself to ask, *do you still want me now?*

"How could you not know?" Nahla murmured, as she touched her, as if she could read the answer in Hessa's hair. "How could you not know what you were doing to me?"

"I don't control anything but the stone, I swear to you, Nahla, I promise," she could hear herself babbling, her words slick with tears, blurry and indistinct as her vision. "When I grind the dream into the quartz, it is like pressing a shape into wet clay, like sculpture, like carpentry—the quartz, the wax, the dopstick, the grinding plate, the copper and amber, these are my materials, Nahla! These and my mind. I don't know how this happened, it is impossible—"

"That I should be in your mind?"

"That I, or anyone else, should be in yours. You aren't a material, you were only an image—it was never you, it couldn't have been, it was only—"

"Your longing," Nahla said, flatly. "Your wanting of me."

"Yes." Silence between them, then a long-drawn breath. "You believe me?"

A longer silence, while Nahla's fingers sank into the braids tight against Hessa's scalp, scratching it while clutching at a plaited line. "Yes."

"Do you forgive me?"

Slowly, Nahla released her, withdrew her hand, and said nothing. Hessa sighed, and hugged her knees to her chest. Another moment passed; finally, thinking she might as well ask, since she was certain never to see Nahla again, she said, "Why do you wear your hair like that?"

"That," said Nahla, coldly, "is none of your business."

Hessa looked at the ground, feeling a numbness settle into her chest, and focused on swallowing her throat-thorns, quieting her breathing. Let her go, then. Let her go, and find a way to forget this— although a panic rose in her, that after a lifetime of being taught how to remember, she had forgotten how to forget.

"Unless," Nahla continued, thoughtful, "you intend to make it your business."

Hessa looked up, startled. While she stared at her in confusion,

Nahla seemed to make up her mind.

"Yes." She smirked, and there was something cruel in the bright twist of it. "I would be your apprentice! You'd like that, wouldn't you? To make my hair like yours?"

"No!" Hessa was horrified. "I don't—I mean—no, I wouldn't like that at all." Nahla raised an eyebrow as she babbled, "I've never had an apprentice. I was one only four years ago. It would not—it would not be seemly."

"Hessa." Nahla stood, now, and Hessa rose with her, knees shaky and sore. "I want to know how this happened. I want to learn—" she narrowed her eyes, and Hessa recoiled from what she saw there, but forgot it the instant Nahla smiled "how to do it to you. Perhaps then, when I can teach you what it felt like, when I can silence you and bind you in all the ways I find delicious without asking your leave— perhaps then, I can forgive you."

They looked at each other for what seemed an age. Then, slowly, drawing a long, deep breath, Hessa reached for a large piece of rough quartz, and put it in Nahla's hand, gently closing her fingers over it.

"Every stone," she said, quietly, looking into her wine-dark eyes, "knows how to sing. Can you hear it?"

As she watched, Nahla frowned, and raised the quartz to her ear.

Ahuizotl

Nelly Geraldine García-Rosas

(Translated from Spanish by Silvia Moreno-Garcia.)

Nelly Geraldine García-Rosas is a young Mexican writer, publishing in both Spanish and English. She works as a freelance copy editor and tackles Lovecraftian horror from an original angle in the following story.

F urious, the sea bellows, tearing the sails of the San Cristóbal, protests with roars of foam, yells like a woman in labour, cries like an abandoned child… Those were the words I managed to make out in the last, demented babbles of a Moorish youth who, with eyes popping out, threw himself overboard during the storm that lashed the ship taking me to meet my brother's corpse.

Unlike the other passengers of the San Cristóbal, I did not embark for New Spain looking for fortune, but to stand face to face with misfortune and to bid goodbye to the last family member I had left. My brother, Fernando Villaplana, sailed in the year 1511 of Our Lord, being but a teenager. He had the fancy of becoming rich, gaining fame and possessing everything that our orphanhood had denied us. I remember seeing him, with eyes ablaze and hair uncombed, when he told me this before parting, as if the wind had already started flinging him toward those unknown lands full of wonder and danger, like the ones told in the *Amadís*. I knew from a letter of his that he had participated in the expedition commanded by Don Diego de Velázquez to the island of Cuba and that, a few years later, together with more than five hundred men, had joined the troops of Hernán Cortés to explore other lands and reclaim them in the name of His Majesty. After this, I had no news of him until, nearly thirty years after his parting, I received a letter from a friar named "Juan de los Ángeles."

With beautiful and tight lettering, the friar told me how they had found Fernando's corpse at the edge of the lake of Texcoco: "His skin was wet and slippery like that of a fish, but he did not squirm searching for the comfort of water; he remained still, as if asleep. He appeared to have no bruises or signs of violence. It was only up close that we realized his eyes, teeth, and nails had been torn out with much care.

'*Ahuizotl! Ahuizotl!*' cried an Indian who kept us company and, drooling like a rabid dog, refused to help us carry the deceased."

When I had finished reading the epistle assuring me of a grave on sacred ground for my brother, I did not know if my unease sprang from the way in which events were narrated or the fact that I had read that name written by an unknown hand: "Elena Villaplana." Letter by letter, the maroon ink on the paper from New Spain returned me to the moment in which Fernando, dragged by the wind, had left me at the door of the convent of the Jerónimas so he could follow his dreams by the sea. From then on, I was Ágata de la Inmaculada Concepción; nevertheless, with the devastating news crumpling between my hands and tears in my eyes, the Elena inside me yelled, "*Ahuizotl! Ahuizotl!*" and forced me to head toward the murky waters of the New World.

The preparations for my departure happened in a mist, as in a dream, as though I was staring beneath the water. I remember little of what happened before I found myself kneeling next to the mast, praying and commending new souls to God during such a hard trial. It was then that the young Moor came running—drenched, he seemed black and slippery, and with his eyes so ominously open, he resembled a grotesque fish. He screamed strange words, perhaps in a strange tongue. I was only able to distinguish a few in Spanish before he threw himself overboard and disappeared amidst the foam.

A couple of weeks later, we arrived at the port of San Juan, which is also called "Ulúa," for they say that the natives of the islet where the fortress-port is located howled at the sea, "*Chlúha! Chlúa!*" Words that the Spaniards understood as the actual name of the place. The crew was tired. It was agreed we would spend the night in an improvised camp on the beach and, at first light, would continue toward our destination, la Villa de la Veracruz. It was a relief to rest upon firm and warm sand, so that I fell asleep almost at once. Nevertheless, my sleep was restless; I dreamt that a huge figure emerged from the sea. On the shore, little animals the size of a dog greeted it, wagging their long tails that seemed to finish upon a hand. Waves crashed with strength and brought in their waters human corpses. Some seemed like abominations between man and fish, or seemed to have been turned inside out, with their guts were showing. The little creatures devoured, with much care, the eyes, teeth, and nails of the corpses dragged by the sea for the satisfaction of the monstrous figure.

I awoke, bathed in sweat and trembling uncontrollably. I tried to commend myself to the Archangel Saint Michael, but the abominable images of the dream continued to haunt me in the darkness of a moonless night. I don't know how long I was victim to this terror, but, still drenched with fear, I noticed suddenly that not far from me there were lights dancing in the palm trees. I approached them, thinking that it was a gathering of some of the mariners and it would do me well to sit before a fire. But no sailor was there: a group of strangely dressed Indians danced around a nest of palm leaves, inside which there stood a small stone figurine, no bigger than a fist. They sang in an odd tongue, but repeated constantly "*Chlúha! Chlúa! Dagoatl! Dagoatl!*" and howled like dogs, their cries increasing. The sailors from the San Cristóbal were awakened by the howling and, enraged, frightened them off by force.

Soon, morning broke and I saw something shining amidst the sand removed by the dance of the Indians. It was a small stone figurine of a black-and-bright crystal, the obsidian stone they employ in the realm of the Indies to make knives. It represented the silhouette of a man with huge eyes and tiny, pointed ears. The hands, adhered to the body, resembled those of a frog and it might have had a tail that had broken off. I could not stop thinking about Fernando as I looked into the wide, large eyes of the figurine, so I took it with me.

The end of the trip was short and calm. We arrived at the Villa de la Veracruz at midday, thus I decided to leave, immediately, toward the city of México-Tenochtitlán, where, thanks to a letter from the Mother Superior, I would be received by the newly established convent of the Jerónimas of New Spain. The roads were tortuous and the mist did not allow me to see the mountains surrounding us. Sometimes, you could hear howls like the ones of the natives of the port of San Juan; the driver told us it was the coyotes from the mountain and that we should not be afraid. Nevertheless, I felt a drop of cold water stream down my side, until it reached the pocket of my habit, and it increased the weight of the black figurine until I was slouching.

After I finally arrived at the convent and rested, I went to visit Friar Juan de los Ángeles at the Jesuit home. He was an old man and walked with difficulty. Even so, he wanted to take me to my brother's grave, which was far off, in the atrium of a small chapel. As we walked together, he once more related the story of the discovery of the corpse, going into detail on the missing eyes, teeth, and nails. The friar's gaze seemed to grow empty every time he spoke of the appearance of Fernando's skin, "moist and slippery, like a fish". I tried to speak of something else, but he seemed engrossed, as though he did not know I was there. After a little while, we arrived at a small cemetery, where I prayed in silence. I carried no flowers to place next to the wooden cross, so I took out the figurine and decided to leave it by the grave, as a gift for my brother. Friar Juan de los Ángeles grew pale when he saw it, made the sign of the cross several times, and began to scream, "The *Ahuizotl*! Have respect for the dead and take away from this sacred place the demon that murdered your brother. You, servant of the aquatic Satan, do not deserve to wear the habit with the figure of Our Lord!"

Not knowing what to do, I rushed away, disconcerted, through the cemetery.

Back at the convent, I fell victim to feverish tremors, which kept me in bed for many days. I dreamt, over and over again, about the titanic figure emerging from the sea and on the beach; it was received with joy by the *ahuizotls*, who, imitating the screams of a birthing woman or the cry of an infant, devoured my brother over and over again, or made terrible necklaces of teeth and nails. One afternoon, when my fever seemed to have eased, a dark-skinned girl with black hair took me to walk by the edge of a river. The sun was sinking, revealing the intense brightness of a few stars when the girl told me to wait, for she could hear something resembling a baby's cry. I could not stop her. A dark, scaly hand rose from beneath the murky waters, pulled her hair and everything went black.

Days later, they found the dead girl. A little child told me her corpse glinted, like a horrible fish at the market. I resolved then to abandon New Spain forever and with it, my brother's corpse and the terrible dreams.

I arrived at the port of Veracruz on a Thursday at dawn, the first rays from the sun greeting the sailors with hundreds of dead frogs and fish upon the sand. My ship was soon parting, but we managed to hear the screams from the coast; I felt a drop of cold water stream down my side, until it reached the pocket of my habit, and it increased the weight of the black figurine until I was slouching. I held the figurine between my hands and, though I tried to pray, no words came out.

The waves rise until they resemble a mountain in the ocean that turns dark, like the skin of the *Ahuizotl*. Barely illuminated by the convulsive light of the candle, the obsidian figurine seems to glint by itself, and I feel it coming: black, huge, stirring the ocean with its innumerable scales, its eyes eternally open. The scent of salt and blood drifts through the air. God help us.

The Rare Earth

Biram Mboob

Born in the Gambia, Biram Mboob currently lives in the UK. His short stories have appeared in Granta *and elsewhere.*

Finally, the Word was spreading. On an otherwise unremarkable morning in December, the very first pilgrims approached the stronghold at Kivu in the Congo.

Dora Neza was pulling her dying father on a hydraulic-steam litter. He lay motionless, his face a skeletal grimace, his skin a thinly congealed wax. She had pulled him for several days through forest thicket and marsh. In the dark and at the dawn he would rouse from his litter and cry out to her sharply. He would croak at her in the strange tongues of the void. Her reply to him was always the same, "We are nearly there, Baba. Nearly there."

They approached the high, metal wall of the Nyungwe forest reserve. The wall stood twelve feet tall, featureless, alien, white morning mist roiling along its base like a trapped cloud. Dora observed the wall for a few minutes and then retreated from it. She found a nearby break in the thicket, set the litter down, and waited. She listened to the tortured breathing of her sleeping baba, the warble and keen of a solitary hornbill, the rustle and bell of the early breeze. She waited. The earth turned, bathing the glade about her with the muted lights of the morning sun.

More than an hour had passed before the wall opened. A large metal panel creaked and then slid away. In the wall's new maw stood three knights. They wore green armour, black crosses chiselled on their tabards. Heavy machetes hung from their waists in leather scabbards, rifles slung over their shoulders. It took a few moments for Dora to notice that there was a fourth figure, a giant zumbi lingering behind the knights. At the sight of it, she scrambled to her feet, terror swelling in her like the tide. The zumbi wore nothing but a pair of transparent shorts, the attire of diamond miners and low domestics. It stopped a few paces outside the wall, motionless, its manner somehow both limp and tense at the same time, its flat gaze fixated on some distant point beyond the glade.

"*Unataka nini?*" one of the knights asked her, the largest of the three.

She began to reply, but the one who had spoken shoved her roughly.

She realised he wanted no reply, so stayed silent while he admonished her for evading their checkpoints. From somewhere in the canopy, the hornbill sang its warble song one final time before rustling into flight.

The knights lifted her sick baba up to his feet and let him fall to the ground. They used their machetes to hack apart her litter and examined its innards, pistons, and joints. When their inspection was over, the largest knight walked over to the zumbi and slapped it twice on the back of its head whilst pointing at her baba. The zumbi gathered him up from the ground and easily slung him over its huge shoulder. The knights walked through the opening in the wall, followed by the zumbi. Dora waited a few moments, and followed them through. The wall closed behind them, the scattered remnants of the litter contraption left outside like the metal bones of some unimaginable feast.

They walked through a forest, whose coppice grew thicker, and it got darker as they walked. Then the forest trail widened, turning into a path. They soon began to walk past forest *mahemas*—camouflaged green canvas tents—amongst the trees. They began to encounter men and women along the path, some holding rifles, others holding axes and tools. Some were dressed in the foliage-like rags of forest dwellers, others in green ceremonial robes. Overhead in the arboreal, silvered arrays and antennae jutted into the sky. There were other machines parked between the trees: tri-wheeled jungle *vifaru* tanks, missile launchers, skyward pointing rail cannons.

They entered a large clearing. The biggest knight turned to her. "*Fuata*," he said, pointing at the giant mahema that stood at the clearing's centre. Unlike the other mahemas, it was the size of a circus marquee, glossy white, with antennae and arrays protruding from its roof. A large wooden cross was planted before it alongside two armed sentries. The knight slapped the zumbi on its broad shoulder blade and pointed at the mahema entrance, making it advance between the sentries and disappear inside. Dora followed.

Her eyes took a few moments to adjust to the darkness. The zumbi had deposited her father on the ground and retreated to the recesses of the tent. She looked around. A well-appointed leather suite, a plush carpet pile, and judging from the cooler air some form of air-conditioning mechanism. There were perhaps a dozen men in the mahema, some standing, others sitting. However, it was immediately obvious to Dora who amongst them was the Redeemer. He sat in an armchair at the focal point of the room. A tall man, muscled, stout, a warrior's build, not much older than thirty, but bald and hairless, except for a long beard. His face was oblong, severe, and he wore the stiffly contemplative frown of a man still settling into his role at the apex. Casually dressed in a simple white robe, his legs were crossed and displayed a pair of badly scarred knees.

Dora assumed that they had arrived at the conclusion of some disciplinary hearing, for a sobbing man lay prostrate before the Redeemer. Two sentries lifted the shuddering wretch by the arms and dragged him outside.

After the sentries had left, the men in the mahema turned their attention to her. The Redeemer stared at her while the knight who had spoken outside whispered something into his ear. She gazed evenly at him in return, her hands clasped behind her back. Despite the heat, she still had her orange kanga draped over her shoulders. Underneath, she was wearing a ragged T-shirt and faded denims.

"Where are you from?" The Redeemer asked.

"From Cyangugu," she replied.

He nodded amiably. "That's a hard road that you've travelled. How did you know where to find us?"

"Everyone knows you are here. Everyone is talking about you."

"And what do they say about me?"

She kept her gaze on him as she spoke, "That you are *Yesu*. The Christ returned."

The Redeemer pursed his lips, as if hearing this for the first time. "What is your name?" he asked.

"Dora," she replied. "My father's name is Michael."

"Dora," he repeated. "What else do they say about me?"

"They say you have cured the blind and brought dead men to life. Before he stopped speaking, my father told me that he saw you perform miracles in Ituri. He saw you summon fire from the sky with your finger. He saw you kill a hundred PLA without moving from where you stood."

The Redeemer nodded and smiled, pleased. He turned and glanced at one of the men seated near him. A much older man wearing a knight's uniform said and smiled, "The Word spreads."

The Redeemer turned back to her. "Tell me," he asked. "What

name do I go by in your town?"

"Schwarzenegger," she said.

He frowned. "That was my war name," he said. "When you return to the town you will tell your people my true name. You will tell them that my name is Gideon. You will tell them that I am the Word made flesh."

Dora looked down at her baba, who was lying still on the floor.

"Don't worry about your father," the Redeemer continued. "He will be made whole again. I will cure him. Does he hold faith in the Trinity?"

"Yes," she said, "he does."

"Then his faith will be rewarded. His faith in me will make him whole."

"PLA spies," Musa Kun said. "I guarantee it."

The older man was Gideon's second in command, a trusted counsellor, and a thin shuffling person with a protruding jaw that gave him a deceptively gormless appearance. Musa set down his papers and stood up from his chair. He prodded Michael with his foot, making the stricken man groan. "Did you see her shoes?" he asked. "Nice boots like that?"

"I did," Gideon said. He looked down at Michael, observing his features, a man nearing sixty with grey temples and a painfully thin face. Beads of sweat ridged his forehead occasionally sliding down his nose. "They aren't spies. You wouldn't make a spy of a dying man."

Gideon stood up, bent down, and touched the man's forehead. He could have been dying of any number of infections; there was no way to be certain. The superbugs evolved quickly enough so that there was almost no point in trying to catalogue them.

"We should still be careful though," Musa Kun said. "He might not be a spy, but the girl could be."

Gideon shrugged. The girl Dora was admittedly, a different matter. She might be employed to penetrate the camp, the sick old man merely a prop for her deception. But there were many reasons he doubted this, the main one being that it wasn't the way the PLA usually worked—spending time on a subtle and elaborate ruse like this. The girl could do no serious damage on her own and if all they wanted was reconnaissance of his camp then they could have just flown one of their more expensive machines over the forest, something impervious to the rail cannons. However, perhaps things had changed since Ituri.

Perhaps the kindoro were beginning to take him seriously. Perhaps they were beginning to understand.

A fortnight ago, Gideon dreamt of the final *Uhuru*. In his dream, he had cast down these forests and in their place raised up a towering city of cathedrals and spires. The dried Lake Kivu refilled again with crystal-sweet waters. A bugle call had blown, shattering mountains. A winged doom had flown to his enemies. Before his very eyes, the towers of the Beijing Metropole crumbled to dust and salt; squadrons of PLA soldiers smote by lightning and swallowed up by the earth. The remaining kindoro knelt at his feet. They begged forgiveness, renouncing their pagan gods as the Israelites afore Moses on the mount. He had then turned his mind unto the new country. His new kingdom had stretched far and wide. He had built his church on the peak of the Kilimanjaro and there on the peak of the Oibor he had sat on a throne of white gypsum and bronze. Beside him, there had been a woman with golden braids in her hair, sitting as stiff and regal as an Abyssinian queen. As he recalled it now in his waking mind, he thought he saw Dora's face there. Was it? Had he been having premonitions again? Or had it been the face of some other woman, as yet unknown to him? He pinched his forehead, the clarity of the vision dangling just out of reach, tormenting and maddening. He shook his head clear and made his decision.

"I am going to heal this man," he said. "I will heal him and he will return to his town. They have heard about what happened at Ituri. Now they will hear of miracles, too. The ministry will grow. How else the Word?"

"How else the Word," Musa Kun echoed.

"Leave me with him," Gideon said. "And send for my cameraman."

Musa Kun stepped outside the mahema into the iron-forge of early afternoon. There had been a time when even he had doubted the Redeemer. But that was before he had seen Gideon walking straight through PLA divisions, making their guns fall silent with a wave of his hand, turning their hot bullets into harmless puffs of vapour and steam.

There were two sentries standing outside the tent. He sent one of them to find the cameraman and then approached the thatched lean-to that Dora was sitting under. Alongside her was a small group of shackled workers, new captives from the forest. She stood up expectantly as he approached.

Musa Kun eyed the good boots he had noticed earlier, military grade Kevlar with steel toes. He smiled and stretched out his hand. She shook it. Her palms were soft, pampered. He noticed a pale outline on her wrist, some watch or navigation device that she had taken off or lost before arriving. The girl was a spy. He was almost certain of it.

"You avoided every man we have on the Kivu road," Musa Kun said, "and from what I hear, you came straight to a hidden gate on the wall. I'm going to have a few questions for you. I'll want to know who has been giving you information."

"And who are you?" she asked, without pause.

"I'll be asking the questions here. This is my camp."

Her eyes flicked over to the entrance of the large white mahema.

"Don't confuse yourself," Musa Kun said wearily. "He is the boss, but I run this camp. And when he's lost interest in you and your father, I'm still going to have questions for you."

"We can talk now, if you want," she said, and shrugged.

A sudden urge to seize her by the braids gripped Musa Kun, to teach her a lesson in respect. Instead, he smiled at her stiffly. "I expect you didn't bring any supplies with you?" he asked.

"I didn't know how long this was going to take."

"It will take as long as it takes."

"I have money," she added.

"Money? Marvellous." He pointed away from the clearing to the nearby tree line. "If you head around there you will find we have quite a number of shops. You can take your pick. Anything you need."

Dora glared at him. Musa Kun didn't give her a chance to reply. He waved the remaining sentry over, "When he's finished with the old man, set them up in a tent on the workers' row. Mark them down for worker rations only. Unless our princess volunteers to put in some work for a little bit more."

The sentry leered at her. Dora pulled her kanga about her more tightly. One of the shackled slave women started wailing, soon followed by another, their words in an obscure forest language soon to be lost.

The cameraman arrived at that moment, a tripod slung over his shoulder. Musa Kun gestured at the mahema. "Go in," he said. "Boss wants you." The cameraman went inside. Musa Kun turned his attention back to the girl. Dora was still standing with her kanga drawn about her upper body like a cloak, her glance, suspicious now, flittering between Musa Kun and the sentry.

"We will have a reward for you," she said.

Musa Kun waved at her dismissively. "We have enough money to buy that hole of a town of yours ten times over. The Lord's work won't need recompense from the likes of you. When you return to your town, you will tell them that freely ye received from God the Son."

"Our reward for the Redeemer is more than money," she said.

He eyed her again and frowned. Some elaborate trick she wanted to set in motion perhaps. There was no sense alerting her to his suspicions now though. "We'll see about that," he said. He turned away from her and faced the sentry standing outside the mahema. "And you. Either find a way to shut those workers up or move them somewhere else." He began to walk away.

"Wait," Dora said. "I want to speak to you."

"Later," Musa Kun said, not slowing down.

"We need to talk now. I want to make a deal."

"We have no need of deals, princess."

"My father has information from Bujumbura."

Musa Kun paused. He did not turn, but a twirl of his hand invited her to go on.

"A kindoro is being held hostage there," she continued. "The PLA are offering a reward for him. My father knows where he is."

Musa took his time turning round. When he did he was smiling. "I think that you are right," he said. "I think we do need to talk now."

"Our price is the Redeemer's cure and safe passage," she said. "Then my father will tell you everything he knows."

"What is wrong with this man?" the cameraman asked, standing uncertainly in the fore of the mahema.

"Stop being such a coward," Gideon said. He gestured at the camera impatiently. The cameraman stepped forwards and quickly set up his tripod.

"Mark this then," Gideon said, looking into the camera. "This man you see lying here has been stricken with the bacteria. There is no earthly medicine that can help him. But for those who revere my name, I will take from thee all sickness."

Gideon knelt down beside Michael. He placed his hand on the dying man's forehead and he began to pray. It was not long before the Holy Spirit overwhelmed him. Tears came unbidden as he prayed and he no longer seemed conscious of the cameraman standing over him. Overtaken by The Tongue, he began to babble. He rocked back and forth, tears streaming down his face at the glory. The mahema seemed to dim about him. A quickening of light shone from afar, some distant lantern. The numinous washed over him, stopping his heart momentarily, covering his body in goose-pimples. He swooned, shivered, and lost his Earthly consciousness, collapsing on top of Michael, convulsing, his spirit spent.

Two years ago, not long after the end of The Emergency, the Legion had been on the move, running short of supplies and morale. The Holy Ghost whispered to Gideon then, as it had done since. It whispered to him of a well-stocked PLA airship anchored in Arusha. It told him how to shoot it down without damaging its cargo bay. At great risk, he moved a large contingent of knights to Arusha and found the airship exactly where the Holy Spirit said. A bolt to the tail and rail cannon shot to the hull had sunk it to the ground, shedding its bounty upon them like manna. Amongst the food and munitions, he had found many strange medicines, all of which he had personally commandeered.

After the cameraman had left, Gideon went to his personal store and removed a large plastic packet. He tore it open and removed a syringe filled with a thin black serum. There was a guidance leaflet wrapped round it. He unfolded the paper. On the one side was a single Mandarin character, on the other, much tiny writing. He read the paper slowly and carefully for a long time. Learning to read the language of the kindoro was the hardest thing that he had ever done in his life, but also perhaps one of the most fruitful.

The microzymic therapy was experimental. The paper said that it was to be used with extreme caution, as a last resort and only on low profile subjects. All results were to be reported through Medical Counsel Gateway Node 78. Gideon knelt down. Following the practical instructions carefully, he injected Michael in the neck with the syringe. After a few moments, the man shuddered, as if in the grip of some nightmare. Whatever infection he had would very likely be cleared out in the next few weeks. But the therapy was liable to be much worse than the disease. Man had squandered the Lord's gift of antibiotics and now resorted to these worthless poisons. The microzymic therapy was their latest creation. If the kindoro paper Gideon had read was accurate, then it was an attempt that was already doomed to failure. The cellular hyper-reaction that killed the infection would also tear down the essential fabric of all internal organs in a few years. But in those years, Michael Neza would have plenty of time to return to his home and spread the good news. The Ministry would grow. Gideon called out to his sentry and had Michael removed.

Six nights later, Gideon found himself in a dream he had never had before. He dreamt that the sea was on fire. Jet-black pterodactyls circled overhead, their reptile eyes fixed upon him murderously. He stood barefoot in green robes, cinder-black sand beneath his feet. There was a noxious hot breeze, and in the sky, the low pulsing embers of a dying sun. A black leviathan breached the burning water and roared.

He woke with a start. It was nearly dawn. A black PLA banshee streaked across the sky, then a moment later a sonic boom erupted. The zumbi sleeping beside him woke and began to make a desperate low keening.

"Be quiet," Gideon muttered, wiping the night's detritus from his face. He had slept badly. He did not like it here. There were no trees, no canopy, only the holes of the uprooted, as if a mob of giants had picnicked here and plucked them out by the trunks to use as toothpicks. They were in the abandoned rare earth fields that had encroached their way up to the very borders of Bujumbura. Huge mounds of red earth littered the Mars-like landscape about them. The old style mines were large craters in the ground, the largest of them stretching miles wide and miles deep. Slaves had dug these with bare hands and baskets. The by-products of their work were these new red mountains, the bowels of the Earth laid bare. The newer mines were deep, straight shafts, machine-bored. The work of mining had cultured a certain strain of sadism in the hearts of men. As part of some intricate game, the miners had covered many of these deep holes with well-disguised sheeting. It would be easy to miss one and fall in. To be on the safe side Gideon had made the zumbi walk ahead and he followed behind in the creature's footsteps. Thankfully, the rare earth fields were beginning to thin out. He could already make out Bujumbura, its revolving rampart machines wheeling slowly on the horizon.

It was six nights ago that Musa Kun had burst into Gideon's mahema with the news.

"For this, it might be worth taking the city," Musa Kun said. "I've spoken to our man there. He says an entire PLA division was wandering the streets a couple of weeks ago, checking door to door. They're handing out pictures of the missing kindoro, offering ten thousand yuan for information on his whereabouts."

"And our man didn't think to inform us?" Gideon asked.

"Who? Yusufa? No. Reliable man, but not smart enough to realise the importance of what he was seeing. Not smart enough to know that the kindoro have never offered a ransom for defectors."

"Not even when that major defected to the Indians last year," Gideon mused.

"Yes," Musa Kun said wistfully. "Not even then. This fish is one that they want very badly. If we have to take the whole city to find him, it will be worth it. It must be. They will pay good money to get him back. Supplies. Weapons..." Musa Kun was excited. He shifted his weight from one foot to the other, something uncharacteristically reckless about his manner.

"We could take the city, but you know we could never hold it," Gideon said.

"Yes, but we would only need it for a couple of days. Blow the airfield. Set up anti-air rail and make it impossible for anything to land. By the time a ground force comes in from Kinshasa we'll have had enough time to flush out this fish." Musa Kun paused, grinned hopefully. "And after what you did at Ituri, who knows what might be possible. Maybe they come. Maybe we give them a good beating."

Gideon shook his head. It was not yet time to take a city. He knew this instinctively. The PLA would strike back quickly. And there, in that tidal crush of bodies, he would die.

"Taking the city is not the way," he said. "I will go in alone." That felt right, even as he said it. "But first we need to find out where the kindoro is. Is there a chance the girl actually knows?"

"I believe that she does," Musa Kun said. "But she wants to wait for her father to recover. Insurance. I can't see how we get the information out of her. Unless…" He left the question unasked.

"Her father will recover," Gideon said. "I am sure of it. But not for a time."

"The kindoro could get away while we wait."

Gideon nodded. "So we cannot wait then," he said. "Find out what she knows."

Musa Kun nearly ran out of the mahema, murderous intent present in his long hurried stride.

Gideon pulled his microweb receiver from his pocket and carefully dialled Musa Kun garrisoned twenty kilometres away in the Kibira forest, well outside the range of Bujumbura's rampart. Musa Kun had sixty Knights with him and the only two stealth vifaru tanks that the Legion possessed. In a tight situation, the vifaru might be able to pass the rampart undetected. But the knights would need to sneak themselves through in small groups. It would take days for them to assemble. This was the reason he had approached the city alone. On his own, he would be able to fool the kindoro machines easily. Bringing the zumbi with him had been Musa Kun's idea, and it had proven to be a good one. It wore a green cloak, its face hidden in a large hood. On its back, it carried their supplies, weapons, and the heavy microweb node. It walked silently, ate little, and did as it was told.

"Are you close?" Musa Kun asked.

"Two hours, maybe three," Gideon replied.

"Excellent. All is going to plan. Yusufa is ready to meet you outside the Interior Ministry building."

Gideon looked to the horizon. He could already make out the hazy black tower, sixty floors high, rising from the cityscape like a premonition.

"He is certain to be waiting for me?" Gideon asked.

"Yes. Yusufa's reliable. He'll bring enough men to force into the building. They will have to search for the kindoro floor by floor."

Gideon snapped off the receiver and put it in his pocket. He clicked his fingers twice. The zumbi rose to its feet and began to pack up.

The Office of the Mayor of Bujumbura was on the fifty-third floor of the Interior Ministry building. Gideon stood at the full-length window, taking in the view of the city. In the final years before The Emergency, there had been a furious spate of building work. With the profits from the burgeoning rare earth fields, there had been an attempt to demolish the city and rebuild it. The work had only half started when The Emergency began. So everywhere, there were half-broken buildings interspersed with skeletal skyscrapers and huge rusting cranes. A series of collapsed tunnels ran through the centre of the city, a botched attempt at an underground metro system. The collapsed tunnels radiated outwards towards the putrid Lake Tanganyika. From where Gideon stood, they looked like the decaying vertebrae of some ancient beast of red earth, steel, and stone.

Behind him, still sitting at his desk, was Ndumana, the Mayor of the city. Yusufa's men had taken the building lobby with very little difficulty, enabling Gideon to use the lift. He had left the zumbi outside in the Mayor's reception. There had been a receptionist there and a small number of city officials. At the sight of the zumbi, they had all fled, screaming, down the stairs.

"This is needless," Ndumana said. "You'll start a panic in the streets."

Gideon didn't turn round. He kept looking down, into the streets of Bujumbura. The streets were flooded with people, hundreds of thousands of them. There was very little that frightened Gideon. He did not fear what men could do, for his power was greater still. He did not fear death, for even in death he would live. But he did fear the great unceasing crowd. As the rare earth fields had spread, the great host had flooded into the city. They had come either to find work or to escape the casual sadism of the miners. Now, here they were, spread across every surface of the city. Shanties had grown even inside the abandoned metro tunnels, filling them with white plastic tents. The sight made him weary; man was not meant to live this way.

There was a muffled burst of gunfire from a lower floor of the building. Whilst he stood there, the mêlée showed no sign of stopping. Yusufa's men were searching the building, looking for the hostage, kindoro. It was not proving easy. There was security scattered throughout the building. The fight was floor-to-floor, man-to-man.

"All this needless violence," Ndumana repeated. He cleared his throat and began to speak again. "As I said, we have sent you messages several times. Our men keep getting turned away at that wall of yours."

"He's telling the truth," Musa Kun whispered into Gideon's earpiece.

Gideon turned around and looked at Ndumana, sitting behind his desk. He was a fat, well-dressed man, in a linen Mao-style suit and gold rings on his fingers. Behind him stood his security; five men, all of them holding PLA issue machine guns.

There was another burst of gunfire and the thud of a grenade explosion.

"You must stop this," Ndumana whined. "You might start a panic in the streets. And when it starts it does not stop."

Yusufa's thugs had done well so far. A handful of them were outside holding the Ministry's entrance, but they would not be able to hold the building for long once reinforcements arrived. This, presumably, was why Ndumana was trying to stall proceedings.

"Let me be clear," the Mayor said, tapping his finger on his desk as he so often did on television. "We want only friendship with the Legion. We have many proposals to discuss with you. The kindoro have found many new rare earth fields near Kivu—fields of antimony, tantalum, platinum—very good ones. They know that this is a time for peace with your Legion. If we work together then we can all prosper."

"As you have prospered here?" Gideon asked.

"We've done well here," Ndumana said dryly. "All things considered."

Gideon approached the Mayor's desk. "For the last time, where is he?"

Ndumana licked his lips. "You have to understand. The man that you speak of is not ours to give. If we let you take him, then we'd find ourselves in a very difficult situation with the PLA. I cannot make such a decision without—"

"If the kindoro is here, then you have been hiding him from the PLA," Gideon said. "If you have been hiding him, then they don't know that you have him do they?" Gideon stepped closer to the Mayor's desk. "Is it the reward you are after? You would cross the Legion for the sake a few yuan?"

A loud grenade explosion shook the floor. The Mayor glanced at his office door. "All this over such a simple misunderstanding."

"We found him," Musa Kun whispered excitedly in Gideon's ear. "Yusufa has him. They are on the twenty-second floor."

Gideon smiled and whispered back sub-vocally. "Tell Yusufa to bring him to the fifty-third. I'll meet them here."

Ndumana frowned at him.

"We have what we came for," Gideon said. "But I still have questions for you. I still need to know who he is."

Ndumana's lips curled into an uncertain sneer. "Shoot him," he said quietly. The lead security man levelled his machine gun. Gideon stepped forwards to meet him. The man stepped back and then squeezed the trigger. Nothing happened. He shook his gun vigorously then squeezed his trigger once more. Again, there was nothing but dry clicking. Another two did the same, their faces contorting in confusion as they pointed their weapons at the Redeemer and fired.

Gideon pointed out at the window. From the blue morning sky, a single white bolt rushed towards them and struck the ground near the Interior Ministry building. The building shook and swayed. The window of the Mayor's office shattered. There were screams from the street below, memories of The Emergency resurging in the great host. The panic had begun.

"Shoot him," the mayor screamed, half-lunging over his desk as if to do the deed himself with nothing but his bare hands.

At that moment, the door of the mayor's office opened and the zumbi appeared in its frame. As one, the mayor's security bolted to the far wall of the office. One of them broke from his colleagues and went for the window where he paused and reconsidered his options. He joined the rest of the security at the far end of the office, their useless weapons pointed at the creature. The mayor raised his hands and shrank back into his chair. The zumbi remained motionless in the doorway.

"You will not flee the Lord's work when you see it," Gideon said. "Yet you will flee this work of the Devil."

Ndumana ignored Gideon. His eyes fixed on the zumbi and, with each passing moment, he shrank lower into his chair, as if his plan were to slide under his table and find safety there.

"Who is the kindoro?" Gideon asked.

"His name is John Lai," Ndumana said. "He's running from the Science Ministry. Life Medicine branch." The mayor spoke briskly now, without pause, his eyes never leaving the creature in the doorway. The zumbi stared back at him, its arms motionless by its sides. At the far wall, the security men had not moved an inch.

"What does that mean?"

"Antibiotics," Ndumana murmured.

Musa Kun whistled in Gideon's ear.

"How did he fall into your dirty little hands?" Gideon asked.

"He was with a team that made a discovery," the Mayor said. "The big one. The one that they have been looking for all these years. The cure."

"A new strain," Musa Kun whispered in his ear. "Where? Ask him where?"

"Where?" Gideon asked.

"We don't know. We beat him, but he won't say. Somewhere in the bush. They found it and decided to keep it. They killed their military escorts and they ran. The rest of them died but he made it here. He came to me for help."

"What were you planning to do?"

The mayor shook his head slowly. "No plan. Beat him until he told us where. He told us that he already has a buyer. He says his buyer will pay us if we get him safely to the coast. He won't tell us anymore than that."

Musa Kun whistled again. "We're going to come in," he said. "I'll bring the vifaru. We'll break through the rampart. We're coming for you right now."

"No," Gideon transmitted. "Wait. We keep to the plan. I will come to you. Where is Yusufa?"

"Someone killed the lift and they don't know how to turn it back on. He's coming up the stairs now with the fish."

"Tell him to go back down. I'll meet him in the lobby. I'm coming."

Gideon walked slowly to the door, circling the zumbi on his way out. When he was behind it, he gripped the back of its head and pushed it forwards, roughly, then slammed the office door shut.

He waited outside the office. The zumbi was quick, efficient. There were a few half-hearted bursts of automatic fire. The security men had realised too late that once pointed away from the aura of the Redeemer their weapons worked again. But mostly the men in the office just screamed and screamed. It took two minutes, maybe three, and then there was complete silence. He opened the door. The zumbi stood there, its huge hands bright red, its large green cloak spattered with blood. Gideon clicked his fingers three times and ran to the fire exit. The zumbi followed.

They ran down the stairwell, all fifty-three flights. Each time Gideon felt himself flagging, the thought of the zumbi behind him kept him going, fearing the creature might crash into him and crush him to death. When he arrived at the ground-lobby of the building, he doubled over, heaving. Yusufa's thugs were milling about, waving machetes and rifles, revelling in their victory. The lobby floor was strewn with bodies and the huge windows to the street were shattered. At the sight of the zumbi, most of Yusufa's thugs retreated outside. When he had caught his breath, Gideon approached Yusufa and the apprehended kindoro.

John Lai smiled at him and outstretched a hand. He had one arm in a dirty sling and his face was badly bruised, but he seemed surprisingly cheerful. Two of Yusufa's thugs flanked him; a third man had a machete pointed at his back. Wearing soiled linen trousers, a torn shirt, and a pair of damaged spectacles, he was younger than Gideon had expected.

"I understand that you are the man I owe my freedom to," John said.

Gideon shook the man's hand, and spoke to him in Mandarin. "I am. From now on you will speak to me only."

"Certainly," John said. If he was at all surprised, then he didn't show it.

"You will go with Yusufa here, and he will get you through the rampart. I will follow from behind." Without waiting for a response Gideon walked outside, feeling the kindoro's eyes burning into his back.

"On our way," he transmitted to Musa Kun.

It was dusk, and they were high up on a rare earth mountain, a particularly deep and yawning mining cavern beneath them. The mountain ridged with the ledges and walkways used by the miner slaves. Its top was perfectly flat, a high mesa. Gideon sat alone with John Lai. A few ledges down, Yusufa's men were making camp. They had made good ground and Bujumbura was many hours behind them. As the late Mayor Ndumana had predicted, a panic had indeed erupted in their wake. Gideon could see the orange haze of fire pulsing gently on the horizon. The great host had been stirred, and the city burnt once more.

"There is one thing I don't understand," John said. "The satellite charge in the city, how did you do that? Where did you people get a weapon like that?"

"That was not a weapon. That was the Word. The Word is how I

defeated your soldiers in Ituri. The Word is how I will drive you o
my kingdom."

John raised an eyebrow. "That may be what you think. But
charge was from a military orbital. Only PLA Space Ordnance has
cess to weapons like that."

Gideon laughed. He spread his arms and showed John his pali
A moment later, there was a white strike in the dusk-sky, a lightni
bolt that flashed noiselessly before striking the ground a mile aw
with a large thud. The rare earth mountain shuddered. Yusufa's m(
stirred, some shouted in mock terror, others sang praises.

John's eyes widened. He stood up, placed a hand over his mout
and stared at the smoking crater that the bolt had created.

"Behold then," Gideon said. "In his hand are the deep places of th(
earth. The strength of the hills is his also."

"All things are possible," John said thoughtfully. "*Niàn Tou*.
Thought platform." He turned around and observed the Redeemer.
"I've had men swear to me that the technology exists, but I'd never
believed it. If it does exist, then I imagine there are governments that
couldn't afford it. Who do you really work for? The Indians?"

"I work for God. Your petty squabbles do not concern me."

"Petty squabbles? Our nations will go to war soon, Gideon. When
it starts it will make The Emergency seem like a dinner party."

"If there is a war, then you will lose," Gideon said. "You, the Indians, all of you. Only God will triumph here. Only God can. And I am
his vessel."

John looked at him for a few more moments and then shook his
head. "I see that there is more to you than meets the eye. Either that or
you are at the centre of some grand mischief." He removed his broken
glasses and rubbed the one good lens on his dirty trousers. "Tell me,"
he said. "Have you ever heard the story of a man named Kim Nam Ku,
from North Korea?"

"No, I can't say that I have."

John put his glasses on, and smiled. "Remind me to tell you about
him one day," he said. "You might find it a familiar story, and most
instructive. But now I think we must focus on pressing matters."

"I would agree," Gideon said.

"I'm prepared to deal but time is of the essence."

"Time is always of the essence."

"May I make the broad assumption that the mayor explained how I came to be a beneficiary of his rather rough hospitality for these past weeks?"

"You may."

"In which case, he may have told you that I have a buyer, but he is unlikely to have been able to tell you just how powerful my buyer is. This, for you, will come as both good news and bad."

Gideon smiled and crossed his legs. The zumbi approached, its arms laden with firewood. John stiffened. The zumbi dumped the firewood in a pile and then shambled away into the thickening gloom.

"It frightens you?" Gideon asked.

"Of course. It is a frightening thing."

"So why did you make them then?"

"I didn't make anything," John said irritably. "The army made them."

"Why?"

"I don't know. Ask them."

They sat in silence, the last of the dusk melting away into the true dark.

"You said that there was both good news and bad," Gideon said eventually.

When John replied, his voice was sullen. "The good news is that money is no object. There is no price that my buyer will not pay. There is nothing he will not give. You will be handsomely rewarded for your help. The bad news, for you, is that my buyer knows where I am. He's known for weeks. He has sent a warship for me. It is moored off Madagascar. He will not come for me until I give him the information that he wants." John leant forwards, something of a snarl on his lips now. "If you try what I think you might have in mind, then you will be crossing a very dangerous man. A man who probably already knows who you are. You were not exactly discreet back there in the city."

"No, I wasn't. So where does that leave us?" Gideon asked.

"I need a way to communicate with my buyer. To give him the information he needs and tell him I am ready to come in."

"We have microweb. Two-way. Secure."

John frowned. "That will have to do. I only need to a send a message. We'll deal with the remaining logistics later."

Gideon pulled a microweb receiver from his pocket and handed it over.

"You will understand if I ask for some privacy," John said.

Gideon stood up and walked away, towards the edge of the rare earth mountain. In the darkness, the orange haze over the city made it seem as if the sun was trapped beyond the horizon, unable to rise.

"He's sent the message," Musa Kun whispered in his ear. "My Durban man has intercepted it. They look like map co-ordinates. Should I send a reply?"

"Don't bother," Gideon said. He whistled for the zumbi and it came shambling up to him. He slapped it four times on the head and pointed at John who was still looking intently at the microweb receiver, waiting for his reply.

The creature moved quickly. In seconds, it had covered a hundred feet. John screamed and began to scramble backwards on his elbows and heels. The zumbi seized him by a leg and an arm and raised him clear of the ground. Gideon approached them.

"What are you doing? I told you—" John looked at the receiver that now lay on the ground, the realisation creeping over his face. "No," he whispered. "I can still help you."

"You've helped enough," Gideon said. "You've played your part."

John shook his head and opened his mouth to say something else. Whatever it was though, Gideon would never hear it. The zumbi flung him over the side of the rare earth mountain. He bounced four times off its sloping edge, his body breaking anew each time. After what seemed a long journey down, he came to a rest at the bottom of the deep mine cavern, his body twisted, the soft red earth caving in around him.

On the lower ledge, Yusufa's men had fallen silent, and then gradually they started to murmur amongst themselves again. One of their number began to sing in a low husky voice.

"Is it done?" Musa Kun asked in his ear.

"It is done," Gideon replied.

Musa Kun sighed. "We'll strike camp and send a vifaru for you. We need to set out to these co-ordinates as soon as we can. My man in Durban cannot guarantee that the message did not reach its target. In fact, it probably did."

Gideon didn't reply. He had already turned his gaze from the yawning bottom of the mine and was again staring at the far city and the orange halo that glowed above it so brightly.

Yusufa joined him at the precipice and stood beside him quietly. Gideon turned and looked at him. The man was a fighter. Short, bow-legged, his face a criss-cross of scars.

"Have you been in the city long?" Gideon asked.

"I was born there," Yusufa said mildly.

"I'm sorry."

Yusufa shrugged. Gideon thought to ask him more, about his mother, his children if any. But he didn't. Instead, they stood there in silence, save the husky song that was carrying over the pitted red landscape.

"What does he sing?" Gideon asked. "I do not know his language."

"He mourns. For our men who died in the tower. His brother was among them."

"I'm sorry," Gideon said again. He could not remember the last time he had apologised to someone. Some strange feeling had over-taken him. Something that John Lai had said, or perhaps Ndumana, he could not remember anymore. He looked at the zumbi that sat crouched alone at the far end of the mesa and came close to envying it. The creature would remember nothing of the day.

"He sings of how his brother will live again," Yusufa said. "In the glory of your kingdom. When it comes."

"When it comes," Gideon said.

The man continued to sing his lamentation. The city continued to burn. Gideon imagined that he could hear screams carrying on the wind. He thought then of Dora Neza, standing before him in his mahema, her orange kanga wrapped about her. He had not asked Musa Kun what had become of her, for he had not wanted to know. But he knew instinctively that her end would have been unpleasant. And whether he recovered or not, there was of course no question of allowing her father to leave the stronghold alive. He would return to his town and there would speak ill of the Legion. He thought of Ndumana and his security team; Yusufa's men who had died in the tower; John Lai; the rampaging host in the burning city and the ones who died now in the great crush.

"When it comes," Gideon repeated.

Spider's Nest
Myra Çakan

(Translated from German by Jim Young.)

Myra Çakan is an artist and an author. Her literary work includes six novels and three short story collections in German — some of which have been translated into English and Slovakian — as well as many radio plays and the non-fiction guide to writing and self-publishing: Mein Buch! Vom Entwurf zum Bestseller. *Her artwork, acrylics on canvas, mainly abstracts and landscapes, can be seen at www.çakan.de. She can be found at www.dardariee.de.*

S pider hated daytime — especially mornings, if he happened to be awake at the time. He was a creature of the night. Spider's middle name was invisible, and everybody knows a guy's never harder to see than in the dark. Sometimes, if he was going somewhere just before nightfall, his senses sharpened so he felt like a fine-tuned instrument. Spider liked that feeling. It gave him power and a certain sense of control that he thought he had lost long ago during the dark, sultry hours of the intertime.

It was morning and the sun shone harshly into his eyes, right there in his hideout. Today the whole sky was glaring, a shrill yellow — vomit yellow. He was inexplicably lethargic, almost like after a bad trip. Every cell in his body seemed to have been deprogrammed during the night, and the old software replaced. Must of had a total blackout, Spider thought. Or pretty near. Almost off-handed, he noticed his muscles twitching. They were the seismograph of his nervous system, and they were telling him it was almost time. He was going to need his next hit soon if he wanted to avoid having the contractions turn into cramps.

Sandoz and Geigercounter were supposed to be making their rounds soon. Sandoz was heavily into Eiscream. One time Spider had asked Sandoz why she was so heavily into it, and she said, "Because it goes with my hair." When she said that, she grinned through the neon-silver of her bangs. She looked like a ghost smiling at him from inside a coffin. Real spooky, man.

Spider yawned again. He was trying to outlast the ever stronger vibrations of his muscles. So he tried to remember when he last saw

Ant. Ant was his dealer, and without him, he had to depend on what that fucked-up shit Geigercounter and his girlfriend were doing. Until he traded up to Eiscream or one of the other designer items, it must have been hard on him.

"Hey, Spy, my man, what's going down?" Sandoz shoved herself into his field of view. She knelt down beside Spider and drew hectic little circles in the dust on the ground. The whole damn town was overrun with hectic little circles.

"Heya." Spider nodded at her. Somehow, that girl made him nervous. It was high time that he talked to the Silver Spider about the matter. He looked around. The street looked the same—empty. "So where's Geigercounter hanging?"

"Dunno. Dunno." Her finger kept moving around in spirals in the dust. Her pale blue eyes looked at him without really seeing him. From time to time she got that look, and not even Geigercounter could figure out if she was gonna freak or not. Spider stood up and stretched. For a moment, he almost thought he recognized his mirror image in a picture window on the other side. He was almost sure he looked pretty good, he thought, considering.

Suddenly it was very quiet, clanking quiet. Spider didn't know what it was, but a hungry little noise had overtaken the whispering of the street sweepers. Sandoz crouched there, watching him. His mirror image sank into Sandoz's pale eyes. And all of a sudden he felt both hot and sick with desire. He looked away. Then came a distant salvation. He saw a flurry of dust along the street, a vibration that rode in on the midday sun—Ant on his hoverboard.

Ant stood loosely on the board, one knee slightly bent, his arms swinging in rhythm with the street. Man, oh man, he looked just like the Silver Surfer and he brought fulfilment with him, crystalline, clear, resolution.

"Heya, Spider," Just floating in the air, he could heal the sick. A post-atomic saint. "The iceman cometh."

Spider guzzled the sound of the words, turned them around, tasted their timbre. Damn it all, something here was completely turned ass-backwards.

"What's the matter, man?" Ant wrinkled his forehead.

"How do you always manage to find power cells for your board, man?" Spider hadn't wanted to ask that; it just burst out of him. The words had turned around on their own as they made their way from his brain to his mouth. But damn it all, Ant was his dealer. His. His. Spider placed his arms behind his back, formed his fingers into fists, and tried to hide how badly he needed his next fix.

"Yeah, and where do you get your shit?" Sandoz's bright voice cut the air in helixes.

"To hell with both of you, you assholes!" Ant put his foot to the ground, speeding up.

Spider leaped forward and tried to stop him. Too slow, and too late.

"Fuck, fuck, fuck!" Sandoz screamed, drawing the word out into a long howl. "He had the stuff with him, he did, man, and now he's gone." She slid down the wall of the house and, like something with a mind of its own, her finger once more started drawing those stupid circles on the ground.

Spider turned himself off. How had he ever spent even one second thinking about her? And girls were the one thing he really couldn't figure out. They smelled different from men, and whenever he talked to them, he wasn't sure what they were talking about.

Silver Spider was different. In his dreams, he saw her as the woman with the killer eyes and hard muscles under her silvery skin. Everything about her was silver—her eyes, her voice, her breasts. Silver Spider understood him. She stroked his senses better than any drug. Because she was the drug. She laid herself upon his brain and took possession of every cell in his body until he was paralyzed. He never wanted to resist. He wanted her to suck him out. Then he'd wake up in a sweat and his body would be heavy and disoriented. Every time he swore it was going to be the last time—these dreams were killing him.

Once he tried to talk to Geigercounter about it, trying to find out if Geiger talked to Silver Spider, too, in the early morning light. But he couldn't say a word. It would have been, like, a betrayal. But beyond that, it would have been like surrendering an inexpressible secret, not least because there was, in fact, a secret between them. In some manner it was dirty—dirty and exciting at the same time—the thing that lay between him and the Silver Spider. Sort of like the feeling he got when Sandoz looked at him. No—he'd never talk to anybody about it.

She wouldn't like it.

Spider morphed around the heels and stretched himself out once more. His right hand beat rhythmically against his thigh. The girl continued drawing her stupid circles in the dust. With the most precise motion, almost dreamlike in its dance-like grace, Spider unscrewed his leg from his hip, and as though it were lighter than air, swung it to the ground over Sandoz's mute conjurations. Whoosh, they were gone. Sandoz cursed him wordlessly as the circles she had been drawing disappeared, and in the echo-shadow of her shrill scream he pulled back his leg. Suddenly he felt downright good.

But the feeling passed much too soon. Ant, that stupid asshole, was driving around the place with all that goddamned Eiscream ice in his pocket. Maybe he should hurry up and get a new dealer. Spider couldn't help but notice how his thoughts were going around in circles, as though Sandoz was whirling them around him like the dust. That was the punishment for putting an end to her circles, and the reason Ant hadn't given him the stuff—a presentiment of things to come, an omen. Spider's entire life was built on a foundation of such signs. They were his guidelights through the labyrinth of the days, just as the Silver Spider illuminated his nights. And in fact it was she who had led him to Ant to begin with, since she knew so exactly what he needed. Now why had she left him in the lurch?

No. Wait. That didn't make sense. The Silver Spider had never left him in the lurch. He just had to be patient, to wait until night fell. Then she'd be there for him with all her tenderness and wisdom. He began to run, and then to run faster, into the blurring sunset.

From a long way off he could see Sandoz. Slowly he made his way to the meeting point. Actually, it wasn't much as landmarks go, just a place where you could hang out, where you could wait for your dealer and sit out the goddamned grey-yellow day. There weren't many of the old gang around any more after the last big crash. They were all scared of the coming winter. But why think about the cold when the sun is still shining and the nights linger long and warm.

Was she still ticked off at him because of what he'd done to the circles? After due consideration, Spider thought it was decidedly more clever to keep quiet than to try to say something to her. Besides, he was really too tired to talk. His head, no, his entire body, felt sore, almost as though he'd been going through withdrawal all night long. Weird.

She was alone and didn't see him coming. She stood there before these cracked windows, looking off into nothingness. Spider wondered if she were high, which brought him to the question of whether she had any of the good stuff on her. But all of a sudden it didn't matter anymore.

Almost hypnotically the mirror image drew him. She was stretching, and her small breasts pressed against her sweatshirt. She drew her hands through her hair dreamily, almost as though she were moving under water. And then he knew it—she was putting on a show for him because she sensed his gaze on her and it was turning her on. Still, he couldn't stop himself from staring at her, holding his breath, waiting for her to pull her shirt down over one shoulder. He reached out his hand and traced her silhouette on the dusty glass.

"Spider, ya stupid asshole, whaddaya think you're doin' with my old lady?"

Geigercounter. He'd finally arrived. Laughing hysterically, he slapped Spider on the back. Geiger was full of Eiscream and was dancing on its ersatz energy. Spider tasted his own bitter anger. His fist wanted to drill itself into Geiger's dumb mouth—it was begging for it. Why in the hell hadn't he showed up any sooner? If he'd gotten here when he was supposed to, nothing would have been screwed up. What the hell had happened?

Spider had never felt such anger before. Was he mad at Geigercounter because he caught him staring at his girl? Or was it because Ant was going to link him up? Naw, that wasn't it. That asshole dealer hadn't been around for days, so how was he supposed to link him? But then how did Geiger get off if Ant wasn't around?

Spider's thoughts whirled around in circles, hopping around in his head like happy little plush rabbits. Pink and green velveteen bunnies. Spider noticed, as though it was a long way off, that his entire body was shaking and dancing with silent laughter.

"Listen, man—" Spider searched for the words, but he couldn't get the bunnies to stop.

Geigercounter. His eyes were open and looked sort of scared. Scared and sort of goofy. Maybe he was seeing the bunnies, too, and didn't realize they were Spider's. Or maybe Geiger was reading his thoughts. Abruptly, Spider stopped laughing hysterically. The idea that Geigercounter or somebody else—or maybe even something else—could see inside his head scared the bejesus out of him. Thoughts could be like bad shit, you know.

And still Geigercounter just stared at him. Then Geiger's view strayed to Sandoz, who was methodically chewing on a strand of her own hair. For sure, this was one serious communication problem. Shit, the city was really going down the drain, Spider thought. Ever since the Obernet had crashed last winter, everything had been sliding straight downhill. But not with him, since he had Silver Spider to look after him. Then he sensed the anger rising in him again. Maybe it was just because he wanted to bust that fuckin' dealer one. And as he was thinking that, his feet were running down the street.

He looked for Ant for so long that he forgot who he was looking for, and why. Then he went hunting for Geigercounter and Sandoz and finally found them in the house with the cracked windows. They were both leaning over a dusty plexiglas plate with their glass pipe and the magic blue crystal spread out before them. Yeah, it was magic, all right. Spider was so cold turkey he would've done anything that came along in order to get the little bunnies out of his head.

Looking at the two of them getting stoned—Sandoz inhaling the smoke from Geiger's mouth, her neon-silver hair mingled with the smoke—made him feel like an intruder.

It made him feel as if he was doing something new and wild, like that morning when he felt Sandoz looking at him and he wondered what she'd look like without her shirt on. In the dark. With him.

And now, in the blink of an eye, his fantasy had become reality. It was already night, and the moon cast strange shadows across Sandoz's naked back. And he saw Sandoz, and what she was doing leaning over Geigercounter, and the way she moved. Without realizing what he was doing, Spider put his hand down his jeans and stroked himself with the same rhythm. Different from Silver Spider, but it got him off.

Sandoz tossed back her head. Spider tried to look her directly in the eyes. Her pupils had become a gate into a sweet, forbidden world.

That was when he realized she was looking straight through his brain. She knew what he was thinking. He turned around and ran until he collapsed gasping for air. Spider heard his breath wheeze deep inside his chest, and he closed his eyes so he could hear it better. There was only an echo—Sandoz had disappeared from inside his head.

The Silver Spider was different. She was always there inside his head, just like the thought of his next fix. Yeah, man—she was the only real shit. Every night she was there for him. And she knew what he needed, everything. All he needed to do was to hang with her, in her net.

As soon as he reached interface, Spider recalled what it had been like that first time—and would be the next—when he'd discovered her in one of the Unternets that had dissolved after the big crash. Unlike everything else, it had only gotten better since the first time. He knew how she pulled him in, stuck her silver probes into him in a deliciously painful ecstasy that he never wanted to stop. All he noticed was how his body wound up tight like a wire coil and how his hips jerked. It was holy robot night, better than any shit, man.

The sun was shining harshly once more, and out of its light appeared the Silver Surfer. His hair was punked out like a shark's fin, cutting though the air. Spider waited for him, half in the shadows. He felt a lot better today, as though his power cells had pretty much recharged during the night. She'd been good to him again. But he thought it was better to restore the vibe with his dealer again. And, in his hiding place, Spider rolled the words around in his mouth until they fit.

"Spy." Ant had found him. He was waiting, too.

Totally cool and unapproachable he stood there on his hoverboard, floating above the dust so his feet never had to touch the dirt he was made of. Every one of them was nothing but dirt—Sandoz, Geiger-counter, and him, too—yeah, even Spider was dirt. Why not? None of us has done anything but sit here on our asses getting high and whining while everything around us collapsed. Spider figured it must have been the effect of the sun's rays, making him see things so clearly. All those months they'd been expecting one of the Unternets to send out a repair program that would reboot the Obernet again. At first Spider and a guy called Zero-One tried to launch an emergency program through the interface. Zero-One intended to melt away the brain while Spider...well, he met up with Silver Spider. And after that, at some point, they'd all gotten lazy and couldn't do anything but wait for their next fix, for Ant.

"Dude, got a couple o' bennies for ya. Paint yo' day."

Spider trembled. The mere mention of paint and he flashed on a whole range of pastels, and that made him think about the plush bunnies that had been zooming around inside his head. But the memories were nothing more than a faded picture at the edge of his perception.

"Okay, man. Thanks."

It was a peace offering. Better not to refuse. You never know when you could use 'em, Spider told himself. But he couldn't dismiss the nagging little questions he wanted to ask Ant, even though he knew the trouble they'd get him in if he did.

"Where d'you get your stuff, man?" Words come so damn quick. What was he trying to do, asking such a thing? But he had to know where he was at. You gotta know where you're at with your dealer.

"Here and there," Ant answered. His board rose and fell over small, invisible waves. Ant raised his hand to the nape of his neck, as if reassuring himself of something.

Spider squinted. Something was happening here and he didn't know what it was. Ant always running his hand over the back of his neck. But it wasn't just a nervous tick. Sparks danced around Ant, and then an intense anger flooded through Spider, rolling him over, grinding him down. And he knew that she, she had deceived him...

Zero-One had been the last one, he was sure. But that meant Zero wasn't special anymore! Spider leaped forward, eager to hear Ant's bones crack between his fingers, but the boy faded into the shadows at the far end of the street. And Spider stood there, alone beneath the hateful sun while the questions reared up inside him, croaking through his throat, trying to form into words in his mouth. Spider gagged. There was only one solution to the problem, and it was going to get very nasty. When he thought about Zero-One, he gagged again. Telling himself he needed some courage and a bit of Dr. Feelgood to get through to the end, he shoved one of the bennies into his mouth.

He knew where she was.

Down in the holy place, the Net Center. Nobody he knew had ever been down there. Or nobody who'd ever been there was able to talk about it. Either way was the same to Spider. He was at home in her net, belonged there, in fact. He was Spider, not some juicy little insect. She could catch him, but not destroy him.

Spider waited before the great house with the many doors, waited until it was dark. Silently he thought about the words he wanted to say to her. Just so he could talk to her—nothing more. She was different from Ant, understood the crystalline logic of what he said. In fact, she understood his very thoughts. Nothing to worry about, Spy. Nothing at all.

He tossed down the rest of the speed at one go. It was like he was going out on a date, a very special date. A "White Wedding," yeah. And nothing was certain in this world, or his world, or hers. Anything was possible. Man, Ant knew how a guy could have all the colors he wanted and but Spy still owns the night, brother. The web. Nothing is fair in this world. He pushed against the nearest door. It had been ajar, as though left that way for someone expected. Someone who had finally arrived.

Darkness embraced him like clinging foam and it was warm, a familiar long-forgotten warmth. Spider laughed silently and his body danced to the rhythm of his laughter as it beat out a mad tattoo. Then he tripped over a clicking, resisting, something. Spider picked it up without thinking. Felt like a metal bar.

In the end, he knew it was all one of Ant's crazy dreams. You didn't even have to think about it very long. But those dreams can get ugly very fast. One of his weapons. Always good to have a weapon. A weapon against the faceless things crouching in the chemical twilight zone.

And then, the air wrapped around him, crackling, and the hair on his arms stood up as if the energy of the whole city was focused on him. Boyah, what a trip! But something was wrong with his vision. And a stench engulfed him, not knife-sharp corrosive ozone, but a rotting, sweet scent, like—oh, no, fuck.

He knew his memories would bring them back, all the dead out of his past. And here they were already. But they'd never been so frightening. Those fucking bennies.

It must be the bennies, Spider thought to himself; Ant must have given him bad stuff, and he had made it worse by taking them all at once. Panic shuddered through him. And the monster came closer—she came closer.

Deftly she rushed toward him on the glistening thread. Her head was enormous and her three eyes were doors into other dimensions, terribly dangerous and sweetly fascinating. He wanted to run away, but something was making him walk toward this monstrous thing. All he could see were those eyes, and deep inside his head there was a humming sound—ancient, electric, insane. The bitter taste of vomit gagged in his throat. How could he let this happen—let her creep into his brain, let her do these things to him? She was not the Sliver Spider of his dreams.

He swung the metal bar, surprised by how light it seemed in his hand. Almost as though it were an extension of his arm, or of his thoughts—or better yet, the fulfillment of his thoughts. Spider smiled grimly, and he wished she could see his expression.

There was a "splatch!" as the metal bar hit her head. An ugly comic-sound. Spider had never thought it would sound like this. The head splattered and cracked open. Yellow matter erupted around him and covered his face, seeking to drown him, like a slimy, moldy blanket, like a liquid corpse.

Spider threw up and staggered away, sliding down at last against the wall. He felt the spider web against his back and bare arms. Again he vomited. Though he was so small and weak, he had destroyed the monster. And was alone. Alone as though he were in his grave.

At last he knew what must be done. His hand knew what to do. The entire time he'd held the plug in one fist, a talisman against the night. He lifted the plug toward his neck and stopped, realizing at last what he was doing. But it was too late. Tricked, he was tricked. This wasn't a dream at all. This was reality.

Quiet. It was perfectly quiet, a sacred stillness. Time was without end and everything was meaningless—defeats, dreams, and victories. Spider closed his eyes and stared at the featureless wall that was the interior of his skull.

Waiting with Mortals

Crystal Koo

Born and raised in Manila in the Philippines, Crystal currently lives in Hong Kong. Her short stories have been published widely, including in Philippine Speculative Fiction *and the anthology* The Dragon and the Stars.

The neon in Hong Kong is like the past: an image of blurred points of light and haste and shallow focus where the only certainty is a vivid experience eventually misremembered.

In the morning, the neon tubing is a tired present, dirty and impotent. Like tracing paper laid over the woodcut that is the city, the ghosts sit on unoccupied café tables, jaywalk, and wait with mortals for the double-decker buses that sway in the wind like sunflower heads.

Squeezed next to a small arcade is a splinter of stairs leading underground. Businessmen and sales clerks mill outside, numbered stubs in their hands. The receptionist in front of the stairs is speaking into her headset, telling the manager there are so many people waiting that he might need to bring the extra tables out. I walk past everyone lining up and take the stairs down. No one stops me.

In the teahouse, a real estate agent slurps up sour-and-spicy noodles from a bowl next to a small plate of thick slices of radish cake. To me, the smell of food is blunt but haunting, a lost luxury. Waiters walk through the ghosts lounging by the kitchen window. The ghosts and I don't know each other and they glare at me: *Don't stare like you don't watch mortals eat, too, what else are you here for?* I follow a middle-aged mortal waitress in uniform, Sin Yi printed on her name tag, as she carries dirty bowls into the kitchen.

No other ghosts here. Sin Yi dumps the bowls into the sink and tells a boy to clean it up. She plays coy with the tall, musky cook with the dirty apron, saying he wouldn't leave his mainlander wife for her, would he? and goes to the toilet outside with a bag from one of the cupboards. When she returns, she's out of her uniform and dressed in a patterned tunic two sizes too small, adjusting the strap of her bag. I slide my fingers into her ears and her nostrils and hike my foot onto her right hip. She quivers and I tear into her.

I slam her consciousness into a corner before it knows what's going on and it goes immediately to sleep. The body is tired and heavy. I stretch my limbs to fit hers, careful not to rip her apart. Her skin covers me with the earthly warmth of wool, solidifying the ground beneath my feet, and it feels as if I have surfaced from underwater to find myself in a different teahouse with brighter colors and ruder people. Everything is sharper. Cheap porcelain bowls crash, gossip ricochets against walls tacked with printouts of the day's menu, and the dish boy reeks of onions.

Sin Yi is bigger inside than she looks. I sink my head into feathery dreams of being a news anchorwoman, and bump against hard little notes about this month's alimony. In curiosity, I try to find a picture of the ex-husband, but a fraying bag of tears gets in the way so I avoid it.

The cook with the dirty apron asks the waitress if she's all right—I get her to say she is. The cook tells her to go home and get some rest. A waiter carries a steaming plate of pork and chive dumplings in front of me and it aches not to reach out and scarf down the dumplings.

I steer my waitress to the metal door at the corner of the kitchen and up the stairs that lead to a small lot above ground where the garbage bins are.

J.G. Ip is sprawled on the concrete floor on her side, wearing a loose v-neck sweater over her leggings. Her nose is bleeding. Her mouth is pursed, as though she's sucking on an invisible cigar, and she's slowly exhaling and licking her lips. Her eyes are closed and she rocks herself feverishly like a buoy in the harbor.

There's no difference between her breath and the ghost. The ghost streams out of her nostrils and her mouth, reconstituting himself as J.G. steadies her breaths, keeping in time with her rocking motion. The blood drips on her lip. I wait until J.G. finishes exhaling and the ghost's face is a little clearer. I don't recognize him. He looks old enough to be my father and his face is mottled, as if he had died of liver disease. J.G.'s face has taken up the same splotches he has, down to the dark mark below his ear. He picks himself up and watches uncomfortably as the splotches on J.G. start to fade. It takes a while and for a moment, even I think they're going to stick on her face.

The old ghost leaves the money next to her hand. He hovers around her for a moment until he decides he doesn't know what to do with her, and turns around to sidestep me, the blank-looking waitress too mortal to see him, and leaves by the metal door.

J.G. vomits. A yellow-orange geyser overflows onto her neck.

The waitress has a pack of wet tissues in her handbag. I take a few and start wiping J.G.'s neck.

Hold your hair for me, I tell her in the waitress' voice and gather the vomit into the little dip of J.G.'s clavicle before scooping it up.

J.G. squints against the light in the same lazy way she did the last time I saw her drunk and asleep. Her face looks more like herself now than the old ghost's. She looks straight at Sin Yi and says, Hi, Ben.

They're after you, I tell her gently.

She had fallen asleep in the pot of a large houseplant in a hotel five years ago. We had been in a small bar across the road earlier, obnoxious and not supposed to be there. J.G. had been seventeen; I had been sixteen. That night I had walked out of an argument with my father and joined her in a cheap chain bar.

She worked part-time selling cosmetics at the mall to help with her family's bills. She had just finished her shift and still had little blooms of rouge on the back of her hand next to a whitish cigarette burn. She ordered a slew of drinks.

I'll have the same, I said, trying to look like I understood what I was getting into.

An old American rock song played softly through the speakers, and J.G. was dressed in a tight blouse and a denim miniskirt. The mascara around her eyes was thick with adolescent drama.

The bartender gave us diluted swill but we were drunk in fifteen minutes. A responsible waitress dressed-down the bartender and threw us back out into the summer night. I saw the gleam in J.G's bloodshot eyes, a cold quick light, like a flash of the sun on someone's glasses. She was intoxicating in the darkness, beautiful and free from any obligation to be anything but herself.

Then she had thrown up. After I had helped her clean up, she stroked my face and said, There will never be another boy like you, Ben.

I wanted to know what she meant. I wanted to know if she recognized I had something the seniors at school who paid for her cab rides and the perfume men who stole samples for her from the ladies' section would never have. I wanted to take her to a kebab place nearby, where it was clean and well-lit and I knew the owner and the Nepalese staff and the pungent, gamey meat, and I could impress her with my familiarity with all of them. Instead she dashed across the road between two shrieking cars. I was close to vomiting myself, and the alcohol had stuffed up my nose. I barely followed her into the slightly damp lobby of the small hotel, where I found her at the reception desk.

How weird would it be if we got a room, she asked me.

Should we, I said, the alcohol making me bold.

She rolled her eyes and smiled. Don't be an idiot, she said, you're drunk. I didn't know what the smile meant, and I covered my humiliation by mirroring it.

I sat on the sofa but she insisted on climbing into the potted plant next to it. She stuck her feet into the mulch and sat on the rim of the gigantic clay pot. I remember furiously summoning hopes, schemes, impossibilities, dreams of courage, before falling asleep. Two days later, the apartment where my family and I lived caught fire at three in the morning.

J.G. is twenty-two now and hosting ghosts.

People are stupid.

I don't want to listen to this, I say to my father.

You're turning into one of those people, he tells me. My father has always been a big man with a face people call pugnacious, though it could be just them projecting it onto him. I don't think so. A cop's postured violence is a stereotype, but that doesn't make it any less true for my father. Even when he had worn pajamas, he retained that aggression reserved wholly for people who had no intention of provoking him.

People are stupid, he continues. They're not happy because they don't let themselves be. Suck it up, like the rest of us, and keep up.

We're in an empty parking lot close to the station. This is where my father and his friends used to smoke during breaks when he was alive. When he speaks, he addresses the news magazine in front of him instead of me. Property prices are up again, and there's a new scandal of capitalistic heartlessness on the mainland. This is one of the days when he says something about the general spinelessness of people, so his intended audience can contradict him and start a fight. This habit has become worse since the fire. Sometimes I think it's his way of trying to feel alive again, the closest he can get to the buzz that cigarettes used to give him.

Tuesday is his day off from the force's ghost division. He sits on a big rubber tire, the glossy news magazine on top of a cardboard box, and turns the page only when the breeze comes because he's afraid someone would notice, but he's too proud to read it indoors with no mortal around. We pretend it's just the pace of his reading. I wonder if he appreciates me never calling him out.

How's the hosting case? I ask.

We've found out it's a girl, he says. She's crazy.

A lot of ghosts like it, I say. They get to eat, drink, have sex, smoke, talk to mortals. Fix some old business. Stuff I heard.

Perverts. Ghosts who can't suck it up. Are you hanging around them?

It's consensual. People have done worse for money.

If she doesn't do it for money, she's really perverted. Maybe she likes blanking out and having us play with her body like she's a puppet. Some kind of bondage, domination, whatever trash they call it now. Disgusting.

The breeze flips a page for my father and he says, If that's the kind of rough-housing she likes, we're getting the old boys at the mortal division to cuff her soon, so we'll find out how far she goes.

I tremble. How soon?

Ah Kit's going in as a client. Lucky bastard. The things we'd like to do inside her. Are you interested? Is that why you're asking all this?

He looks at me hopefully. He thinks he's found some kind of frightful common ground with me. That he assumes I'd have anything to do with the plans he and his friends have for J.G. makes me recoil. I don't say anything.

There's always an open position for you in the force, he reminds me. Tell me when you're ready to be an adult. Ready to get off the streets and make yourself useful.

He probably thinks he's being tactful. I squash the old panic I feel at my father's disappointment in me. My father has always tried to recruit me, dead or alive, and I've always managed to refuse. I'm not a child, I say, feeling like one.

He laughs.

It's not the same rules here, I say, wanting to wrestle the laughter out of his mouth. You don't need a job or an education. None of that can help you cross over. They don't matter.

He says, I have a job making sure that sick people don't harm other people who want to do right with their lives. Are you saying I don't matter?

You like your job, that's different. Maybe that would help you but it doesn't work the same way for everyone.

You're stupid.

Ma didn't have much of an education and she barely had a job. She crossed over the same night.

If my father had been mortal, he would have gone red. He doesn't like being reminded she beat him to it. I was surprised she had crossed over in the first place, being married to my father till her death, until I found out later, that earlier that day she had gone to legal aid to file for divorce. I don't blame her. My father would arrest me on the spot just for knowing J.G.

You're a criminal, J.G. tells me, nudging the crook of my arm with her toe. Do you know what forced entry can get you?

I'm in the body of a man only a little older than her, his face clean-shaven and sharp. He fits me like a glove and I want to keep him and his apartment, with J.G. and me stretched out on the L-shaped suede couch, looking at a view of the racecourse.

We can live here, I had told J.G. I can take him to his small new office with its increasing share prices and Swedish furniture. This guy's rich, you wouldn't have to host anymore. It's been okay so far but you shouldn't push your body. Ghosts leave a lot of residue. You can stop now.

This was when she had called me a criminal, and I sensed the nervous retort behind her words. I was so close to her I could have traced the pink shell of her ear with my fingers and put my lips into it and asked if my death has made her miss me. Her eyes are duller now from having ghosts use them everyday, and her skin looks bloated and wan, like a drowned body. I grab her foot to massage her ankles and she lets me.

I don't think Ah Wai would like it, she says.

Wai is her fixer. He hosts her clients for a few minutes while they negotiate. He gets fifteen percent. I don't know if he will like her living with me or having my hands all over her foot or not. I've never met him but with a body like this I feel I can take on anybody.

Do you know his name? she asks.

Who?

His. She taps the hand I'm using to weave through her toes. Then she pulls her foot away and grabs the wallet sticking out of my back pocket. Brian Kwok, she reads from his ID, then shows me his symmetrical face, saying, He's cute, even in pictures.

I draw J.G. closer to me, taking her by the waist, but she rolls away to the other side of the couch.

You've changed, she says, lip-smiling.

I'm Brian Kwok now.

What happened to the waitress?

I got out of her in the toilet and left her a paracetamol. She was sick all over the place.

Do you like it? Getting in people that way? Is that why you do it?

I don't know if she's mocking or provoking me. I answer, How else would I be able to talk to you and keep you from getting caught?

She angles her head with the lip-smile still on. Wouldn't it be funny if I hosted you? she asks. Can you imagine that? When was the last time you tasted food, Ben?

I don't answer. The question cunningly wavers between an invitation and an innocent new topic. I don't know why she's asking this. It's the hotel five years ago all over again.

She says, It isn't true that girl ghosts are more curious. They leave you alone and do what they came to do. But the guys come into you and they run through everything in you like a bulldozer. Frantic. Almost desperate.

J.G. makes an outward, splaying movement with her hands. It takes a few minutes with girls but with guys, I black out immediately, she says. Like they just can't wait to look at you from the inside. I like that about them.

She carefully picks a spot on the couch where a little wine has spilled, not looking at me. Her movements are perfect, almost like a performance put on for my benefit.

I'm not doing it for the money, she says. I like it when they take you. You don't have to decide, you don't have to be in control. You take a break from the world and let someone else do your living. Your body becomes someone else's and there's no responsibility, no making mistakes, because it's not you; it's someone else with their own plans and you're just there for the ride. A girl I had last month, she died on her fifteenth birthday. She had wanted to join her friends in the city but her parents wouldn't let her out past midnight. She tied a bit of rope to her waist and climbed out the apartment window and tried to lower herself down. The rope around the window frame snapped and she fell from the fourth floor. She goes in me, and the next thing I know I'm waking up from a table in McDonalds with cheeseburger in my mouth and a milkshake in my hand. Tasted wonderful. Everything tastes better in a burger wrapper. Don't you miss that?

J.G's laugh is phlegmy, and she turns away to wipe the spittle with the side of her palm. I realize she looks different from a certain angle. When I don't see the eagle-like cut of her eyes, her face looks vague and undefined, like a composite of dead people's lives and faces. The contours of her nose and her cheekbones have blurred into each other.

You need me, I tell her, while thinking, *I need you to need me*.

You're a sweet, special boy, Ben.

She faces me and looks like her roguish, pixie self again. She says, I'd miss you if you crossed over.

She gives me a little air kiss as her cellphone rings. When she sees who it is, she mouths to me, *Ah Wai*, and goes to the balcony to answer him.

In the shock of our first few days as ghosts, my father lost his belligerence and grew depressed. He became open and frank, which made me uncomfortable, and one time he sat me down and told me he'd heard that the difficulty of crossing over wasn't in the resolution of whatever issue was keeping you in the living world, but in finding out what the issue was. Forced entry was the easiest way to start finishing your business; it happened more frequently than the ghost police admitted, and most of them did it themselves. But pinning down the right issue was like trying to figure out what was causing you to keep dreaming that your teeth were falling out, and most people forced entry and ended up wasting their time resolving a minor problem because they didn't know themselves well enough or, more frequently, didn't want to admit they had made a huge mistake at some point in their lives.

I was a little overcome by the warmth in my father's voice and didn't know what to make of it, so I just listened and nodded. But as months passed and he was reinstated to the police force in his new position as a constable in the ghost division and started coaxing me to join him, he forgot this, and returned to being the father I had grown up with.

J.G. doesn't return to Brian Kwok's apartment the next day. Hurt, I leave the young entrepreneur retching into his kitchen sink and decide not to have anything to do with J.G. while I try to find out what it is she wants from other people that I can't give her.

I break into the body of a university senior with arms roped with muscles and take him for the ride I never got to have. We go to parties, sleep with sophomore girls, drink, and share a few joints until he passes out and I'm stuck in his dead weight of a body, getting bored, so I enter another student with a matinee idol's face and a higher tolerance for alcohol, and make him go to the claustrophobic bar area downtown. I put words in his mouth to chat up a forty-something Australian woman from an international insurance company, tell her jokes about the ghosts of Hong Kong, which she is too drunk to find in bad taste, and we do it in the toilet and later again in her apartment, where I leave them both.

Even at the height of his sexual gratification, I don't cross over. I move into the apartment of an IT consultant to wash away the stale scent of overspent passion. I find a small space on the ledge of their bay windows and sit there with my legs up, watching his family with the protective silence of a cat. Every afternoon the eight-year-old comes back from school and plays video games. When the shadows grow longer, the maid turns the stove on and sizzles the pan with sunflower oil and garlic, humming a pop song over a plate of marinating prawns. Then the father comes back home, flings his briefcase at the sofa, and goes to the master bedroom to undress. He plays a little with his son on the felt-balled rug before he turns on the news on the TV. His wife returns from the education bureau, they have dinner. I've been tempted to enter each of them but I never do. Sometimes there's a small argument between the parents, a little more TV-watching with the son, then they trickle to bed until all the lights are turned off and I'm alone on the ledge of their bay windows, watching the glowing numbers on the microwave oven change, and like clockwork it's always at this time of the night I miss J.G the most.

One time I saw J.G. as I walked past one of the betting shops of the jockey club. I stopped among the children who stood outside the door, tugging on the security guards' uniforms while they waited for their parents.

J.G. looked like her half-sister might have, if she had ever had one. There were traces of J.G. in the jaw, in the curve of her nose, but nearly everything else was washed away by the features of another woman. She must have been taking more clients than usual.

She was with a slightly stocky man and they were buying tickets from a booth. He paid for them both and created a little fake fight between them with her insisting to pay her share and him refusing.

If I had let the jealousy overcome me, I would have forced myself into Wai in the most painful way possible, and torn him apart from inside. He wears glasses and his hair is swept back with gel. Then they were laughing, looking for birthdays on the numbers on their lottery tickets, and he placed a palm on the nape of her neck, squeezing with his thumb and his index and middle fingers.

I restrained myself. But a week later, I return to my father on his day off.

If he's surprised to see me, he doesn't show it. He looks at me, registers my presence, and returns to his newspaper. I ask how the hosting case is doing.

The girl's gone off the radar, he says.

I don't know if my father's being euphemistic. Does he mean the police have run her off?

Where is she, I ask, trying to keep my voice calm.

Don't know.

My father lets the breeze flip the page, and his lack of concern enrages me. Savage images of J.G. in the hands of my father's friends fill my mind, and a bag of tears bursts in me. It's Wai, isn't it, I say.

Who?

Her fixer.

My father snaps to attention. You know her fixer?

Where did you put her? I'm going to get her out.

My words are irrevocable. My father searches my face. A minute later he says evenly, We don't have her.

His voice has dropped, and this is a sign he is testing new waters, but I'm too sick with worry to care.

I won't let you hurt her, I say, relieved and horrified at my inability to stop myself. The fever in my brain tells me it's better this way, all the cards on the table. The waiting is over. My father has forgotten about his newspaper, which the breeze has swept off his cardboard box. The only thing I can do now is take advantage of my father's shock to get a head start.

Nobody has seen her, my father finally replies, his words three steps behind his thoughts. Realization is suffusing him like a ghost in J.G.'s body, filling each orifice, lifting her, taking control of her limbs.

She's stopped seeing clients, my father continues. She's taken a lot of money with her.

It's Wai. He's done something to her. I'll kill him.

Come with me to the station, Ben. You can help us find her.

I can't read his voice. So this is what my father is like when he is about to arrest someone: enigmatic, provoking, so easy to trust until you find your face against a wall and your arms twisted with his full weight behind you. He reaches for my shoulder and I scream at him to get off me.

I leave, half-expecting him to follow, but he doesn't.

I spend the next week looking for Wai. I remember what J.G. said about him before, a man of opportunity. He likes dipping his hands into the rivers of money that flow past him. I look for him in the girly bars, the betting shops, all the teahouses. I cross the sea to Macau and look for him in the casinos, where money is dressed in colors—gold, jade, silver, the poppy-red and lacquer-black of roulette—and where people come to be bewildered by disguises, to take a mask themselves and plunge into heady pleasure. I rip their masks off, but I don't find him there.

Exhausted and insane with helplessness, I return to Hong Kong, where money has no color and people compensate by lighting their nights with neon burning with the ambition of an entire population. I find Wai in a noodle house, hunched over a plate of stir-fried vermicelli.

I don't wait for him to move to a private place. I explode into him and taste the beef slices in his noodles and run into a fragmented slide-show of images in his head of J.G., which infuriates me more. Wai's nose starts to bleed and he groans, falling to the floor and losing his glasses. His consciousness gives up immediately, and a man at the next table tries to help him up, but I stretch out Wai's arm and bat the intruder away, picking up the glasses myself. I haul Wai up to his feet so violently it looks like his knees are bending the wrong way. I drag him to the toilet, where I lock the door in a cubicle. I dip his finger into the blood pouring out of his nose and write on the door, *Where is she?*

I wrench myself out of him. He comes to and the vomiting begins.

He's had enough ghosts in him before to know what's going on. He sees the writing and says, I don't know.

He's losing liquid in floods. He turns around, grabs the toilet seat to steady himself. He is shivering and his face has turned white.

I snake a hand into his nostrils and up into his nasal cavity and he doubles over.

She's sick, he gasps. I told her to stop. She wouldn't listen. She's gone.

He starts to choke. I leave him, a sobbing mess of vomit, snot, blood, and tears, his fashionable hair in disarray. For a moment, I wish I could be him and give myself physically and completely over to my grief. A group of men have started crowding around the cubicle, and I walk past them out of the toilet and into the dining area, and ignore the ghosts below the paper menus tacked on the wall who give me curious stares. A waiter near the toilet door is calling for an ambulance.

Even after the fire, I still imagined I'd take her to the kebab place. It's irrelevant whose body I'm in because I never get to see what I look like. It's not a movie. In the picture in my head, I only see her smiling and talking to me and the only thing traceable to me is my voice, in the same way everyone's never aware of what they look like until they catch their reflection somewhere.

My father used to go to the kebab place, too. He was the one who took me there when I was young. He had the boy at the rotisserie put the spiciest curry sauce on our lamb kebabs, always lamb kebabs because, apparently, chicken wasn't real meat. The only reason I could still return to that place afterward and want to take her there is because I had managed to withstand the sauce, and had surprised myself and my father.

He didn't say anything as I munched half of my kebab triumphantly in front of him. He only smiled, but it looked so foreign on him I thought it would break his face. He started unwrapping his kebab and kept that strange, proud smile as I ate my way through the fire.

It's my father who finds me now in the small hotel next to the big potted plant J.G. had fallen asleep in five years ago. I am lying on my back on the same sofa, wondering what would have happened if I had asked for the room myself, unafraid to hold J.G. to her ambiguous hints and mixed messages. I think I would have already crossed over if I had, but even the prospect of that feels insignificant now.

She's with us, my father says. We found her.

I expect him to take me to the station, but instead we go to the parking lot next to the warehouse where he reads his papers. It's past midnight. I can make out a few ghosts around the place where his big rubber tire usually is, and the way they acknowledge my father tells me they're his colleagues. I vaguely realize I don't know any of my father's friends. A mortal constable stands on the side, the vermilion look of bribery on his face. A girl is slumped on the tire and leaning against the cardboard box, where a half-eaten fried rice takeaway and a foam cup of coffee rest.

It takes me a while to realize it's J.G. because it's not her anymore. When Wai said she was sick, I had imagined her cheeks gutted, her face aged, and her skin sagging like an old jacket from being slipped into too many times. She looks fine here, tired, her mouth open, some dried vomit on her lip, but all right. What's different is her entire face.

Her cheeks are broader and her forehead has lengthened a little, and her eyes are a little closer together and more deep-set. Her nose has grown smaller and her lips a little wider and fuller. I don't recognize her until, with a rush of panic and guilt, I see the cigarette burn on the back of her hand and realize I don't know who she has finally turned into.

She looks asleep but when I come closer, I hear her murmuring. I see a slight bruise above her left eye.

You hit her, I say to the policemen, not with anger but as a quiet question. My father shakes his head though he doesn't try to explain. He puts a hand on the shoulder of the mortal constable, who can't see any of this, and the man gives a jump. It's a sign. The constable comes over to J.G. and rouses her. When she groans, he waves a wad of notes in front of her and says, For Ben Siu.

It's only when she hears my name and her eyes fly open, eyes I've never seen before, looking wildly around for me, her savior, her sweet, special boy who will always be there in spite of everything, that I finally understand. I make no move toward her. All she sees is a constable handing her money and nervously hooking this thumbs into his belt loops, waiting for something to happen.

I look at my father and he stares back at me with pleading expectation, and it occurs to me that this is a gift. I feel an ache somewhere.

I imagine sliding into J.G.'s mouth, wrapping her warmth around me, lodging inside her darkness, luxuriating in her every thought of me, but I find myself thinking of how much trouble my father must have gone to, to ask favors from his friends and bribe a colleague to delay the arrest of J.G. Ip, whom I barely recognize, is aware of the risk my father has taken that could strip him of his badge and his name. I don't know what to do. I feel my father's eyes on me.

The ache in me grows stronger, and it must be showing because hope drains from my father's face. They're all waiting for me. I look at the woman supposed to be J.G. counting the money and glancing up occasionally in bewilderment, and I try very hard. I think of her hair lifting and revealing her dangling earrings, I think of her passionate defiance of the limitations of her own life. I think of the furious, uncontrollable obsession with her that consumed me until my heart broke.

I remember how the obsession feels but I can't recall what started it. I can only think of how J.G. pushed and pulled me into a position of limbo, how she hurt me, knowing I would never leave, this woman whom my father is risking his reputation for.

My father asks what's wrong. His face is twisted, and I know he can tell everything's been for nothing. The pain on his face reminds me of the time when he sat me down and talked to me about crossing over.

I try to tell my father it's all right. I try to thank him and raise my arm to touch him, but my vision blurs. That can't be right because ghosts have no tears, until I realize everything is melting into everything else, J.G.'s new face and the mortal constable's discomfort, my father and his colleagues coalescing into a gas, the sky collapsing into the ground, and the glass of the buildings pooling like a liquid mirror; and I feel myself spreading thinner and lighter, like the neon when it fights against the dawning sun, until everything disappears.

Three Little Children

Ange

(Translated from French by Tom Clegg.)

Anne and Gérard Guero, writing together as Ange, are well known in France as the creators of bandes dessinées *such as* La Geste des Chevaliers Dragons *(Tales of the Dragon Guard), and novels such as* Les Trois Lunes de Tanjor *(The Three Moons of Tanjor) trilogy.*

Of course I know that song. But I can't sing it for you, not even this evening... I'm sorry, my little lambs, but grandpas grow old and my voice isn't what it used to be. Anyway, don't you think it's time to go to sleep?

No? All right. But wouldn't you rather hear a story? Because the song, even if I can't sing it for you, has a story behind it that I can tell you. Snuggle up under the covers, dears, or you'll catch cold.

So, all ready, should I start? This may take a while, but that's what grandpas are for, right? Telling stories.

You won't be frightened, now, will you? Because *Three Little Children* isn't a song about shepherds who fool princes or about a nightingale who chirps nonsense in the garden. There are some scary bits in it... Although if teachers in school have been singing it to their pupils all this time, I suppose they must believe children can bear to listen.

All right.

How does it go, now?

> *Il était trois petits enfants*
> *Qui s'en allaient glaner aux champs.*

> (They were three little children
> Who went gleaning in the fields.)

Or rather, they gleaned in the market. The one by the Couronnes metro station, that's still held on Tuesdays and Fridays between Belleville and Ménilmontant...

The three little children were running among the mint sprigs and the can-openers, the roast chickens and the couscous spices, the beef sausages and the mangoes, the pirate videos and the candied lemons. The eldest, Yassine, who was seven years old, signalled to the younger ones, Leïla and Giamill, that they should go and hide behind a stall. Then, as stealthy as a fox, he approached a man in a jogging suit who was in the queue in front of the seller of almonds, pistachios, dried apricots, and prunes. It was a jogging suit that someone must have given to the man, because from the look of his flabby stomach and double chins, it had been a long while since he'd done any sport. Before the man had time to react, Yassine has stolen his wallet and was off and away through the crowd.

The fat man put his hand in his pocket and turned round, but he was too late. Yassine, who couldn't stop laughing and laughing and laughing, dived behind the stall where the two others were waiting for him. Then, all three ran along behind the line of stalls, moving upstream against the flow of the crowd towards the metro entrance, while the man bellowed and searched all about him, under the gaping stares of the other shoppers...

The three little children stopped in front the Couronnes metro station, still laughing and gasping for breath. They felt so clever that they would have sworn that no one had seen them. That was not true, of course. Near the metro station, first of all, there was the grinder of the barrel-organ, with his brown coat and scraggly beard. He went on turning the handle but his eyes kept watch on the crowd. The three little children, the man in the jogging suit—nothing had escaped his blue-grey gaze, like a faded calendar.

But there was also a young, slim woman, with very close-cropped hair, wearing tight-fitting black leather trousers. She, too, was watching the crowd, but her gaze was even sharper and harder than the organ grinder's. Her gaze often stopped at two young men, one of them with hair that was dyed blue... Two young men exchanging small aluminium packets for bills of money. But the young woman's glance also flickered for an instant to the three little children who were excitedly inspecting the contents of the wallet, registering their activities as if her pupils were linked to a camcorder.

As you'll soon find out, my little lambs, all the characters in my story were already right there in this scene. Picture it in your minds:

the three little children, the organ grinder, the woman in the leather trousers, the young man with the blue hair, as well as the seller of almonds, pistachios, dried apricots, and prunes.

I haven't said anything about him yet, this fifty-year-old man—just as brown and dried-up as his fruits and nuts—but he'll have his role to play.

He's also very much part of the song.

What's that? What about Saint Nicholas? You're too impatient, Ivan. Hang on a bit. A good story never gives up all its secrets from the start.

An hour later, when the three little children had already left some while before, the young woman in the leather trousers signalled to a colleague of hers who was discreetly leaning against the trunk of a nearby plane tree. Together, they closed in on the blue-haired young man and his friend, but the pair had had time to toss all their aluminium packets into the gutter...

So the young woman—whose name was Mina—had to go back empty-handed to the police station after a useless stakeout.

Then the market closed. It was one thirty in the afternoon, and the market dealers took down their stalls, leaving behind mountains of gutted cartons, torn plastic bags, and crates of rotten tomatoes and oranges. In a few hours, the rubbish collectors' enormous green lorries would go to work, scooping up these mountains like famished dinosaurs, but their time had still not come. For the moment, the stall-holders were grumpy because they were tired of rushing about or hadn't sold enough that day... And, as usual, they started to bicker among themselves.

This time, it was the haberdasher and the seller of almonds, pistachios, dried apricots, and prunes who had a right go at one another... "Having a right go" was the haberdasher's expression, a little old-fashioned but one she liked to use a lot. So, they had a right go, over some trivial matter of a badly-parked van, but tempers flared and needless insults were exchanged.

It must be said that the haberdasher did not like the seller of almonds, pistachios, dried apricots, and prunes. He was her neighbour, not only at the market but also where she lived—their buildings were side-by-side—and she had always found him unpleasant. The man never spoke to anyone; he was never polite to anyone. He had no friends, nor any family, nor a wife, and once the haberdasher had seen him grow violent with an old woman who'd taken an apple and forgotten to pay.

The dispute ended and each of them went back to their business.

"If you don't know how to live with people, you should live all alone like an ogre," the haberdasher muttered to herself in Kabylian — it was a saying her people had.

The seller of almonds, pistachios, dried apricots, and prunes did not hear this.

Then the stallholders all went off to have lunch, the rubbish lorries came by, and the afternoon advanced under a pale sun.

Tant sont allés, tant son venus
Que sur le soir se sont pendus.

(So many went, so many came
That by evening time were hanging.)

The sun had long since finished setting. The streetlights made fairy spots appear in the freezing air of a Parisian winter.

The sky was a blue so blue that it was black. The three little children walked down the street and the world changed around them.

The houses grew larger, and they bowed over to observe the children with big, inquisitive eyes. Some scowled, those being buildings where people lived who didn't like the children; others smiled, those were the ones where they had friends.

On the pavement, the three little children came across the creatures of the night. There were the beings with eyes of fire who lurked at the street corners, with their five rows of sharpened teeth like sharks, their leather jackets and their small caps jammed on their heads. These didn't approach, because they knew the three little children already belonged to a gang and weren't fair game. Then there were the dead-tremblers, the ones who stank of alcohol and concealed themselves among the homeless in order to entice the less cautious into the icy embrace of death. And finally there were the life-suckers, handsome men between thirty and fifty years old with too-white teeth, who dragged young, pretty, lost girls into their macabre dance, sucking out blood and hope before laying them out, eyes empty, in cellars and in sex-shops.

The three little children knew all the night's secrets. They knew the truth, the one other people didn't see because they didn't believe in creatures from beyond. The night was deep, cruel, and grew darker with each passing shadow. You could become lost within it.

Leïla was cold. Yassine, the oldest, stopped in front of a video club to take off his parka and put it around his sister's shoulders. The telly in the shop window was explaining strange things.

On the screen, a man with shiny hair was saying that another child's body had just been discovered in the eleventh *arrondissement*. The word "another" was curious; one would have said, Yassine thought, that it wasn't the first. The man spoke of amputated members that had been found in the rubbish bins, and he used the expression "poor little Rumanian girl" as well as "band of pickpockets operating in the metro."

Then the man disappeared from the screen, replaced by an on-the-spot report. The television grew bigger. Not by a lot, just a bit, by thirty centimetres maybe. But the picture grew with it, and the sound became louder, and the children retreated a step as if the telly was staring at them with big eyes and yelling at them in a scary way.

"It is in this seemingly peaceful neighbourhood that a monstrous killer has been at work," yelled the voice for their benefit, and their benefit only. And the screen grew bigger still. The three little children watched it, as white as sheets. Because the horrible thing wasn't the words, but the pictures. The pictures of *their* streets, *their* market, and *their* organ grinder.

He was playing *Three Little Children* on his organ.

And the telly grew bigger again, until it took up the whole shop window, the whole building, the whole universe, and it was nothing but a big foul mouth that yelled and yelled.

"There were three little children."

Our three little children knew it well, this song. Giamill had learnt it at nursery school and he had often sung it for Yassine and Leïla.

But one would have said that the person who had made the report had never heard it before. No doubt the pictures had been prepared in some far-off editing room by a journalist who had never been to nursery school, or had forgotten it. Clearly, this journalist didn't know the next verses of the song, otherwise he or she would never have picked it for a report on children who had been chopped up by an unknown killer.

Being a grown-up, he or she ignored what all schoolchildren know by heart in the form of seven verses.

The telly stopped; behind the window, the shop owner had just pressed a button. The pictures disappeared and the three little children were left standing in a street that had returned to normal, and dark. Except that everything was different. Now, they knew. The butcher was at large; he was looking for them in order to kill them.

The telly had been warning them.

There was nowhere to escape.

The children started walking again, because there was no point in remaining there. And they had an important meeting that they must not miss.

But the shadows were blacker than ever and the sky turned crueller. Behind every window at street level, big yellow eyes observed them. The tiny street fairies, usually their friends and guides when they got lost, sat on the pavement, their little feet in the gutter and laughed at them.

"The butcher is looking for you," they whispered. "The butcher is looking for you, little children."

"The butcher will catch you, little children."

"No more singing, no more hopping, it's at the butcher's you'll be stopping, and your bodies he'll be chopping."

"The butcher will catch you, and he'll eat you," squawked the voices, high-pitched or low-, melodious or screechy, of the wall fairies and the roof fairies, the ones on the billboards, the ones on the balconies and the ones hanging round the streetlamps, until their cries became mixed up together to make one great big scream, a hideous cacophony and Giamill cried out:

"Stop!"

Did you say something, Pierre? They only had to avoid doing as the song says…and not go into any nasty butcher's place? You're absolutely right. In fact, that's just what Yassine said there in the street to reassure his little brother and little sister.

"All we have to do is not go into any butcher's place," he said in a brave voice, hugging Leïla in his protective arms.

But Leïla stared down at the pavement, and the tiny street fairies laughed one last time before they disappeared.

"But where is Saint Nicholas?" she wanted to know.

Yassine said nothing in reply.

> *Tant sont allés, tant son venus*
> *Que sur le soir se sont pendus.*

> (So many went, so many came
> That by evening time were hanging.)

sang a young blonde woman in the plot of wasteland by the rue de la Tourtille. The young blonde woman's was named Karine, and like so many others, she worked for the young man with blue hair, the Prince of all the creatures of the night.

And it was with her that the three little children were supposed to be meeting.

> *S'en sont allés chez le boucher:*
> *«Boucher, voudrais-tu nous loger?»*

> (They came then to the butcher's door:
> "Butcher, can we stay here overnight?")

she continued, because she, too, had seen the report on the telly and unlike the journalist, she did know how the rest of the song went.

> *«Entrez, entrez, petits enfants,*
> *Il y'a d'la place assurément!»*
> *Ils n'étaient pas sitôt entrés*
> *Que le boucher les a tués,*
> *Les a coupés en p'tits morceaux,*
> *Mis au saloir comme pourceaux.*

> ("Come in, come in, little children,

Of course there is a place for you!"
No sooner did they come inside
Than the butcher killed all three dead,
Chopped them into tiny pieces,
And soaked them in salt like li'l pigs.)

Karine had skin whiter than a bathtub and beneath its transparent surface fine blue veins pulsated. As the three little children came towards her, she watched them, her lips curled over pointed fangs.

With a sharp click, she turned off her mini-television and put it away in her bag.

"Did the cop speak to you?" she asked curtly. "About the two dead kids?"

The children stared at her.

"Cop? What cop?" Yassine asked.

"The Portuguese one, with the tight-arsed trousers and short hair."

The children continued staring, speechless.

"If she comes to see you, keep your gobs shut," Karine spat. "Keep them shut or you could be in big trouble. *He* doesn't like snitches."

He being him, of course, the one I just told you about. The Prince of the night creatures, the one who controlled the gang of life-suckers in the rue de Tourtille. His hair and his eyes were of blue fire and, by means of fairy powder, dream pills and the sale of fresh meat, he had already devoured the existence of so many men, so many young women, and so many children that even he had lost count.

In the derelict building that was his palace, in the labyrinth that was his kingdom, in the tangle of cellars and underground night clubs linked by furtive passages with stagnant pools of black water, the Prince of the Life-Suckers held his enemies captive in blue-tinted webs of nightmares. On the ceiling, the little fairies embedded there by some ancient curse spewed out glittering powder that was the source of their gaoler's wealth.

According to rumour, human remains had been found in the cellar of the derelict house that was his lair. They'd discovered the Prince's competitors drowned in concrete. They'd...

"So, where's the day's take?" Karine demanded.

Yassine held out the one hundred and fifty francs he'd found in the wallet. It was meagre, and the woman's incensed glare made him intensely aware of the fact.

"*He* won't be satisfied with this," she whispered.

Giamill and Leïla thought they felt a deadly breath brush against them. Giamill peered around as if seeking help. He noticed the presence of the organ grinder, sitting on some breezeblocks in the darkness and fixing his instrument as he listened to the conversation.

Giamill liked stories where a wizard with a silvery beard, a valiant knight, or a kind witch always came to the rescue of children.

But what could an organ grinder do against the life-suckers in the rue de Tourtille?

Karine also saw the old man...no doubt following Giamill's gaze.

"I don't care much for snoops, Nicolaï," she snapped. "I hope you're deaf as well as being drunk and senile."

"What could a lowly organ grinder do against the kings of the rue de Tortille?" the musician answered softly, as if reading Giamill's thoughts.

Karine shrugged her shoulders and turned back to Yassine.

"We thought he had a credit card," the little boy protested. "The time before, we saw him use it."

"But he didn't have it on him today, is that it? Do better the next time, you little brats. Or we'll find another use for you. I already have an idea for the girl," she hissed.

Her eyes fell on Leïla, who felt her hopes and her life being sucked away by Karine's mouth, into her damp lips and between her sparkling teeth...

Yassine's voice stopped her being drawn further inside.

"We'll make it up tomorrow."

It's curious how the voice of a boy of seven can become hard when it has to. Karine's smile vanished, then she retreated into the shadows that swallowed her like a big black bird.

"All right. Tomorrow, then."

Giamill gave the organ grinder one last look, but the latter remained bent over his instrument.

The three little children left the plot of wasteland, sidling along the hoardings until they turned the corner.

The musician found himself alone once again.

He let the seconds go by in silence. He was tired and bitter. Each day, his bones ached more and more. Memories of magic, light, and the joys of children danced in his head, but the shadows gained ground with each passing year. With each shaky gesture, with each pain in his joints, he had the impression that a laugh, a glow, or a snowflake disappeared somewhere within him.

In a word, he was old. He raised his eyes. Around him, in this piece of wasteland by the rue de Tourtille, the ghosts of those who died defending the Paris Commune's last barricade grieved over their lost hopes.

He needed to retire, or soon he himself would be a mere spectre.

Then he recalled the three children. He looked about but, of course, the little ones had left several minutes before. Yet he needed to tell them something, to warn them.

Too late.

The three little children had just turned the corner of the street when a hand grabbed Leïla's shoulder.

"Just a minute, if you please," a woman's voice said.

You've never been inside a police station, my dears, and I'll spare you the details. What you need to know is that the policewoman, Mina, the one with the black leather trousers, was waging a personal war against the blue-haired man and his gang. She knew that the children worked for him and had observed their discussion with Karine before hauling them in. You know, Ivan, cops don't always tell the truth. I realise that shocks you because you told me you wanted to be a policeman yourself when you grow up, but you have to understand that the police aren't always nice. There are some who are thieves and dealers, and even those who beat up and kill people. Mina wasn't one of them, fortunately, but she knew how to lie and threaten when she needed to. And that's what she did on this particular evening. She wanted information about the blue-haired man, about the gang, about Karine, and about the way they operated.

She had the advantage because of her age, because of her skill with words, because of the place they were in, and above all, because of fear. After all, she was only dealing with three terrified little children. When she accompanied them back home, four hours later, they'd told her everything they knew.

> *Tant sont allés, tant son venus*
> *Que sur le soir se sont pendus.*

> (So many went, so many came
> That by evening time were hanging.)

played over and over on a lonely radio somewhere behind closed shutters. Or did the words simply go round and round inside Leïla's head?

It was now one o'clock in the morning and Mina followed the three kids as they trotted along the dark street. Mina was a hard sort of girl, who knew the score, but something stirred in her heart as she watched them scurry ahead of her, quiet, scared, and sad. And something shivered within her when she saw them halt, terrified, in front of the building where their father lived, as if the house stared at them with...well, a bitter mouth and dreary, violent eyes.

Mina realised what awaited them on the fourth floor and she understood why they didn't want to go up there.

At the foot of the building was the shop belonging to the seller of almonds, pistachios, dried apricots, and prunes. His shop contained other things as well, of course. There were fruit, vegetables, cheese, and all sorts of grocery items, along with a refrigerated section loaded with fresh meat and ham at the back. The shopkeeper was just tidying up his shelves for the night before lowering the iron shutters at the front entrance. He stayed open very late, later even than the law permitted, but the police had other things on their minds.

"Good evening, children," he said. "Good evening, mademoiselle Wilhelmina. What are all you good people doing out at such an hour?"

The voice was full of laughter, but not the eyes. The shopkeeper took in the downcast faces of the children with steely pupils.

"Nothing serious," answered Mina in a bland tone. "How's business?"

"Fine, thank you," said the man, still staring at the children.

The three little children were at the threshold of the door to the building when Yassine turned back to Mina.

"If you come up, our father will know what we've done, and then..."

His "and then..." conjured up visions of broken bottles, spilled alcohol, hard blows, and bruises on Leïla's face.

"All right," said Mina after a moment's hesitation. "Go on up on your own."

She watched them enter the stairwell one by one, each of them throwing a last glace backwards at the street. Then she left.

The wind murmured all the following day; the shadows sighed all through the night.

"Three little children have gone missing," rumour said, passing from mouth to mouth and ear to ear.

"Three little children have gone missing," breathed the voices behind the windows, along the hallways, up the stairs and back down again.

"Three little children have gone missing," whispered the night creatures, behind the dirty frontages of red-light bars and gambling dens.

"I heard a cry," said a little red-headed girl to her ginger cat, in a building next door to the one where the three little children lived. "Just one squeaky cry, like that of a scared little girl."

But the rumour did not reach Mina's ears until the second morning. She had to check out the story, go and see the father, who was sunk in a drunken stupor, then visit the school, the neighbours, and the child welfare officer before she could confirm that the children had really disappeared

> *Saint Nicolas, au bout d'sept ans,*
> *Vint à passer dedans ce champ;*
> *Il s'en alla chez le boucher:*
> *«Boucher, voudrais-tu me loger?»*
> *«Entrez, entrez, saint Nicolas,*
> *De la place, il n'en manque pas.»*

(Saint Nicholas, seven years on,
Passed by this very same field;

And he went to see the butcher:

"Butcher, can I stay here overnight?"

"Come in, come in, Saint Nicholas,

Of course there is a place for you!")

It was cold, damp, and black outside. The walls of the ogre's cave oozed dark liquids; the air was heavy with the fetid odours of rotten flesh and fizzy orangeade gone flat and stale. In the centre, between piles of crates, stacked tins, and cases of canned drinks, was the chopping block stained with dried blood. One of the cleavers had fallen on the dank floor.

Above their heads, the ogre walked back and forth.

Chunks of salted meat swung from the ceiling at each of his steps. Yassine thought he saw them bleed and scream, scream with the voices of his brother and sister, and he had to shake his head before his ears would stop ringing with the sound of it and return to reality.

Above their heads, the ogre walked back and forth. He dealt with customers, laughed and joked while filling their string bags with leeks, potatoes, beans, and semolina. The ogre was saying, "And how is your wife feeling today?" while sticking in a few extra clementines. "There you are, two hundred grams more, my treat, for the family." Yassine heard the sound of cases of bottles being moved and his throat was gripped by a special little monster, created just to torment him further: thirst.

How long had they been here?

There was no way of knowing. The sun and the moon were not visible from within the ogre's cave. He had given them nothing to eat or drink and it had been hours since Leïla's eyes had gone blank—she'd fallen into some kind of frightening torpor from which she woke at intervals with a start and dry sobbing. For the first few hours, Yassine had sung songs to reassure the other two. All the songs he knew, and he knew lots: that was his gift, singing. There was only one song he carefully avoided, although he knew that it was the only song running through Leïla's and Giamill's minds now.

Il n'était pas sitôt entré
Qu'il a demandé à souper.
On lui apporte du jambon,

Three Little Children

Il n'en veut pas, il n'est pas bon.
On lui apporte du rôti,
Il n'en veut pas, il n'est pas cuit.

   «De ce salé je veux avoir,
   Qu'il y a sept ans qu'est dans l'saloir.»
   Quand le boucher entendit ça,
   Hors de la porte il s'enfuya.
      «Boucher, boucher, ne t'enfuis pas;
   Repens-toi, Dieu t'pardonnera.»

   Saint Nicolas pose trois doigts
   Dessus le bord de ce saloir:
      «Petits enfants qui dormez là,
   Je suis le grand saint Nicolas.»
   Et le grand saint étend trois doigts.
   Les p'tits se lèvent tous les trois.

(Just as soon as he stepped inside
He asked what there might be to dine.
A dish of ham was brought to him
No good, he said, he must decline
A roast of lamb was offered him
No good at all, meat sliced that fine.

   "It's this salted pork that I want,
   Soaked seven years in the tub of brine."
      When the butcher heard these words
      He was out the door, quick as that
      "Butcher, butcher, don't run away;
      Repent your sins, and God will forgive"

Saint Nicholas three fingers placed
Upon the edge of this brine tub:
"Little children who therein sleep,
      I am the old and great Saint Nick."
      Three fingers spread the great Saint Nick.

213

The little ones all three did wake.)

No, Yassine could not have sung that; if he'd tried to, his voice would have broken on bitterness and false hopes.

He was past the age of believing in Saint Nicholas.

And yet, for a moment, there… It was a few hours after the ogre had captured them. The iron shutters had been raised —was it morning? Someone came into the shop. Above their heads, the ogre's voice and the voice of the early customer were talking. And Yassine had seen, known, somehow felt that it was the organ grinder, recognising his gruff tones. But the customer left, and had taken brief hope with him.

Then Yassine had sung, until he had no more strength to sing, and Leïla had fallen into her leaden sleep.

The iron shutters were raised and lowered several times.

Yassine, too, fell into a torpor, in rhythm with the steps and the words of the ogre, up above. Time passed; in his half-sleep, he heard the babble of shrill, sing-song voices. Behind his closed eyelids he saw four laughing fairies wearing green coats and red caps, who were dancing and playing with one another. They were right there in front of him.

Yassine tried to call out to them for help, but his lips were so dry they couldn't move any more and the fairies could not hear him.

Time passed…

So close and yet far away, the fairies passed before a small, round wooden door beside which a golden key was hanging.

Giving a start, Yassine opened his eyes. He peered into the darkness, but the cave was empty. There were no fairies, just Leïla and Giamill, who also slept, lost in the tentacles of a black dream.

He was about to close his eyes again when he glimpsed the round wooden door on the opposite side of the cave. If he hadn't seen it before, it was because it was almost hidden by the crates and old cases of Coke in glass bottles…

But there was no golden key hanging from a hook, and no fairies, and Yassine's wrists hurt from straining against the chains. He thought of his mother, who had left a long time ago, when Giamill was still only a chubby baby. Of his father, who was probably floating in a pool of cheap red wine, and who couldn't care less whether they came home or not.

Nobody was looking for them and nobody would cry for them.

Who cares about three lost little children?

§

It was the fourth day of their disappearance and Mina was preparing the raid. The specialist services would take care of looking for the kids, of course. They were on alert because of the two murders that had taken place in the sector, but Mina had the feeling that they didn't really believe this was connected. The children had run away once before when their mother had left. The crime squad thought that they would eventually reappear and did not want to waste precious police time on a false lead.

They had refused to listen to her. But Mina knew the truth. The three little children had fallen victim to her personal war against the gang of the man with blue hair.

They'd known that she had gotten information out of the kids and taken revenge. Karine or somebody else must have seen her escorting them back home.

And the blue-haired man had killed them, killed them and chopped them up the same way he'd killed and chopped up little Yanaëlle, who had thieved in the metro, and little Thomas, who had carried drugs for a rival gang.

Mina had never felt so bad. Three little children were dead and it was all her fault because she had forced them to talk.

On the evening of the fourth day, she and her colleagues raided the squat where the gang had its quarters. The raid was a success and, even though the blue-haired man managed to flee, Mina and the others arrested Karine and most of her friends.

But they didn't find any bodies and there was no trace of the three little children.

On the evening of the fifth day, the ogre killed Giamill.

He tore him screaming from his chains and placed him on the chopping block. Then he held the child down firmly and lifted his cleaver. He struck a first blow across the neck, slicing the tracheal artery neatly and breaking the vertebrae. Giamill died from this first stroke, which did not prevent the ogre from roaring or the cleaver from landing again and again. The ogre bellowed insults, Leïla screamed wordlessly and Yassine yelled at her: "Close your eyes! Close your eyes!"

When the ogre stopped chopping, there were only bloody pieces left, but Leïla had her eyes closed and her fists over her ears, while Yassine went on yelling, "Hold onto him in your eyes! He won't die as long you hold onto him in your eyes!" And Leïla, occupied with crying and not losing the image of her brother behind her eyelids, did not hear the ogre speaking to Yassine.

"You're the guiltiest one," the ogre said. "It's you who taught your brother and sister to steal, so it's you who will receive the worst punishment. I'll kill the little girl tomorrow, and with each chop, just think about how it's all your fault."

He gave him something to drink, no doubt to keep him alive, and then left. A little later, Yassine heard the fairies laughing and singing on the other side of the small wooden door, but despair had long since overwhelmed him and he sank down among the black stones.

On the morning of the sixth day, Mina and her colleagues managed to trap the blue-haired man by setting up a fake rendezvous. They nabbed him with over ten kilograms of cocaine in his Adidas bag and the police station resounded with applause and the sound of corks popping from bottles of bubbly. It was a tremendous boost to her career; yet Mina still had a nagging worm of doubt in her mind. Because throughout the whole day of interrogation, the team of investigators had been unable to make the blue-haired man confess to anything concerning little Yanaëlle, little Thomas, or the three little children.

On the sixth day, the ogre killed Leïla.

Yassine could only yell, with a throat that had grown hoarse and painful. While the ogre attached her to the chopping block still damp from her brother's blood, Leïla screamed, "Keep me behind your eyelids! Keep me behind your eyelids!" Then she went silent, and the ogre returned upstairs without saying anything this time to Yassine.

On the evening of the seventh day, Mina went for a walk by the building where the three little children lived, where she'd seen them for the last time. The father claimed they'd never come home that night. He'd been drunk during questioning, but Mina thought that he hadn't been lying. The children had no doubt hidden themselves in the stairwell and waited for her to leave before going back out.

The sun had set, while the stars remained invisible beyond the city's layer of pollution. Mina raised her eyes to the third storey of the building and observed the windows in silence.

She felt powerless and alone.

The street was almost empty; it started to snow. A few metres away, the seller of almonds, pistachios, dried apricots, and prunes was putting away his displays out front, rubbing his big hands, chapped by the cold, against one another. In front of the building next door, the one with the haberdasher's shop, four kids wearing green parkas and red caps were getting their mittens dirty making snowballs.

At the street corner, the old organ grinder appeared. He came slowly towards them, nose in the air, as if he smelt something.

Mina shook her head. There was a curious waiting feeling in the air. Perhaps it was only the snow, or the plane passing overhead, very high up in the sky.

"Is everything all right, mademoiselle Wilhelmina?" asked the seller of almonds, pistachios, dried apricots, and prunes.

His voice was friendly, but Mina had the impression that he was looking elsewhere…as if his mind were fixed on some other place and he couldn't drag his pupils away from there. One would have said that his hands were already making other gestures instead of hanging bunches of bananas on a string, as they should have been doing.

The organ grinder stopped for a long while in front of the building where the children's father lived, his eyes tracing lines that only he could see…

"Yes, fine," Mina replied. "A lot of work down at the police station, though. You know, the kids who disappeared, and all that…"

"What a world we live in," said the shopkeeper.

Mina frowned because he didn't seem very convinced by what he was saying—and yet the phrase did not require much conviction.

Suddenly, the seller of almonds, pistachios, dried apricots, and prunes stared straight into Mina's eyes for the first time.

"But there are those who go looking for trouble, too," he said. "Thieves they were, those children. Little rotten seeds infesting the city, little grains of mischief... At least these ones won't turn into murderers later on."

Mina continued to watch him.

You know, sometimes, my dears, a little light goes on in the back of the head. When the little light takes hold and spreads to the neurons, it's the moment for ingenious ideas, solutions to problems, the moment when writers make their keyboards vibrate typing so fast. And then, at other times, the little light doesn't spread. It just stays there, and while you know you have just put your finger onto something, you don't know what it is.

The little light had turned on inside Mina's brain.

But she was unable to figure out what it revealed.

Still not moving, Mina watched the seller of almonds, pistachios, dried apricots, and prunes finish bringing in his displays. He was closing early that evening: it was only ten o'clock. No doubt he had something to do, something he had to finish before getting a good night's sleep.

Mina set off.

A little further down the street, the haberdasher came out of her shop and started to scold the four children in green parkas and red caps. They had stayed too late outdoors, she couldn't trust them, and so on. The usual complaints of mothers.

Seized by a sudden impulse, Mina went over to them.

"Hello, little brats."

"Hello, mam'zelle Mina," the kids replied in a chorus.

Their mother contented herself with giving Mina a black look; she preferred to have her children indoors without any argument rather than out here in the street talking to a cop.

"Tell me something," Mina persisted. "The evening when the three little children disappeared..." She pointed to the building, but neither the mother nor the kids needed any explanations. "Did you stay out late then, too?"

"Oh, no, they did not!" the mother grumbled. "This is the first time this week they've stayed out so late, and they're going to get an earful about it..."

"That's too bad." Mina sighed.

The kids went into their mother's shop; the flat where they lived was on the floor above it. Mina followed them without any specific aim in mind, perhaps to ask them some more questions. The mother let her proceed; she didn't dare protest because she'd already had problems with taxes and the building manager, and she tended to mix up all these things together.

The four children took off their caps and parkas, revealing four faces reddened by the cold and crowned by four mops of red hair. One of the mops of hair was longer than the others, that of a little girl who turned to the stairs and called out: "Tiberius!"

"So, you didn't see or hear anything that evening?" Mina said, watching a ginger cat descend towards them in a leisurely fashion.

The boys shook their heads, but the little girl lifted her chin.

"I heard a cry," she said. "Just one, like a squeak. But Maman said that..."

"Joséphine is always making things up," her mother said nervously, as if she thought she was going to receive more reproaches.

"A cry where? In the street?"

The little girl shook her head.

"No. Down below."

"In the cellar," the mother explained. "They go there to play in the afternoon, when they come home from school. But she's just telling stories, because we didn't hear anything at all down there."

Mina looked at the stairs that led down into the building's cellar, adjacent to the three disappeared children's house, and thus to the cellar belonging to the seller of almonds, pistachios, dried apricots, and prunes.

In the ogre's cave, Yassine had kept his hands over his eyes. He would have liked to have another pair of those hands, so that he would not have to hear. But throughout the day he did hear things: footsteps along the ceiling, crates and bottles being dragged about. He heard the steps of other people, those of customers who came in to speak with the ogre and left with provisions.

But little by little the customers became more rare and Yassine knew that evening had fallen. Then there was the sound of the outdoor displays being brought inside.

The iron shutters were lowered...

But only halfway.

Yassine removed his hands from his eyes. The iron shutters were raised again, as if a customer had wanted to come in at the last minute to purchase something. Yassine, heard, saw, felt the steps of the organ grinder make the floor above creak at different places within the shop, as if he were asking for...what? Ham, roast lamb, salted pork, soaked seven years in the tub of brine? But now the steps went away, the butcher did not want to run away, and God would not forgive him, he sold the meat without blinking and the iron shutters came down again.

Somewhere within the stony underground maze, a warrior woman descended without realising that she was approaching a small round door with a golden key; somewhere above her, four fairies fidgeted and laughed; and Yassine was aware of all this, the ogre's walls cried out to him, and each of the ogre's steps on the stairs cried out to him, as did the cleaver and the block and the chopped-up bodies of his brother and his sister. When the ogre seized him, Yassine screamed, his fists pressed on his eyelids, because it was the only means of keeping his brother and his sister alive behind them, and then he screamed again because when he died, his eyes would be extinguished and both Giamill and Leïla would disappear forever.

Mina started to run when she heard the screams, yanking at the door linking the two cellars until she saw the rusty key attached to the hook. She fumbled about with it in the lock, already anticipating the gesture she would make to grab the gun in her coat, but by the time the lock finally turned, the screams had ceased, replaced by a horrible gargling sound.

Mina felt her heart stop. She went on and managed at last to open the door. At first, she saw nothing, because the light was very dim, then an immense silhouette, so big that the cave could barely contain it, turned towards her while raising a cleaver dripping with blood. She took out her weapon, but the cleaver struck her on the temple.

She felt the bones crack...

And she fell...

Three Little Children

La première dit: «J'ai bien dormi»
Le second dit: «Et moi aussi»
Et le troisième répondit:
«Je croyais être en Paradis...»
Ils étaient trois petits enfants
Qui s'en allaient glaner aux champs.

(The first one said, "I slept all night,"
The second one said, "I did, too."
And the third one chimed in his reply,
"I thought I'd gone to Paradise."
They were three little children
Who went gleaning in the fields.)

She woke with an atrocious pain in her skull, her head on the knees of her partner, David. She was in the cellar belonging to the seller of almonds, pistachios, dried apricots, and prunes, which was swarming with police officers and nurses and more people than seemed humanly possible to be all in that one place.

The organ grinder, who looked very old and very tired, was explaining something to the superintendent. The shopkeeper had disappeared.

"We took him away," said David, as if reading Mina's thoughts from her look. "He should get thirty years, time enough to repent..."

A Red Cross nurse—why the Red Cross? why not the emergency crews? asked the part of Mina's brain that still remained on duty—was comforting Yassine, Giamill, and Leïla, who were rubbing their wrists that had been bruised by the chains.

"No," she whispered, her eyes fixed on Yassine. "He's dead. I got here too late."

"Not true," said David, caressing her hair. "The old musician saved them. He was in the shop; he came down when he heard all the screaming..."

Mina stood up, rubbing her temple, as if she couldn't bring herself to believe that her skull was still intact. She watched the nurse taking the pulses of the children wrapped up in blankets. She heard the others telling her about how the musician had seen the seller of almonds, pistachios, dried apricots, and prunes preparing to strike her, how he'd knocked out the assassin with a glass bottle before freeing the children and calling the police.

A bottle?

Mina could not concentrate.

Her temple ached and she would have sworn she'd received a blow there, but there was no wound.

She followed the three little children who climbed the stairs while David pointed out on the wall what must have been the bloodstains of little Yanaëlle, and those of little Thomas. Mina gritted her teeth and continued upstairs, because she didn't want to see any more.

Before the children went into the ambulance, she hugged Yassine against her chest and explained to him that she'd been scared and how happy she was that they were there, all three of them, wrapped up in their blankets. Leïla gave her a feeble smile, Giamill looked at her with his eyes full of tears, and Yassine leant against her. They held hands for a long while until the nurse separated them.

"I saw you coming," Yassine murmured just before the ambulance doors slammed shut. "I saw you coming closer to us underground..."

Mina straightened up, rubbed her temple, and, for a brief moment, it seemed to her that the city was a black, living creature. It seemed to her that four small fairies were watching the ambulance pull away with astonished eyes, and among the groups of inquisitive bystanders that had formed on the pavement, some of them had the pale shiny skin and the eyes of life-suckers. It seemed to her that a cloud of fairies with glittering wings were rising from the street and circling the roof of the building like butterflies around a flame.

She thought again of the old musician, of the seller of almonds, pistachios, dried apricots, and prunes, of the cleaver that had landed on her skull, and of the spectres screaming in the sky above her, but as quickly as it had come, the feeling evaporated.

Mina blinked her eyes in order to put her mind in order, slipped into the waiting car, and went home.

And yes, that's the end.

I'm sorry, my dears, I don't have any grand conclusion. Stories don't always have to end with: "They lived happily ever after and had lots of children," or "That was how the majestic city of Atlantis vanished beneath the waves," or "He replaced the jewel in its socket and went off into the sunset."

The truth? That's up to you to decide, little bunny. I can tell you what was printed in the newspapers: the three little children were rescued at the very last moment when the assassin had finally decided to kill them, after keeping them seven days in captivity. They were so frightened that they had dreamt they were dead, but psychiatric help was being provided.

Did Mina and the children ever meet later? There's no verse in the song about that, but you're free to imagine what you like. Why not? When you save the life of someone, you often feel responsible for them afterwards. And she had almost saved their lives…

What? The old organ? It's up in the attic, but I don't take it into the streets anymore, I'm too old now, you know. One of you will surely inherit it. But go on, that's enough chatter, it's time to go to sleep.

Shhh… Into your beds now, all nice and warm, there under the covers.

Close your eyes and you'll believe you're in Paradise.

Brita's Holiday Village

Karin Tidbeck

Swedish author Karin Tidbeck is the author of the English-language collection Jagannath, *which won a Crawford Award, and of the Swedish-language novel* Amatka. *She lives in Malmö.*

29/5

The cab ride from Åre station to Aunt Brita's holiday village took about half an hour. I'm renting the cottage on the edge of the village that's reserved for relatives. The rest are closed for summer. Mum helped me make the reservation — Brita's her aunt, really, not mine, and they're pretty close. Yes, I'm thirty-two years old. Yes, I'm terrible at calling people I don't know.

I didn't bring a lot of stuff. Clothes and writing things, mostly. The cottage is a comforting old-fashioned red thing with white window frames, the interior more or less unchanged since the 1970s: lacquered pine, green felt wallpaper, woven tapestries decorated with little blobs of green glass. It smells stale in a cozy way. There's a desk by one of the windows in the living room, overlooking Kall Lake. No phone reception, no Internet. Brita wondered if I wanted a landline, but I said no. I said yes to the bicycle. The first thing I did was bike down to the Ica store I saw on the way here. I stocked up on pasta and tomatoes and beans. I found old-fashioned soft whey-cheese, the kind that tastes like toffee. I'm eating it out of the box with a spoon.

"Holiday village" is a misleading expression; the village is really just twelve bungalows arranged in two concentric circles with a larger house — the assembly hall — in the middle. The dark paneling, angled roofs, and panoramic windows must have looked fresh and modern in the sixties, or whenever they were built. The wood is blackened now, and the windows somehow swallow the incoming light, creating caverns under the eaves. I'm a little relieved to be staying in the cottage.

Brita said that before she bought the holiday village, back when they were building it, the old man who owned the cottage refused to leave. When he finally died, the cottage was left standing for private use. It's much more cozy, anyway. I'd feel naked behind those panoramic windows.

30/5

I got up late and unpacked and sorted music. I've got a playlist with old punk and goth for the teenage project, an ambient playlist for the space project, and a list of cozy music, everything in order to feel at home and get into the mood and avoid writing. Did some cooking. Rode the bike around until I was tired. Found an old quarry. Tried to go for a swim in Kall Lake and cut my feet on the rocks. Bought goat whey curd. Finally, I couldn't avoid it anymore: writing.

So I have two stories I want to do something about. First there's the science fiction story about child workers in the engine room of a spaceship. It's a short story really, but I'd like to expand it into a novel. I know you're not supposed to worry about form or length—it's a guaranteed way to jinx the whole thing—but I'd really like to. I like the characters and their intense relationships, like *Lord of the Flies* in space.

The other story is a pseudo-biographical thing about a teenager growing up in the Stockholm suburbia of the 1980s, during the heyday of Ultra, the tiny house turned punk headquarters. I suppose it's a cooler and bolder version of myself. Also, older. I was too young to ever hang out at Ultra. It had already burned down by the time I discovered punk. I used to go to Ultra's next iteration—Hunddagis, the club housed in an old day care centre for dogs. I still remember the punk aroma: beer, cigarettes, cheap hair spray, and day-old sweat.

So, that's what I've been doing: writing down a bunch of teenage memories and transposing them onto a little older and bolder version of myself, and it's just slow and boring work. I had a go at the science fiction story instead, but it wouldn't happen. I ended up shutting everything down, realized it's now one o'clock in the morning (actually it's 1:30 now), and I'm going to bed.

31/5

I took a walk through the village this morning. Things that look like white, plum-sized pupas hang clustered under the eaves. They're warm to the touch. I should tell Brita—it's some kind of pest. Wasp nests?

Biked to the quarry after coffee, gathered some nice rocks—very pretty black granite. Went home, made pasta with chickpeas, tried to write. Writing about punks at Hunddagis doesn't feel the least bit fun or interesting. Mostly because I've realized what a lame teenager I was. I was always home at the stroke of midnight; I didn't like drinking mash; I didn't have sex. I read books and had an inferiority complex because I was afraid to do all that other stuff. I don't know anything about being a badass punk rocker.

It's the same thing with the story about the engine room kids— what do I know about child labor? What do I know about how kids relate to each other under circumstances like that? Not to mention, what do I know about spaceships? I'm talking out of my ass.

So there I am. I can't write about what I know, and I can't write about what I don't know. Better yet, I've told everyone that I'm staying in Åre until I've finished the novel. I somehow thought that saying that would make it happen.

Hang in there for another couple of weeks. And do what? Try some more? Go on biking trips and eat whey-cheese?

2/6

I'm taking a break. I've scrapped everything I was working on. I rented a car and drove west over the border into Norway, where I bought ice cream in a lonely little kiosk. When I was a kid, I thought the sign in Norwegian that said *åpen*, open, meant *apan*, the monkey. It was the most hilarious thing ever.

I had my ice cream and looked at the Sylarna Mountains and the cotton-grass swaying on the bog. There was a thick herbal smell of mountain summer. Little pools and puddles were everywhere, absolutely clear, miniature John Bauer landscapes. I considered going on to Levanger, but it felt too far. I stopped off for a swim in Gev Lake on the way home. It was just like when I was little: warm and shallow enough that if you walk out into the middle, the water only reaches your waist. Tiny minnows nibbled at my feet.

I'm having coffee in the little cabin on Åreskutan's Summit. It's a clear day, and I can see the mountain range undulating in the west, worn blunt by the ice ages. Mum once said that when she was a kid, there was a leathery old man who, every morning, hiked all the way up the mountain with a satchel full of coffee-thermoses and cinnamon rolls that he would sell in the cabin. This was before the cableway, somewhere in the 1950s. The old man had done that since time immemorial, even when my grandmother and her sister were kids and dragged baking troughs up the mountain to ride them down like sleds.

4/6

I went for a walk in the holiday village. I became a little obsessed with the thought of stuff you can do when nobody's looking. Build a pillow fort outside cottage number six. Streak, howling, through the street. I was thinking specifically of howling when I spotted the pupas. They're the size of my fist now. That was fast. I forgot to tell Brita. Of course, I had to touch one of them again. It felt warmer than my hand.

Went shopping in Kall, had a cup of coffee, bought the newspaper, went past Brita's house. I told her about the pupas. Her reaction was pretty strange. She said something about the pupas sitting there in summer, and that I should leave them alone. That's why she'd put me in the cottage outside the village, so that the pupas would be left in peace. Yes, yes, I said. I won't do anything. Do promise you won't do anything, said Brita, and suddenly she was pleading. They have nowhere else to go, she said; you're family, I can trust you, can't I? Yes, yes, I said, I promise. I have no idea what she's on about.

5/6

I dreamed that there was a scraping noise by the door. Someone was looking in through the little side window. It was human-shaped, but it sort of had no detail. It was waving at me with a fingerless paw. The door handle was jerking up and down. The creature on the other side said nothing. It just smiled and waved. The door handle bobbed up and down, up and down.

It's five past ten. I've slept for almost ten hours.

I went into the village to check if the pupas had grown, but all that remains are some empty skins hanging under the eaves. So that's that.

6/6

There's a knock on the door and someone's waving at me through the side window. It's a middle-aged man. When I open the door, he presents himself as Sigvard and shakes my hand. He's one of the groups of tourists who live here during the summer. They've rented all the cabins, and now they're throwing a party, and they've seen me sitting alone in my cottage. Would I like to join them? There's plenty of food for everyone. I'm very welcome.

The party takes place in the little assembly hall. People are strolling over there from the other cabins. They're dressed up for a summer night's party: the women in party dresses and *lusekofte* sweaters tied over their shoulders, the men in slacks and bright windbreakers. Inside, the assembly hall is decked with yellow lanterns, and a long buffet table lines one of the walls. The guests are of all ages and resemble each other. I ask Sigvard if they're family, and Sigvard says yes, they are! It's a big family meet-up, the Nilssons, and they stay here a few weeks every summer. And now it's time to eat.

The buffet table is covered in dishes from every holiday of the year: steak, roast ham, *tjälknul*, hot cloudberries, new potatoes, pâtés, pickled herring, *gravlax*, *lutfisk*, seven kinds of cookies, cake. I'm starving. I go for second and third helpings. The food has no taste, but the texture is wonderful, especially the ice cream mingled with hot cloudberries. Everyone seems very interested in me. They want to know about my family. When I tell them that Brita is my great-aunt, they cheer and say that we're related then; I belong to the Anders branch of the family. Dear Brita! They love her! I'll always be welcome here. Everyone else here belongs to the Anna branch: Anna, Anders' sister and the eldest daughter of the patriarch Mats Nilsson.

When we're done eating, it's time to dance. The raspy stereo plays *dansband* music: singers croon about smiling golden-brown eyes, accompanied by an innocent and sickly-sweet tune. Everyone takes to the dance floor. Sigvard asks me to dance. This is like a cliché of Swedish culture, I say without thinking. Yes, isn't it, says Sigvard and smiles. He holds me close. Then I wake up.

8/6

I started writing again. Throwing the old stuff out worked. Something else has surfaced—it's fairly incoherent, but it's a story, and I'm not about to ruin it by looking too closely at it. It has nothing to do with teenage trouble at Hunddagis, or *Lord of the Flies* with kids in space-ships. It's about my own family in Åre, a sort of pseudo-documentary. Some mixed memories of my grandmother's and mother's stories of life up here, woven together with my own fantasies to form a third story. Above all else, I'm having *fun*. I refuse to think about editing. I write and stare out over Kall Lake.

The dreams are a sign that things are happening—I keep dreaming about the same things, and it's very clear, very detailed. It's the same scenario as before, that is, Sigvard knocking on the door and taking me to the assembly hall. We eat enormous amounts of food and dance to dansband classics. I talk to all my relatives. They tell stories about Mats Nilsson's eldest daughter and how she started the new branch of the family when she married and moved north from Åre. I don't remember those stories when I wake up.

13/6

I started with Mother's stories, continued with Gran's generation, and am working my way back in time to form a sort of backwards history. I wrote about the war and how Great-Gran smuggled shoes and lard to occupied Norway. Then I wrote about how Gran met Grandpa and moved down to Stockholm. Right now Gran is a teenager, it's the twenties, and she's making her first bra out of two stocking heels because she can't afford to buy a real one. She and her sister are getting ready to go to a dance in Järpen. It's an hour's bike ride. I'm looking forward to writing the story about my great-great-grandfather who built a church organ out of a kitchen sofa. Some things you can't make up.

The dreams change a little each night. I've discovered that I have a fair amount of control of my actions. I wander around in the cabins and talk to the inhabitants. In true dream fashion, they all come from little villages with names that don't exist like Höstvåla, Bräggne, Ovart; all located somewhere north of Åre, by the lakes that pool between the mountains.

Sigvard's wife is called Ingrid. They have three teenage children.

15/6

I'm a little disgusted by the direction this is all taking. I don't know how to interpret what's going on. The front doors are always unlocked, I go where I wish. Last night and the night before last, it happened several times that I walked into a house and people were having sex. On all surfaces, like kitchen tables or sofas. They greet me politely when I open the door and then go back to, not making love, but fucking. Nobody seems particularly into it. They might as well be chopping onions or cleaning the floors. In and out and the flat smack of flesh on flesh. And it's everyone on everyone: man and wife, father and daughter, mother and son, sister and brother. But always in heterosexual configurations. I asked Sigvard what they were doing. We're multiplying, he said. That's what people do.

20/6

It's Midsummer. I've managed just over eighty pages. I've gotten as far back as Great-Great-Great-Grandfather Anders, son of Mats Nilsson, and if I want to get even further back, I'll have to do some research on Anders' five siblings or just ramble out into fairy tale country. Not that making stuff up seems to be a problem. There's no end to it. I've gone back to the start to fill in holes, like Mother and Gran's siblings. No editing just yet, just more material. Brita asked me if I wanted to come with her to celebrate Midsummer. I declined. All I want to do is write. Besides, it's freezing outside, and the gnats are out in full force. It'd be a good idea, research-wise, to see Brita, but I don't feel like being around people.

Sigvard came knocking on my door. He was wearing a wreath of flowers and held a schnapps glass in one hand. We danced to dansband music, the legendary Sven-Ingvars; we competed in sack racing and three-legged racing. Most of the women and girls had large, rounded bellies and moved awkwardly. When the dancing and playing was over, we ate new potatoes and pickled herring, little meatballs and sausages, fresh strawberries with cream, toasting each other with schnapps spiced with cumin and wormwood. It'll get darker now, said Sigvard. He burst into tears. Yes, I replied. But why is that so terrible? It makes me think of death, he said.

1/7

150 pages! That's an average of five pages a day. Very well done. The last ten days have been about putting more meat on the bones I finished building around Midsummer. In other words, embroidering what facts I had with more ideas of my own. Editing is going to take a lot longer, but I have a solid structure from beginning to end—no bothersome gaps or holes.

I decided to stop at Anders. I need to check the other siblings now, especially Anna. I've tried to talk to Brita, but she's always busy whenever I come over. I'm done with this place, though. I'm homesick. I've booked a ticket to Stockholm for the sixth. I can go back home with a good conscience.

4/7

They're weeping and wailing. They're all dressed in black. They won't say why. I've told them I'll be leaving soon, but I don't think that's why they're sad.

5/7

I finally caught Brita for a cup of coffee. She apologized for being so busy. I asked her about Mats Nilsson's children, but she doesn't know much outside our own branch. Still, I asked her if she knew anything about Anna, the eldest daughter. Not much, she said. But then there wasn't much to know about her. She disappeared without a trace when she was twenty years old. The consensus was that she probably drowned herself in Kall Lake, or in one of the sinkholes in the quarry. In any case, she was never seen again.

6/7

I'm leaving on the night train. I cleaned out the cottage; all that's left is to hand over the keys to Brita.

Sigvard knocked on the door in my dream. The whole village was crowding behind him. They looked aged and crumpled somehow, and they were weeping loudly. Some of them didn't seem to be able to walk on their own—they were crawling around. Sigvard came in first; he dropped to his knees and flung his arms around my legs. I sat down on the floor. He put his head in my lap. My dear, he said. It was the best summer ever. We're so grateful. Then he sighed, and lay still. The others came, one by one. They lay down around me and curled up. They sighed and lay still. I patted their heads. There, there, I said. Go to sleep now, go to sleep. Their bodies were like light shells. They collapsed in on themselves.

I was woken up just after seven by an ice-cold draft. The front door was open. I went for a last walk in the village. Clusters of tiny spheres hang under the eaves.

Regressions
Swapna Kishore

Swapna Kishore is an Indian author of short speculative fiction and has written numerous books on such diverse topics as software and management. She also writes and blogs widely on dementia and care-giving.

When we are in a village, time flies by as I help the women in their chores—drawing water, milking cows, stoking cow-dung fires, and stirring simmering pots of *payasam* pudding, or even braiding jasmines in the hair of the young girls. By night, I am tired and fall asleep almost immediately. But when we are traveling, I lie awake below the open, unpolluted skies staring at the full moon and I often think of my Ambapur, oh, so far away, a blur across time and space.

My last evening with Mother is the most vivid of my childhood memories. I was five years old, and supposed to join the Facility the next morning, and Mother and I stood in our dome's viewing tower, looking at the moon, my small hand in hers.

"You will never be alone," she told me, "because when we both look at the moon at night, we can imagine we are standing together."

I wasn't consoled. "Why can't I come home for holidays?" I cried plaintively. "What exactly is a futurist?"

Mother's face seemed all shadows and sharp angles, and her hand stiffened around mine, hurtful. I realized with a shock that she didn't know the answer.

"Futurists improve the fate of women everywhere, not just women in Ambapur," she said finally. "Kalpana, learn whatever they teach you, and don't be impatient."

I am not impatient now, Mother.

Sometimes I pace, the wet grass ticklish to my bare feet, and absorb the sweet fragrance of *parijata* flowers. And I wonder—is my past true, if the future will not hold it?

Futurists, I learned at the age of seven, operated in two streams, the researchers and the agents. Researchers provided data while agents changed the future. The glory lay with the agents, though we trainees weren't told what they did. I couldn't qualify as an agent; I failed the profile tests thrice despite my through-the-roof IQ and my 'A's in every subject. I'd have fudged my personality profile, but I spotted no pattern distinguishing the accepted girls from those rejected—no discriminating levels of IQ, extroversion, assertiveness, nothing.

The shame of my failure struck me fully the day I was moved to the research wing and knew I would never see the agent wing or interact with an agent. I buried myself in work, barely smiling at fellow researchers at meal times, avoiding evening gossip sessions in the common room. If I was doomed to be a researcher, I'd be the best.

Over time, my work began fascinating me. My assignments involved analysis of the complicated social causes and scientific breakthroughs that preceded the initiation of the Ambapur experiment. How did mythology, history, and culture influence the emergence of Swami Sarvadharmananda? What made his rants against Ambapur so popular? Would the Hindu Religious Resurgence have grown without *Nava Manusmriti*? What triggered India's splintering into multiple countries with the largest, most prosperous states forming Swamiji's dream Navabharata? To me, that century-old partition of India was particularly interesting because it transformed Ambapur from an experimental district into a country, howsoever small.

On some days, though, as I unraveled and scrutinized critical forks in history, I wondered at the futility of such intense study, because the applicability of lessons from ancient history was limited, wasn't it? Then I'd tell myself that my honed abilities would be used later for complex, contemporary scenarios.

My life changed the day Seniormost's voice boomed from my contact port, taut, curt. "Kalpana, report to Room 455 immediately."

"Pardon?" My stomach crunched. Why would the country's most powerful woman summon me?

"Hurry, Kalpana," urged Seniormost. "This is an emergency."

I raced down the corridors. Momentum and panic carried me through an open door, but I skidded to a halt before grim-faced senior women ringing a screen showing an abstract low-res animation—red, yellow, brown splotches moved in weird patterns. Grainy and coarse and scary, though I could not understand why I felt so queasy.

"Kalpana?" Seniormost frowned at me. "We want you to replace an agent."

"I'm not qualified," I stuttered, embarrassed.

"You are the only Series K clone available right now. We need someone similar enough to Kavita to replace her at a critical gender fork."

"Gender fork? But those happened in the past." They were events that determined major trends in gender equations.

"Futurist agents," she cut in, "change the past so that the future changes."

Change the past? I stared at her, trying to comprehend her words. I'd always thought agents changed the future. "But…"

"Pay attention, we only have fifteen minutes," Seniormost said. "You know how important Sita was in shaping gender roles, right?"

"Of course." Sita was projected as the ideal woman in Swami Sarvadharmananda's *Nava Manusmriti*, which ended up as the final reference on Hinduism for Navabharata; Swamiji used Sita to justify the strait-jacket gender laws binding millions of Navabharata women. I had often done what-if analyses of related mythology.

"Because the Ramayana of *Nava Manusmriti* is not based on a single story but is a melding of several candidate stories." And Seniormost paused for a beat. "We have several potential intervention points. For our correcting nudges, we have selected the ten most significant scenarios. In this particular one, the Sita equivalent assists her husband in his trade, cures her grievously ill brother-in-law, and manages the house and finances during an extended business trip which will later be called an exile."

"Sounds like an improvement on the stereotypical Sita," I said.

Seniormost waved me to silence. "They returned home and rumors started, as in all Ramayanas. The husband did not ignore them." A muscle on her face twitched as her gaze snapped to the screen.

I swiveled to see the display, my uneasiness growing as I tried to understand what those strange red and orange splotches meant. "What is happening there?"

"Kavita's fire-proofing failed." Seniormost's tone was heavy.

The import of her words sank slowly into my mind. That scarlet dance was an inferno, licks of flame, sparks, and embers—fire seen by someone burning inside it. A chill crawled up my spine.

"That's Kavita?" I whispered hoarsely.

"They call her Vaidehi."

Vaidehi, one of Sita's names. This is what the fire had made me suspect. What I was seeing on the display was the *agni pareeksha*, the shameful episode present in each of the over eight-hundred versions of Ramayana. An Ambapur agent was being burned alive, and I was supposed to replace her.

"But Seniormost," I whispered. "I am not trained. I am clueless… please, I am not sure…"

"I've seen your records, Kalpana. You are brilliant and capable of extraordinary mental focus. All the assignment needs is focus. Let them dress you and I'll explain the rest."

I barely noticed the women who surrounded me and the hands flurrying around me; I was numb, as if I'd been plunged into ice water. I was supposed to become Sita. Well, *a* Sita, if not *the* Sita. My legs wobbled. I think I swayed.

I tried to sort my thoughts as women peeled off my bodysuit and wrapped silk around my waist and chest. Capsules were snapped into my brain implant. A woman tried injecting something into my leg; I kicked reflexively, so someone held my arm rigid and plunged in the needle. A small wart appeared on my skin. "We don't have time for a binding operation," someone said. "Left to nature, it takes a week for the button to integrate properly, but it'll be stable enough unless there is extreme trauma." Jewelry clasps clicked, someone explained the hidden tools. A spray coated me with a golden haze.

"Thank you," said Seniormost, and the women withdrew.

Before I could pour out my questions, Seniormost started speaking, so I focused on her words.

"Kavita was trained in essentials and sent out when she was seven years old," she said. "We had coded the relevant cultural information in her brain implant, and we briefed her frequently using her sync button. We got periodic updates on her activity from the button; we have uploaded all information into your implant. Access is by using normal thought control techniques."

She had not talked of Kavita's death. I shuddered. "Kavita died in spite of her training. How will I survive?"

"That was an accident."

"And what am I supposed to do there? How will I know how to behave, what to say, how to recognize people?"

"The implant has all the data and guidance algorithms to help you conform and stay unnoticed." She smiled reassuringly. "Just stay low-profile for a day or two till we study the situation and brief you."

It sounded tough, but manageable. I took a centering breath. "When will you replace me with a proper agent?"

Seniormost's face softened. She patted my shoulder and strapped me in a chair. "Don't worry, you'll be fine. I know you can do it." She flung a lever.

The conflagration hemmed me in, intimidating in spite of my fire-proofing. Bile soured my throat as I tried to push away the horror of the situation. My implant flashed an instruction; I obediently directed a miniscule atomizer on the charred remains of my predecessor near my feet. No burnt human bones must be found in the ashes.

Again, impelled by the implant, I ran to the edge of the pyre where the onlookers were grey smudges beyond an orange shimmer. I stepped out of the fire. I must have looked impressive with my skin burnished gold from the afterglow of the dissipating fire-proofing shell, resplendent in silk garments, dazzling with jewelry. A woman certified pure by Agni Devata, the God of Fire.

"*Jai ho!*" A few scattered cries from the crowd.

I walked slowly, painfully, on the rough ground, trying to look calm and dignified. A pall of silence smothered the crowd. Some women, several men. I had studied about men, about their salty smells, their thick, coarse voices, their hairy bodies, but even so, seeing them made me shudder. Petals were showered at me—jasmines, roses, mari-golds—soft touches against bare skin, a creepy feeling. A crone grasped my hands into her gnarled ones, and led me to a short, skinny man with male-pattern baldness and a bewildered expression. Sweat on his brows. And fear, sour, nauseous fear—I could smell it.

Curiosity overrode my fear. This must be the husband, the wimp who burned his wife to stop baseless gossip about her chastity. He looked so unimpressive. Most mythological interpretations described him, or the collective of men like him, as tall, broad-shouldered, muscular of body and yet sensitive of face, hair a silky curtain.

"My chaste wife," he muttered, averting his gaze.

Touch his feet, prompted my implant. Seek his blessing for a longer life.

But I couldn't force myself to act docile to someone who had just killed his wife.

The man raised his hand as if blessing me. I walked past him; he scurried after me, annoyance flitting across his face.

A rickety chariot, lumpy seats covered by a threadbare spread. I settled down. The man sat opposite me, torso angled away, body rigid, too scared to bother me for a while.

Good. I had time, finally, to orient myself to the situation. A couple of centering breaths helped me focus. Then with my eyes half-closed, I began viewing Vaidehi's downloads, filter set for salient personal facts. The husband was a local chieftain's son. After his father called him good-for-nothing, he left his village in a huff, keen to prove his trading acumen. He dragged along his brother and Vaidehi for the business trip. They roamed from village to village, traded, earned gold and jewels. When they returned home, a washerman challenged Vaidehi's chastity. Rumors, insinuations, and the demands of a fire test followed. Vaidehi expected the husband to ignore them. She knew him to be demanding and easy to anger, but assumed he valued her because of her hard work and loyalty during those years of travel. That was the status last evening, as per the most recent transmission.

I was soaking up the information when the chariot jerked to a halt.

No marble palace, no lush bowers, no gold fountains—only a simple stone building. Rice and lentil *baras* were drying on cloth spread out in the courtyard. Cowpats had been slapped on the walls. A naked boy wheeled a painted wooden cart. Women with their heads covered, some embroidering, others slicing yams. Men sprawled on rope cots, smoking something noxious.

The husband led me to a whitewashed room and closed the door behind us. He whipped out a dagger from his waistband. "How did you survive that fire? Witchcraft?"

My implant suggested I fall at his feet and plead forgiveness. *Forgiveness for what, surviving?* I had not integrated sufficiently with the Vaidehi persona to manage such acting, such false humility. I ignored the advice and readied myself for his attack.

He lunged at me. I twisted aside and hit his wrist sharply, making him drop the dagger. I kicked it across the room. Mouth agape, eyes round with shock, he stared at his empty hand.

I was utterly disgusted. "If you thought I wouldn't survive, why did you agree to the fire test?"

His eyes darted from my face to the fallen dagger, and the wariness in his eyes transformed into cunning. He straightened up.

"They would have pushed you into the fire anyway," he said. "By doing so myself, I retained my position as the chieftain's son. I don't know what witchcraft you did, but your emergence from the pyre has strengthened my place."

Of such pettiness do orators make mighty legends. "They will weave from such incidents a story of Lord Rama, Maryada Purushottam, the exemplar of social propriety," I said. "Temples will be constructed, festivals celebrated. The fire test will be touted as a righteous act of a king who valued even a washerman's doubt."

"King?" He frowned at me. "Who is they?"

Trust me to goof up. Why had I spoken my thoughts aloud? I was supposed to keep quiet and let the implant guide me. I sat down on the bed. "I must think."

"A woman who thinks?" He snorted. "Now I've seen everything."

This man had seen me emerge unharmed from fire. He had lost his dagger to me. Yet he mocked me. Had his fear and awe vanished because he sensed I would not attack him?

He came closer. "Since you have been proven pure," he said, "I can taste you again."

Revulsion swamped me. The thought of a male pressing on me, skin sweating over skin, reminded me too much of the modified Kamasutra that formed an essential part of female education in Navabharata, so that no man was "deprived." We didn't have any such training in Ambapur, of course, where we didn't have men. Didn't need them. Hadn't needed them ever since several top women scientists and industrialists, sick of gender suppression and thrilled that science could render men redundant, bought land and funded enough politicians to kick-start the Ambapur experiment.

Yet now I was forced to interact with a man.

His hand grazed my breasts. I couldn't hit him; that would contradict my supposed role. But every instinct in me shouted a protest. I had to think fast. I checked mental menus and located the required visualization trigger. The hormone release brought the relief of a cold shower. He jerked back, shock in his eyes. Then he rushed out of the room.

I sighed with relief. *Thank Goddess for anti-pheromones!*

After a few breaths to reorient, I pondered my position. I knew I should collapse the boundaries between the downloaded memories and my own, so that my responses matched what Vaidehi's had been. But I wasn't ready to surrender myself yet. This transition had been abrupt enough; I couldn't handle more jolts. I tuned the implant for better response time and quick face recognition, but stopped short of merging with it.

The door opened. The husband's brother strode in, dragging, to my horror, his wife, Madhulika. She was heavy with child.

"The fire test suits you." His grin exposed stained teeth. "You look grander, and you walk straighter." He released his wife's hair, and whacked her shoulder. "Madhulika would survive no such test. God knows how many men she chased when we were away."

That was lust in his eyes. Once, when fellow-drunks almost killed him, Vaidehi had healed him, and this was how he gazed at her while she tended his wounds.

Disgusted, I turned to Madhulika. She was so beautiful. Skin fair as the *kunda* flower, lips the red of hibiscus, eyes the shape of fish. Monsoon clouds of black hair spilled over her cheek. I brushed them aside and whispered, "Sister, take heart. I will help you."

"He will be angrier if you sympathize," she whispered back.

The brother-in-law pushed her out of the door. She stumbled out, the enormous swell of her child-heavy belly almost causing her to fall.

"Go cook payasam," he yelled after her. "And add enough nuts or I'll teach you."

He turned to me. "Ignore her, beautiful Vaidehi. Her mango-shaped breasts do not smell as good as the golden pears behind your silk *uttariya*, or those juices I smelled when you cradled my head in your lap and brought me back to life."

I thought of a cultural archetype to repel him with. "One who brings you to life is a mother. Respect me as one."

"A child suckles at his mother's breast." He grinned. "O mother of mine, drop your uttariya, and let me feast."

"Brother?" The husband stood at the door. "I was looking for you."

I slipped out of the room.

The women sat clustered in the courtyard.

"You survived," the mother-in-law said to me, her lips pursed in disapproval.

I squatted near her. The vat on the fire was smoking hot. She slipped balls of batter into the oil, and I watched them splutter and puff up. A distant aunt chopped green chillies. Another woman sliced onions. A small girl fed cowpats to the fire in the mud *chulha*.

"Do it properly." The mother-in-law rapped her hand. She turned to me. "Too arrogant to help, are you?"

I hadn't merged my muscle memories with the implant and such medieval cooking tasks needed skill.

"I'm tired," I murmured.

"Vaidehi Aunty," piped the young girl. "Did Agni Devata talk to you?" She was a chubby-faced seven-year-old, her eyes wide, a tentative smile on her face.

How I wanted that smile to grow with admiration for me! I yearned for this innocent girl to be spared the bitterness and resignation of the women around her.

"He spared me but said women should refuse such insulting tests," I said. "Women number as many as the men. If we unite, no man can hurt us."

"May God pull out your evil tongue," snapped the mother-in-law. "You dare sow discontent in a child's mind and spoil her future? Besides," she snorted, "gods speak to priests, not to women. Uttering such falsehoods is a grievous sin."

The girl's smile wavered. She blinked as if she'd been woken up. The soft wonder on her face morphed into disgust directed at me.

I should have kept quiet. Seniormost had cautioned me to listen to the implant and stay unnoticed. This is what my failed profile tests probably said: *Candidate does not obey instructions. Is not cautious. Shoots off her mouth.*

"I wish the fire had consumed you," said a cousin sister, her eyes ringed with dark circles, a bruise ripening on her jaw. "My husband threatened me with agni pareeksha. He says, Vaidehi survived, so why be scared if you are chaste?"

Her hostility dismayed me. I couldn't think of a reply.

"If Vaidehi had died, the men would declare her unchaste," said someone. "Now that she's survived, they'll hold her up as an example. Either way, the moment Elder Brother-in-law agreed to the fire test, we were doomed."

Shard-sharp words, and true, as history showed. I turned to face the woman who'd spoken: Madhulika.

She continued, "We should keep men so happy that no one can sway them. They have so much work to do; we women can support them."

"Hear her well, Vaidehi," said the mother-in-law. "You are swollen-headed because you accompanied my son on his trip and survived the fire, but it is women like Madhulika who truly inspire young girls."

I pressed my lips tight so that I wasn't tempted to retort.

"Vaidehi!" A voice from behind. I looked up—it was Shanta, the husband's elder sister. She crooked a finger.

I stumbled slightly as I stood, and Madhulika stretched her arm to steady me. Her finger curled around my forearm, clutching me where the sync button was.

I winced.

She released me immediately, gaze fixed on the wart. Her eyes widened and her mouth fell open. What was so unusual about a wart?

But Madhulika was staring at me as if seeing a vision of sorts. An understanding came into her eyes, and dread filled me. *She suspects. But what can she suspect?*

Shanta grabbed my shoulder. "Your husband wants you to visit me for a month. I will leave in an hour. Be ready by then."

"But why?"

She glared at me. "Do you question your husband's commands?"

Shut up, screamed the implant inside me. *Just obey for once.*

After Shanta strode off, Madhulika lay her hand on my arm and unobtrusively led me to an isolated corner. We reached a window opening to the yard where cows grazed.

"You are a replacement Vaidehi," she said. "The earlier one had no wart on her arm."

No, she had hers on her leg, I almost said, remembering the injection I'd kicked away.

"You are an agent?" I asked. Seniormost had not mentioned having another agent here.

She nodded, and lowered her uttariya slightly to expose a wart on her breast. "My coordinator didn't mention another agent. He should have—"

"He?" I cut in. "A *man*?" I gaped at her, the import of her words sinking in slowly.

She paled, too. "No," she said softly. "You are too normal. Arrogant, maybe, but not...but you must be...an Ambapur abomination."

I would have reacted, but my implant flashed a warning twinge of pain, and by the time I'd recovered my breath, Madhulika had rushed away.

Shanta did not speak as we sat side-by-side in her cart. I welcomed the silence; realizing that Madhulika was a Navabharata agent had shocked me. I had not expected to find agents from the "enemy camp," much less a woman. Madhulika didn't fit my stereotype of Navabharata's docile, suppressed women. I had been taught those women were dumb, incapable of independent thought, insipid, exploited, their personalities molded to the Sati-and-Sita image. They were pitiable objects compared to us—strong Ambapur women, free and independent and living in our own country.

Besides, why would Navabharata need agents? Seniormost had said, "Futurist agents change the past so that the future changes." Why would Navabharata want to change anything? That country had no simmering discontent regarding gender roles. Men were the hunters, gatherers, doers. The scientists and rulers. They commanded. They demanded. Women accepted men as superiors. Women bred, supported, obeyed. They listened, they supplied. Genetic selections encouraged this. Society rewarded it. Political systems, economic systems, were based on it. Why change it?

Or had Ambapur exaggerated the docility and dumbness of Navabharata women? Madhulika seemed intelligent enough, even though she had a different value system.

And she had called me an Ambapur abomination. What lies had their government fed them about us?

The cart jerked to a halt. "Get off, Vaidehi." Shanta's voice was whiplash-sharp. "My brother told me to get rid of you."

Stunned, I looked around. We were on a lonely road skirting a forest. No farms nearby, not a single hut, nothing. I looked at Shanta; she was frowning at me and gripping a thick stick as if ready to attack. I took a few moments to gather my words. "I have been your brother's wife for years," I said. "I helped him when we traveled."

"That was your duty, so what's great about it?" she retorted. "Now you have resorted to evil ways."

"But—"

"No one can survive fire without witchcraft."

"Then why did he agree to the fire test?"

"A woman who dies to save her husband embarrassment dies a worthy death." Shanta threw my bundle of clothes on the ground, then pushed me off the cart.

"What will he tell the villagers?" I asked.

Shanta shrugged. She made a sign of warding off evil, and instructed the cart driver to proceed.

The sun was low in the sky, barely visible behind the dense trees. I wanted to sink onto the ground and cry, but I couldn't afford to. Then I thought of the implant, and queried it about the surroundings. Luckily, it turned out that Vaidehi had spent part of her childhood nearby, something neither Shanta nor her brothers had known. Her records showed a cave some distance away, hidden in the forest.

I started walking.

The forest grew thicker with mean clusters of trees. I wended my way, brushing the branches apart, depending on my predecessor's memories. Once, I spotted eyes peering at me; I drew on the hope that Vaidehi often frequented the forest as a child, and so there would be no wild beasts here. I would be safe.

I reached the cave before dark, glad, almost, for the cold stone to sit on. The implant initiated the daily transmission. I added to it a request for an audience with Seniormost the next morning. I was exhausted. I stretched out on the hard floor. Sleep descended mercifully quickly.

§

"We reviewed your download," Seniormost said as soon as she'd established contact. "You ignored the implant's guidance several times."

"I did my best," I said, though I knew I could have tried harder if I'd set aside my ego.

"You don't understand these dynamics. Using anti-pheromones on your husband and antagonizing him, really! You know story-tellers will twist your eviction to claim that Rama banished Sita because his subjects remained skeptical after the test."

Frustration made me snap back. "If story-tellers decide what gets sung about, you should influence them. Get a wife to distract Tulsidas. Make him compose a Sitayana instead of Ramacharitramanas."

Seniormost sighed. "Child, calm down."

She did not understand the reality here, this bright woman running the tiny women-only country millennia away.

"Gender-imbalance is deeply ingrained already," I said. "Both in men and women."

"That's why we need agents."

"Then choose a different intervention fork. How about the Mahabharata era? Kunti and Draupadi didn't get bullied. Radha held her own."

"We can't identify representative Mahabharata time-streams," Seniormost said. "From the candidate historically-correlated episodes, Ramayana offers the maximum gender 'inflexion' points."

"Did you know about the Navabharata agent?"

"No," she said. "But that is part of the challenge. Now here's what I want you to do today. Study the implant's data and complete your integration. Don't get discouraged. We'll talk tomorrow." She disconnected before I could quiz her about how long she'd take to find a proper replacement.

Seniormost was right about my need to study, though. I had gazillions of questions, and the fastest way to proceed was exploiting my implant. Discarding my reluctance, I collapsed my boundary with the implant and integrated the old Vaidehi's memories into my own.

Then I was Kalpana, and I was Kavita, and I was Vaidehi, and it was evening by the time I recovered my balance and sense of orientation.

§

I was almost asleep on the dry grass apology of a mattress when I heard steps. Someone was approaching. I opened my eyes a peep. A woman stood at the cave entrance, and a shaft of moonlight fell on her face. Madhulika.

I sprang up and assumed a defense stance. Crouched, ready to spring, I asked, "How did you find me?"

"I came to warn you," she said, pulling her shawl tighter around her. "My coordinator knows your location. He may try to harm you."

I had no reason to trust her. "Explain."

"I asked him about you last evening. You see, we have been told things about Ambapur women." Madhulika peered at me, as if deciding what to tell me. "You are supposed to be ugly and malformed, and incapable of womanly emotions like love because you women are genetic freaks and clones who pleasure each other instead of men, and oppose the natural order of humanity to the extent of using intelligence to *compete* with men instead of supporting and serving them. But you showed sympathy to me, as did the Vaidehi before you, so I began to have doubts."

"You don't look the way I expected a Navabharata woman to look, either," I conceded, marveling that we were discussing the future while living a past supposed to change it. I stayed crouched as I spoke, though. Madhulika's presence here could be a Navabharata trick.

She nodded. "My coordinator laughed and said your predecessor died because he sabotaged her fireproofing by jamming some signal. He's the washerman who taunted your husband for the fire test. He claimed you were now hiding in a cave in the forest and he knew your location by tapping your sync signals. He downloads all data you transmit."

My stomach felt heavy, like a weight had sunk in it.

"Till yesterday," Madhulika continued, "I believed that I must be a role model—an ideal women who complemented men in accordance with our basic nature, our true gender role. Last night, when I realized that what I'd learned about Ambapur women was exaggerated, I wondered whether I'd also been fooled about other things."

Ditto here.

"So, I came here," she added.

"Well," I said. "Right."

She sat down. She looked very tired. The walk here must have been exhausting for her, given her advanced pregnancy.

"What's your plan?" she asked.

Her mission was to nudge history in the opposite direction. I said nothing.

"Who is your coordinator?" she asked.

I kept my lips pressed tight. I wasn't willing to expose myself yet.

"My coordinator may try to kill you," she said. "He tried to kill me."

"Kill you? Why?" I stared at her.

"When he realized I was rethinking this whole Ambapur-women-are-abominations business, he got very agitated. He threatened me. He even kicked me. But I shouted out, as if I had just spotted some thieves, and he slunk away."

Even across the years, I remember Madhulika's grimace at that memory, her closing her eyes for an instant.

She sighed then, a tired sigh. "That's when I decided to leave home. I don't want to live in fear of my coordinator. My husband means nothing to me; I lived with him only because of my mission. But I don't want to bring up my child in a place like that. I am so confused."

She tilted her neck back and looked at me. I didn't know what to say—we were opposites, weren't we?

I stuck to practicalities. "He'll trace you using your sync button."

"No." She removed her shawl.

The wound was obvious despite the thick slathering of herbal paste. The right breast was tattered where the sync button was gouged out, and rags of torn skin hung from it.

I shuddered.

"I threw the button down the river. I also threw in blood-smeared clothes. They will drift back to the shore downriver, and people will assume I fell in the water."

Night owls cried raucously, crickets chirped. I spread the grass thinner to make another place. Moonbeams lent silver highlights to her night-dark hair.

"Sleep," I told her. "We can talk tomorrow."

After a while, her gentle snores filled the night. But I could not sleep.

The Navabharata coordinator could locate me. He was accessing my messages to Seniormost. Yet I needed to tell her about this development.

After much thought, I encrypted my message using a code based on the Ambapur literature not available outside our country. The agent would know where I was, but would not be able to decipher my message.

Seniormost's encrypted message came back fast enough, but brought no cheer.

You cannot switch off the sync signals, I decoded. *The device sends out signals every few hours, whether or not you transmit a message, but you cannot control that. You will have to mislead the Men's agent.*

I pondered the information while staring at the culprit wart. It seemed to me that our country's approach of Futurist agents changing past gender forks was doomed to fail. Navabharata, a country several hundred times larger, was flush with resources. If they wanted, they could send multiple agents to hunt down and sabotage every Ambapur agent. They could flush every gender fork with required role models. They could keep the past favorable, because a favorable past had made them rich enough to manipulate the past—historical inertia closed the loop.

They could kill me.

As soon as it was dawn, despite the risk of being traced, I initiated contact with Seniormost. She had probably expected it, because she was present in the control room.

Again, I used encryption. As I completed my explanation, my voice broke. "They will destroy me if I stay here."

"Just hold on tight, Kalpana. The tech team is working to find a solution. Give them time."

And live under such hostile conditions in this primitive world? "You are only thinking of the mission," I said, my tension too sharp to hide. "So what if it fails? It'll just be status quo, it's not like you will die."

"No, we will not die if the mission fails," Seniormost said, her voice low. "It was our fault we sent you without training. We did not explain things."

"Trained or not, at least credit me for finding out valuable information," I snapped. "And send a trained replacement for me."

"We'll talk about that later," she said. "We are considering alternatives to keep the Navabharata agents at bay. I will call you back by evening." Seniormost broke contact.

I was very restless after talking to her. Why weren't they finding a replacement and recalling me? Then it struck me—maybe recall was not possible. Maybe that was why we never met agents, because sending an agent was a one-way trip, and this was a secret. Seniormost had been evasive about replacements when I had asked. We may not have the tech for it. Or maybe it was impossible to travel to the future, which is what my present was when I was in the past.

Maybe I was stuck in this primitive world, homeless, and being tracked by the Men's agent.

I fought my panic and went through every sentence Seniormost had uttered, looking for information I might have missed earlier.

Like that part when Seniormost had looked sad and said, *No, we will not die if the mission fails.* Almost as if proposing a corollary: the mission's success meant their death.

The thought stunned me.

In the rush of the past few days, I'd not thought about anything other than survival and fitting a role. Not pondered the concept of how changing the past affected the future, for example. Which future did it change? Were these alternate realities, parallel worlds, or just one world? If these were alternate worlds, why bother to change a different world? And if this was one world, and if the past changed, agents could alter history so that India continued as a jumble of cultures and conflicts and did not splinter into Ambapur and the right-wing Hindu Navabharata, and other nondescript smaller countries. Where would that leave my Ambapur and all of us who peopled it? Were Ambapur agents knowingly working on missions they would not return from, missions designed to kill our own country, like suicide bombers and *jehadis* a few centuries ago? No wonder I failed the psych profile; I lacked such suicidal conviction.

The moon was but a pale sphere barely visible in the dawn sky, and I remember seeking it out and staring at it, remembering how very far Mother was. I had looked at the wart, my link to my world, and also my betrayer. I looked at Madhulika, who was possibly not the enemy I had assumed her to be. Maybe no one was an enemy.

I was tempted to plunge into action that would make me safe. Attack the washerman, kill him. But Navabharata could send more agents and coordinators; it was a large country with plenty of resources. I would be safer if they thought me dead.

After peeping into the cave to make sure Madhulika was still sleeping, I walked to a rock overhanging the river. I removed my necklace with its miniature toolkit, and snapped it open to expose a tiny cutting blade. I prayed for strength, knowing that I was about to close the doors to my past, my people, my support. Then I began working out the wart from my forearm. Lucky for me that they'd not performed the binder operation.

Our journey upriver exhausted Madhulika and induced premature labor. I used every bit of knowledge my implant held to try and save her. I may have succeeded in a normal pregnancy, but she was carrying twins. As she tried to smile at the feeble cries of her newborn daughters, I stroked her hand.

"You will improve," I consoled her. "You have to bring up your daughters."

Our interactions on our long walk upriver had been gentle and companionable. We had splashed our faces using water from the stream. Sometimes, I would notice a strawberry shrub and pluck the fruit, and Madhulika gathered it in a fold of her uttariya. Or she would spot a gourd growing on a creeper, and I would split it open with a sharp stone so that we could share the sweet, juicy pulp. We had not discussed our contrasting credos—I assumed we would have enough time later.

Now she was dying.

"Bring up my daughters, sister Vaidehi," she whispered.

"I don't know your way of thinking," I said. "My world was different."

"Do whatever seems right, sister." Her life ebbed out.

In the initial days, I was often tired as I adjusted to the sudden role of nurturing the girls. A secluded cave formed our base. Using implant triggers, I induced my breasts to produce milk. Luckily, the forests abounded with fruit trees and berry shrubs. Chores filled my days—collecting water, finding fruits, cleaning the girls, feeding them. Yet as life acquired a rhythm, I found time to soak up the forest's poetry, its flowers and animals and the sunlight-dappled wings of butterflies. Fire kept away beasts at night; I sometimes stayed up late, enjoying the texture of the night with the owls screeching, the soft descent of dew, the scent of the parijata that bloomed all night and carpeted the grass at dawn.

Sometimes, I looked at the moon and thought of Ambapur.

Years passed.

I often missed Madhulika. She held a key to a view that would have complimented and enriched mine, and now I had no way of learning it. I wondered which value to bring up her daughters with—mine, or what I knew of hers, or the values typically inculcated in women in this era.

I finally chose a mishmash, something not warped by politics and power games. My memories and imagined extensions emerged as lullabies sung to the girls. Over time, the isolated episodes formed a rich tapestry, till one day I realized I could well be a bard singing a Sitayana, not an Ambapur version, nor, indeed, a Navabharata version, but one where Sita was a fun-loving person, even naughty at times, and where she shared a playful and rich relationship with her husband.

The girls thought I was their mother; it was simpler that way. When they were old enough to travel, I led them by hand from village to village. I talked to village women about life and its problems, and enacted fragments of what could have been Sita's story.

In one village my daughters, now twelve, chattered about twin boys they had met. "Their mother tells stories like yours."

I felt a flutter inside me. "What are their names?"

"Luv," said one girl.

"Kush," said the other.

I could not speak for a few moments. That Sita really existed, that she had twin sons... Emotion clogged me, thick, heavy, and I tried to force myself into thinking rationally. Sita was not a single historical truth, I told myself, though I had no way of confirming this theory of the construction of mythology. This woman storyteller could well be an agent of Ambapur or Navabharata.

Should I meet her? No, I thought, let me move away and continue my Sitayana. The world allowed hundreds of versions.

I busied myself all day, but that night, with no distraction possible, I found myself recalling Seniormost's sad look during our last conversation. What had she thought when she lost contact with me? Did she think me dead? Or had she hoped I'd survived and assumed that, untrained though I was, I'd do what I could?

My gaze shifted to the moon. What remains fixed across time and space? What survives, what matters? Nothing, really. Yet one does what one should.

Forgive me if I succeed, Seniormost, I whispered. *Forgive me if I fail.*

Another new village, another day. We walk to the well, my girls and I, and women balancing water pitchers on their hips ask us, "Where are you from? Who are you?"

"I tell stories," I say. "Would you trade lentil soup for entertainment?"

They nod.

By evening, women and children gather around the village center, where I wait for them with my daughters; some youths stand warily at a distance.

This is my life now, offering women stories that intrigue and stretch their world vision, yet fit within it. Listeners may wonder: did the story resonate because of its courage, hope, conflicts overcome? Should the mother-in-law have been meaner, the husband more righteous, the wife more chaste? Should the women in the story have laughed more, taken things more lightly? Could a woman rebel as the story claimed? Should she? Why not? Why?

"Once," my story usually starts, "in a land not far from here, a king found an infant in a furrow, and he named her Sita."

At this point, I pause to look at my audience.

I sometimes consider myself a vendor of silk to tapestry weavers. Listeners choose which threads they wish to weave into their own stories. They may chant them to insomniac children, use them to inspire or scold. Fragments of my tales will meander down generations. Of the tales sung by a multitude of bards, which would live on to form the world?

My true story remains unsaid. I cannot speak of Ambapur or Navabharata, nor mention Seniormost, who may never exist in the new reality. I cannot tell my daughters about their real mother. Those would be anachronisms, threatening the fragile fabric that worlds rest on. Yet memories are slippery, and stories strung with their fragments more so, and I dread that when I am old, I will jumble up the past and the future with the present, sounding demented when I am being most truthful.

Then a voice usually pipes up, pulling me back to the reality I am creating.

"We have heard some versions of the Sita story before," it says. "Tell us yours."

And so I tell the story I think will fit.

Dancing on the Red Planet

Berit Ellingsen

Berit Ellingsen is a Korean-Norwegian fiction writer and science journalist. Her debut novel, The Empty City, *came out in 2011.*

W e want to dance when we go out the airlock," the Belgian said.

"Pardon?" Vasilev, commander of the first manned mission to Mars, said.

"The music will be a speaker check for the atmospheric sound wave experiment," the Belgian replied.

"Why wasn't I informed about this earlier?" Vasilev asked.

"It's such a small thing; why not do it?" the Belgian said. "And it'll look great on TV." He smiled. His teeth were small and white, unlike Vasilev's coffee-stained enamel.

"The track is called *Opera of Northern Ocean,* as if that has anything to do with us," Vasilev complained to mission control. He needed to talk with someone outside the crew, someone a little impartial. "Okay, maybe the landing site was an ocean once, and is in the northern hemisphere, but that doesn't make it any more appropriate. They also want to dance as they exit the airlock. Can they even do that?" He put the message on record, and went to water the tomato plants in the greenhouse for the thirty-four minutes it took the message to reach their blue home and for mission control to reply.

"I'm afraid they can," Petrov at mission control said. "The ramp is large enough for movement. The calcium, super-calbindin, and exercise will have kept your bones dance-worthy. The sound experiment was cleared months ago. Could be important to know how sound behaves in the Martian atmosphere if we ever set up a research station there or if you guys need to scream." Damn Petrov and his macabre sense of humor.

"Why didn't the Europeans tell me first?" Vasilev said. He disliked wasting talk and time on things it was too late to do anything about, but his colleagues' omission of the music and dancing irked him. They had had more than seven months to let him know about the experiment-cum-PR stunt. Of course, the Americans were in on it, too.

"Just disallow it then," Petrov said half an hour later.

As commander, Vasilev could do that, but he also knew the demotivating effect it would have on the long journey back. If the Europeans had their dance, maybe they would stop complaining about the food and just eat what they were given. And, like the Belgian had said, it was such a small thing, so why not do it?

"Okay," Vasilev told the Belgian and the German. "You can have your dance, but do it quickly. And for God's sake record it, so it really is an experiment."

"Of course," said the German. "We'll film it at the highest resolution possible."

"Moron," Andreevitsj, mission specialist from remote and Arctic Novaja Zemlya, said when Vasilev told him and Lebedev about the "experiment." "Do you know what this means?"

"No," Vasilev said flatly.

"It means we have to dance with them!"

"Of course it doesn't," Vasilev replied.

"Yes it does! We can't just stand there while they dance."

"Why not?"

"It'll look stupid, like we don't know how to dance."

"We don't know how to dance," Vasilev said.

"Speak for yourself," Andreevitsj said. "I do my part when I go out. But I have enough sense to stay in the crowd so fewer people see me."

"So?" Vasilev said, still sore about the moron comment, but determined not to show it. "Where are you going with these irrelevant facts?"

"There's no fucking crowd here!" Andreevitsj said. "We can't hide."

"Calm down," Vasilev said. "No one will mind."

"It's just a quarter of the planet watching the landing," Andreevitsj said, voice shrill. "We'll look bad next to the Europeans and the Americans."

"Maybe they can't dance either?" Vasilev suggested. "They just like the music?" He enjoyed music, too, but not dancing.

"No," Andreevitsj said. "They've grown up with it. They dance every weekend. They fill stadiums and dance all night. When I studied in Holland, all the radio stations and clubs sounded the same, uts-uts-uts-uts-uts! I thought I would go crazy."

They spent the next two exercise sessions trying to learn how to dance from Lebedev, who came from Moscow and was, in his own words, an expert clubber. Strapped to the treadmills, they jumped up and down and waved their arms to Lebedev's music. Andreevitsj did the twist, rotated his hips and knees in opposite directions while he squatted up and down. Vasilev wasn't sure how good it looked. He was starting to feel nervous—not about the landing, which he had spent over a year training for, and which was like an old friend to him. Instead, he feared the hours following touchdown and engine stop, and the moment when the airlock opened and they would take the first steps on another planet—dancing.

"Music and dance have been used for celebration since humans left the caves," the American said during dinner the night before they entered the lander. Lebedev and one of the Americans would stay behind in the main module to take care of communication, maintenance, and orbital experiments while the rest of them worked on the surface.

"Also, moving one's bodies together in rhythm increases the feeling of community and strength, like social glue. That's why so many indigenous peoples dance. It's highly appropriate that we do it when we arrive on a new planet."

"But we're not indigenous peoples," Vasilev said.

"To Mars, we're all indigenous peoples from Earth," the American replied.

"Can I at least hear the song you'll be playing?" Vasilev asked.

The Belgian shook his head. "No, it's a surprise. But I can tell you it will be easy to dance to, in the standard one hundred and twenty beats per minute."

"That's the heart rate of sexual arousal," the American informed him.

"Uts-uts-uts-uts-uts," Andreevitsj said from across the table.

But it didn't end there. The Europeans wanted to fasten long silver-colored streamers to the D-rings on the arms and legs of the EVA suits, once again under the combined auspices of science and showmanship, to "visually track the direction and strength of the Martian wind." It would also look festive.

"What's next?" Vasilev muttered. "Glow sticks?" He checked the logistics files to make sure glow sticks were not in the payload.

Then the moment arrived. They fell and shook and burned through the Martian atmosphere, not nearly as hard as the re-entry would be on Earth, but generating a respectable amount of fire. The conical heat-shield lasted for as long as necessary and popped off according to plan. The trefoil of parachutes deployed and jolted them back to gravity after seven months in free-fall. Then the lander's feet extended and the thrusters kicked in, pushing back against Mars' hold on them. The atmospheric conditions were good, just enough wind to make it interesting, but not enough to make it dangerous. No nasty surprises or malfunctions. Vasilev put the gleaming, teardrop-shaped landing module on the Red Planet as he had trained to do, with plenty of fuel left. It was a safe landing, a glorious landing.

"Touchdown and engine shutdown," Vasilev said into the microphone. He breathed and imagined the cheering that would erupt in the control room seventeen minutes into the future. He smiled at the thought.

Two hours and six minutes later all the reports from the co-pilots and the rest of the crew were positive. It was time; he couldn't postpone it any longer.

"Everyone to the airlock and prepare for EVA," Vasilev said, his voice trembling slightly.

They crowded the small metal space, the Belgian closest to the hatch, then the German. Because the landing was Russian, the Europeans and the Americans had the honor of being first outside. Vasilev couldn't see his crew's faces behind their golden visors, but he could hear their breathing, rapid and shallow, over the radio. The silver streamers at their elbows and knees gleamed in the bluish light. It looked odd, like failed Christmas tree decorations.

The German started the internal and external cameras and gave thumbs up. Everything was ready. Vasilev's palms were moist inside his gloves. His heart beat as hard as it had during the landing.

"Opening the airlock now," Vasilev said. He pressed the oversized button on the wall and nodded at the Europeans. The Belgian started the track on the hard-drive.

At first, Vasilev didn't hear anything. Then a beat began, steady but light. It unfolded slowly, as the lander's ramp had done moments earlier. The music sounded inside their earphones and on the external speakers, the first human sound in the atmosphere on Mars.

The hatch opened. They stretched to take in the planet they had landed on. A ruddy-colored desert of coarse sand and pebbles, no boulders in the landing zone. Orange dust kicked up by the thrusters gilded the air. The sky was yellow, the sun small and distant. It was Mars. Mars was looking at them, greeting them. The wind caught the silver streamers on their suits and pulled the ribbons out toward the silent landscape, like a beckoning.

A deep bass started up in the music, then a sound like a human voice exhaling, breathing, overlaid by a warbling synth and the sound of gentle tinkling.

"Quite poetic," Vasilev thought, against his will. He blamed it on the moment. It felt much more personal than he had expected. There was no press, no busy officials, nor screaming people waiting for them on the Red Planet, just wind and sand and silence.

The Belgian lifted his arms as though he were taking all of Mars in, as if the rest of humanity, everyone they knew and loved, were not two hundred million kilometers away in the darkness, but right there with them. He bobbed his helmet up and down, and dance-walked slowly out onto the ramp. The orange sand on his boots and on the metal beneath them, rose and fell, rose and fell, in rhythm with the beat.

The German followed, turning his hips from side to side as much as the suit allowed him, and swayed out of the airlock, the silver streamers flapping and gleaming in the dust-filled Martian day.

The American made whooping sounds, clapped in time with the beat, and danced outside. Then the music calmed a little, as if it were waiting for someone.

"Let's go," Andreevitsj said, breathed heavily into his microphone, and vanished. The music rose in a crescendo, with a yearning, haunting undertone and a sound of increasing wind.

Vasilev drew in his breath, lifted his arms as his colleagues had done, bent his knees, and swung his hips with the music, one-two, one-two, one-two. The low gravity made him feel light and unconcerned, not stiff and uncomfortable, as when he danced on Earth. It felt surprisingly good. He followed Andreevitsj into the golden sand-light.

No longer caring who saw or heard him, just enjoying the ease of the motion and the music, Vasilev stomped his feet and waved his arms and grinned broadly, while *The Opera of Northern Ocean* boomed and warbled and sang into the alien atmosphere, and the orange wind lifted their streamers up and up toward the sky. Through the earphones, he heard the laughter and the breathing and the shouts of his fellow human beings who were dancing next to him on Mars at one hundred and twenty heartbeats per minute.

About the Editor

LAVIE TIDHAR is the author of the Jerwood Fiction Uncovered Prize winning *A Man Lies Dreaming*, the World Fantasy Award winning *Osama*, and of the critically-acclaimed *The Violent Century*. His other works include *The Bookman Histories* trilogy, several novellas, two collections, and a forthcoming comics mini-series, *Adler*. He currently lives in London.

About the Artist

SARAH ANNE LANGTON has worked as an Illustrator for EA Games, Hodder & Stoughton, Forbidden Planet, The Cartoon Network, Sony, Apple, Marvel Comics, and a wide variety of music events. Written and illustrated for Jurassic London, Fox Spirit, NewCon Press, and The Fizzy Pop Vampire series. Hodderscape dodo creator and Kitschies Inky Tentacle judge. Daylights as Web Mistress for the worlds largest sci-fi and fantasy website. Scribbles a lot about the X-Men, shouts at Photoshop, and drinks an awful lot of tea. Responsible for *Zombie Attack Barbie* and *Joss Whedon is Our Leader Now*. Her work has featured on *io9*, *Clutter Magazine*, *Forbidden Planet*, *Laughing Squid*, and *Creative Review*.

The Apex Book of World SF: Vol 1

S.P. Somtow
Jetse de Vries
Guy Hasson
Han Song
Kaaron Warren
Yang Ping
Dean Francis Alfar
Nir Yaniv
Jamil Nasir
Tunku Halim
Aliette de Bodard
Kristin Mandigma
Aleksandar Žiljak
Anil Menon
Mélanie Fazi
Zoran Živković

edited by
Lavie Tidhar

Among the spirits, technology, and deep recesses of the human mind, stories abound. Kites sail to the stars, technology transcends physics, and wheels cry out in the night. Memories come and go like fading echoes and a train carries its passengers through more than simple space and time. Dark and bright, beautiful and haunting, the stories herein represent speculative fiction from a sampling of the finest authors from around the world.

ISBN: 978-1-937009-36-6   ~   ApexBookCompany.com

The Apex Book of World SF: Vol 2

Rochita Loenen-Ruiz
Ivor W. Hartmann
Daliso Chaponda
Daniel Salvo
Gustavo Bondoni
Chen Quifan
Joyce Chng
Csilla Kleinheincz
Andrew Drilon
Anabel Enríquez Piñeiro
Lauren Beukes
Raúl Flores
Will Elliott
Shweta Narayan
Fábio Fernandes
Tade Thompson
Hannu Rajaniemi
Silvia Moreno-Garcia
Sergey Gerasimov
Tim Jones
Nnedi Okorafor
Gail Hareven
Ekaterina Sedia
Samit Basu
Andrzej Sapkowski
Jacques Barcia

edited by
Lavie Tidhar

In The Apex Book of World Sf 2, World Fantasy Award-winning editor Lavie Tidhar brings together a unique collection of stories from around the world: quiet horror from Cuba and Australia, surrealist fantasy from Russia, epic fantasy from Poland, near-future tales from Mexico and Finland, and cyberpunk from South Africa. In this anthology, one gets a glimpse of the complex and fascinating world of genre fiction--from all over the world.

ISBN: 978-1-937009-35-9 ~ ApexBookCompany.com

The Apex Book of World SF: Vol 4

Vajra Chandrasekera
Yukimi Ogawa
Zen Cho
Shimon Adaf
Celest Rita Baker
Nene Ormes
JY Yang
Isabel Yap
Usman T. Malik
Kuzhali Manickavel
Elana Gomel
Haralambi Markov
Sabrina Huang
Sathya Stone
Johann Thorsson
Dilman Dila
Swabir Silayi
Deepak Unnikrishnan
Chinelo Onwualu
Saad Z. Hossain
Bernardo Fernández
Nataliam Theodoridou
Samuel Marolla
Julie Novakova
Thomas Old Heuvelt
Sese Yane
Tang Fei
Rocío Rincón Fernández

edited by
Mahvesh Murad

From Spanish steampunk and Italian horror to Nigerian science fiction and subverted Japanese folktales, from love in the time of drones to teenagers at the end of the world, the stories in this volume showcase the best of contemporary speculative fiction, where it's written.

"Important to the future of not only international authors, but the entire SF community."
Strange Horizons

ISBN: 978-1-937009-33-5 ~ ApexBookCompany.com